the Wilds Exile

RANGER OF THE TITAN WILDS

BOOK FOUR

J.D.L. ROSELL

This is a work of fiction. Names, characters, places, and incidents either are the product of the author's imagination or are used fictitiously. Any resemblance to actual persons, living or dead, events, or locales is entirely coincidental.

Cover illustration © 2025 by Joemel Requeza
Cover design by Shawn T. King
Interior illustrations © 2024 & 2025 by Sutthiwat Dechakamphu & 21
Book design by J.D.L. Rosell
Map © 2022 by Keir Scott-Schrueder

ISBN 979-8-348561-08-6 (first edition hardcover)
ISBN 978-1-952868-55-9 (hardcover with dust jacket)
ISBN 979-8-869137-86-9 (first edition paperback)
ISBN 978-1-952868-54-2 (IngramSpark paperback)
ISBN 979-8-307794-33-3 (KDP Print paperback)
ISBN 978-1-952868-47-4 (ebook)

Published by Rune & Requiem Press
jdlrosell.com

ADDITIONAL RESOURCES

You can find appendices on the characters, creatures, and world of Ranger of the Titan Wilds located near the end of the book.

There are also additional resources on my website, including series lore, commissioned art, my recommended reading order for all Ranger stories, and summaries of the previous installments. Find all of those at *jdlrosell.com*.

Six other novellas and short stories are associated with Ranger of the Titan Wilds that are presently only available through the occasional series Kickstarter. Catch the next campaign by signing up on my website.

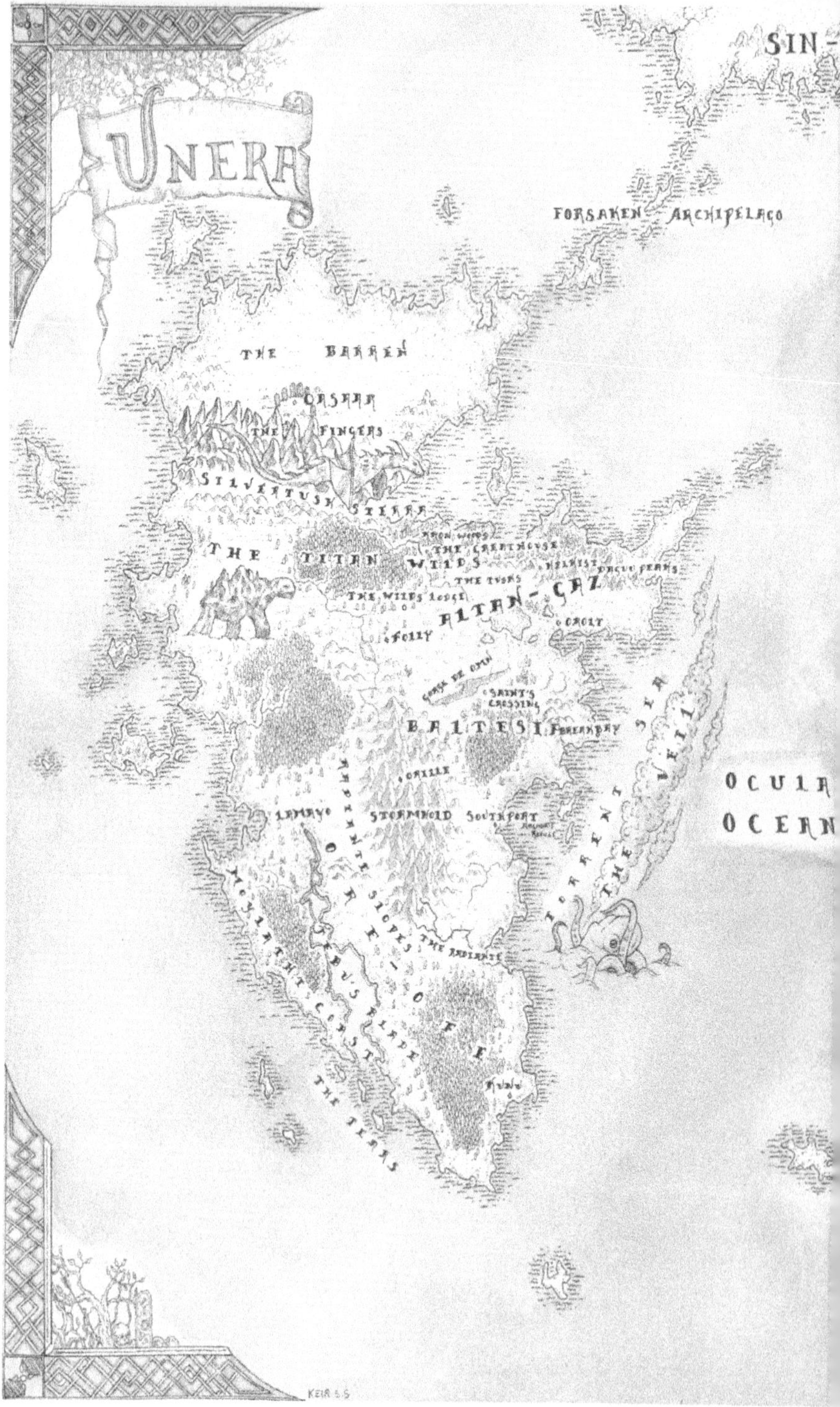
UNERA
SIN-
FORSAKEN ARCHIPELAGO
THE BARREN
THE FINGERS
SILVERTUSK SIERRA
THE TITAN WILDS
THE GREATHOUSE
THE TUSKS
THE WILDS LODGE
ALTAN-GAZ
FOLLY
SAINT'S CROSSING
BALTESI
LAMAYO
STORMHOLD
SOUTHPORT
TORRENT SEA
THE VEIL
THE RADIANTE
RADIANTE SLOPES
THE TEARS
OCULA OCEAN
KEIR S.S

N
W
E
S
REFUGIO
TIBERIA
VASARA
THE ANCESTRAL LANDS
THE SKY SEA
EYT
MUMSI
THE EYRIE
GAIKHIA
KAIGA
BETGOL

"I know how men in exile feed on dreams...
and know such food is vain."

—*Aeschylus, Agamemnon*

PROLOGUE

Ayda stepped onto the balcony to behold the rising sun.

When outside of her private chambers, she bore the weight of her titles: Gran Ayda di Inhoa, Mother of Mercy, the Bride of Heaven. Holder of the Office of the Altacura. Head of the Holy Catedrál of the Ilberian Union.

But here, alone on her balcony, she was only Ayda. A woman who had grown up a mason's daughter until a passing priestess beheld her potential. A woman who appeared young for her nearly nine decades of life but whose bones ached with the fading chill of winter. A mortal woman who sinned in the pursuit of immortality.

How far away immortality seemed that morning.

She allowed her eyes to rove over the town below. Bayo Sol appeared as radiant as ever, its limestone pavers swept and marble fountains sparkling. Ships moved in and out of the docks, ushering in offerings of gold and silver from temples across the Union and bearing away trinkets and statues to raise more funds in Omn's name. They brought pilgrims, too, come for the first altar erected to their deity, where it lay high upon

Monte Ardiente, the peak soaring above the Hallowed Isle. Paupers came as well, seeking the charity of the Catedrál. She had maintained a benevolent reputation since first accepting her office, and she always would. The generous hand was more readily forgiven after it delivered just judgment.

This town, this campus, this island—they were the beating heart of the Catedrál. Refugio, where San Inhoa long ago ascended the mountain and tamed the volcanic Ardiente. Tamed it and built her altar to a god none had yet known.

It was a seat of power to befit a queen, yet in that moment, she took little pride in her Golden Harbor. Ayda placed her hands on the smooth marble balcony and closed her eyes. Tilting back her head, she let the light rising over the ocean wash over her face. The sun's warmth seemed a benediction as it played across Ayda's bared skin.

Omn blesses this day.

She willed it to be true. The Unknowable One had Its moments of caprice, but she had glimpsed Its plan. Ever since, she had dedicated herself to that mission. Every spring since first donning an acolyte's robes, she had given to the Holy Catedrál. The rest, she would gladly yield.

She had spilled blood in Omn's name. Enough to dye the seas red from the Hallowed Isle to the Tricolonies.

And beyond, Saints willing.

Her morning scripture lay open beside her hands, barely a passage read. Less and less, she found comfort in those ancient pages. The wisdom of her forebears lay upon it, yet did she not initiate a new aeon? Did she not Ascend the stairs of the heavens to join their revered ranks?

No, it was not to the Saints she should look for guidance, but another. A more visceral authority.

Her attendants had suffered the edge of her agitation that morning. She had sent them from her chambers claiming a need for solitude and meditation yet had not seated herself upon the cushions before Omn's altar, nor taken up the prayer beads of her matron Saint, San Inhoa. Pacing the balcony provided more comfort, and the sight of her paladins lining the white walls of the campus below the Basilica Sóveran was a firmer cornerstone for strength. She kept her veil pulled up, even that thin barrier seeming to restrict her need for air.

Her Shrouded Eye prickled with his arrival.

"Ayda." A voice as timeworn as Monte Ardiente itself spoke behind her. "Do not say you were waiting for us?"

Us. Her mind caught on that unexpected wording. World King Baltesar might claim the royal address, but she had not thought to hear it from these ancient lips.

But she had not become the highest priestess in the Holy Catedrál by letting every errant thought show. Wishing she had thought to lower her veil, Ayda kept her expression placid as she bowed to her visitor. "Undying One."

A glimpse of him made her grateful for the moment to regain her composure. The Saints' Servant had always been capable of shifting his form, but the changes she witnessed now were greater than any before. His skin, once cracked and blackened as if by flames, had smoothed and gained the sheen of umber wood. His slim physique beneath his luxurious robes and sanguine sash had swelled like a soldier recruit after months of training. Most startling was his essence. To her Shrouded Eye, he shone as bright as Omn Itself, many thousands of souls contributing to its radiance. Painful even to behold.

"Undying...yes. More than ever before." The immortal twisted his lips, suppler now than when she had last seen him.

Mockery. She quelled a ripple in her soul. Decades of his visits had taught her to bridle her pride. Even the Altacura could be humbled before one such as he.

She recited her mantra silently, as she did each time he

came. *He does Omn's will. He ushers in the Epoch of Belief. No sea of sin is too dark or deep for the world's deliverance.*

The Saints' Servant moved past to peer beyond her balcony. For how cavalier he was with his presence, it was a wonder so few had seen him. Those foolish enough to mention it once had never spoken again.

Doubts assailed her as she remembered ordering those deaths.

He does Omn's will.

Silence pooled within her chambers. Ayda moistened her lips before breaking it.

"Undying One, how may I serve you this day?"

He turned his gaze upon her. His eyes had also changed. Before, they had appeared like twin abysses, and staring into them felt like glimpsing into Legion's black hells. Now his gray eyes were as hard and unyielding as his skin, if veiled like an elder going blind. With piercing intent, they chiseled into her, body and soul.

"Unless we have erred in our judgment, we shall soon have...let us call them *visitors*. Perhaps they will come this season. Perhaps the next."

"Visitors?"

"Oh, yes, Ayda. Of a most cordial variety." He smiled, each sharp tooth as gray as a tempestuous sea. "They will be few in number, but you are not to underestimate them. Take every precaution."

"It shall be done, Undying One."

Trepidation shivered through her. Did this mean more of his kind were coming? How many more hid in the depths of Unera, only now revealing themselves after untold centuries?

They feel the changes we bring. The last thrashes of Legion before the devil's fall.

Whatever their form, she would meet their enemies and overcome them. She, Gran Ayda, who would become a Sacred

Saint before her time on this mortal sphere was through. When she unified with Omn in eternal bliss—decades in the future, Saints willing—she would be welcomed with all the adoration suited to a Bride of Heaven. Her sins would be burned away by the Blinding One's light.

The Saints' Servant slapped his hands together. The ensuing *crack* overcame even Ayda's self-possession. He cast her his too-wide smile as she startled.

"Now," he spoke as the echo faded, "we are ready for our refreshment."

Refreshment. A soft word for such a sinful thing. But who was she to defy a messenger of the divine?

She bowed her head and looked to the adjoining chamber. "Instrument, join us."

A hand swept aside the curtain that separated it, revealing a gray-robed man, head shorn of hair. His expression didn't shift as his eyes fell on the visitor, nor did he hesitate to approach and stop before them.

Little disturbed the placid minds of odiosas. Yet another aspect for which Ayda found them as odious as their name.

The Saints' Servant stalked around the man as a cat might fuss over its meal. Lifting a long, taloned finger, he traced the odiosa's jaw and neck until he completed his revolution. A thin red line followed his touch as the sharp nail parted skin.

The Instrument did not flinch, only stood there, eyes staring forward, both attentive and absent.

The immortal's smile evaporated. The life in his eyes brightened as he stood before the odiosa once more, hand falling away.

"So empty," he murmured. "So pliant. Though useful in his own way. But there is satisfaction to a challenge, do you not think, Ayda?"

She ignored his question. Experience had taught her to

ignore his macabre imagination. "If he does not please you, Undying One, another may be found."

"Oh, we can find plenty of prey on our own." His smile flashed again, feral as any beast's, before he faced the enrobed man once more. "For the moment, he shall suffice."

Then the immortal lunged at his prey.

Only his spirit moved—the Saints' Servant did not assault by the flesh—but the violence was no less for it. Ayda watched as the divine messenger ravaged the odiosa. The man crumpled as his body went dark and lifeless. A corpse not yet grown cold.

Ayda kept her expression placid and her body still. Could he hear her racing heart? Her repressed breaths? No matter how many times she witnessed this sacrifice, she never grew accustomed to it.

The immortal tilted back his head and closed his eyes. His arms spread, much as Ayda had done when welcoming the sun's touch. For a moment, he was perfectly still as only his kind could achieve.

Then he sighed. Remnants of the odiosa's spirit wafted on his exhalation.

Opening his eyes, the Saints' Servant let his arms fall back to his side and faced her. His body, writhing with yet one more spirit, seemed engorged by it.

"Once these visitors are dispatched," the Servant said, "we have another task for you."

"I do your will, Undying One."

Those gray lips smiled. "Burn the colonies down. All of them. Only from ashes can faith grow anew."

Ayda could not hide her surprise. "Burn them? Is there no other way?"

"Not until the harvest is finished." The Servant gestured to her, a casual flick of his hand. Even that felt a threat knowing the strength and speed latent in the limb. "You are our storm; we are the scythe. Only together can we cull humanity into a devout congregation."

She bowed again, hoping to hide the fear trembling through her being. "If it is within my power, it shall be so, Undying One."

Though the Saints damn me for it.

"Do not fail us, Ayda." His tone was light, almost pleasant, but his eyes darkened the words with portent. "We shall return upon their arrival. All shall be as we command."

Before she could respond, the immortal ripped the world asunder and vanished.

Ayda, still on the verge of speaking, swallowed her words and stared at the empty space. With a shake of her head, she returned to the balcony and let her hands rest on the stone. Still cold from the wintry night, but Omn's return slowly warmed it.

She basked in the light, hoping to banish the chill quivering through her. To sear away the sins clawing ever deeper into her soul.

PART I

THE EXILE'S HOME

1

EMBRACE

The jungle huddled around Leiyn as she tailed her quarry.

He walked ahead, unhurried and unbothered, demonstrating little care for what might linger in the dense forest. Not once had he turned to examine his surroundings since she followed him. Single-minded in his purpose, he left himself open to ambush.

And pursuit.

Still, Leiyn took every precaution to escape notice. She breathed through her mouth, measured every step, and avoided dead branches and fallen fronds. Winter was mild in the Ofean wilds, but its influence had discarded shriveled leaves from the canopy, making a hundred hazards necessary to avoid. Like a jaguar stalking prey, she slunk around trees, shrubs, and ferns, careful not to let her clothes snag.

To be discovered might spell Batu's death.

Guilt threaded through her at tailing her friend, but she saw scant other choice. That he had snuck off under the cover of darkness was telling of his intent. A mission that Leiyn knew could only lead to danger.

So she pursued him, unseen and unheard. She even veiled her lifeforce. Though Batu did not possess lifesense as she understood it, in the months spent at their refuge, he seemed to have attained some glimmer of it. Even when she approached with her softest footfalls, she rarely surprised him. He would turn with that solemn stare of his, eyes a reflection of the emptiness in her own heart.

Hollow, both of us. Like two rotted stumps.

She banished the thought. Thinking of their shared loss would not help. Distraction could imperil them both. Though Batu would never intentionally bring harm upon her or their party, intentions could be corrupted.

Particularly with what the plainsrider sought.

Leiyn followed Batu across an overgrown stream, its water trickling through a carpet of mossy stones, then up the opposite bank. They traveled next to the rivulet uphill. With her shoes muddy, it was difficult to keep her footsteps silent, but Leiyn managed as best she could. The growing gloom in the shrouded jungle made it trickier still. The creatures amid the branches provided inadvertent assistance, birds and insects filling the forest with their muffled, repetitive songs.

She yearned to open her lifesense. To be part of it all. The absence inside her yawned widest when her walls separated her from the web of surrounding life.

Yet she resisted. If she alerted him to her presence, he would turn back, then return another time without her.

She could not lose him.

They continued to climb, heading east toward the Ofean side of the Radiante Slopes. Leiyn had guessed their destination from the start, but her conviction grew with every step. So, too, did her foreboding.

Don't do this, she willed to Batu. *Don't throw your life away.*

He would not have heeded her even if she had spoken. Be it a taint in his blood or the sorrow in his marrow, her friend was lost to any insight she could offer.

The cave eluded her at first. Covered with moss and overhanging vines, it blended into the verdant hillside. But as Batu neared the mouth, Leiyn detected the beckoning darkness beyond the vegetation.

Darkness was not all that lay within.

Her heart crowded into her throat, choking her. The urge to cough became nearly irrepressible. Fear pulsed through her as Batu strode on with that same resigned determination, shoulders bowed and eyes lifted.

Should she cry out, stop this before it went further? What if she saved his life now only to doom him tomorrow?

Rarely had she suffered from indecision. It chafed all the more for its unfamiliarity.

Leiyn ghosted behind a fallen trunk. Between the fresh saplings growing from their fallen kin, she watched Batu, hardly daring to blink. Moving so slowly her muscles ached, she shrugged her longbow into hand, drew a broadhead arrow, and nocked it. Better if she did not have to use it, but it was a comfort to be prepared.

The pressure against her veiled lifesense presaged its coming.

Batu stopped a handful of paces from the entrance. He did not reach for his battle axe, tucked into a loop at his hip, but continued to wait, unshifting as a rocky outcropping in a storm-riven sea.

The mouth of the cave was three strides tall and twice as many wide. The beast that emerged nearly filled it.

Leiyn tensed her bowstring as the creature came into view. A bear, by all appearances, yet so large she might have mistaken it for a titan. Was it five times Batu's weight? Six? On all fours, the beast rose no higher than Batu's chest, but standing upright, it looked to double that. Even the snow ape they had encountered on their way to Qasaar had not loomed so large.

A swipe of its paw could break bones. A bite could tear through limbs, enchanted armor be damned. This was no creature to be trifled with.

More perplexing than its size was its fur. Pale as snow, it seemed ordinary until a stray moonbeam fell on its coat. It struck like a spark on dry brush. Light spread across the bear. In moments, all of it glowed with a pale luminescence.

Even with her lifesense closed, there could be no doubt to its nature. This was a spirit beast like her silver fox, Chispa, and Ketti's emerald hummingbird. One not entirely of Unera.

Back away! she urged Batu silently. *Spread your arms and make yourself seem large!*

Even as she thought it, she doubted the usual tactics for warding off bears would work. This creature wielded innate magic, straddling the line between worlds. It would be too much to hope it could be intimidated by a paltry show of force.

Batu did not attempt any such tact. Flouting his plainsrider training, he lifted his chin to stare the pearlescent bear in the eyes. Set in the large, pale face, those fuchsia eyes appeared like pits into fiery hells. She imagined all manner of foul feeling lay behind them. Malice. Ravenous hunger. Affront at this blatant invasion.

But Batu had not yet finished his foolishness. Leiyn watched, helpless, as her friend raised his hands to the white bear's face. The hulking beast beheld him, neither growling nor retreating. Its claws did not paw at the ground. Its ears remained upright rather than folded back.

But she could not trust her eyes. Leiyn raised her bow. Her mahia's walls trembled, the need to lower them battling with prudence.

Batu paused and glanced over his shoulder. Leiyn almost called out a warning, for the bear chose that moment to move. Yet it did not strike as she feared, but drew back, its hackles rising.

Before the words could press past her teeth, the former plainsrider faced forward again. To her relief, he let his hands fall to his sides and stepped back. She began to hope this foolhardy endeavor was at an end when Batu folded onto the ground in the middle of the clearing. Crossing his legs, he sat facing the spirit beast.

The white bear's hackles dropped. For several long minutes, it regarded the intruder with an unreadable stare. Then it, too, sat back on its haunches.

The bear set to cleaning itself.

Leiyn let her bow fall and loosened her drawhand. As the creature licked its fur with methodical leisure—*his* fur, she saw as he displayed his sex—she realized neither Batu nor the bear intended to move soon. She funneled a sliver of esse throughout her body, easing the stiffness already setting in. But as a ranger of the Wilds Lodge, she had trained in such vigils.

How long they remained in their standoff, Leiyn could not say. Night set in. The moon that had shone on the beast hid behind clouds, and the illumination of his fur faded. The bear progressed from cleaning his chest to twist around and attempt to reach his back.

He had moved to licking his paw to clean his face when Batu rose again. The bear regarded his visitor with fresh interest. Leiyn swallowed, the sound loud in her ears.

Batu approached. Again, his hands lifted as he closed the final feet between them.

Leiyn caged her tongue once more behind her teeth. She watched her friend take that last damning step, then reach his hands out to touch the reclining bear.

His fingers brushed the white fur lining the bear's muzzle.

His palms pressed against the flesh. The beast did not strike him, but held Batu's stare, unblinking.

Feshtado *fool!* she railed. *What in Legion's hells are you doing?*

But she had known from the beginning what this was. An exploration. A delving into the buried parts of himself.

An acceptance of his heritage.

Batu had been told he carried a taint in his blood. Much like Leiyn had with her magic, he had regarded this sliver of Iritu within himself with horror and revulsion.

But it was still part of him. And as she had discovered with her mahia, denying a part of yourself only led to ruin.

A fresh sensation brushed against her mahia's walls, ending Leiyn's trust.

Carefully, she lowered her walls and extended her lifesense past them. It was a struggle to comprehend what she felt. Batu's lifeforce leaked from his body in a way she had never felt from him, flowing into the bear. And the bear's esse flowed into him.

Tainted.

Beastfolk, most called people like Batu. Ata had named them wildsouls. The name did not matter to Leiyn.

She only knew she could not lose him.

"Batu!"

Leiyn stood from her hiding place as she shouted. She kept her bow lowered, but the nocked arrow told of her readiness to harm.

The bear jerked back, startled. She aimed, fearing its aggression. It did not strike at Batu but bared its teeth at her. Slowly, she lowered the bow again.

Batu retreated a dozen paces. When he was out of immediate danger, he turned to her. She flinched at his expression.

"Come on," he snarled. "We need to speak." With a final

glance at the spirit beast, Batu stalked back down the path away from the den.

Fear of a different flavor filled Leiyn as she followed her friend down the slope.

2

HAVEN

"You shouldn't have come."

They were the first words Batu had spoken since leaving the bear's den. Silence hung between them, thick as moss gathered on the boulders along the verdant stream.

Shame should have driven her to an apology. But Leiyn had rarely behaved as she should.

"What would you have done if I hadn't?" she countered.

Her friend paused and looked back over his shoulder. The beard thickening across his jaw lent him a wilder look of late, exacerbated by his unrelenting scowl. She could not help but flinch. Rare was the occasion when Batu became angry with her.

"Whatever I deemed right." He spoke through clenched teeth. "You cannot choose for me."

Too late, Leiyn adjusted her tact. "Batu, please try to understand. I know this is something you have to explore—Saints, I know better than anyone. But doing *that,* when we don't know the consequences... It's dangerous."

The plainsrider laughed, a harsh, biting thing. "You're one to speak against being rash."

"I'm the authority on it," she retorted. "Who better?"

"Just what did you think I was doing?"

Leiyn moved around Batu, tired of speaking to his back. "Bonding with it."

He failed to meet her gaze. It was all the confirmation she needed.

She wanted to seize hold of him, break the solitude that swaddled him, but did not dare. Instead, she adjusted her longbow where it hung from her shoulder.

"We don't know what would happen if you did that. I can't..." Leiyn swallowed and looked aside, not daring to voice that fear. "Isla wouldn't want that," she said. "She wouldn't want you harmed."

"Isla's not here." His words were soft, but they seethed with feeling. Like sharks swimming beneath the surface of a black sea. "She doesn't get a say in what I do. Not anymore."

"Batu..."

"The rest of you can fight." Batu stared into the dark jungle ahead, his lifefire sputtering. A campfire trying to remain lit amid a downpour. "Fight *him*. If I'd been stronger, I could have..."

"Don't." She spoke more harshly than she meant to. Casting aside caution, she grabbed his shoulder and shook him, as if that might banish the thoughts in his head. Her esse touched his, another layer of conviction. "Don't go down that path. We didn't kill her. Don't take blame that isn't yours."

She spoke as much to herself as to him. How often had she condemned herself for what happened that day? Counterfactuals haunted her sleepless nights. Nightmares came when she finally slept, taunting her with her failures.

Each time, she saw Isla's lifeless eyes staring back at her. Her friend's blood staining her hands.

Batu looked askance at her. "I don't," he said, softer now. "But it doesn't change the facts. You have your mahia and Clouded Fang. Ketti has magic. So does Ekosa. Teya has enough to get by. And Ata is Ata. You all can fight lyshans and odiosas and titans. While I..." He shook his head. "I can't. Not as I am. But my tainted blood—my heritage," he corrected himself, adopting the word Ata used to refer to it. "If I embrace it, I can fight with you. I can take down that bastard."

Leiyn let her hand fall away. She wanted to deny his reasoning, but he was right, in part. Batu's lack of mahia made him vulnerable.

And what if we lose you? she wanted to ask.

But she feared what his answer might be. Instead, she addressed the pain they shared. What drove them each day toward the edge of despair.

"I miss her, too."

He jerked his head. Agreement and acknowledgment was in that gesture, yet a trace of denial as well. As if he refused to let Isla go.

Have I?

She bumped him with an elbow. "Let's head back. Don't want the others to worry more than they already have."

Leiyn passed him to take the lead. After several strides, Batu followed.

The jungle thinned as they neared their sanctuary.

Even set in a clearing, Leiyn might have missed their refuge in the gloom had she not known it was there. Haven, they called this place. In a way, it resembled the hollowed maple of the dryvans' Glade, a house formed of a living tree. Every balcony, ceiling, and floor was the wood of that grand kapok. Its leaves, yellowed but clinging to the branches, shaded them in a draping canopy. Ridged roots congregated to form a ramp up to its upper levels.

At another time, she would have marveled at it as a wonder. Now, she only saw it as a ruin. In the scant light, she could have almost believed it haunted. No campfire warmed its mossy lengths, nor did life glow from within beyond a few animal inhabitants. Yet she felt those lingering out of sight, an untouchable itch.

Leiyn continued striding forward as she reached her mahia deep into the ground.

Clouded Fang.

The ash dragon roused to consider her with his searing gaze. For a time after Isla's death and Leiyn's exile, grief had dampened her power so that she wondered if it would ever return. But in the months after, the formation of grottos came easier than ever. No longer did she fear becoming lost in the tangle of life spread across the world. If anything, part of her longed for it.

The same held true of her titan. Each time she summoned him, more of the ash dragon swept through her. Threatening to consume her, should she let him.

She always clawed her way back to herself. Just.

Even with the titan fathomless leagues below, their bond was strong enough that Clouded Fang did not need to rise to lend her his strength. A shock of power rolled into her, then burst through the air.

Their refuge transformed.

No longer was Haven cold and dark but illuminated by firelight. The windows, empty before, echoed with the sound of conversation. Ketti's laugh carried across the clearing, spiking irritation through Leiyn. All amusement did that of late.

She stifled it, as she had these past three months. A necessary measure lest she drive her friends away.

Those few who remain.

Batu's step barely stuttered as they entered the grotto. He could not achieve the transition on his own, but he had undergone it enough times to be inured to its effects. Little rattled him these days.

It was she whose heart still squeezed. Whose fear threatened to whip her temper into a fury if she loosened her grip on it, even for a moment.

Grief makes monsters of us, Tadeo had told the rangers once after losing one of their own to a titan's awakening. *You must guard against it as any foe.*

Ever before, she had warded it away. Even when she lost Tadeo and the rest of the Wilds Lodge, she had kept going.

Now, she wondered if she could.

Breathe, just breathe.

Leiyn steadied her breathing as she climbed the sinuous ramp to their home, Batu trailing behind. By the time she reached the main chamber, her mind had faded back to numbness. As much relief as she ever felt.

Beyond the archway awaited their comrades. Ketti and Ekosa nestled together on a curved bench beside the bonfire burning within the central pit. The months had worn subtle changes into the Eteman. She had relaxed and laughed often with her beloved. Occasionally, when Ekosa whispered in her ear, Leiyn caught a blush warming her face.

Leiyn had to squash the resentment that flared up. Unfair though it was, witnessing a blossoming love grated against her grief.

Ekosa provided no relief, for he matched Ketti's warmth. Yet during their stay at Haven, the *eesu* had shown himself to be as steady and thoughtful as Leiyn had first estimated him to be. Toward Ketti especially, he was gentle and caring, and toward the others he showed sensitivity to their troubles.

Many was the night he spent with Batu, distracting the plain-srider from his loss.

The months had wrought physical changes upon Ekosa as well. His hair grew out thick as a shrub, and the braid down the back of his neck widened. A beard spread across his face, though he did not let it grow as wild as Batu's. Only Ekosa's thin frame remained untouched, the jungle during the winter months providing too poor of fare.

At their entrance, the pair looked up. Ketti's smile slipped away, expression smoothing with expectation. Biqqa continued to flutter above their heads, the emerald hummingbird's long beak dipping into honeysuckle flowers that had crept through a seam in the ceiling.

Leiyn did not look at Ketti yet but raised her chin to stare at where Teya stood. Out of sight, she leaned on a balcony, peering into the gloom—or, with her limited lifesense, glimpsing the shimmering haze of the jungle's esse.

Below the Gast scout and under the cover of the treehouse sheltered their four mounts, fetched for them by Ata in the days following their arrival at Haven. Teya's draconion, Bane, lay still, his lifefire reduced to what would have been a worrying level in another beast. Almost, the huge reptile seemed to hibernate. His stillness did not prevent the three horses—Feral, Saikan, and Isla's old mount, Mottle—from skirting to the far side of the shelter, their lifefires radiating vigilance. For Mottle and Saikan, Leiyn could muster pity. That proved more difficult for her own ornery horse.

With Chispa and Ata departed, she had the full count. Everyone was safe.

For now.

Leiyn faced Ketti. "You should have warned me."

The Eteman stood and met her gaze. The precious stones dotting her skin sparked in the firelight. "We are each free to do as we would," she murmured. "Is that not so?"

Heat swirled through her like fire building in Clouded Fang's belly. "It's not safe to wander at night."

"Don't blame her." Batu angled between Leiyn and the Eteman. "It was my choice."

She met his eyes before looking back at Ketti. Neither of their expressions shifted.

Ekosa stood beside his beloved. "Please, everyone. It is late and we are all weary. Perhaps this is best discussed in the morning."

Leiyn knew he spoke wisely, but she could not contain her fraying fears.

"So what?" she snapped. "I'm just supposed to let you get killed by lyshans? Sharo knows where we are—he has to. Every time we step outside this grotto, we're taking a risk. We have to make sure it's worth it."

At her raised voice, Biqqa fled through a window to hover outside. The chamber filled with quiet, broken only by the crackling of the fire. Leiyn felt Teya approaching before she filled the doorway on the opposite side of the room.

"Redlock."

Warning rang in the scout's voice. Leiyn cast one more look at their companions, hoping her words had gotten through to them. Their expressions told otherwise.

"I must do this, Leiyn." Once, it had been Batu's habit to speak so softly he was difficult to hear. Now, his baritone filled the room. "It will be worth it."

She did not look at Ketti and Ekosa, knowing what she would find. Their agreement spread like an odorless vapor.

Leiyn gave the best compromise she could. "We'll discuss it when Ata returns."

"As you wish," Ketti replied, her tone implying that much was left unsaid.

Weariness washed over Leiyn. *Saints, I'm tired of this.* Each day, the beast caged inside her lashed out at her friends.

The fear she would drive them away only made it more unruly. Did they not see she only tried to protect them? That she could not keep them safe if they put themselves at risk?

"I need rest," she muttered. "Night." Apologies tumbled through her head, but she could not find the energy to voice them.

Her companions returned her farewell as Leiyn moved around the fire pit to where Teya waited. The scout inclined her head toward the archway, then led her through.

They traveled across the balcony to where the mass of thick vines collected. It served as a ladder, allowing them to reach the loft above. Grown used to the climb, Leiyn managed it easily even with her bow slung over a shoulder. Pulling aside the curtain of ivy after Teya, she hauled herself into their room.

The loft was shaped like a bulb just beginning to blossom. The narrow opening at the top of the curved walls of smooth wood was covered with a thick growth of vines that served as well as a thatched roof. For all the wonder of Haven's construction, its furnishings were modest. Lacking wardrobes and chests, they had strewn their belongings across the floor, the months eroding habits of preparedness. What sparse furniture there was had been grown from the wood and was strangely proportioned. Designed for bodies not quite human.

The primary piece was the canopy bed in the middle. Ivy hung in curtains around the sides, providing a modicum of privacy and, more importantly, shelter from bugs. Though only made of moss and wood with their bedrolls spread over the top, the hum of heritage, Iritu magic imbued in it long ago, made it as yielding and comfortable as any bed Leiyn had slept in.

Teya stood at the foot of the bed, staring at her. An invitation in that look.

"Not too tired?" she asked as she parted the hanging ivy.

Leiyn shrugged off her bow and leaned it against the sloping wall next to the rest of her gear, then deposited her weapons belt and quiver next to it. Standing, she held Teya's gaze as she approached with purpose. Her hands found Teya's hips and swayed her closer before murmuring in her ear.

"Suppose I have a minute or two."

Teya smiled. Just enough light infiltrated the room for Leiyn to notice that the smile only touched her mouth. She focused on her beloved's lips and leaned into them.

Teya came alive against her skin. Their lifefires leaned toward one another, extending from their bodies to merge.

Lips pressed together. Tongues darting. Esses flirting, twisting, twining.

Teya encircled Leiyn in her arms and moved them onto the bed. Their limbs entangled as much as their lifeforce. Flames raced along her skin, soothing, invigorating. Burning away all other thoughts.

Leiyn yielded to the moment. Escape lay in Teya's embrace. She drank it down, thirsty for even the faintest taste.

Fleeting though its comfort proved to be.

3

COLD CLAWS

Night, Leiyn's father once told her, *is when fear comes out. Cage it, lion cub. Deny it. Don't think of your fears—think of me. Of your home. Remember what brings you joy.*

Perhaps that was why she hardly slept. Fear had swallowed what little joy she had.

She forced herself to lie next to Teya long after she knew sleep would not come. Leiyn had hoped their intimacy would morph into rest. Instead, sorrow clawed back in, raking across her soul.

She had already tried inhabiting her senses to clear her mind. Inhaling the earthy perfume of their surroundings and Teya's scent lingering on her skin. Listening to the songs of crickets and potoos, the wind rustling through the leaves.

But when her focus drifted, in the pause between thoughts—there, fear pounced.

Her other practice of listing the tasks needing to be done the next day was similarly ineffective. Inevitably, thinking of the future led to her worries for it. That they had delayed too long here in the Ofean wilderness. That she was incapable of action. Paralyzed by doubt.

Each day, she pressed back against that drowning tide. She had not lain idle, but striven to harness the power that could keep her and her friends alive. And she had mastered the forming of grottos in a season when it had taken Ketti years to learn. Clouded Fang was a part of her, no more than a thought away.

She prepared to battle her fear. But still, she feared meeting it.

You're not enough, a voice resembling Sharo's whispered during the sleepless nights. *You'll never be enough. How could you be? You weren't enough to save her.*

As with every night, there came a point where she could no longer endure it. Leiyn rose silently, ducked beneath the curtain of ivy, and drew on her clothes. She scarcely knew why she bothered taking them off.

Slipping on her shoes, she climbed to the balcony below and leaned on the railing. Only Young Chiuni, the smaller moon, was out that night. Its scant light draped over the clearing but failed to penetrate the foliage beyond.

Leiyn closed her eyes and spread her lifesense, immersing herself in the jungle. Claiming what comfort she could in the web of life. When that did not ease the ache in her chest, she reached for the pouch at her hip and drew out the fox figurine. Its features had begun to smooth from her constant touch, but it was the faint spark within that mattered more. The last remnant of a man who had been as good as a father.

Tadeo, she called to him through her mahia. Beseeching him to respond.

Too little of him remained.

Since first sensing him as she drowned in Anchor's Refuge, she had reached for more. To communicate with his spirit and know him as she had in life. Yet all she could sense was that vague spark of lifefire. Only that the lodgemaster had held it while he died assured her it was him.

Even with so little of him left, to feel him with her, to know it was Tadeo...it was enough. Enough for her to press on.

We're ready. I am ready.

She had purged herself of shortcomings. Her ash dragon was ever ready to be summoned. She sensed Unera in its entirety, and from that awareness, could form and step through grottos. Her aim with an arrow and her skill with her Iritu falchions had never been keener.

She was ready to hunt.

Only one flaw remained to undermine her. The fear that found her when she let down her guard.

If you let her die, that insidious voice whispered, *how can you save any of them?*

She had learned to ignore her doubts. Now, purpose was what she needed most. A target to sight.

Still, it was denied to her.

Though Ata spent most of her time away from Haven, departing for days and weeks at a time, she had little to show for it. Only hints and rumors of where Sharo might have been. The sly lyshan remained as elusive as before.

They suspected the same could not be said of themselves. Practicing with mahia outside their grotto—Leiyn in harnessing Clouded Fang, Ketti and Ekosa leashing other titans—was too conspicuous to hope otherwise. Ata could sense mahia across much of the Veiled Lands. She claimed her fellow Iritu had similar capacities.

Sharo was not coming after them. There would be no luring him to his fate. They had to seek him out.

Leiyn clenched her hands into fists and pressed into the smooth, wood railing. Time. The more time they gave Sharo, the deeper he burrowed into human society. He and his lyshans might devise ways of beating them. New, dreadful techniques that would end their stuttering rebellion.

Then who would stop him from enslaving humanity?

They could not give him more time. Still, Leiyn doubted her motivations. Ever had she been rash. Impatient. The arrow hastily aimed rarely found its mark. They had to know where to go before conducting an attack.

But if I don't find a target, she thought, lifting her chin, *I might just shoot for the moons.*

"I thought I wore you out."

Leiyn turned as Teya descended from their loft. She had felt her stirring above but had not dredged up the will to face her. Now, she painted on a smile.

"Sorry to wake you, my sky."

The scout waved a hand, feigning nonchalance. "I would be a poor *situal* if I could not go one night without rest."

Quiet fell. Neither acknowledged that, after Teya's decision to follow Leiyn into exile, she was a *situal* no longer.

Leiyn traced constellations with her eyes. Teya had given up everything to be here. They all had. Each was an exile, self-imposed or by decree. Their goal was nearly all they shared in common.

It cannot be for nothing.

"The exile has no home." The words left her lips before she could reconsider them. "Ekosa said that before, I think."

"It sounds like the very definition of the word." Teya kept her voice light.

Leiyn raised an eyebrow. "You know it's more than that."

The former *situal* inclined her head and looked out over the jungle. Leiyn faced forward as well. Limned with moonlight, lush green leaves transformed into scythes of silver. Beautiful but deadly. Cold.

Once, they would have huddled together against the night. Now, each warmed themselves with lifefire alone.

A bitter laugh worked free of Leiyn. "You know, with everything that's happened, I'd almost think we're all cursed by Omn. But that'd be a shit god to do all this."

A breath passed before Teya murmured, "Then what do you believe?"

Leiyn's smile slipped away. She had seen the teachings of the Holy Catedrál unravel, one after the other, since she had embraced her mahia. Seen Gast and Eteman worldviews affirmed by the formation of grottos and the bonding and commanding of titans. The Altacura, leader to all Omnists, was a puppet made to dance to Sharo's whims. Even the Saints were held suspect, for had not most of them served as the Altacura in their time? Perhaps none were as virtuous as the scriptures made them seem.

She shook her head. "Does it matter? Doesn't change what we have to do."

"It matters." Teya glanced at Leiyn, an emphasis to her words.

Silence fell again, a smothering curtain. Leiyn endured it as long as she could. Uttering what she knew she must almost came as a relief.

"Think we'll find him?"

The former scout did not have to ask whom she meant. "We might," she said, each word as stiff as a marching Suncoat. "If we do not remain in hiding."

Leiyn hid her flinch. She should not have been surprised by the bite of Teya's bitterness. She had not only lost her people, but her authority as a Spear. Her purpose. Yet, coming from Teya, that sting hurt too much to prepare for.

"You're right," Leiyn said at length.

Teya turned to her. "Am I?"

"Yes. We've waited long enough." Leiyn pushed away from the railing. "Once Ata returns, we're going. And if we still don't have a destination, then we'll figure out where to start searching."

Teya straightened. "May she return tomorrow, spirits willing."

Leiyn suspected no spirit gave a damn—those traveling with them being the exception. She nodded toward their loft.

"Come on. Let's see if we cannot catch a few hours still."

She climbed after Teya back into their loft, praying Omn would hurry Its ascent and bring an end to the interminable hours to come.

4

BEYOND SIGHT

Ata did not return the next day, nor the day after. Leiyn tried filling the time as best she could. After martial training with Batu and Teya, she practiced her mahia against Ketti and Ekosa. Reaching out to Clouded Fang, she formed grottos a dozen times over before she was satisfied that their bond remained strong and accessible. She hunted for their meals and pretended to make merry around the nightly fire. In the spare moments between, she indulged in sketching, focusing on replicating the perfect lines of the flora and fauna around Haven.

For a time, she drove out the intrusive thoughts. But her chest never loosened.

Her only relief was that Batu did not return to the bear's cave. He only bided his time, no doubt, but any delay was welcome. As she lay awake at night, she pictured all the ways bonding with the pale beast could go wrong.

But the more she sat with it, the less she could justify her resistance. Only the plainsrider neglecting to mention it kept her from having to confront it again.

The third day finally saw Ata's appearance.

The dryvan came in the middle of the afternoon while Leiyn and Ekosa were out fetching water. Even amid a city, the dryvan would have been difficult to miss, and neither she nor the *eesu* could fail to notice her blazing into being in the quiet glade. Loading up Feral with the waterskins, they hurried back to Haven.

The others were still gathering around when Leiyn and Ekosa arrived. Depositing their loads in a corner of the central chamber, they joined the others. Ata looked no worse for wear from her journey. Scars marred her face and body, marks from their recent encounters with lyshans—most notably the eye taken by Khamo, the armored devil who had nearly done them all in. Leiyn had never extracted a straight answer from the Iritu on whether she kept the scars intentionally or if she truly could not heal them. If any crossed Ata's chest, they were hidden by Chispa's silver fur. Each time she ventured out, the spirit fox went with her, allowing her to reenter Haven without Ketti or Leiyn's intercession.

"Much the same as before," Ata was saying. "Suncoats burrowing in along the coast, stranded and desperate. Your consul trying to secure his borders. Conflict between the colonies." She waved one elongated hand, her eyes—one white and blind, the other chartreuse—traveling to Leiyn. "Rebellion things, as you'd expect."

Leiyn tightened her jaw at that. Once, she had dedicated her life to Baltesia. Protecting its borders, its people. That was a ranger's duty, and she'd embraced it wholeheartedly.

No more.

Their "secessionary conflict," as Lord Consul Mauricio had once termed it, meant little to her now. That war paled next to the greater struggle against Sharo and his allies. A distraction from broader stakes. The continued existence of humanity trumped any other concerns.

And Baltesia was no longer her home. Its leader had betrayed her.

As you betrayed him.

Leiyn pulled her thoughts back from the brink. Follow that thread and the despair she'd fought for the past season would swallow her again. She needed to rise above it, now more than ever.

"What of Sharo?" Leiyn interjected. "Any leads on the bastard?"

Ata cocked her head, a tilt too far to be natural. "No. Not yet."

Her chest ached with fire; frustration coated her tongue like ash. She swallowed it back down. Better she burn than hurt those undeserving.

"And a way across?" Teya asked from the opposite side of the circle. By the way her eyes caught on Leiyn, her frustration had not gone unnoticed.

The dryvan started to answer when she shuddered and pressed a hand to her chest. Leiyn tensed with instinctual fear as her esse grew fever-bright, but relaxed as a creature took shape from her. To her eyes, it was a baffling sight. Silver fur peeled from Ata's skin to ravel into a snout, then a head, then the fox's lithe body.

The transformation might have been grotesque but for her mahia. Through the lifesense, it was a dazzling transition. One lifefire separated into two, the characteristics of each diverging, the individual flames dimming.

In moments, Chispa hopped to the ground, then pranced over to nestle against Leiyn's leg.

Even at her lowest, the fox could bring out a smile. Leiyn kneeled and ran a hand along him from head to tail. As ever in grottos, his coat resembled meadowgrass yet remained soft to the touch. She reveled in the nudge of his esse against hers, as warm as a friend's embrace.

"Hello there, little one," she murmured as she looked down into his apricot eyes. "Glad you're safe."

He watched her a moment longer before giving her a final nudge, then racing down the ramp.

Rising, she looked up to see the others smiling. She wondered how long it had been since she had truly smiled. Not since Chispa last left, most likely. But as she remembered the topic at hand, it slipped away.

"You were saying?" Leiyn prompted Ata.

"Ah, yes—a path to your so-called Ancestral Lands." The dryvan tapped a claw to her chin, which made an odd thudding sound against her wooden flesh. "For mortals, a ship from Altan Gaz remains your most promising avenue. Braving the northern wastes would not be comfortable, I think." She flashed them a mouthful of teeth, sharp even without Chispa's influence.

"That is no more than we knew before," Ketti pointed out.

"No. But as I explored the desolation of that city, Breakbay, a thought occurred to me. You might take a marine Vast One instead."

Leiyn frowned at the thought. *Sail atop a titan?* Breakbay was dangerous enough without that dubious goal. Overrun by titans during the Titan War against the Gasts, the Ilberian port had been abandoned to the colossal creatures ever since.

Teya seemed to share her thoughts. Crossing her arms, she shook her head. "I know Ketti accomplished this before, but she nearly drowned on that whale. Those without *semah* would fare poorly, I think."

No one looked at Batu, but Leiyn knew whom the former *situal* referenced.

"Not as I am," Batu said. "But as a wildsoul, I might endure it."

She should have seen it coming. Too late, she saw the inevitability of the topic's resurgence.

"No." Leiyn stepped forward. "We're not doing this again."

"Leiyn," Teya interceded, warning in her voice.

She kept her eyes on Batu. Once, he would have crumpled under her withering look. Now, the plainsrider met it with an unflinching stare.

"Oh-ho," Ata breathed, her mismatched eyes sliding from one person to the next. "So we have finally come to this." The dryvan turned to Batu and sniffed, then grinned. "You have been to the moonbear! Let me guess—our little fox followed you to its den?"

Moonbear. A fitting name for the beast. Leiyn grimaced, but she did not look away. "Someone had to."

Batu's glower made his thoughts clear on the matter.

"Everyone," Ekosa said, his hands raised, "please, let us discuss this calmly. We are allies, no? It would be better not to leap at each other's throats."

"I agree," Teya said. "Besides, we have more important matters to discuss. Such as how Batu came to choose a bear for his spirit beast when it is also his lifemark. A bit obvious, no?"

Their companions chuckled. Batu's expression lightened to a margin less thunderous.

"I don't know that I chose him," the plainsrider murmured, "so much as he chose me."

Leiyn did not smile with the others. Sucking down a breath, she let it out in a ragged stream. Fear and anger continued to spawn ice and fire throughout her body.

Cage it, lion cub.

"It's dangerous," she said with forced calm. "None of us know what will come of it. Bonding with a titan can be fatal. The same might prove true of...wildsouls and spirit beasts."

Using that term, "wildsoul," felt as if it legitimized something best forgotten. But Batu deserved better than her deriding his heritage.

"Undoubtedly. But, my friend, you forget to whom you speak." Ata tossed her head, and the blossoms tipping her vineyard hair released a shimmer of pollen. "I'm something of an authority on our shared Inheritance and transformations. The joining will not be bloodless. The little wildling may be required to prove himself to the beast. But he shall come to no true harm under my guidance. So long as you still wish to try it?"

This last question Ata posed to Batu. Leiyn turned back to Batu to find his gaze still trained on her.

"I do," he answered. No hesitation.

Cage it.

Only then did Leiyn realize the source of her fear. Of course, she wanted no harm to come to Batu, but it was more than that. Change—she feared him changing. Becoming a person she no longer recognized.

She feared him seeking revenge.

Hypocrisy, in another's eyes, yet she had more authority than most on the matter. Who better to understand its perilous pursuit, its scant fulfillment? Even as she longed to make Sharo pay for all he had done, vengeance was no longer her master. Hope for a better life, a better world—that was why she still fought.

Rage cut both ways. It had forged her into a weapon her enemies feared. But you could only bleed for so long before it hollowed you.

Before her companions' gazes, however, Leiyn could find no way to express what she'd learned. They were lessons only experience could teach. The best she could do was pull Batu back lest he tip over the edge of the abyss.

"We cannot delay anymore," she spoke into the silence that had fallen. "We have to press on and find Sharo. If Batu needs to do this, I won't stand in his way. But we must do it tonight."

Batu stared at her, his brow furrowed. Almost, she thought she detected a flicker of fear in his eyes. The others seemed similarly off-kilter, though they recovered quickly.

"Tonight." Ata nodded. "Tonight, Batu Kinblood shall become a true wildsoul."

5

WILDSOUL

The moons witnessed their return to the albino bear's den.

Batu stepped forward, Ata tailing his step. Leiyn remained at the periphery of the clearing with the others. She had brought her longbow, but kept it slung over her shoulder. Threatening overtures would only hamper their efforts.

The former plainsrider stopped several steps from the cave entrance. He wore one of the few sets of ordinary clothes they possessed at Ata's advice. Being deprived of his Eteman garments made him all the more vulnerable.

Her misgivings grew with every moment. Only the dryvan behind him kept Leiyn from pressing forward. She had seen how swiftly Ata could move when need required.

He's safe. Trust them.

As they waited, she wondered what Isla would have thought of this. Would she have approved of Batu embracing his tainted blood or shared Leiyn's fears? She felt for the sparks of her mother and Zuma, warm coals lost amidst her lifefire. If only she had been able to claim a piece of Isla before she slipped away, perhaps she would have known.

But she had not. Isla could not guide her or Batu any longer. They decided their own fates.

The bear was not long in coming. His bright presence had roused at their arrival, yet he emerged from the cave at a slow saunter. Unconcerned by the beings intruding on his territory. Unthreatened, she could only hope.

His amaranth eyes flickered over their party, his gaze lingering on Ata, then coming to a rest on Batu. With measured steps, the moonbear approached the plainsrider, every stride a reminder of his considerable bulk. The spirit beast's lifefire was unlike any Leiyn had witnessed before. Colorless and translucent, it made the bear seem more phantom than animal.

Batu advanced on the bear. Slowly, he raised a hand. Leiyn clenched her fists and pitted her will against her instincts. The others tensed beside her. Ketti and Ekosa twitched with nerves. Teya's posture remained relaxed, but her esse stirred with readiness, cerulean flames flicking outside her body as she extended her lifesense.

Only Ata defied the atmosphere. Examining a talon, she picked at it with all the fastidiousness of a chickadee cleaning its nest.

Bear and man neared each other. Batu's hand hovered next to the albino's snout.

He pressed it down.

The moonbear flinched. His lips parted to reveal yellowed teeth. A rumbling growl worked up from his belly to fill the glade.

It took all of Leiyn's will to remain where she was.

Ata ceased to preen but made no move. After several moments, the beast quieted and sealed his lips shut. Leiyn felt the bear's spirit quest forward, translucent flames curling up and around Batu's arm.

He stiffened as if the bear's touch burned, but he did not

retreat. Still as summer mountains, the plainsrider allowed the creature to explore him, within and without. The bear's nose twitched as he sniffed him, his unnatural eyes boring into Batu.

Leiyn barely saw the paw rise before it battered Batu to the ground.

She lunged, snarling, hands reaching for her weapons. But someone had thrown their arms around her to hold her back.

"Stop!" Teya hissed in Leiyn's ear. "Remember what Ata said? This is a test!"

"It's killing him!" Drawing on the amber beads at her hip for a spurt of strength, Leiyn threw off the scout and slipped her longbow into hand.

But she paused at Ata's gaze from across the clearing. The dryvan had not moved from her position, but she no longer stood in repose.

"Observe, Awakener," the dryvan commanded her.

Leiyn looked back to the scene, stomach twisting. Man and beast circled one another, Batu having regained his feet. Her friend was bleeding from a trio of tears in his shoulder, but he scarcely seemed to notice.

He's going to die.

"Leiyn," Ata cautioned again. "Do not interfere."

Batu flickered his eyes toward her, emphasizing the Iritu's words.

Only at that look did Leiyn subside. Lowering her bow, she watched, foreboding churning her stomach. A volcano simmering, waiting to erupt.

The spirit beast rumbled again, then lumbered forward before rising onto his hind legs. Batu dodged the swiping paws, then threw himself against his adversary. Even catching the moonbear blindsided, his shove had no effect, the beast far outweighing him.

The moonbear roared again as he collapsed upon Batu, driving him to the ground.

No! Every part of Leiyn yearned to leap forward. She only realized she raised her bow again when Teya's hand arrested it. Once more, Leiyn relented, striving against her instincts. Fighting down the fear.

Cage it.

The monstrous creature had Batu pinned. One great paw pressed down on the plainsrider's chest, crushing him. Yet Batu struggled on. His hands on a thick leg, Batu pushed against it. His face, littered with scrapes and cuts, was a mask of resolve as he kicked and bucked.

Futile, all of it.

She was losing him. Watching him die. *Letting* him. Her bow tried coming up on its own.

Teya pushed it back down.

The moonbear lowered his broad face to loom over Batu, snout inches away. His lips parted so it slavered over the plainsrider. Another moment, and the beast would sink his teeth in, kill and devour their friend in front of them.

But the bear did not. Instead, their boundaries bled away.

In contrast to moments before, this sharing was as gentle as the first exchange she had observed. Batu's sage lifefire and the moonbear's pale flames twisted together, melding into a ghostly green. He yielded more of himself to the spirit beast.

They were becoming one.

Instead of her fears waxing, relief washed through her. The moonbear would not kill him. Batu had passed its test. Not to overcome it, but to display just as fierce a spirit.

At last, fear gave way to curiosity.

She wondered how this merging felt. Was it as natural as her bonding with Clouded Fang, powerful and true? Or more like Chispa's soft comfort? When she embraced her mahia, she had exposed herself to all it could offer. But this went beyond anything she would experience.

Teya pressed tighter on her arm. A warning.

Leiyn blinked, reasserting her vision. Lost in lifesense, she only then realized what the former scout already had.

Batu was changing shape.

The bonding did not stop at their spirits. Like Chispa with Ata, the two joined in body as well. Where the bear's paw pressed on Batu's chest, its fur and flesh flowed over him, like sap melting down a tree trunk on a blistering summer day.

She recoiled even as it captured her fascination.

Batu's skin bulged, then pale fur burst forth. His muscles rippled and swelled, tearing through his ragged clothes. Her friend threw back his head, face twisted with agony. The transition was not devoid of pain.

Yet this was what he wanted. She had no choice but to accept it.

More and more of the moonbear went into him. Following the paw and leg, he sank in at the shoulder; then the rest followed, deflating the massive form like a doll deprived of its filling. Batu grew as he absorbed the beast, writhing and moaning all the while. He lengthened and broadened until he rivaled the bear's size.

How long they watched, she could not say. But it seemed an interminable time later that the transformation was finally complete. For a moment, the clearing lay quiet. Leiyn stared at what had become of her friend. He lay, mutated and exhausted, on the moist ground. The pale fur covering him had gone dark in places; from blood or dirt, she could not tell.

Then he roused and flipped onto his hands and feet that had transformed into elongated paws. Rising on his hind legs, he loomed over them, twice as tall as Leiyn. Batu's brown eyes were tinged pink as they peered over their group, small amid his expanded face. Some of the human she knew remained in his features, the shape and suggestion of him.

But it was a beast that looked down upon them.

Batu threw back his head and bellowed. Leiyn retreated a step with the others, then held her ground.

Her friend fell to all fours and observed them again. Then, moving at a swift lumbering lope, he fled into the jungle.

They listened until his crashing faded from hearing before any spoke. Ketti muttered something under her breath in the same manner as devout Omnists warded off evil spirits. Teya was more explicit with her curses.

"*Gresht!* I do not know what I expected, but it was not that."

Leiyn shook her head in silent agreement. Part of her followed Batu's flight through the dense forest, her lifesense tracking his progress.

Ata smiled as she sauntered back to them. "He'll be at it until the moons set. A bit like the 'teething' you mortals go through. Has to sort out the snags and twists." She rolled her head around as if to work out kinks in her neck. "No need to wait here. He will find us when he is ready."

"He'll be safe?" Formidable as he now appeared, Leiyn doubted Batu could take on a lyshan alone. Especially not when he was still unpracticed in this new form.

"Safe as any of us." The feathers fluttered on the dryvan's shoulders with her shrug.

Teya pressed a hand to Leiyn's back, guiding her down the path by which they had arrived. "You cannot protect him from this," she murmured. "Come. Let us wait where it is warmer."

With a last look after Batu, her friend growing more distant by the minute, Leiyn sighed and turned away.

6

THE UNTROD PATH

True to Ata's prediction, Batu did not return until long after moonlight faded from the sky. Gray twilight foretold dawn's coming when Leiyn caught sight of him. The others had entered the grotto, but she had kept her vigil from without. Other spirit beasts could allow admission into the grotto, but she did not know if the moonbear had that capacity.

How little she knew of any of this.

The moonbear did not return with him, however. After roaming the woods, Batu looked as ragged as his esse implied. Emerging into the clearing surrounding Haven, she saw he was nearly naked, mere scraps of clothes clinging to his frame. Scrapes and cuts crisscrossed his body, and bruises were evident on his chest.

But she was happier to see him injured than covered in pale fur.

She descended the ramp to meet him. His hair, normally bound atop his head, fell in a sweat-soaked curtain about his face as he met her gaze.

"You alright?" She scanned his shabby appearance.

He smiled. His shoulders were bowed, but only from weariness. No shred of shame of who he was remained.

He's come a long way.

She was about to lead him up the ramp when he spoke. "I feel...complete. More than I have since losing her."

Her. Between them, there could only ever be one "her."

"While with Sarryl," he continued, "I—"

"Sarryl? The moonbear?"

He nodded, eyes vague, his gaze seeming to reach beyond the treehouse. "'Moonlight' in my tongue. He revealed it to me, I think. Or perhaps I invented it." Batu shook his head. "While together, it's difficult to know which thoughts are his and which are mine."

Almost, she envied him that. "Strange," she murmured. "That's not how it is with Clouded Fang."

Even after months spent strengthening their bond and plumbing his depths, the titan remained opaque. Distant. Their joining was more of vitality and power than of twinned souls. She still did not know why he yielded to her or bore any interest for a mortal. In some ways, he felt more a force of nature than an animal. A storm tentatively tethered.

Batu did not seem to hear her. "I didn't feel incomplete before. But somehow, with Sarryl, I'm whole."

"And without him, you're naked." She gave a meaningful look down. "Come on. The others will be wondering about you."

This time, he understood, and a wry chuckle broke free of him as he took in his state of undress. "Maybe you're right."

She started to reach for her ash dragon, then paused. "The bear—where is he now?"

"Back at his den. It will be some time still before he wishes to leave it." His eyes, returned to their usual warm brown, grew sharp as he looked into hers, seeming to read her unspoken question. "But when I call for him, wherever the moon shines, he will come."

She envied that confidence with which he spoke of Sarryl. She had faith in her bond to Clouded Fang, but it had taken a season of practice to achieve.

Though I need not become the dragon.

"Good," she said aloud, then jerked her head back toward the living house. "Ready?"

As they set up the ramp, Leiyn reached down for her titan. One burning eye opened to stare at her. Esse raced through their bond and burst from her in a shimmering cloud.

The hidden grotto materialized from beyond reality's veil.

Early the next morning, the others rose and gathered around their rekindled campfire. Even Ata was present, the dryvan perhaps sufficiently interested in Batu's experiences to battle her boredom and remain in place. Chispa curled around Leiyn's legs, warming them. She stroked his fur from head to tail. A faint trail of lifefire curled from the silver fox into her, bolstering her after her sleepless vigil.

Once Batu was awake, they pestered him for an account of his strange experience. Despite having little rest, the former plainsrider was bright-eyed as he told of his moonlit wanderings. While merged with Sarryl, they had hunted a red deer, gorged themselves, then slaked their thirst and bathed in a small waterfall. Simple acts all, yet to hear Batu speak of them, each sounded like a spiritual awakening.

He was not just a plainsrider now. He was truly a wildsoul.

When their questions ran dry, Ekosa spoke into the silence. "We decided to leave before. But where will we go?"

They looked at one other. Leiyn was never one to stay

directionless, yet she was at a loss. Where could they go when Sharo could be anywhere?

Only one place remained. The one to which Ata sought a path.

"Ilberia," she said, drawing the gazes of the others. "Find the World King in the capital, Vasara. The Altacura might be there as well if we're fortunate. Maybe Sharo, too. But even if he's not there, we'll still take away his puppets."

Ata laughed and strode off toward the balcony. What she found amusing, she did not see fit to share. Chispa nestled under Leiyn's legs, his lifefire pressing into her.

Teya spoke hesitantly. "If we intend to venture to unknown shores, we should be prepared. Let us go to Qasaar first."

"Qasaar?" Ketti cast her a quizzical look. "Are you not... That is, would we be welcome there?"

The implication was plain: Teya was as much an exile as any of them. Leiyn harbored similar doubts. How willingly would the Many Tribes aid them when they traveled with a Spear who had abandoned her duty? And if they remained allies with Baltesia, as she hoped, could they aid Leiyn without breaking faith?

But as the former *situal* stared across the campfire, Leiyn tried for optimism. "We helped the chieftains once. And they know better than anyone the importance of our mission."

Teya nodded, looking more doubtful than assured. Ketti and Ekosa exchanged a look. Batu leaned his elbows onto his knees, looking more like the man he had been the past few months than the spirited wildsoul from the night before.

"We may acquire more Iritu artifacts there as well," Teya continued. "Khamo was not the last of the lyshans serving Sharo. Though you have your titan, the rest of us may be served by carrying more weapons."

Leiyn flinched. Words sprang to her tongue like venom to

a snake's bite. *Isla wore Iritu clothes, used Iritu arrows. Where did that get her?*

She swallowed them so they sat hard and unspoken in her gut, then spoke tempered words. "Best hope they're feeling generous, then."

"We need not only rely upon their generosity." Ketti wrung her hands. Her small frame seemed vulnerable, almost like a child's, even as her esse burned high and bright. "Let us return to Solace. Etemans may not be warriors, but there are none more skilled in mahia throughout Unera. And we have long known our enemy."

"Very long, indeed," Ata called over her feathered shoulder. Taunting.

The Eteman did not rise to the goad. "If we do not find weapons there, we may recover knowledge. A hint to where Sharo lies."

A hint. That was all they could hope for now. Leiyn swallowed a sigh and nodded. "We'll visit there as well. Briefly," she added as Batu raised his head, eyes smoldering with need. "Only as long as we must."

He bared his teeth, feral ferocity crossing his features. Then it was gone. He lowered his gaze once more, animal instinct fleeing before lingering human grief.

Teya stood and stretched. The sight distracted Leiyn, though the urgency of their mission banished the baser thoughts.

"We take the morning to prepare," the scout said when she subsided. "Come the afternoon, we depart."

"Do as you must," Ata said, still facing the forest. "I shall be waiting."

Omn's eye hung high above their refuge by the time they gathered around their mounts. Leiyn stroked Feral's snout and was surprised when she did not snap at her hand.

"You know, don't you, old girl?" she muttered in her ear. "Know we cannot take you with us."

The mare eyed her, a warning that Leiyn tested her limits. Subsiding, Leiyn watched Batu, the last to come down the ramp. His shoulders were bowed with weariness, the night's trials weighing on him as the day passed, but he did not plead to delay. If anything, in his bloodshot eyes lay more determination than the rest.

Including you? part of her taunted. *Where has your flame gone, Firebrand?*

As Batu took Saikan's reins, Leiyn turned for one last look at their refuge. Haven had become comfortable and familiar over the winter. Its living roof had given them shelter from the constant rain, and the grotto kept them safe from the many threats without. It had hidden them from the world when she could not bear to be part of it.

But an exile had no home—none but the one they had lost. Without Isla, without the Wilds Lodge, Leiyn doubted she would ever feel at home again.

Spotting Chispa approaching from the jungle, where he had departed while they packed, she crouched and held out her hand. The silver fox nestled his head against it, then twisted up to look at her with guileless affection. Biqqa had emerged with the silver fox, and the green hummingbird flew circles around Ketti's head. The Eteman smiled at the spirit beast, her mahia reaching out to her in greeting.

"Thanks for staying near," Leiyn murmured. "For always being there."

Chispa purred like a cat as he rubbed against her leg, then yipped. Startled, Leiyn laughed and rubbed down to his bushy tail, making him prance a step back.

"Lay low," she said, sobering. "And keep safe out there. It might be a while before I see you again."

She brushed his lifeforce with her mahia in farewell. Though their communication sounded nothing like what Batu had shared with Sarryl, she thought they shared some understanding as Chispa reciprocated her touch.

Without warning, the silver fox turned and fled into the jungle. Biqqa was close on his trail, a flash of emerald before she dove into the shadows. Both vanished to her lifesense as they found a new grotto to shelter within.

Leiyn rose and turned to Ata. "Ready when you are."

The dryvan nodded, her gaze trailing after where the spirit beasts had vanished. "We'll take it in shorter strides," she said vaguely. "Wouldn't want to lose any of you along the way."

"Or break any legs," Batu noted, running a hand along Saikan's flank. His horse snorted and bumped his head against his master.

Ata ignored him and looked out over the forest north—to Qasaar, their destination. She wondered if the Iritu could sense it even from where they stood. For all the months they had spent together, she was only vaguely aware of the shapeshifter's limits. And, by extension, those of her twisted kin.

"Stay close." It was Ata's only warning before she dragged them into the unknown.

PART II

LEGACY OF DUST

7

A DREAM OF MIST

To an Iritu, Qasaar was but a few steps away.
Yet even a single stride can falter.

Leiyn kept her esse tucked around her. The grotto resolved around them to reveal a vine-draped forest, not unlike the one they had left behind. This one, however, fell away to either side so that gaps between the vegetation revealed hills rolling into the distance. Attempting to orient herself, she looked in the opposite direction and found snow-crowned peaks towering above them.

Ata seized them again, and her senses shattered.

Frigid air greeted her, the bite of winds no warmer for spring's coming. Bile sat on her tongue, her body rejecting the abrupt passage. Gales howled in her ears. Cold seeped through her shoes, snow sapping her heat.

Her vision returned, unveiling the Silvertusks surrounding them. They had appeared atop one of the taller peaks, affording them a view for leagues around but for the haze cowling the range.

She gripped Feral's reins and worked up saliva, trying to

rid her mouth of its sourness. Qasaar would not be far now. One more leap, and they would arrive.

Before she could spit the foul taste away, Ata moved them again. And in the breath before arrival, Leiyn peered through eternity.

She burst free of her body's moors, spread across the continent, thin and translucent, a cloud dispersing under Omn's glare. To the coast she traveled, where the ocean winds dragged her beyond the shores and across the writhing mass of its unsettled waves.

A bank of mist stretched below her. Though as insubstantial as herself, it seemed a wall. She felt its wariness as they soared above it, glimpsed a sinuous slide through it, feathery fins fluttering above the fog before subsuming back into mist.

The winds beckoned her on to another land, sent her soaring up its coasts. At the far end of the continent, she halted. She had not known it was her destination, but looking down upon this place, she knew. Some part of her recognized it, memories welling up from untold depths.

This was where she was meant to go.

An island, it appeared, but she recognized it for what it truly was: a slumbering giant. No, not slumbering—dying. Its body remained warm, but it was a corpse slowly cooling. A mountain was buried in its chest like a stabbed knife. Its collapsed caverns were like closed eyes.

Sorrow flooded her, making her heavy—so heavy it bore her down like rain. She fell to the murdered colossus and shattered on its face. Over and over, she broke, each shard of herself endlessly fragmenting.

Only once she had soaked into the earth and inhabited its million specks did she flow down the side of the gargantuan cadaver. Leiyn reached the sea, melded with it, and was glad for it. Only in losing herself could she feel whole.

Slowly, inevitably, the current carried her away from that isle of death, back to the lands from which she had come. To the body that beckoned her. The duty that bound her.

Back to life.

8

STAMPEDE

Sand gritted between her teeth. Wind lashed her skin. Leiyn cracked open her eyes to behold the storm.

Qasaar was nowhere near the size of Southport, but it was a substantial city in its own right. Still, the sandstorm dwarfed it. Looming high in the sky, it was not wholly sediment and wind, but a maelstrom fueled by sentience. Esse wept from it, flogging her lifesense. Thundering hooves and a glimpse of colossal beasts amid the clouds told her the source of the tempest.

A sand stampede. A titan of the Barren.

Leiyn tore away the dreams still clinging to her mind and scrambled to understand. Did lyshans once more siege the Many Tribes? Had they captured Mother Xepi, turned her against her people? She had been the final shaman remaining when Leiyn left. Unless the Iritu had brought a maha from another place, only she could be commanding this assault.

"*Takah*, I come!" Teya stumbled down the road, her draconion dragged behind, heedless of how the ground fell away to her left. Only then did Leiyn recognize where they had landed: the upper entrance of Qasaar.

"Teya, wait!" Leiyn cried.

Feral's whinny and yank on her reins had her spinning back. The mare tore free of Leiyn's grip and made to bolt up the path. Leiyn lunged, just catching the straps. Digging in her heels, she wrestled the unruly horse to a halt.

"Damn it, old girl, not now!"

Leiyn pressed her mahia into the horse to calm her as she took stock of the others. Though she would do all she could to break the siege, her first duty lay to her comrades. Her chest loosened when she saw they had all arrived unharmed, their mounts as well. Batu had fallen to his knees, barely keeping hold of Saikan's reins. Ketti and Ekosa still stood, leaning on each other and Isla's horse.

Only Ata remained unconcerned. A taloned hand propped on her waist, ivy fluttering across her wooden body, she stared into the sandstorm stretching into the beige sky.

"Futile," she declared, barely audible over the roar.

Leiyn spared her no more thought. Tugging on Feral's reins, she pulled the uncooperative mare down the road after the scout.

"Come on!" she shouted over her shoulder.

Her companions followed in her wake. Ata remained above, but only for a moment before she disappeared.

"*Fesht.*" There was nothing for it but to keep going.

Leiyn's lifesense came in fits and starts as she went down the cliffside road. As ever when traveling through grottos, it left her feeling dazed and stretched thin. She tried to focus on the storm, to see who raised it, but only the same ominous guess as before greeted her.

Clouded Fang. She reached for her titan and was relieved when the connection remained stable. Grasping it, she felt the attention of the ash dragon settle upon her.

Be ready, she told him, stealing only a sliver of lifefire to steady herself.

Gasts poked their heads out of the doorways and windows carved from the ocher cliff. Spotting her, they shouted out inquiries.

"Outlander! Ranger! What comes for us? Do they return?"

She waved away their questions and pressed on, her foreboding piling up like the sand did on the road. Her only assurance was that this storm could not have raged long for them to be so ignorant of it.

Only after three switchbacks down the cliffside did she understand. One figure shone brighter than all the others in the city from the top of the Whisperspire, the tower at the heart of the city on the canyon floor. Her hopes surged as she recognized her.

Xepi.

That the shaman was the source of the titan grew ever clearer, for as her mahia dimmed, the sandstorm subsided. As they reached the end of the winding cliffside path, only a dusty haze remained. Daytime turned dun, the titan behind it dispersed to the Barren.

Leiyn released her hold on Clouded Fang. Coughing, she covered her mouth and followed Teya into the heart of the dust cloud. Both the *situal* and her reptilian mount seemed impervious to the conditions as they strode forth, heading for the tower standing tall amid the open plaza. Beyond them loomed the stone gates of Qasaar, still broken from the titan attack during Leiyn's previous visit. Likely, they would remain that way for many years, for mahia beyond any of their skill was required to mend them.

"Sorry, old girl," Leiyn rasped as Feral emitted fresh whinnies, her eyelids crusted and eyes irritated and bloodshot. "Teya needs me."

She caught up with her beloved at the base of the tower

where Teya spoke with a *situal*. The man was no one Leiyn recognized, though he wore the scarlet of Teya's tribe, the Red Hawks. Teya spoke with him as she would to a relation.

"Let me through, Moyo. The Tetrad needs to hear from me."

Moyo lifted his chin in defiance. "You are no longer Spear, Teya of the Hunt. You do not command."

Leiyn hurried forward, fearing the way her beloved's shoulders tightened. Teya was not immune to rashness; after all, they had begun their courtship with a duel.

"I may no longer hold authority, but I can still wallop you." Teya's smile was a vicious promise. "Would you like to chew on your own teeth, *kuit-ka*?"

"We've enough sand to chew on," Leiyn interjected in Ilberian as she reached her side. Fearing she was already too late to avoid a confrontation, she pressed a hand to Teya's shoulder. The scout shrugged her off, a rare rejection of her touch.

She's just angry. Doesn't mean anything.

"We must speak with the Tetrad," Leiyn said. "Urgently. And I don't think they'd appreciate you delaying us."

The *situal* turned his glare on her. "The chieftains have spoken. This one"—he jerked his chin toward Teya—"is not welcome among the Many Tribes. She is *kilakt*." He spat at the former Spear's feet.

Kilakt. Leiyn did not know the word, but it was like the one they used for oath. "Oathbreaker?" she asked.

Teya did not look at her. In place of anger rose something both softer and sharper. Not the steel of a knife blade, but the shards of shattered pottery.

"Forsworn," Teya corrected.

"Huntress."

Leiyn turned at the address, spoken with a familiar gravelly voice. Acalan Tikau strode toward them like a revenant of the desert, flanked by two Jaguar warriors. He wore his usual grim expression, though a shade darker than before. The Iritu armor adorning him from foot to neck was a stark contrast. Made of tightly woven reeds, it was the deep green over old growth forest. Huge violet feathers trailed down his back like a cape, feathers that could only have been plucked from a tempest hawk's plumage. Only his head he left bared, the light green tattoos of the Jaguar tribe spider-webbing across his skull.

Acalan had always treated Teya with respect, but now he spared her barely a glance before stopping in front of Leiyn. Teya's nostrils flared, but she kept her lips pressed tightly together.

The urge to defend her beloved clawed up Leiyn's throat. *She did it for me! It's not her fault! Don't you see that?*

But such words would go unheard. In the eyes of the Many Tribes, Teya had committed an unforgivable transgression. She had abandoned both them and her duty. She could expect no less than this.

So Leiyn swallowed the words, though they smoldered like sunbaked stones in her chest. They needed Acalan and his fellow chieftains to comply with their requests. Offend them, and their chances of assisting plummeted to nothing.

So you won't defend her, that insidious part of her whispered. *Just as you failed to defend Isla.*

With the storm subsiding, the air took on an eerie calm. Leiyn spoke as much to quiet that voice as to break the tense silence.

"You're not supposed to be here," she said to Acalan.

A smile, barely more than a lift at the corners, touched the chieftain's lips. "Neither are you."

She hated giving voice to her fears. But what else could she speak of these days?

"He broke it, didn't he? The alliance. Mauricio turned you away."

All trace of a smile dissipated. Acalan rested a hand on the hilt of his weapon. An Iritu blade replaced the *macua* he had once wielded. No doubt the shapeshifters did not fashion such uniquely Gast weapons, and he had been forced to compromise.

"We bled for them," he said. "Died on their behalf. And, as ever before, your people proved treacherous."

Leiyn looked aside, jaw clenched. What could she say? She had feared this would happen. Mauricio was too clever and ambitious to give up land he might keep. He knew the weakness of the Many Tribes, how their shamans had been culled down to Xepi alone. He knew they would not have the strength to fight both the Tricolonies and the lyshans.

Cruel, clever bastard.

Reluctantly, she met Acalan's eye. "I never wanted this."

"No," he acceded. "You did not. But you remain the cause."

Taking an arrow could not have hurt worse. Stunned, Leiyn let the chieftain push past her to enter the stone tower. At the entrance, he paused and spoke over his shoulder.

"Eloxo, Cual, take their mounts. Huntress, with me."

The warriors accompanying Acalan stepped forward, hands outstretched. Leiyn placed Feral's reins in the young woman's hands, then turned to Teya. She could have been a ghost for all her people acknowledged her now. The scout who took Bane's reins did not look at her as he did so. Even Acalan, with whom she had shared a warm camaraderie across tribal lines, refused to speak to her.

Leiyn tried to give her a reassuring smile, but it could not lift the stiff mask her face had become. At her gesture, Teya moved forward, and Leiyn followed. It came as a small relief that the quarrelsome guard of the Whisperspire did not step in their way.

The rest of their companions had reached the bottom of the cliffside road, taking their time to descend. Leiyn did not wait for them. With Ata already among the Tetrad, any delay might give the dryvan time to cause further rifts between them and the chieftains, and they could ill afford that.

Whispers from the stones ushered her up the spiraling stairs. As they reached the open-air chamber atop the tower, shouts drowned out the Whisperspire's spirits.

Outrage had spread in Ata's wake. Ilaoti leaned over the map table, the Red Hawk chieftainess glaring at the dryvan as if she would enjoy nothing better than cutting Ata apart limb from limb. Zyanya of the Moonfish tribe looked similarly upset, arms crossed and a glower further lining her aged features, though she remained seated. Tinoch, the Uman chieftain, smiled in a way too strained to be believed as he leaned back in his chair. The precious metals and jewels adorning his teeth glinted in the scant light.

Only Ata and the shaman standing near her appeared unmoved. Xepi looked up at their arrival, charcoal eyes seeming to pierce through Leiyn, as they always had. Leiyn glanced away. The middle-aged woman had before borne a healthy dose of extra flesh, but she had lost it all in the year since she had seen her. Now, the shaman's skin pulled tightly over her bones, her fringed robes loose over her diminished body.

Acalan stopped as he reached his place at the table. "*Sach'aan.* You have caused great alarm appearing unannounced."

"Am I to be blamed for your fright?" Once, Ata's teeth had been flat and dull. Now, as she grinned, they were sharp. A smile fit for a predator. "Your alarm would not save you."

"What trickery is this?" Ilaoti demanded. Her generous

frame lent her fury additional weight as she glared at the shapeshifter. "Why have you come?"

Ata started forward, her rectangular pupil dilating. She seemed to loom over the chieftainess across the table. "I have only ever protected you, mortal. Because of my people's assistance, only I remain of our grove." The dryvan placed her hands upon the table, talons digging into its face. Even stone was not hard enough to defy her. "And this is the gratitude I receive? Empty threats and emptier insults? I wonder why I bothered."

Leiyn stepped forward. Too long, she had let the moment spin away from her. She had to hope the hostilities had not grown too tall.

"Ata, please. Toa Ilaoti, Chieftains of the Tetrad—we are all on the same side. I only ask that you listen to me."

The Red Hawk chieftainess turned her scowl on Leiyn, then seemed to notice Teya for the first time. Her features twisted. "First you beset us with this *sach'aan*. Now you bring this *kilakt* into our midst? Your insolence goes too far, outlander!"

Blood throbbed in her head, narrowing her vision. When she had first visited Qasaar, she might have lost her temper. But she was a different woman now. Harder. Colder. Tempered by loss and sorrow.

How far can they push before you break?

She sighed out a breath before speaking in the Gast tongue. "I am responsible for the consul breaking his promises. I am to blame for Teya leaving her duties as a Spear."

"Leiyn—" the disgraced scout started.

Leiyn silenced her with a pleading look. "I do not come to ask forgiveness," she continued. "For all I have done, all that my actions have led to, I do not deserve it. But she does." She nodded at Teya. "Everything she has done has been in defense of your people. The enemy we hunt is a threat to

Qasaar and the Many Tribes, as you know well. If she believes her people hate and scorn her, she will fight the worse for it."

The leaders exchanged looks. Acalan bent his head as if deep in thought. Tinoch seemed on the verge of speaking but kept looking at Ilaoti instead. Teya's chieftainess did nothing more than glare at the former Spear, her feelings plainly unchanged.

The sinkhole in Leiyn's gut grew, threatening to swallow her whole. She did not let it show, silently enduring the torment. Waiting for them to speak.

Zyanya broke first. "Given the circumstances, I would be open to allowing penance from Teya of the Hunt upon her return. If Toa Ilaoti is amenable, of course."

The Red Hawk leader raised her chin. "If she returns."

Leiyn glanced at Teya. The pain in her eyes burned in Leiyn as well, but pride nestled next to it as the scout bowed her head with control and grace.

"Thank you, Honored Tetrad. Undeserving though I am, I welcome this chance. If we succeed and I survive, I shall do all I can to prove worthy of your mercy."

Ilaoti looked back at Ata, a blatant snub of Teya. She addressed the dryvan's back, for Ata had turned away as if bored with the proceedings. "What did you mean, *sach'aan*, when you said Taht Xepi's *kainox* could not save us?"

Leiyn glanced at the shaman to find Xepi's gaze on her. She nodded, a brief acknowledgment of all that remained to discuss, and was relieved when the shaman returned it.

At least one person here doesn't hate me.

Ata looked back over her shoulder. Her profile cast against the dusty Barren, feathers ruffling in the dying winds, made her seem all the more like some avian monster. "The barriers my kin and I erected over Qasaar, those meant to protect you—they have fallen with Eld's passing."

Murmurs rose from the chieftains. "Impossible," Ilaoti scoffed, though she kept her affront quiet.

The dryvan turned back to stare blandly at the Red Hawk leader. "You would be the authority in this, would you not?" Her mismatched eyes slid over to Leiyn, as if to invite her to share a jape.

Leiyn found little amusing in it. "So lyshans can appear here anytime they wish."

"Just so." Ata turned her head to an unnatural degree, her body still mostly facing away. "You are only alive from Sharo's negligence—or indifference, more like."

"Indifference?" Acalan raised his head. "Man'nah and his *sach'aan* assaulted Qasaar for decades. They stole our shamans, killed our scouts. I would not call them indifferent."

"But the war has changed, has it not?" Ata turned around, then started pacing, every movement as sinuous as a snake slithering through grass. "Sharo reaches into every mortal realm. He has no need for your last paltry shaman—he has hundreds and thousands from which he may select the choicest morsels. You are not the threat he fears." She pointed one long talon at Leiyn. "She is. Her, myself, and others of which you know little."

The Etemans, she could only mean. Leiyn appreciated her keeping their secret. She trusted the chieftains as much as she could trust anyone in power, particularly after Mauricio's deception. But that was a decision best left for Ketti, and she remained at the base of the tower with the rest of their companions, clearly not being given admittance.

"Then we are vulnerable." Acalan crossed his arms and looked around at the other members of the Tetrad. His brow was furrowed, but Leiyn detected no fear in him. Even in the face of eternal malevolence, the war chieftain remained unbowed. "Xepi will do what she can, but the hunt for the lyshan Sharo is our best hope for survival."

"Them, our hope?" Ilaoti's scorn remained, but it looked to be doing battle with impending dread—and losing. "A skin-walker, a *kilakt* Spear, and a handful of outlanders? I would not place our fate in their hands!"

Ata laughed and turned away. "You speak as if you have a choice!" she flung over her shoulder.

Not waiting for a reply, the Iritu strode toward the window, stepped out—and vanished. Dust spun in her wake, outlining her figure for a moment before a gust dispersed it.

The Tetrad gazed after her before Acalan turned back to Leiyn. "We must discuss this in private. If you would await our decision below, you and your mounts will be provided for."

"Thank you, Acalan." Bridling her patience was never easy, but Leiyn managed it as she complied with Gast custom and bowed. After Teya rose from her bow, she followed the disgraced scout down the stairwell.

9

REACHING

They did not have to wait long for the Tetrad. No sooner had the rest of their mounts been taken to the stable and Leiyn caught up their companions on the brief discussion than she sensed Acalan descending the Whisper-spire, Xepi close behind. They awaited them in silence, Leiyn trying to read their expressions for the verdict, but neither had ever been easy to read.

The war chieftain spoke first. “The Tetrad has agreed to aid your hunt, little as that aid may be.”

The tightness in her chest loosened. “Thank you, Acalan.”

He nodded, then scanned the rest of them. His gaze came to a rest on Teya. “I trust you wish your party to remain small?”

Leiyn felt the ripple through Teya’s lifeforce at being addressed. “That would be best,” the former *situal* answered.

“Though you would be welcome,” Batu added, “if you were offering to come.”

The war chieftain smiled. “My duties keep me here, though I wish it were otherwise.”

“So do we.” The depth of her disappointment surprised

her. Acalan had no command over mahia. As mighty a warrior as he was, he remained mortal and comparatively frail for the fights to come. Yet there was a solidness to his presence, a practicality to his mind, and a breadth to his experience that she would miss.

Brow furrowed, Acalan acknowledged it with a nod. "Then all we might offer are talismans and guidance. Our cache of Iritu objects has grown scarce. We claimed much from within the barracks grotto, but our enemies returned to take what remained. If they reappear here, we must have some way of defending ourselves."

Leiyn held up a hand. "We don't need much. Only what you can spare."

"Taht Xepi can speak to that." He turned to the shaman in invitation.

Xepi looked at Teya, lips pursed. Leiyn suspected she studied the scout's lifeforce. By Teya's discomfort, she guessed the same.

"I once judged you insufficient to be a shaman," Xepi said at last. "And so it has remained to this day. But you, Teya Chitlaam, must become more than what others made you. What I have made you."

The shaman tapped her feathered staff on the packed dirt, pulsing her mahia as she did.

Teya seemed hardly able to breathe. Even her lifeforce stilled, though there was a frantic flutter around the edges of her. Leiyn recognized that which froze her: the fear of trying and being found wanting.

The shaman reached into her robes and withdrew a pouch, then held it out in offering. Teya slowly accepted it, still dazed.

"Amber," Xepi explained. "Ten beads of it. Train. Grow your potential. And use them well." She gave the scout a nod, then turned to Ketti and Ekosa. "I shall bring beads for both of you. And for you," she added with a glance at Leiyn, "if you could use them."

"I could. Thank you, Xepi." Leiyn hesitated, glancing toward the ruined gates of Qasaar. "The titan at the gates, the sand stampede. How was it here? Have the wardstones failed?"

"Can you not sense it?" As Xepi frowned, Leiyn winced. She knew that look: that of a teacher noticing a fresh shortcoming in her student.

Chastened, Leiyn extended her lifesense over the leagues to the arc of black pillars that marked the end of the Fingers and the beginning of the rest of the Barren. Some remained full of fire, but all had dimmed. In some, esse had extinguished entirely. She turned her focus back south toward the arc littered among the mountains. Those, at least, still glowed with lifeforce.

She returned to Xepi's expectant gaze. "You're protected to the south, but vulnerable to the north."

Her old teacher nodded, as much approval as she was wont to give. "With only myself as our remaining shaman, it is too much of a risk for me to leave Qasaar, particularly to travel where we have lost shamans before. Though," she added with a distant look, "if our protections are gone, I am at risk anywhere."

"You protect the city from titans," Acalan said. "Your presence is required here."

Xepi nodded. "We risk it only to visit the mountain wardstones, but they require much less maintenance. Fewer titans roam the Silvertusks than the Barren."

"How do you keep away the titans?" Leiyn pressed. "And the sand stampede—you called it as if it were waiting."

It took Leiyn a moment to recognize the feeling stirring through Xepi's esse and lifting her expression. Pride—how often had she witnessed the shaman indulging in it?

"Though I cannot bond a titan, I have leashed one." Xepi held up a hand to forestall questions. "No, I cannot draw its power as you can, nor is our connection strong. But it is sufficient that it remains near Qasaar and rises in our defense."

Leiyn laughed, feeling lighter than she had since their arrival. "I'd like to hear how you managed that."

Xepi smiled. "Perhaps I will tell you, if we have time." She sobered as she looked back to Teya. "But first, I must speak more with Teya. I believe I have lessons from which she might benefit."

Leiyn glanced at her beloved to find her nodding stiffly. Frightened though she might be of exploring this avenue, she did not back away from it.

She never does.

"Taht Xepi," Ketti spoke up, "if you would allow it, I would be delighted to accompany you both. I believe I might learn much."

Her mastery of the Gast tongue was admirable, superior to Leiyn's clumsy handling. With that, the precious stones embedded in her flesh, and her potent mahia, Leiyn wondered if Xepi had not already guessed that one of the Gast ancestors stood before them.

If she did, the only sign the shaman gave was bowing her head. "I would be honored by your attendance." She paused, the question implicit.

"Ketti," the Eteman replied. "Ketti Ta'Rul."

"Taht Ketti." Xepi bowed again.

Leiyn crossed her arms, caught between bemusement and irritation. Xepi had never treated her with such respect.

Ketti took it all with her usual grace. "I am no shaman, but I appreciate it all the same, Taht Xepi."

"My pardon," Ekosa said in Ilberian. "But if we might converse in a colonial language?"

Leiyn grimaced. She had forgotten the *eesu* did not know the Gast tongue. "Sorry. Ketti's attending Teya's lesson."

"I see. If it is permitted, I would be delighted to attend as well."

"Of course." Xepi eyed him with wariness rather than the respect she afforded Ketti. Leiyn could hardly blame her. She knew little of the history between the Eyin Empire and the Many Tribes, but she had to imagine it was as saturated in blood as the one shared with Baltesia and the Union.

But that was a matter for them to settle. Leiyn turned to Acalan. "You said you have few artifacts to spare. I thought I might look inside the barracks and see if I can find more."

Teya hissed her disapproval. Xepi stared. Leiyn kept her gaze on the war chieftain, ignoring the others.

His expression tightened. "That poses a risk."

"No more than anywhere in the world," Leiyn retorted. "Sharo can find me anytime he likes, the same as his lyshans. If anything, I'm safer in a grotto than out here."

Acalan hesitated, then nodded. "Very well. But go prepared."

Leiyn rested a hand on one of her falchions, belted at her hips. "I always do."

"I'll go with her." Batu stepped up beside her.

The war chieftain nodded at once. She tried not to feel irritated at how Acalan did not hesitate to accept his risks. Whether their understanding stemmed from manly camaraderie or being kindred spirits, she appreciated their bond more than resented it.

"No point in wasting daylight." Leiyn met Teya's gaze and reached out her mahia to brush her esse. Not so subtle a gesture among so many with the lifesense, but her beloved reciprocated it all the same.

Stay safe, that touch seemed to suggest. *Stay alive.*

Nodding at the others, Leiyn turned and strode toward the

rise up Lualli, the cliffside road leading to the waiting barracks. Batu fell into step beside her.

Until they reached the ascent, they remained silent, listening to the sounds of Qasaar rousing. Gasts had begun filtering out into the streets and plaza once more, and many eyed them with curiosity. She gave them small acknowledgments but engaged no more than necessary.

"Isla wouldn't like this," her friend murmured as they began up the road. "What we're doing."

Leiyn faltered a step before resuming her stride. "Isla didn't approve of much that I've done."

She hoped he would leave it be, but something drove Batu to speak again. "I wonder what she would have thought of me. Of me embracing my...heritage."

"She accepted my mahia." If they had to have this conversation, Leiyn knew she could not back away from it. She grasped his shoulder and gave him a fond shake. "She would've done the same for you."

"And still wanted me as her beloved?" His eyes were bloodshot as he glanced over. The sleepless night and travel by grotto had not been easy on him. She wondered if it was wise to let him go with her.

As if you could keep him away.

She batted his arm. "Don't be daft. She loved you."

He laughed, the sound of it rough as bark. "Is that enough?"

It was a relief to reach the barracks and find a familiar figure awaiting them. "Ranger Leiyn! Plainsrider Batu!" Tozi grinned and bowed before remembering their own customs and extending an arm to shake. "A pleasure to see you both!"

Their old caretaker looked well compared to the other residents of Qasaar, still as full of vitality and optimism as ever. His lazy eye wandered off, already tiring of looking at them.

"Good to see you, Tozi." Leiyn returned the smile and gestured to the barracks. "They still keeping you here?"

"No, not since you were last here. I return to prepare rooms for you and your companions." Tozi peered down into the canyon. "Will they be along soon? Your belongings have arrived, but I have only two beds made."

"Xepi claimed them for the moment. And we won't need rooms yet." Leiyn jerked her head toward the doorway. "Got another appointment."

Tozi's expression fell. "Within the walls? I cannot advise this, Ranger Leiyn."

"Just Leiyn, remember?"

If he heard her, he pretended otherwise. "The last expedition lost nine men and women. Fine warriors all. Who is to say *sach'aan* do not wait for you there at this very moment?"

Though her earlier declaration that lyshans could surprise them anytime remained true, Tozi was right on that point: the grotto within the barracks' walls made for a fine place to lay an ambush. She had seen how patiently lyshans could wait. They had been like statues when she first visited where Man'nah had kept them in the ruins of a second Iritu city. Sharo might feel it worth sparing one or two of his people—though, given their estimate of his remaining forces, even that might stretch them too far.

"Can't know till we see." Not waiting for permission, Leiyn took the stairs into the old barracks, then up to the second floor.

The sand blown in through the open windows had layered thick inside, though she saw Tozi had swept the doorways of several curtained rooms. Somehow, her footsteps through the grime made it seem as if she walked in a dream, a memory brought to reality around her.

She paused. A dream—is that what had gripped her when Ata had pulled them across the continent? It had felt more real than that, not unlike when she had seen the vision of Sharo speaking to the Altacura on that distant shore. That, according to Ata, had been a glimpse of true happenings, her essence reaching across Unera to Ilberia.

Had she truly passed over the Ocula Ocean in that shattered moment? And did that mean the slain giant, the one clinging to its fading life and impaled upon a mountain, was real?

"Leiyn?"

She took another step and spoke over her shoulder. "Fine. Just thinking."

"And here I thought you could think and walk."

Leiyn flashed a rude gesture over her shoulder, then swept aside the curtain to step into the room. Her former bedchamber was not one of those Tozi had yet cleaned, but she barely spared it a glance as she strode to the wooden mattress, stepped upon it, and examined the square of stone set above it. Esse still shimmered within the panel. The window into the grotto beyond remained open.

"Going somewhere?"

Dust puffed into the air with Ata's appearance. Leiyn startled and glared at the dryvan. Ata leaned against the wall, a smirk twisting her lips.

"Where'd you go?" Leiyn demanded.

"Reconnaissance." Ata flicked a dust mote from her feathers. "Or would you prefer Sharo take us unaware?"

Leiyn only huffed out a breath, then coughed. The sediment in the air was making her lungs feel heavy. "Fine. You coming?"

"To the armory?" The shapeshifter shrugged. "If I must."

She hesitated, then looked back at Batu. The former plainsrider had his axe drawn and still breathed heavily. At her glance, he lifted an eyebrow.

She shrugged, then gestured to a torch lying among the

dust, no doubt discarded after a venture into the barracks wall. "Grab that and light it."

Batu nodded and complied. After several strikes of flint and stone, the torch burned merrily, and he approached her with it and his axe in hand.

Leiyn gripped him by his elbow, then faced the wall once more. With a last look at Ata, who gave no sign of following, she pressed her palm to the panel.

In a swell of mahia, the wall sucked them in.

10

EVOLUTION

The transition took the bat of an eye. Leiyn blinked at the sudden gloom. To her lifesense, the hallway came alive, the Iritu frescos seeming to dance along the walls. She detected no other presence with them.

Batu raised the torch, the firelight illuminating no farther than a dozen strides. "Let's go."

She drew a falchion and started down the hall after him. They went the same direction she had gone before. The Gasts had known about these chambers in the barracks, so she did not expect them to have missed much, though it was worth checking. After that, there were other parts she had not ventured to, many more, by how much she sensed of these halls. If the rest contained what these chambers had, there might be artifacts to loot still.

They reached the first chamber and found it much as expected. The stands lay empty of the weapons they had once held. Some had been knocked over, speaking to the haste with which they were left. By the torchlight, Leiyn saw dark stains upon the stone.

Blood. Gasts died here.

A person materialized not three paces away. Leiyn had her sword raised and pointing before she recognized Ata. Heaving out a sigh, she lowered it. She sensed Batu doing the same behind her.

"Good of you to join us," Leiyn said.

If the dryvan noticed their alarm, she did not acknowledge it. Striding among the stands, she brushed the tips of her claws along them in a gentle caress. Seeming as if she looked for something lost and long lamented.

"They have been here," she murmured. "Recent by our reckoning."

Leiyn's skin rose in bumps. "How recent?"

"Not days. Perhaps a season, maybe two." Ata shrugged, then drifted to the next chamber.

It was in much the same state as the first. Empty rack after empty rack showed where armor had once hung.

Moving on to the last room she had visited, Leiyn saw the talismans had also been taken. Remembering their potency, she hoped the Gasts had claimed more of them than the lyshans.

"Nothing here," Batu murmured. He trailed behind her, axe lowered and torch aloft, dark eyes scanning the filthy corners. Searching for anything they might have missed.

Leiyn belied her disappointment. This was what the Tetrad had told her, what she had expected. But there remained other chambers to explore. They might still discover something of use.

"What's in the rest of this place?" She gestured with her free hand toward the other rooms and corridors she sensed.

"I had not visited for many years before I last accompanied you. Hundreds? Thousands?" Ata laughed, the sound sharp as an elbow to the ribs. "To live so long, then evaporate in a blink. Existence is strange, is it not?"

"Ata."

"Not in a mood for philosophy, I see." The dryvan cast her a droll look before swinging her gaze to the unseen rooms. "Baths—dry now, I suppose. Groves, though those are dead, too, of course—"

"Groves?"

"For one's growth." Ata looked back with one mossy eyebrow arched. "You did not think I naturally appear this way, do you?"

"That was my thought."

The dryvan sniffed. "Think of it as...ah, the thing where you sit and do nothing."

"Meditation?" Batu offered.

"Yes, that. Groves stimulate the growth of esse and thus, our bodies—for they are connected." Ata waved a hand, the movement fluid as a willow in a breeze. "It is of no consequence; it shall not help us now. Takes too long to grow, if it would even work for you mortals."

She paused, eyes distant as her heritage walked the empty halls. "There would also be the *nappahi*—workshops, if you like. There we forged our weapons and armor and deadly devices." She plucked at a vacant stand as if to materialize one of those absent artifacts.

"Those sound promising." Leiyn nodded to the corridor leading beyond. "This is the fastest way?"

"For you, perhaps." Ata smiled, then started loping for the entrance.

Batu exchanged a look with Leiyn, then shrugged and headed after her. Leiyn followed, then winced and clapped a hand to the back of her neck.

A sting? Tadeo had spoken of insects and other creatures that could lie in stasis for years, even decades, before coming alive. But she sensed nothing of a wasp or anything else that might be behind it.

Yet as she brought her hand before her eyes, by the torch's flickering light she saw a speck of blood dotting her finger.

Leiyn spun with her falchion leading. Her blade cut through air. Yet several steps afar, standing amid the accumulating shadows, she saw...something. She did not recognize the silhouette, hunched and hulking, but a being so strange could only mean one thing.

"Lyshan!"

She drew her second blade and reached for Clouded Fang. The titan responded at once, rising from rivers of lava to ascend toward her. As Batu came running back and his torch fully illuminated the room, Leiyn expected the shapeshifter to flee.

But the lyshan appeared content to remain hunched where it was. It watched them, eyes unblinking. Then a moist, rasping sound gurgled up its throat. Laughter, she could only assume.

Ata materialized at the opposite entrance, mismatched eyes hard on the newcomer. They had blocked all exits to the room, little good though it would do if the lyshan decided to leave. As easily as the dryvan, it could will itself in and out of the grotto and flee this chamber. For now, it seemed content to cackle.

Leiyn suppressed her irritation and took stock of their enemy. As its silhouette had suggested, it was the most malformed lyshan she had yet to meet. Sharo appeared almost human but for his cavernous eyes and pitted skin. Even Man'nah and Khamo, monstrous as they were in size, approximated their same shape.

This lyshan was more like those that had ambushed her and the Gast patrol in the Fingers, their distortions moving beyond anything natural. Its legs, bent backward and scaled like a bird's, ended in vicious talons. Instead of feathers, its thighs were lined with mangy fur, a dirty white that seemed smeared with mud or worse. The torso curled over itself, leading to one arm that ended in a paw like a jaguar's and another like a lizard's.

Its limbs did not end there. Wings, leathery like those of an enormous bat, fluttered off its shoulders as if eager to take flight. Two twitching black legs like those of a spider protruded from the creature's sagging chest. And then there was the head, shaped like a boar's, with a flat snout and tusks falling from its mouth. Its eyes were beady and dark and flicked about the room.

Grotesque as its appearance was, Leiyn feared its magic most. As it lowered its walls, she saw esse boiling inside the lyshan in a way that reminded her of a witch's cauldron from one of Ranger Gan's nighttime tales. It seemed anything might catalyze from that caustic brew at any moment, a chaos and changeability to it that Leiyn found deeply unsettling.

More than any other, this lyshan was a monster fit for fireside tales.

Clouded Fang neared the surface. *Wait*, Leiyn sent along their bond, stalling the titan. *Be ready.* In such crowded quarters, the ash dragon would be more hindrance than help. But she would need him if she were to grab Batu and flee.

Though Saints knew she craved the fight.

"Osmet?" Ata narrowed her eyes and hunched, as if to spring—or to evade if attacked. "That cannot be you."

"Osmet? Osmet!" The lyshan cawed like a crow. "I was, I was, and now I *am*! But you, Atastimina—you were, you were, and *will not be*!"

"Mad," Batu breathed. His axe never wavered, but his torch betrayed the wobble to his hand. The firelight danced and flickered, the movement making the shadows all the more menacing.

"Mad? Mad? What is mad?" Faster than Leiyn could follow, the creature shifted forward, crossing half the distance separating them. Its stench wafted over them, one of rotting vegetables and sour meat. "That which is unseen, no? That which is beyond reach, no?" It tittered again. "Yes, yes, I am mad! But the mad survive while the sane are swallowed, no, no, no?"

Her sanity had certainly been swallowed. Leiyn edged forward, falchions held at the ready. Killing this one now would mean not facing her later. That the lyshan meant them harm was evident from the blood crusted on the back of Leiyn's neck.

Why prick me instead of killing? Her blood chilled at the thought of all Osmet could have done.

Ata, at least, still seemed intent on conversing. "Osmet, you must focus. Did Sharo send you? Did he mean for you to spy on us?"

"Osmet! Osmet!" The lyshan shuddered, filthy fur falling to the ground around its raptor feet. Its spidery legs worked even faster as they brushed up against one another, over and over. "She Who Remains, I am! Ata Who Was, you are!"

The dryvan seemed to run out of patience. "She Who Remains," she spoke through bared teeth. "Do you serve Sharo?"

"Sharo, Sharo! Brother beloved!" She Who Remains laughed. "Sniff, sniff, can you smell? Can you hear? Should I tell?"

Ata lunged, talons leading. Leiyn followed with her falchions, her movements swift from esse. She Who Remains evaded them both, disappearing then reappearing deep inside the chamber. Her snickering never ceased.

"Stay close," Leiyn called over her shoulder. "Bringing that bear of yours?"

"No moon," Batu grunted from close behind.

Fear cut deeper. Her breathing raced like Feral in a gallop. How could she protect him from this?

I failed Isla. I'll fail him.

She blinked, her vision fuzzing. *Focus, Firebrand.* Losing control would be the surest way to doom him. Each moment felt like clinging to the reins of a terrified horse bucking to win free.

Still, she clung on.

Ata skirted around to cut off the lyshan's new position. Leiyn moved opposite to her, Batu coming behind. She Who Remains had worn her laughter through and watched them with black eyes catching the firelight. Her layered lifeforce writhed. Her gaze fell upon her fellow Iritu.

"Poor, poor Ata, stuck in the past." The lyshan's tongue, black and thick, darted out over her scarred lips and snout. "Have you forgotten all we learned long lost seasons ago?"

Her leathery wings flapped once, gusting fetid air over Leiyn's face. She flinched, expecting an attack, but the lyshan remained where she was.

"Adaptation is justification!" She Who Remains roared. Spittle flew from between her fangs. Her eyes protruded farther from her face. "*Kasadum il denu*—did you forget? We deserved our fate! We should have been eradicated. Existence demands evolution! The Mothers showed us from the beginning." A curdled laugh ushered from the tortured lips. "Our first failing. Yours and Eld's, and Man'nah's as well. But Sharo knows better—as do I."

Ata shrieked as she pounced her monstrous kin. Too late even before she moved—the lyshan's esse rippled, then her skin. Their enemy twisted, her shape shrinking with a wet squelch like feet stuck in mud.

The dryvan's claws met air. She Who Remains, now an ugly bat no bigger than Leiyn's head, darted through the air.

An unseen blow rocked Leiyn forward. For a moment, she was too stunned to turn back. A specter loomed in her mind, shadowing even Clouded Fang. Its words were like if Omn spoke, like the Sacred Saints had descended to Unera to speak with one resounding voice.

"Mortal! Pathetic. Weak. Frail. Your kind has survived past your time. You can never adapt!"

"Get. Out!"

Leiyn surged to her feet, falchions raised, whirling to seek her opponent. Only the sight of Batu, alarm written across his fire-limned features, greeted her.

The lyshan was gone. She sensed nothing of Osmet, by lifesense or her natural senses.

Ata snarled and battered an empty stand, sending it skidding across the room. Leiyn watched in silence, her mind still buzzing.

She spoke to me. In my head. A deeper fear settled in. *Can I keep her out?*

Her mahia's walls had been her surest protection. She had always kept claim over her mind. Yet this lyshan had breezed in as if she had left the door unlocked and open. Leiyn had been powerless to stop or even resist her.

Never had she felt so mortal.

"Go." Ata's voice was like a tree stripped of bark. "It is not safe for you to be here. I shall see if there is anything to reclaim."

At another time, Leiyn would have protested. But even if she did not feel so exposed, there was Batu to think of.

"Be careful," Leiyn said.

The dryvan did not seem to hear. Setting off at a languid lope, she moved down the corridor and out of sight.

"Are you alright?" her friend murmured at her back. "When you fell, it was like you'd been struck. But the lyshan wasn't there."

"I'm fine." Resolutely, Leiyn pushed the chilling thoughts from her mind. "Come on. Let's get somewhere safer."

Letting Batu move ahead with the torch, she sheathed one

falchion and touched the back of her neck. Her mahia had closed the small wound so only dried blood met her fingertips. Chipping it away, she felt at the smooth skin. Her lifesense delved beneath the surface.

Nothing. No dark roots of infection. No foreign substances intruding.

You're alright. You're fine.

Reaching the panel, Leiyn gripped Batu's arm, then left the dark corridor behind.

11

TRUST

Leiyn and Batu wasted no time in exiting the barracks to the street without. She could not be away from those haunted halls soon enough.

Tozi caught up to them at the threshold. "I am glad to see you well! Nothing to find within, it seems?"

"Nothing worth taking." Leiyn resisted the urge to touch the back of her neck again.

"A pity, a pity. But what matters most is your safety." The caretaker waved them away. "I am certain you have other important things to do—I shall see you tonight. And by then, my good guests, this place shall be swept of every last speck of dust!"

Leiyn only waved in response, distracted as she reached her lifesense across the city in search of their companions. Xepi had taken them up the western cliff to her hovel at its farthest edge. They were still crowded inside and seemed to practice mahia.

Withdrawing, she turned to Batu. "Ready for another hike?"

He shrugged and led the way down.

Qasaar had recovered from their startling appearance, and the people of the Many Tribes filled the central plaza and streets. There had been a time when they had greeted Leiyn with warmth and admiration. Her feats against the lyshans had spread in extravagant tales through neighborly gossip and at ceremonial gathering halls.

But in the wake of Baltesia's duplicity, her popularity had waned. Her passage was met with icy stares and reluctant nods. It was Batu who received salutations, most coming from the *situali*, with whom he had briefly trained. Batu returned these with swift smiles and curt nods, as much affability as he seemed capable of mustering.

They crossed the plaza to ascend the opposite cliff. As the crowds lessened, their pace sped up. Whispers rose from the surrounding stone, soothing as the susurrus of a river. Sweat filmed her brow. With the sky clearing of drifting sand, the sun beat down on them with renewed vigor. Months of living in the shadowed jungle made it burn all the more.

She grounded herself in the sensations. Slowly, the horror of their encounter with Osmet seeped away.

They crested the final ascent to bring Xepi's round hut into view. The others would have noticed their coming, but it was only as they arrived at the door that they exited the building. There seemed a new sense of camaraderie between the four by their shared glances and smiles. Leiyn tried not to feel jealous. How often had she longed to smile with Xepi?

Don't be a child, she scolded herself. *Better we be bound together and not just through you.*

Exchanging greetings, their companions showed what they had gained for their time spent with the shaman. Ketti and Ekosa produced satchels filled with amber beads, ten each, the same as Leiyn had received when she first departed. Teya had also received beads, but in addition bore another item.

"An Iritu talisman," Teya confirmed, relinquishing it to

Leiyn's inquiring look. "Xepi says it can kill when awoken. Perhaps even kill a lyshan."

Leiyn held the artifact gingerly. It looked different from the other talismans she had glimpsed in the Iritu barracks. Sinew, dull and yellowed, pulled in a webbed pattern across a circle of bone; remnants of titans, like many Iritu weapons and armor. It was uncomfortable to touch, a stickiness to it that adhered to esse rather than skin. Should she relent her walls while holding it, she felt it would drain her essence to the last drop.

She passed it on to Batu's inquiring touch. "Like carrying a scorpion."

"Good." Teya flashed a hard smile. "We need venom."

"Save it for Sharo. No need to sting the rest of us."

Xepi moved to stand before Leiyn, two more pouches clutched in her hands. "For you," she said, handing ten more amber beads to Leiyn along with the other pouch. "And this as well."

Leiyn tucked the beads into her belt next to the others, then pried open the ties of the second bag. The earthy musk made her dizzy with a single sniff. Retying it, she looked up at the shaman.

"*Nacatl* mushrooms. Guessing there's *peyotl* in there, too. When did you get a sense of humor?"

A smile crossed Xepi's lips, fleeting as a deer spotted among the brush. "As before, it will expand your awareness of *Tlalli*. You have grown in your time away, but many tasks still await you. May this assist if you should have need of it."

The need would have to be dire for her to subject herself to such intoxication again. Leiyn only nodded and tied it in next to the beads. "Thanks, Xepi."

"What of your expedition?" Ketti asked, violet eyes darting over them. "Did you find nothing?"

"No artifacts." Batu's gaze slid to Leiyn. "But we discovered something else."

They told of their encounter with the lyshan. Both struggled to explain her peculiarities. Ata's reaction, too, seemed perplexing upon recollection. The dryvan had shown moments of rage in the past, but the unbridled fury with which she had engaged Osmet seemed a step beyond ordinary anger. A flavor more personal.

What did she do to you, Ata?

Xepi bowed her head. Ketti chewed her lip. Ekosa looked out over the Barren, gaze distant. Only Teya met their words with hard resolve.

"We shall kill her as we have killed the others, no matter their history."

Leiyn nodded and rubbed at the back of her neck.

Ata did not reappear for the rest of that day. Stranded until she returned, they spent the night in the barracks. Leiyn was not entirely disappointed. After the events of the day and the dream-riddled travel, she was grateful for the chance to rest.

While not spotless, their residence of old was far cleaner for Tozi's efforts. The caretaker cooked for them as well, a meal of mutton and corn and spices that evoked memories of the months she had spent in Qasaar. Teya all but moaned upon tasting it.

"What?" she protested at Leiyn's teasing smile. "It has been too long since my last proper meal."

Ekosa, who had prepared many of their meals back in Haven, pretended affront. Everyone, even Batu, joined in the laughter.

Acalan visited soon after with a pair of their surviving *situali* comrades, Nahui and Coyoti, in tow. The diminutive female scout was as gregarious as ever, greeting them with a blaring welcome and two jugs of fiend's nectar. Soon, the slimy alcohol banished any lingering sobriety. Even the more reserved Coyoti began spouting enigmatic philosophies with abandon, to the chagrin of all. If either took issue with Teya's degradation in status, they did not show it.

Nahui, for her part, seemed more interested in Ketti. "Tell me of these," she demanded, poking at the pearls dotting the Eteman's arms. "You are like an Uman, decorating yourself with jewelry. They are pretty, but very, very strange. And you speak just as strangely! What lonely tribe birthed you?"

Embarrassed, Ketti stuttered through an explanation. Leiyn laughed with the others as the Gast scout grew increasingly perplexed. Finally, she threw up her hands and poured another helping of the milky liquor.

"I know not of what you speak," Nahui declared. "But another cup might make sense of it!" Then she tipped her head and drank it all.

Two more *situali* that Leiyn did not know had accompanied them. They did not join in the cheer but stood watch outside the barracks doors. Leiyn caught them darting baleful looks inside at Teya. When Teya noticed Leiyn glaring back, her beloved turned her away, then pressed a fresh cup into her hands.

"Drink," Teya said. "Help me forget."

Leiyn took the cup and pretended all was well. "How could I refuse that, my sky?"

Together, they drank. Enough, almost, to forget the shame cast from outside the door. To ignore the monsters lurking within the barracks walls.

The night's revelries pulled them back in when Coyoti revealed a second gift: a set of Iritu clothes for Ekosa, the only member of their party still wearing ordinary fabric. His *eesu* robes had long since tattered during their months of wear, yet the Ofean remained hesitant to don the gifted garb. They comprised articles he was unused to wearing: trousers, a long tunic, and a jacket in garish colors.

The odd *situal* was little help in convincing him as he pressed the set into his hands. "They shall fit you," he said with a circling gesture below his waist. "Like a swaddled babe."

Eventually, Ekosa relented to their intoxicated jeers and donned them. After he put them on, they coaxed him into spinning around once.

"You look dashing!" Teya laughed and clapped him on the back, causing him to stagger. She looked happier than Leiyn had seen her in months. "And better for running from lyshans, eh?"

Ekosa smiled, and though Iritu clothes adapted to one's form, Leiyn caught him plucking at them for the rest of the night.

When she was five cups in, Acalan pulled Leiyn aside and pressed a sheaf of arrows into her hands. Her lifesense confirmed her guess: these were Iritu-fletched and imbued with corrosive magic.

"May they aid in your hunt," he rumbled.

"Thank you, Acalan." She set them next to her seat. "It could still be your hunt, too. We'd be glad to have you."

The war chieftain afforded her a small smile. "You honor me, Huntress, but my place is here. And without *semah*, I would only slow you."

"You always kept up before." At his look, Leiyn held up her hands. "Fine, fine. I had to ask."

He nodded. Despite the merriment, his expression turned grave. He leaned in and spoke in a harsh whisper.

"Remain wary of the Iritu, Leiyn. Ata has done much to earn our trust but remember what they are capable of. Do not rest all our hopes on her. Your mission cannot fail."

"We won't." She put all the force of her conviction into the words.

Acalan smiled again, this one as sharp as desert glass. Clapping her on the shoulder, he rose and went to speak with Batu.

Leiyn remained where she was at the periphery of the revelries, her thoughts turning somber. Promise what she would, the fact remained that they were severely hampered without Ata. Should she choose not to aid them, what hope did they have to succeed?

We have to. She drank down the rest of her cup.

It was long after dark before they relented to sleep. Those with mahia burned away most of the inhibiting alcohol in their blood. Though scouts guarded them, at least one lyshan lurked nearby. It was not worth risking impairment during a night-time ambush.

Leiyn left only a pleasant buzz to her thoughts, hoping it would help her sleep. She listened to Qasaar's whispers, then Teya's breathing as her beloved eased quickly into sleep.

For herself, it was not until light edged the sky before she drifted off.

12

SURVIVE

Leiyn awoke to Ata in their room.

Heart hammering, irritation rising, she snatched up her discarded clothes from beside the bed. Though the Iritu did not share human sensibilities and did not balk at nakedness, it still made Leiyn feel too vulnerable to tolerate.

"Do you try to needle us?" she snapped as she pulled on her garments.

Teya roused and sat up. She did not move for her own clothes but stared, blinking, at the dryvan's back.

"Only when I require amusement." The shapeshifter did not turn around, nor did she inflect the words. One of her dark moods possessed her. Even her lifefire burned low.

The sight of it cooled Leiyn's anger. "Something wrong?" she asked, tying her weapons belt around her waist.

"Wrong?" Ata twisted back, a fey smile stretching her features wide. "Why, I was not aware anything at all was *wrong*."

"Have it your way," Leiyn muttered, settling her falchions against her hips.

"The rest of the armory," Teya spoke up. "Was it also empty?"

"Empty as a milked udder." The Iritu faced forward again and leaned far out the window. Leiyn's stomach fluttered, though Ata was at little risk from the fall. "Our legacy," the dryvan shouted inside, "evaporated, confiscated! Requisitioned for utilization in their malevolent crusade!"

Ata pitched from the window and out of sight. Leiyn tensed, then relaxed as her lifesense informed her of the dryvan standing unhurt below.

Teya, still swathed in blankets, arched her eyebrows. "She is 'in a mood,' as you outlanders say."

"Best hurry, then. Don't want her taking off without us."

After Teya dressed, they shrugged on their equipment and packs, lightened to the bare essentials for the next stage of their journey. The rest of their party met them in the corridor below. Hunger gnawed at Leiyn's belly, but with Ata as she was, she did not dare spare time to break their fast.

Batu, Ekosa, and Ketti picked up on the atmosphere, sharing worried glances as they went outside. Leiyn could only wince and pretend all was well.

As well as it ever is.

The scouts standing guard at the entrance barely greeted them. Their wary gazes remained on the dryvan striding up and down the dusty road. Ata shot them an impatient look, but continued to pace. Leiyn guessed those she saw walking up the path to be the reason for the delay.

Acalan and Xepi had come to see them off.

The war chieftain paused to have a muttered word with the guarding *situali*, after which they went jogging up the cliff path. Leiyn stared after them, hoping they went to do as she desired.

"Hunt well," the war chieftain said as he came before them, a heavy hand resting on the pommel of his Iritu sword.

"And survive," the shaman added with a smile. "We have need of you after this war."

Teya bowed deeply to each of them. "Thank you, Toa'Yao, Taht Xepi. May the sky lift your spirits."

Leiyn heard the emotion in Teya's voice, felt it in the flutter of her lifeforce. Her own throat ached for beholding it. Teya had come to Qasaar expecting to be rejected by her people. That these two esteemed members of the Many Tribes not only acknowledged her, but honored her, meant more than Teya could give voice to.

Still, Leiyn knew.

"And the hills bury your fears," Acalan rumbled. He and Xepi bowed their heads to her, then the war chieftain extended his hand to each of them, clasping their forearms with a strong, calloused grip.

With Teya, Acalan leaned in close. Only from her nearness did Leiyn catch his words to the *situal*.

"Survive. Even *kilakt* can be redeemed."

As he leaned away, Teya stood stiff and tall. She nodded to him before glancing away.

To Leiyn, Acalan said, "Hunt well, Huntress."

"I will."

He nodded. The force of his gaze and heat of his esse against her hand imparted a more visceral message.

Kill them. No matter the cost.

Leiyn pressed his arm, then moved to Xepi. The shaman peered into her eyes, seeming to search them for something. She nodded, then caught Leiyn by surprise when she pulled her into an embrace. Leiyn relented, even letting down her mahia's walls for their spirits to brush.

"You are not alone," the shaman whispered. Images accompanied her words.

Xepi poured her lifemark into Leiyn.

Again, Leiyn saw the eviscerated draconion representing

her son's death, but the latter two scenes had changed. Where the hearth had once been a dying fire, now it filled with renewed flames. And the broken spear was whole and clutched by a tanned woman. A hand that might have belonged to Teya. Or Leiyn.

Blinking, Leiyn gave the shaman a final squeeze, then pulled back to cuff her eyes. That Gasts could feel like family would have been incomprehensible to her younger, hateful self. But the world felt fuller for it.

If only Isla were here with us.

"Shall I let you leak more liquid from your eyes," Ata cut in, "or is it time to depart?"

The harsh words came like a knife through one of Leiyn's drawings. Leiyn glowered at the dryvan, but prudence tempered her response.

"Not yet." She nodded up the path. "Just a few minutes more."

The *situali* were already returning, their party's mounts in tow. As they had discussed with Acalan the night before, they would leave them in Qasaar. Horses and draconions were more of a liability than an asset when traveling by grotto and sea, as had been shown when Saikan had broken his leg while coming up from Ore-Ofe.

But the jaguar chieftain had thought to have them brought here for a final farewell.

Leiyn took Feral's reins and ran a hand along the mare's snout. She was nearly bit for the gesture, the roan in nearly as foul a mood as her rider that morning.

"Stop that," Leiyn snapped, surprised as tears again sprang to her eyes. Disregarding the risk, she leaned her head against Feral's and closed her eyes, then sent forth with her spirit to touch the horse's. "Do you want to leave things like that?"

The mare tried pulling away again, then settled. Hesitant,

she returned Leiyn's gesture, the tips of her lifefire leaning toward her ranger.

Leiyn smiled and spoke quietly, not wishing to startle Feral. "At least part of you will miss me."

As if in defiance of the words, the horse jerked free of her grip and loosed a frenzied neigh. With a final wild look, Feral went galloping up the rise.

One of the Gast scouts sprinted after her, shouting commands to stop. Leiyn might have reached out with her mahia to halt her mare; instead, she only laughed and watched her run free. It was a scene worthy of a sketch, should she ever have a moment to put it down.

The others concluded their more sedate goodbyes with their mounts, then gave over the reins to the remaining scout and Acalan. Under Ata's baleful gaze, Leiyn congregated with the others around the Iritu. Xepi, Acalan, and the *situal* stepped back as if afraid of being swept up in the Iritu's magic.

"At last," Ata snapped, "we go!"

Then the dryvan ripped the world away.

PART III

RUST & RUIN

13

A DREAM THAT NEVER WAS

Swift as a summer storm, they leaped over Unera's landscapes. Leiyn tried keeping her footing as the sandy streets of Qasaar were replaced by the uneven rocks of the Silvertusks, then the root-ridden ground of a Titan Wilds forest. Her senses collapsed before the maelstrom. Darkness swooped in.

Then, all at once, the storm calmed.

Leiyn opened her eyes to a wooded clearing. It was much like the glades she often came upon in the forests surrounding the Wilds Lodge. Dappled sunlight fell upon the toppled tree whose collapse had created the break in the canopy.

On that log sat a woman.

Leiyn advanced, hesitant. The woman's head was turned away, her features hidden by a mane of auburn hair. Her clothes were the simple homespuns worn by many a Baltesian on the frontier. Yet for as little as she could see, there was something familiar about the woman.

"Hello?" Leiyn approached like she would a deer who might bolt at any moment. "Do I know you?"

The woman turned toward her. The full view of her face

struck Leiyn to a standstill. She had only seen it once before, and she had been far from clear-headed then. Yet she remembered every detail. The angled, sky-blue eyes. The strong jaw and generous nose. The unfettered beauty of a woman comfortable in her own skin.

Leiyn could only breathe the word. "Mada."

Her mother smiled. That she was middle-aged was enough to tell Leiyn this was an illusion, for she would have been near Leiyn's age now when she died. This was a dream that could not be real.

Yet she longed for it enough to pretend that it could be.

"How are you here?" Tentatively, Leiyn scooted onto the log next to her. All she wanted was to take her mother's hand, to feel her warm embrace. But she could not make herself reach out. Afraid nothing would greet her touch.

Her mother's lips parted. Leiyn watched them, waiting for the words she knew she would commit to memory.

"Remember."

Only that single word did she speak. Then a gale whipped through the glade, strong enough to knock Leiyn from the log

Falling to her hands and knees, Leiyn twisted back, desperate to look upon her mother again. Already, the forest had begun dissolving under the heavy wind. Leaves tore free of the branches, then shredded to nothing. Her mother's hair blew back before her face, hiding it from view again. Only her lips remained visible, repeating that word once more.

Remember.

Leiyn tried standing, but her feet left the ground. The forest glade and its occupant disintegrated into detritus.

Then the dark storm stole her away.

14

OLD STONE, FRESH BLOOD

At last, the world settled.

Leiyn collapsed to the ground. Her pack dragged where it hung to one side. Drawing on her quivering esse, she put strength back into her limbs and struggled back to her feet.

Remember. Her mother's word echoed in her head, as enigmatic as in the vision. *Remember.*

Remember what, Mother?

Someone behind her retched, rousing her from her daze. Glancing around, she saw it was Ekosa who had fallen sick. The *eesu* was slumped over and moaning, spittle dribbling from his lips. Ketti kneeled next to him, a hand rubbing over his back, speaking in soothing wordless murmurs.

The others fared better. Teya looked unsteady, the former scout leaning on her spear to remain upright, but her jaw was set and gaze sharp. Batu already strode up the ruined road that led to where Solace lay hidden above, head turning as he scanned the surrounding area.

The fetor of vomit wafted over her. Leiyn wrinkled her nose and turned to Ata. She had expected the dryvan to watch them with amusement, but the Iritu was devoid of her usual perverse humor. Alert, she stared into the forest, her eyes unshifting.

Focus, Firebrand. What does she perceive?

She followed Ata's gaze and parsed the area with both vision and lifesense. All she could detect were plants and the attention of a few curious creatures.

"Can you not see?" the shapeshifter breathed. "The trees have eyes."

Pulse quickening, Leiyn investigated the trees themselves. Even if the Iritu had limitations to their transformations, when dealing with shapeshifters, there seemed a fair chance she meant the phrase literally.

A bat alighted from a branch.

Only then did Leiyn understand. Slipping her longbow from her shoulder, she fumbled for an Iritu arrow. She had just nocked it when the creature disappeared from her senses.

"*Fesht.*"

The immediate danger had passed, but Leiyn did not replace the bow or arrow. Looking to Ata, who still stared after the vanished creature, she asked, "Our new friend, I'm guessing?"

"Yes. Osmet. She Who Remains." The dryvan's lips twisted, a hint of sharp teeth peeking through, then spun toward the ruins. "Come. We shouldn't delay."

Without waiting for a reply, Ata strode away with her limber lopes. Leiyn lingered, telling the others of their lyshan tail and waiting for them to muster before guarding their rear. The lyshan may have disappeared, but she had veiled her essence so entirely that Leiyn had not distinguished her from an ordinary bat. Until she knew the limits of her enemy, it paid to take every precaution.

Clouded Fang. She touched on the bond to her titan. As he roused, she drew upon the vast well of his esse. The ash dragon turned one burning eye up at her, his mind as smoky as his form. Her body swelled with his lifeforce. She cast off the last vestiges of weakness. Her senses sharpened. Nervous energy filled her so she twitched as she looked this way and that.

They proceeded up the curving slope to the entrance of the ruins, quickening as Ekosa drew on an amber bead to recover his strength. Once, Khamo had ambushed them here with a contingent of Suncoats and driven them into the ruins. None appeared now. Yet even with Osmet's departure, she could not banish the feeling of wrongness. Spreading her lifesense, she searched for further signs of danger.

The first crackled against her awareness from the ruins rising before them. The tempest hawk who guarded them was never far from the senses, but Mehu'Ra was more present than he should have been.

Perhaps he senses our approach. Or the return of a Ta'Rul.

A flash of emerald startled them. Leiyn had drawn and aimed before she realized its source. Hissing out a breath, she glared balefully at Biqqa as the hummingbird fluttered madly around Ketti's head.

"What is it?" the Eteman whispered to the spirit beast. "*Deq ama*, Biqqa. What has upset you?"

But the little bird seemed to have reached her limits. With a final revolution around Ketti's head, Biqqa flew away, vanishing midair.

"What was that?" Teya's voice snapped through the silence.

Ketti's lavender eyes had rounded as she looked about them. "I do not know."

Leiyn scanned the shadows, searching with her natural senses for what might be hidden from her mahia. There was nothing—no glint of metal, no cloaked figures, no lyshan lying in wait. No sign of what had upset Biqqa.

"Wait." Ketti's voice pitched high. "What is that?"

Leiyn looked around as Teya stalked forward and peered

at the ground. Ata had strode past and scanned the ruins with a slight hunch to her posture. As if she meant to spring at any moment—or expected to be sprung upon.

"Blood." The scout straightened and took her spear in both hands, gaze casting about for enemies. "A day old, two at most."

Fresh blood. Leiyn tensed her hands on her bow and raised it higher. "Ata," she called across the ruins.

"I heard, Awakener." The dryvan twisted her head around to study their group, her features a mask of fury. "Can you not smell it?" Ata pivoted her gaze to Ketti, who had begun trembling. "Take us through, Eteman. At once!"

Leiyn edged closer, her back to her comrades. Far below, Clouded Fang stirred, his form solidifying with her trepidation as he prepared to rise to her defense.

The others had drawn their weapons. Batu clutched his axe in both hands, a feral look in his eyes. Ekosa had his belt knife out and his mahia held in readiness. Ketti had drawn a knife as well, yet she seemed in shock, her gaze distant and her mouth hanging ajar. Her chest heaved with shallow breaths.

"Ketti!" Leiyn said.

The Eteman roused, then nodded. "Yes. I am ready. I will take us through...now."

At the word, the ground lurched underfoot. Leiyn clung to her connection to Clouded Fang through the transition. The village of Solace replaced the ruined castle.

Yet ruin still surrounded them.

Rain pelted her face. The sky, always overcast in this grotto, had darkened to a slate gray.

It failed to hide the devastation that had been visited upon the marketplace.

Once bustling with cheery colors and vendors, it lay ravaged by violence. Stalls had toppled, fruits and vegetables spilled and split open on the flagstones. Banners and clothes were scattered, torn, and tangled. Some were ashy and dark, signs of a recent fire.

Amid the disarray sprawled the bodies.

There were dozens of them, unmoving and lying in twisted heaps. Some wore the golden colors and armor of Suncoats. Most had the clothes and gem-spangled skin of Etemans. They had not been dead more than a few days, for the stench of decay remained mild, and the bodies had only just begun to bloat.

A scream split the air.

Leiyn flinched and looked toward its source. Ketti had fallen to her knees. Her hands twisted into her wet curls, wrenching at her hair, her face twisted like the Catedrál's depictions of the demonic Legion. Her esse was worse still to behold, folding inward again and again. Tearing itself asunder.

"Ketti, Ketti!" Ekosa fell by her side, hands held up before him. "Please, speak to me!"

The Eteman was beyond hearing. "How?" she gasped, staring at everything, at nothing. "How did they get in? Did I...?"

"Not you. This was not your fault!"

Leiyn tore her gaze away. Forcing herself alert, she sloughed off her rucksack in readiness for whatever—or whomever—they might find. Batu and Teya followed suit, then stood over their companions, rain running down the furrows of their faces. Ata strayed from their party, mismatched eyes lingering on the corpses. Over the drumming rain, Leiyn picked up the dryvan murmuring to herself.

"Brother, *Ahu*, have you no mercy?"

Sharo. Hatred, buried and dormant, flared up to heat her through. Leiyn gritted her teeth and looked for their enemy without hope. If any lyshan were here, they would not have evaded her notice for this long. Not unless they were already in hiding.

But Solace did not lay lifeless. At the far end of the town, toward where Hold Ta'Rul lay, a dozen people had taken shelter. Their esses remained firmly inside their bodies and appeared dim like those without mahia.

She knew who they were. What they had done.

"Suncoats," she spat, jerking her head in the direction of the Ilberian soldiers. "They're hiding."

"From what?" Teya shouted back.

Before Leiyn could answer, lightning split the sky, illuminating Solace as brightly as day. Thunder followed on its heels, trembling through her bones. Esse shuddered over her skin, sparking and numbing where it landed. Telling her what lay behind the storm.

Leiyn freed her drawhand to point at the sky. "Mehu'Ra!"

Even as she shouted, the tempest hawk burst through the clouds. His brilliant blue and purple plumage were radiant with lightning. His eyes shone with stormy light. As he shrieked and dove, thunderous booms washed over them, paralyzing them where they stood. Only her connection to Clouded Fang allowed Leiyn to sprint away.

Rise! she called, sending esse racing down their connection. *Come to me!*

The volcanic titan surged upward, flapping smoky wings through the earth toward her. He could not move fast enough. The storm titan was upon them, diving, deadly talons reaching. Leiyn dove out of the way and twisted back to ensure the others had followed.

Ketti had not run. Shoving Ekosa sprawling, she stood with her arms spread wide.

"Mehu'Ra—*ama ek akkir!* I am yours!"

Leiyn had but a moment to wonder at the words before the tempest hawk crashed into the Eteman.

Or so it seemed. The titan filled Leiyn's vision and took up the whole of the plaza. Energy shuddered off the wings as they spread overhead, making Leiyn's muscles spasm and twitch. "Ketti!" she gasped with what breath remained in her flattened lungs.

Yet her lifesense told a different story. The Eteman still stood before that mass of feathers and fury. Her mahia spread from her body, reaching up and into the titan before her. And the tempest hawk flowed back into her.

They're bonding.

"Wait!" Leiyn gasped, sending a warning down to her rapidly approaching titan. Clouded Fang banked to a halt just short of the surface. Incandescent eyes settled on her, seeking to understand. She did not know how to share it with him, so she repeated the command.

Wait. Friend.

The others, drenched and frightened but alive, had skirted the edge of the tempest hawk's tail feathers to stagger over to Leiyn. Ata was not among them; vaguely, she sensed the dryvan elsewhere in Solace through the pervasive presence of Mehu'Ra. Standing together, they watched as the enormous bird folded its wings, revealing a head bowed toward the diminutive figure before it. Ketti had her hands clenched in the head feathers of the titan. Her quivering body told of continued sobs.

The implications of their bonding rolled through Leiyn like thunder clouds. As far as she knew, only one person could bond with a titan at a time. Mehu'Ra had been bound to Oro Ta'Rul, Ketti's great-grandfather and the patriarch of her household.

Not him.

Leiyn fanned the flames of her rage and glanced back toward the hiding Ilberian soldiers. "I'm going after them. Teya, with me. Batu, Ekosa, keep watch over Ketti."

The men nodded. Leiyn shared a look with Teya.

Together, they loped down the debris-covered street, making for their unsuspecting prey.

Leiyn tried not to see the slaughter, but it was all around them. Blood darkening the puddles. Cadavers, split open and tossed to the side. The Etemans had not been a martial people, but they had been as formidable as she in mahia. For all of them to fall would have taken more than Suncoats. Odiosas had been here. Lyshans as well.

You'll pay for this, she swore to Sharo, *you* egreshti *bastard.* She wished the lyshan stood before her then so she could extract his debt in flesh.

They slowed as they neared the soldiers' hideout. They had holed up in Hold Ta'Rul itself. Its broken tower loomed above, exposed to the elements.

Teya motioned to a nearby alley, and they ducked into it. "How should we enter?"

Leiyn set her bow on the stones and replaced the Iritu arrow in the quiver on her hip. She drew her falchions, the titanbone blades emerging seamlessly from their scabbards. "I'll break us in."

Teya eyed her, brow furrowed. "How?"

"Just stay with me and keep them off my back."

Clouded Fang had followed them through the village and hovered just below the surface. Leiyn drew more of his esse into her body, then channeled it into her muscles and bones. Strength shuddered through, almost too much to bear.

She rose, then jerked her head forward and set off at a run. Teya remained close on her heels.

Blades pumping with each stride, she charged for the front door. Pavers slick with rainwater endeavored to make her slip, but her enchanted shoes kept their grip. The door, solid wood, fast approached. Their slapping footsteps must have been audible, for Leiyn felt the soldiers stirring through her life-sense, aware of something amiss.

She picked up speed and lowered her shoulder, channeling esse to pad it. A snarl broke across her face.

She rammed the door.

Pain ratcheted up her left shoulder as it dislocated with the impact. Wood splintered around her as the hinges tore free of the frame. Her mahia rushed to repair the wound.

The sharp edge of an axe greeted her.

Leiyn caught it with her right falchion. Titanbone cut halfway through the haft before stopping the weapon.

In her left shoulder, bone and ligaments pulled back into place. Screaming with the pain, Leiyn whipped her left sword around to remove the head from the stricken Suncoat.

As blood sprayed from the decapitated body, pandemonium spread throughout the Ta'Rul's atrium. Leiyn kicked the corpse aside and knocked the axe free of her blade before diving into the melee. Soldiers, frightened and haggard, raised shields to block her blades, but steel could not withstand bones harvested from titans. Two more fell in screaming, bloody heaps, their arms removed along with the top halves of their shields.

Two were charging down the stairs, only to be met with the point of Teya's spear. Though anxiety for her beloved tore at her, Leiyn had no choice but to leave the pair to Teya and face the remaining seven. Leiyn's savagery had sent them scuttling back, none were eager to engage an adversary whose weapons could cut through their armor like a machete through brush.

"It's her!" one gasped. "The Wilds Witch!"

Dread-filled prayers issued from the Suncoats' lips. Had she not witnessed Solace's slaughter, had Ilberia and its allies not killed Isla, Leiyn might have smiled. But whatever satisfaction that had come from the hunt was gone.

All that remained was grim resolve. The butcher's duty.

She charged. Two cowered away, while the other five

rallied their flagging courage. She took their attacks against her vambraces, the Iritu armor repelling the sharp edges, then whipped her falchions across, carving through chins and collarbones.

The line of soldiers broke. Those who had not perished outright clutched at mangled jaws, blood spurting from cloven bone. Leiyn left them to die and stepped past them to the two cravens. One was a young woman, the other a graying older man. The fear in their faces gave her a moment's pause.

Then she remembered Isla, lifeless on the bloody planks. Tadeo, stabbed and sliced amid the blackened ruins of the Wilds Lodge. The mangled bodies of the rangers, the staff, the apprentices.

She killed the man where he stood, stabbing through his chest too quickly for him to dodge. Withdrawing the blade, she closed in on the girl.

"Leiyn, wait!"

Teya wrenched her back by the shoulder. Leiyn twisted around to snarl at her, but her beloved's expression gave her pause.

Still full of fire, she shrugged off the former scout's hand and turned back to the huddled young woman. Her trousers had darkened, a wet patch quickly spreading. The acrid stench of piss cut through the sweat and blood of the fallen soldiers.

Shame choked out the flames.

"Question her." Leiyn turned back to the soldiers still clinging to life, throat tight. It was a mercy to end them, but it darkened the cloud filling her. She coughed as she skewered the last of them, choking as though smoke filled her lungs.

Spitting the bile free, Leiyn wiped her blades on one of the stained yellow coats and reached out with her lifesense. The others still appeared safe in the plaza. If lyshans lingered in the grotto, they had not come out yet. Withdrawing her mahia, she turned to where Teya kneeled before the remaining Suncoat, her spear pointed at the ceiling. The *situal's* posture and tone were unthreatening, but the young soldier panted with panicked breaths, her wide eyes staring at the blood dripping down the shaft.

Leiyn wondered where Ketti's parents had died. Where Oro Ta'Rul lay. In this house? Had they slaughtered the patriarch on his throne? The building did not reek of decay like the rest of the village. If they had been killed here, the Suncoats must have moved their bodies.

"How long have you been here?" she heard Teya ask the girl soldier. "How long ago did you attack?"

The young woman whimpered, her head lowered, not meeting Teya's eyes. She looked to be eighteen years old. Old enough to enlist, but young enough to know nothing of the world.

Leiyn looked away and leaned against the wall. The Suncoat reminded her of another soldier they had taken prisoner, one just as young and naive. Whose arm she had lopped off at the wrist. Yet Arias di Carille had escaped them when she let down her guard.

She would not make the same mistake twice.

Leiyn kept her falchions drawn and at her side. Ready to strike.

"We will not kill you," Teya murmured. "We will not harm you. Please, just answer my questions."

How the *situal* could be so gentle after killing, Leiyn could not know. She still felt the thrum of battle pulsing through her. Clouded Fang flew through the earth below, agitated and impatient. Though she could never know the titan's mind for certain.

"I didn't know," the girl soldier whispered. "Didn't know what they... When these people were..." A fresh sob worked free of her, hunching her over. "I never wanted this. I just want to go home."

A laugh cut free of Leiyn. Both women looked up at her, Teya with weary resignation, the girl with sharp fear. That look of fear almost silenced her, but bitter words pressed out all the same.

"You want your home?" Leiyn spat. "So did we. But you Suncoats stole that from us."

Leiyn held the girl's gaze until the soldier looked away. Only Teya's reproachful stare made Leiyn relent.

"We will find you a way home," the scout promised the Suncoat. "I swear by my ancestors' spirits, and that is not an oath I would break."

The young woman drew in a shuddering breath. "Alright. I'll talk."

"Good. How did your company come to be here? How long have you been in Solace?"

Unable to help herself, Leiyn glanced at the Ilberian soldier. The young woman flinched, then turned back to Teya. She opened her mouth several times before she spoke.

"Three days ago, I think. That's when our captain—"

Her words ended in a scream as the wall imploded—and a giant claw clamped over the Suncoat's head.

15

FEATHER & CLAW

Leiyn stumbled back from the broken wall. The claw that emerged from the hole was glossy and cobalt blue: the claw of a crab, though a hundred times larger than any she had witnessed. It was dead to her lifesense, yet its rapid movement showed it was very much alive.

With the claw clamped over the Suncoat's head, there was only one end. It tensed, and like a melon left in the sun, the young woman's skull split open. Blood spurted around the claw.

The dead woman slumped to the ground as the claw released her.

"*Sach'aan!*" Teya jabbed her spear at the armored appendage.

As she pierced its shell, the rest of the lyshan became visible to Leiyn's lifesense. It was massive, bigger than either Khamo or Man'nah, though it contained fewer souls than either. A hundred, she guessed at a glance.

Leiyn launched herself at it, blades leading. She landed glancing blows on the shelled arm before the pincer drew back.

"Back up!" she shouted at Teya. "Away from the wall!"

Barely had she spoken before four more pincers thrust through. Stone crumbled; dust flooded the atrium. Leiyn coughed and squinted, trying to see their enemy through the cloud. Her mahia proved a better guide than vision as she launched a fresh attack.

Each of these pincers was like the first: as large around as her chest and reinforced with glossy plate. Withdrawing again, they tore through with impossible speed and strength. Even a single hit promised to kill, punching through enchanted armor and flesh as easily as they did stone.

Leiyn skirted out of range and into the Ta'Rul kitchen. Teya followed, backing up the stairwell.

The crustacean lyshan was not content to remain outside. Breaking fully through the wall, it scuttled in to close them off.

The tower could not take much more abuse. Already, the ceiling buckled and the walls groaned. Desperate, Leiyn drew on her connection to Clouded Fang, flooding her body with yet more esse. The ash dragon flew impatiently below, fiery eyes set on their enemy.

Be ready, she told him, then charged for the door.

Teya screamed at her back, but she put her out of mind. The lyshan thrust its pincers forward. Leiyn sidestepped and bumped into the wall to avoid the explosive attacks. Then she was through the door and moving to flank the skin-walker.

Teya was still trapped. Only by drawing the lyshan away could Leiyn free her.

The lyshan turned to face her. She dared to come closer, lashing with her falchions. "Fight me!" she shouted at it, trying to land hits on its plate and crack through. "Fight me, you Saints-damned devil!"

She never saw the blow land.

Next she knew, Leiyn lay crumpled on the ground. She wheezed, trying to breathe, but all the wind had been knocked from her. Panicking, she looked down, expecting to see a gaping hole in her chest. Blood painted her clothes, but she could not tell if it was hers or the Suncoats' she had cut down. Neither the jacket nor tunic was torn, though their esse had dimmed.

Thunder boomed in the distance. Teya cried out, her voice seeming distant. Fear levered Leiyn up even as her lungs refused to expand. She grasped for strength from her mahia and rose to her feet.

Not her. Don't take her!

But Teya had not been yelling from pain, but in warning. The lyshan scuttled toward Leiyn, four pincered arms tucked against a broad, plated body. Its head rose as a stump above it, pitted eyes glinting with esse. Four spindly limbs supported the rest, some revolting amalgamation of a crab and a spider.

Black spots dotted her vision as the lack of air took its toll. But for a time, she could live on esse alone. Stumbling, Leiyn made to stay out of its range. She delved into the earth, to where her titan waited, and drew yet more lifeforce from it.

Come, Clouded Fang!

The ash dragon swept upward. The lyshan, sensing it coming, rushed forward with its claws upraised. Leiyn struck with her falchions, desperate to keep them at bay. Titanbone and chitin clashed, numbing her arms and driving her back.

Clouded Fang broke the surface.

Soot and smoke morphed into scale and tooth. Enormous jaws closed around the lyshan. Long, yellowed fangs drove through its plated torso.

The shapeshifter shrieked, an inhuman sound that filled the alley. It was powerless to escape; the titan held it with both mahia and jaws. Though it beat against Clouded Fang's maw, the titan's grip only tightened. His esse pulsed like lava flowing through the heart of a volcano, every bit as destructive and inescapable.

Leiyn was thrown back as the rest of the dark dragon emerged and soared into the sky, taking the lyshan with him. She watched him burst through the low dome of clouds as breath finally rushed back into her lungs. Wracked with coughing, she steadied herself before rising back to her feet. Clouded Fang burned in her awareness as he soared behind the clouds.

She felt the moment his jaws closed. When the lyshan's layered being went dark. From the sky, pieces of it tumbled down into the village below. Amber ichor fell with the rain.

One shard of chitin crashed into the ground before her. Leiyn bared her teeth at it before kicking it aside and striding forward.

Thank you, she sent to the titan along their bond. If it understood gratitude, it gave no sign of it but only continued to circle above.

Teya had stumbled from the ruins and ran toward her, spear in hand. Dust layered her, but she looked unharmed.

"Are you hurt?" she asked, looking Leiyn up and down. Leiyn felt her mahia probing her as well.

Leiyn shrugged. "Nothing that stuck. You?"

"Fine." Her beloved pressed her arm with a fleeting smile, then nodded back toward the center of Solace. "We must hurry."

Absorbed by her own struggles, Leiyn had neglected to keep track of the rest of their companions. Her throat clamped shut as she noticed Batu's esse. Something was attacking him, some beast many times larger than he, and it sent his lifefire into chaos. Yet he did not seem to suffer injury for it, and the esse of the creature seemed familiar.

Sarryl. His moonbear.

This was no attack—it was a wildsoul joining. Somehow, even with clouds hiding the moons, the spirit beast had found a way into Solace.

Yet she was scarcely reassured. Beyond the merging man and bear were more than Ketti, Ekosa, and the tempest hawk.

A second lyshan stalked their friends.

For the moment, it seemed held at bay. Crackling lightning told of who was responsible for that. But all it would take was one mistake to end their lives. Especially with Batu vulnerable during the transition.

Leiyn took off at a sprint, Teya matching it.

Clouded Fang! she beseeched her titan, sending her need along their bond. The ash dragon banked where it soared in the air, making to dive at the central plaza.

"He'll buy us time," she panted to Teya as they turned the corner. Though she had mostly healed, her lungs still struggled to expand.

"Your *kainox*?" the scout asked between breaths.

She nodded.

A second battle sprawled before them. This lyshan was only slightly less grotesque than the one she had fought. Snorting and huffing, it tossed a head like a bull's and stamped a hoofed foot into the stone, sending spiderweb cracks through it. Shaggy blonde fur covered its bulky frame where aqua armor did not cover it. A line of yellowed bone ran over its skull between two wickedly curved horns. Claws such as a lizard might have extended from its arms, gray scales blending haphazardly with the fur coat.

Leiyn put on a burst of speed, trying to reach them before the lyshan charged, but they were too far. With its horns lowered, it bellowed and bolted forward, aiming for her companions.

A mass of pale fur whirled into view, knocking it off course.

Leiyn could scarcely follow the melee. Batu, merged with his moonbear, wrestled the lyshan. His esse was not as bright, nor was he of a size with the bestial lyshan, yet he held his own. Bright red and amber sprayed as claws and horns landed on their hides. Batu roared, and the cry was more bear than man.

Hang on! she willed her friend. Pride and fear for him wrestled for supremacy.

As they reached the edge of the plaza, Clouded Fang broke through the clouds, diving toward the melee. At the speed he flew, he would kill everyone there.

Not yet! she cried at the ash dragon, sending the plea through their bond. *Pull up!*

The titan seemed as if he would not heed her, but as he came level with the broken rooftops, he banked and made for another turn through the clouded sky.

She had no time for relief as they reached the fray. Falchions in hand, Leiyn circumnavigated the turbulent match between wildsoul and lyshan, looking for an opening. Teya joined her, spear held at the ready. Though she wished the scout would fall back with the others, Leiyn knew better than to try convincing her. From the corner of her eye, she saw Ekosa standing with Ketti beneath Mehu'Ra's spread wings. Every caw of the tempest hawk sent violet lightning rising all around. From what she could tell, her comrades merely observed—without martial training, there was little else they could do. Where Ata was, she could not tell.

The answer came at once when a third lyshan appeared behind the others.

"She Who Remains!" Leiyn shouted, pointing a sword at the skin-walker.

The twisted lyshan screeched in what might have been a laugh, then sent forth an arrow of mahia. Ekosa crumpled, body limp.

Her breath caught. Only the weak glow of his esse reassured her he was still alive.

Ketti screamed in Eteman as she faced the lyshan. Her

tempest hawk shrieked with her. Lightning wreathed both the woman and titan. Mahia writhed in and through them.

Together, they attacked, their magic aimed like a ballista bolt at the lyshan.

Osmet did not wait for it. As quickly as she had appeared, she was gone again. Ketti's onslaught met nothing but stone. Mehu'Ra's lightning scorched the pavers black.

But the lyshan had not entirely disappeared; she reemerged on high, clinging to a parapet.

"Puny ancestors!" Osmet cackled. "Ponderous mortals! Have you not adapted in all these years?"

Ketti shrieked back something in Eteman. Power crackled over her skin, her body overflowing with her bonded hawk's might. A titan caller like the Gast stories of old, in full possession of her power.

The Eteman never had the chance to land an attack. Ata lunged from the air behind Osmet. Her talons gripped her enemy's leathery wings and ripped them free. The lyshan squawked and pitched off the wall, vanishing just before she hit the ground.

Ata, snarling, dove after her, disappearing as well.

Batu's pained gasp and a heavy thump brought Leiyn's attention back around. The bullish lyshan had thrown him off, sending him rolling in a spray of blood. White fur had been dyed pink. Jagged wounds crawled up and down her friend's morphed body. For the moment, he would survive—so long as the lyshan was given no opportunity to finish him.

Snarling, Leiyn moved forward. *Clouded Fang!*

The dragon banked and headed toward them. The lyshan turned to her and bellowed before charging. Even with a titan's power, she could not hold up to that charge. She kept her feet light and slashed as she dove past him.

Narrowly, she evaded the charge. The stones pounded her shoulder as she landed awkwardly, then rolled back to her feet.

The skin-walker turned back, snarling visage facing her. His hooves dug into the stone, tensing thickly corded legs.

Teya jabbed her spear into his side, then sprang away.

The lyshan was on her in moments, too swift to evade. Leiyn screamed as she drove forward.

But she was not swift enough.

A clawed hand rent into the Gast. Teya went spinning into a collapsed stall, her lifefire dimming.

Leiyn was on him a moment after, swords slicing through hide and armor and horn. The skin-walker lashed at her and tossed his head, trying to gore her on a horn, but twin strikes lopped off the tip of one. She took two clawed fingers with another strike and cut deep furrows into his left leg. Yet even the light blows he landed sent her stumbling, undeniable power behind them. A full blow might shatter bones and put an abrupt end to the fight.

The lyshan closed in—then halted as lightning washed over him.

Leiyn stumbled, staring as the blonde fur turned black and smoke rose from its flanks. Her hair stood on end. She knew well the pain of that lightning; she had suffered Mehu'Ra's attacks on their first encounter.

Yet the Iritu was not felled. With a pained bellow, it rose and dashed—not toward Leiyn and the others, but away. The tempest hawk's attack broke off as it turned the corner.

Then the lyshan disappeared as it fled the battle.

16

HEIR OF AEONS

Leiyn stared after where the lyshan had vanished. Clouded Fang had been diving toward the spot, but at a thought from Leiyn, he turned aside and winged back skyward. Satisfied they were safe for the moment, she ran to her beloved.

"Teya!"

The former scout groaned and sat up slowly. Leiyn's chest loosened as she saw Teya's armor had borne the brunt of the damage. Threads of black spiraled through Teya's head and body, betraying her injuries, but they were nothing that could not be quickly mended.

"I am fine," Teya managed after a moment, waving back toward the plaza. "Go to Batu."

Though reluctant to leave her side, concern for her other friend drove Leiyn back to her feet. Batu and his moonbear remained joined. As she probed his esse, she found it difficult to distinguish where one ended and the other began. Like the twisted trunks of a tree, they had intertwined so they almost became one being.

She reached his side and looked down at him. Low

moans escaped him, yet he raised his head and met her eye with a steady gaze. She tried not to cringe at how he had transformed. Tried not to think "beastfolk" and "tainted" when staring at him. Yet the strangeness of his appearance, the suddenness of the transformation, his sheer ferocity and size—all of it conspired to make her wary.

She forced herself to kneel next to him.

"It's alright," she murmured, placing a tentative hand on his side. "I'll help you, Batu. But you need to change back."

His mouth, elongated into a snout, pulled back to bare teeth painted with ichor. Leiyn tensed, ready to spring away.

Then the moment passed. Batu closed his eyes, the snarl fading before his weariness. She felt his esse quiver, then pull away from the bear.

Leiyn rose and moved back, watching as one being turned back into two. Sarryl emerged like a fleshy tumor being removed, peeling off the fur and shrinking Batu's features as it did. The humped back came first, then the head reared up. Four legs pushed out, parting their bodies from one another. Tan skin and white fur separated, wounds covering both in a mirror to one another.

Sarryl stood and stared in challenge at Leiyn. Separate from Batu, his fur had turned to luminous mist, his lumbering frame seeming as light as a cloud. It was a similar unnatural appearance to that which other spirit beasts gained within a grotto. Batu curled onto his side, covering his nakedness. Of the two, the plainsrider seemed to suffer the worse for their wounds.

"I won't harm him," she told the moonbear. Like with Chispa, she wondered how much Sarryl understood. Enough, it seemed; the albino beast shifted, allowing her to move to her friend's side.

Batu cracked open his eyes to look up at her. "Damned

strong, that lyshan," he said through clenched teeth. "But Sarryl held his own, didn't he?"

"You both did." She raised an eyebrow with a glance at his bared chest. "Any clothes left?"

"In the alley behind you." The former plainsrider closed his eyes again.

"I will fetch them." Teya came tottering up behind Leiyn, movements slow but esse burning steadily. Leiyn sensed that several of the amber beads on the scout's hip were drained and assumed them to be the source of her renewed strength.

Leiyn nodded, then set her hands on Batu's arm. He tensed, then relaxed, too exhausted for wariness.

"This'll sting," she told him, then set to mending his wounds.

When she finished, Leiyn supplemented her lifeforce with Clouded Fang's, then stood on stiff legs. Teya brought over Batu's clothes, and they both turned away as he dressed.

While they waited, Leiyn let her gaze wander to where Ketti kneeled by Ekosa. He had not yet risen, but a glance at his lifefire showed he would survive. Ata remained absent, ostensibly hunting after her Kin.

So long as she returns soon.

At a word from Batu, they turned back to him. "Think he'll let me help him?" Leiyn nodded at the moonbear, who had set to licking the wounds layering his hide.

Batu shrugged his jerkin into place. "Don't know." He peered at the moonbear. She wondered if they had some invisible method of communication, like she did with Clouded Fang. If her experience with other spirit animals was any guide, it would not be by language, but a shared understanding.

"He'll let you try," the former plainsrider said after several moments. "But go slowly."

Leiyn nodded and edged toward the albino bear. He

watched her with wary, intelligent eyes, pink as if with fever. As she set her hand on his shoulder, he shifted and loosed a grunt. Leiyn tensed, ready to bound back.

"Sarryl," Batu murmured, moving to his side and running a hand through the cloudy fur. "Please."

The tension in the moonbear's body subsided. Leiyn sent her mahia in slowly, feeling for his injuries. Bloody rents tore up and down his sides, turning to a red mist where it met his incorporeal form. Already, they had begun to heal and showed no signs of infection. The innate mahia of spirit beasts, demonstrated by how they passed in and out of grottos with ease, seemed to afford them resistance to disease. Gently, she closed what wounds remained and fed Sarryl esse to supplement what he had lost.

When the moonbear finally shifted away, the aggression had faded from his stance. He gave her a considering look, then moved over to nestle his head against Batu's chest. The smile Batu gave him as he scratched behind his ears was as bright as any she had seen from him since they lost Isla.

Her pleasure at the sight could not last. Leiyn looked to where Ketti and Ekosa huddled under the tempest hawk. The *eesu* had risen to his feet, arm clasped about Ketti's waist, as much to remain standing as to lend her support. He still had a dazed look in his eyes, but his concern for his beloved overrode any lingering injuries.

Leiyn turned toward them. Reluctance gripped her, but she forced herself to look at Ketti. The Eteman's eyes were red-rimmed, and though she held herself upright, there was a fragility to her stance. A statue of glass in danger of fracturing.

How well she knew that feeling. It was the same that filled her when she had woken to the Wilds Lodge burned, its occupants slaughtered. Home was supposed to be steady and safe. For it to be violated, for everyone you knew and loved to be ripped away in a moment—how could it not shatter your world?

She stopped several paces off, mindful of the looming titan. Mehu'Ra had subsided the rainstorm, but the violent purple of his eye was hard upon her, promising to raise thunderheads again at the slightest provocation. He was not as large as Clouded Fang, but his hooked beak could easily bite off her head, and his lifeforce could overwhelm her as it almost had in the past.

"Ketti?" Leiyn asked. Her friend's sorrow nestled in her chest, heavy and aching, but Leiyn knew no words to express it.

The Eteman blinked, then separated from Ekosa. The *eesu* looked stricken and haggard, but he did not cling to Ketti as she moved away. With his master's departure, Mehu'Ra leaped into the air. Leiyn flinched from the buffeting of his wings, then watched as the gigantic hawk took to circling the sky with Clouded Fang. Dark clouds gathered again, swirling together with the smoke trailing the ash dragon, forming an ominous whirlpool above.

As Ketti made to pass her, Leiyn grasped at the first question that occurred to her. "You've bonded, then? With Mehu'Ra?"

Ketti flinched, then pushed past. "I must find my family."

Leiyn watched as her friend plodded through the devastated plaza. The Eteman's gaze drifted from body to body left in the wake of the attack. At some, she paused, kneeling and gently turning them over to examine a face. Ketti had known each of them. All in Solace had appeared to send her off when she left. The town had numbered no greater than a few hundred people, all capable of surviving for centuries.

They had been friends. Family. Tied together by shared space, history, culture.

All gone, thanks to Sharo.

Leiyn clung to that flicker of anger, cupped it in her hands like a candle flame in a gale. At least it cast off a little light, a little warmth. At least it was not this pervasive, numbing darkness.

Ketti continued her search, murmuring words for each of the dead as she went. Leiyn followed with Ekosa for several minutes before breaking off to fetch her bow. A vague sense of dread filled her. Solace was no longer a place of shelter. Somehow, lyshans had devised a way to come and go from it as they pleased. The sooner they left, the better.

But she could not rush Ketti's grief. All she could do was remain vigilant and hope their enemies had suffered enough for one day.

At least we killed one of the bastards.

Her bow retrieved, she returned to the plaza when Ata appeared beside her. Leiyn flinched away before she recognized who it was. At odds with the somber atmosphere, the dryvan wore a fierce, satisfied smile.

"That was a blow they won't soon forget! Shu'eil, crushed in a Vast One's jaws. Ram'bal wrestled down by a wildsoul. And Osmet!" A wild laugh jangled down the broken alley. "I hope she still feels the lack of her wings!"

"Ata, please." Leiyn glanced toward the plaza. "Think of Ketti."

The dryvan's glee dimmed, but it did not leave her mismatched eyes. "Ah, yes. The demise of the Etemans is unfortunate." She tilted her head, and Leiyn felt her mahia pulse out, light as a summer breeze. "Does she seek her kin? The previous master of the *kainox* I can sense near..." Ata narrowed her eyes. "Near the husk of an *Ialadt*."

"One of your Mothertrees?" Leiyn realized what she spoke of. "The seeing pool."

"Of course they would have twisted it for their own purposes." The dryvan strode down the street, not sparing a glance for the bodies she moved around. As Leiyn followed, she wondered if Ata regretted the Etemans' deaths at all.

Informing Ketti of Ata's insight, they moved off together for the tower where the seeing pool lay. The prospect of finding her great-grandfather alive animated Ketti. The death and detritus lining their path swiftly doused it. Leiyn tried not to stare at the bodies. To see if she recognized any. That path only led to despair.

Ketti, however, could not help herself. She peered at each of the villagers, murmuring words under her breath. If they were names, words of departure, or curses at those who committed the massacre, Leiyn did not know. With each corpse passed, her shoulders sagged lower.

When the ruined tower rose before them, Ata stopped, wooden features twisting. "I shall remain without," she announced as she turned away.

Batu stopped next to her, Sarryl by his side. His expression was a match to the Iritu's. "We will as well."

Seeing little reason to insist otherwise, Leiyn nodded and moved forward, then tarried at the entrance. Foreboding slowed her. She was not the only one to notice the trail of dried blood on the stone.

Ketti pushed past, barely glancing at the smear. A gasp and a plaintive plea told of what she found within.

"*Etaro anni*... Not you, too, Ab-Abi..."

Leiyn trailed in after Ekosa and Teya. There he lay, face-down next to the ancient tree stump. His feathered staff was next to him, the wood stained dark with blood. The pearls lining his skin were dun to her lifesense, along with the rest of his body. One arm lay at an awkward angle, as if he had been reaching for the scrying pool in his last moments. She wondered why. Wondered if he reached it.

"Ab-Abi, please... I cannot do this without you..."

Ketti cradled her great-grandfather's head in her lap. Ekosa kneeled next to her, a hand on her back, despondency bowing his head.

A flash of memory struck Leiyn. In place of Ketti, she once more saw Batu cradling Isla's corpse.

Grief, barely diminished by the seasons, clawed inside her chest. Leiyn stalked around the edge of the room to the other side of the pool, desperate to escape the scene. Seeking distracting, she peered into the hollow and observed the swirling waters, moving without cause for a current. Esse shimmered within. Violet light danced upon the ceiling, emitted from the enchanted waters.

Watching the pool slowly stir helped calm the creature within her. The pain of losing Isla receded to its usual dull ache.

Leiyn tensed as she noticed something new to the pool, something that had not been present during her first visit. A dark tendril whirled through the water, almost black amid the lighted pool.

Blood.

"Ketti." Reluctant to interrupt her grieving, Leiyn spoke in a whisper. She forced her voice louder. "Ketti, I think you should see this."

The Eteman sniffled, then slowly extracted herself from her great-grandfather's body. Eyes puffy, tears streaming down her face, she rose and looked at Leiyn.

Leiyn nodded down at the pool, unable to meet her eyes for long. "I think he reached into the pool."

"Ab-Abi?" Ketti sniffed, staring into the eddy for several moments.

"What does it mean?" Ekosa stood at his beloved's side, supporting her. Recovered from Osmet's blow, he stood as strongly as he spoke.

The Eteman did not answer but leaned over the hollow.

Leiyn felt a pulse of her mahia enter the waters. A moment later, Ketti set her hand within.

"I feel him." The misery did not leave her face or voice, but a fragile smile lifted her lips. "He is here."

"Oro?" Leiyn scarcely dared breathe. As if an errant exhalation might banish the spirit of the patriarch still lingering in this place.

"Come, everyone, gather." Ketti spoke eagerly. "Come with me."

Leiyn met Teya's raised eyebrow with a nod. The former *situal* wordlessly joined, pressing her hand into the water with Leiyn. Ekosa had already placed his next to Ketti's.

"Oro Ta'Rul," Ketti whispered.

As before, the water rippled into impossible lines, acting like a creature alive. Leiyn watched a man take shape in intricate detail. Even with as brief as she had known the patriarch, she recognized his features. The prominent brow. The stooped stance. The wise, plum eyes.

Ketti spoke a sentence in Eteman, then in Ilberian. "Take us to him. Please."

Leiyn felt the invitation rise. When they had been tossed in Anchor's Refuge, the bay off of Southport, she had felt a powerful undertow pulling her down. The sensation now was similar, though gentler. More an invitation than a drowning current.

Leiyn drew in a breath, then dove into the pool.

17

A BREEZE ACROSS THE SEA

Leiyn spun down into the pool. When the turning slowed, a scene painted itself before her in shifting pastels.

A shimmering ocean, cornflower blue and bathed in sunlight, spread below a cliff. On an outcropping overlooking the sea grew a tree, deep-rooted and high-reaching. Peach-pink blooms tipped with white blossomed across it, their petals layering the grass beneath.

At the base of the trunk sat an aged man.

The others were there as well. Ketti moved forward, seeming more to drift than walk. Leiyn took a wobbly step after her. The more she tried moving her body, the less it seemed to comply. Only when she willed herself under the swaying branches did she appear there.

This was a place not of the body, but of the spirit. By will alone could she move.

Ketti moved to stand next to her great-grandfather. Teya and Ekosa, grasping the rules of this place, appeared at Leiyn's side. Oro was not covered in blood and wounds here, but whole. Happy. The smile he wore jarred against all they had witnessed that day. Almost, it transformed the wizened man into a boy.

"Ah, be welcome, all of you. Is this place not..." Oro smiled out over the ocean, not seeming to notice he had not finished his thought. "'The sight stole the wind from my lungs,'" he continued. "A phrase borrowed from one of our ancestors. Now, who was it..."

He's fading. If she had not heard it in his speech, she saw it in his form. Ketti's was strong and solid; Oro's became indistinct at the edges, parts of him pulling and fraying away. Like a tattered blanket soon to be relegated to rags.

"Ab-Abi." Ketti sat and clasped Oro's hands. She smiled, though fresh tears trickled down her cheeks, the pervasive luminance making each droplet crystal bright.

"At-Iti." He turned his smile upon her. "This was my treasured place to visit." Oro looked back over the water and sighed. His figure grew mistier for a moment before solidifying once more. "I did not allow myself to come often. An indulgence, I believed it. Perhaps I should have enjoyed it more."

"You can enjoy it now," his great-granddaughter murmured.

"For a little while, perhaps." Oro freed a hand and held it up. The tips of his fingers trailed off into a fog that was blown out to sea. "Not long now. But at least I may share this moment with you."

"I did not expect to see you again."

Oro turned to cup his great-granddaughter's cheek. "Ah, but I knew you would come."

Ketti buried her face in his hand. Leiyn turned her gaze up, focusing on the pink flowers rippling in the gentle sea breeze. She inhaled the salty air, trying to forget the despair written in furrows across her friend's face.

"I am sorry," Ketti whispered, choked with emotion. "I did this, all of this. It is my fault."

"No, no, Ketti Ta'Rul. The fault lies with me."

Leiyn looked back at the patriarch to find his eyes closed and his face tilted up to the sky. The sun filled in the wrinkles on his face, banishing every shadow.

"This was always my favorite place," he said, eyes still closed. His form blurred, a cloud dispersing.

Loath to interrupt, Leiyn saw their last chance for answers fading. "The lyshans," she said. "How did they enter Solace?"

Oro opened his eyes and looked back at her, Ketti turning with him. Leiyn kept her eyes on the elder. She must remain resolute. Even if it robbed Ketti of these final moments.

"It was my error," he said at last. "'Those with the highest power commit the lowest follies'—so did Arwia believe. Or was it Eshun?" He shook his head, his features softening again, then firming as he stilled. "I believed myself secure in my *semah*, protected by my bond with Mehu'Ra. But that did not insulate me from deception."

"What deception?" Ketti asked. Tentative. Afraid to know.

The patriarch looked back at her. "They imitated you, At-Iti."

Ketti bent over, wracked with fresh sobs. Oro continued, hardly seeming to notice. Now that he had begun, he appeared incapable of stopping.

"They stole your voice, your face—or so it seemed when I peered through the *ara'buru*." Another sigh released more of himself to the wind. "Trickery by *semah*, I know now. But I believed myself above deception. And what would I not risk for you, the heir of Hold Ta'Rul, the light of our future?"

Silence swarmed them, buzzing in Leiyn's ears. Desperate to break it, she said, "You went after her."

Oro nodded. "Mehu'Ra was not enough to ward against their ambush. I was nearly slain that first moment. They tore into me, through me..." His brow creased as he pressed a hand to his stomach. Leiyn was glad she had not inspected his body. Picturing his spilling innards was enough to make her queasy.

"They stole parts of me," he continued. "My blood and essence. They...became me. Enough to pass as Ta'Rul. Enough to pierce our protections and enter Solace."

His eyes closed. His image wavered. But as Leiyn thought Oro would disappear, the Eteman elder opened his eyes and continued.

"I was dying. Even with Mehu'Ra, I could not heal from the wounds they dealt me. And I could not bear to see them butcher our people. So I came here." Oro smiled as he looked at the tree swaying above him. "Came here to..."

A gust rushed from behind them, stronger than before. Like a candle's flame, the patriarch's spirit flickered and sputtered. Threatening to extinguish.

"Ab-Abi, please." Ketti clasped his hands again and kneeled before him. "Stay with me."

He did not seem to see her now. "This was always my favorite place to visit."

Ketti bowed her head to his chest. Leiyn looked aside, gritting her teeth. Hardly able to bear it.

"I cannot do it," the younger Eteman whispered. "I am not ready to live without you. For the wind to steal you away."

Oro seemed to see her once more, though his voice was thinner as he replied. "But that is all we ever are, my light, my blossom. A breeze wending across a vast sea. As every wind ceases to be, so must we."

A pressure came on her skin. Leiyn looked down to see Teya had clasped her hand. Her beloved peered into her eyes. Beseeching.

Leiyn nodded. It was time for them to leave. For the last two Ta'Ruls—the last two Etemans—to spend Oro's final moments together.

Ekosa turned at Teya's touch, but he lingered. They all heard Ketti's whispered words.

"You do not have to remain for me, Ab-Abi. *Ama ek ammar*. I will carry our legacy. Be at peace."

Leiyn turned away and released her hold on the scene. Let the wind bear her up and away.

18

CARNAL HONOR

Leiyn tore free of the pool and stumbled back.

"Are you alright?" Batu kneeled next to her, dark eyes full of searching. His gaze flickered to the others, who roused from the vision more gently.

"Fine." Burying her embarrassment, Leiyn looked him over. "Came in after all?"

"Ata was concerned. I worried..." He grimaced at the *ara'buru*. "What happened?"

Leiyn followed his gaze. "He was in there. We spoke to him."

"Oro?"

"Yes. Or part of him." She saw the glittering sea again, the bright sun. The magnolia blossoms quietly shedding petals around him. "He died... content."

Batu went quiet, absorbing her words. Sarryl huffed from the entrance where he paced. The moonbear's impatience reawakened hers. Reminded her of the perils lingering among the whispering stones.

Teya and Ekosa were not far behind, blinking and shaking their heads. Ketti delayed only a minute longer. When she emerged, she fluttered her eyelids and stared, unseeing. Ekosa moved back to her side, murmuring words Leiyn could not catch.

At length, Ketti raised her head. When she spoke, her gaze settled on Leiyn.

"I must usher the dead to their next life, if it is not too late."

Leiyn hesitated, then nodded. Though it multiplied their risk to stay, she understood why Ketti wanted it done. She had not been able to do the same for those of the Wilds Lodge and had regretted it in the seasons since.

"Tell us what you need."

Ata was less sanguine when they announced their intentions.

"All of them?" She swept her gaze over Solace. "There must be hundreds."

Ketti flinched at her callousness, then turned, stiff-shouldered, to the first body in sight. Kneeling next to them, she murmured a phrase in Eteman and pulsed her mahia, then pulled free one of the stones embedded in their flesh. That appeared to be all she required, for with that, she moved on to the next body.

"Please, Ata, try to have some tact." Leiyn had her bow in hand again, though she did not yet nock an arrow. "She lost everyone. She needs this."

The dryvan twisted her wooden lips before giving an exaggerated shrug. "Osmet and Ram'bal won't be returning soon. We made certain of that." A savage smile spread her mouth wide, but it proved fleeting. "Likely, they are all that were not otherwise indisposed, else we would have seen the rest of my wayward kin. We have gained a temporary reprieve. I would not see it squandered on superstitious rituals."

"Ata."

The dryvan relented with a short laugh, striding down the street opposite of where Ketti had gone.

After a brief discussion, Leiyn and the others moved to gather their discarded packs, then began searching Solace for supplies. Though doing so felt too close to looting the dead for her liking, Ekosa reassured them that Ketti had mentioned her intention to do the same. "'They have no need of it,' as she said," he relayed. His pained expression, however, betrayed less sanguine feelings.

Still, their need remained, particularly with the dearth of artifacts to be found in Qasaar. Leiyn moved through the hidden town with Teya, entering house after house to discover fresh tragedies. Several times, they were forced to withdraw, the bodies too horribly mangled or children killed too young to tolerate.

Despite the setbacks, they scrounged up some dried fruits and vegetables, sorely lacking in their diet for the past season. They also pilfered more clothes, their journey thus far foretelling the necessity of backup garments.

As for weapons, they found little beyond household cutlery and farming implements. Leiyn remembered the sword at Hold Ta'Rul, but though she braved the wreckage to search for it, she found no sign of it among the rubble. Most likely their enemies had recovered it first and borne it away.

With a poverty of options, they settled on the longest kitchen knives they could find. Though made of horn, they were enchanted to retain their edge and resiliency so that they became stronger than steel.

Leiyn raised an eyebrow when Ekosa took two for himself and Ketti.

"We must learn to defend ourselves," he said with a look of distaste. "In case they find us again."

Leiyn did not say what he must have known: *A knife won't*

stop a lyshan. Instead, she nodded and said, "I'd be happy to teach you."

It took Ketti hours to claim a stone from each person in Solace. By the time she summoned them, Leiyn itched to be on their way, but the resonating pulse of esse from the Amber Altar was too compelling to resist.

They streamed down the castle walkway to where the living arches encircled the golden platform. Even Ata appeared, leaning against one henge with a peculiar expression, at once amused and solemn. The rest of them gathered around the edges, gazing upon Ketti standing in the middle.

Around the Eteman spread hundreds of precious stones. Most glimmered with a vestige of esse. Leiyn wondered if they contained sparks of those who had borne it. She reached for Zuma and her mother, buried deep within her own lifeforce, then touched the carved fox that held a glimmer of Tadeo. Even having a piece of a person could be a comfort.

But that did not appear to be Ketti's intention. Crying out in her native tongue, she pulsed her mahia through the disc of amber once more.

Ekosa murmured into the reverberation of her words. "She says, 'Come, come—feast upon our souls. Return us to the womb so we may be reborn.'"

Leiyn had known Ketti taught the *eesu* some of her language, but he had progressed farther than she imagined.

Teya screwed up her eyes. "They believe in rebirth? That their spirits will return anew?"

"Not as Etemans," Batu muttered, his brow furrowed.

The conversation broke off as everyone looked beyond the circle of archways, sensing what Leiyn had. Newcomers approached the dais; scores of them, perhaps a hundred or more. They appeared in the grotto from thin air, but she did not fear them. These were no lyshans or Suncoats, but creatures that belonged here.

Spirit beasts of every species and size padded toward them. Like all such animals in grottos, their fur and hides took on a semblance of flora. A pair of mice boasted budding flowers at the tips of their tails, the rest of them tiny bushes. An owl flew in to land on an archway, a tangle of orange vines with scarlet leaves. Its hoot echoed as if emerging from the bottom of a hollow trunk. Wolves, sable as darkness, stalked forward, roots twisting through their sinuous bodies. Elk strode forward with forms of fallen leaves, intricate toadstools sprouting in place of antlers.

Predators and prey alike walked beside one another, heedless of their roles in nature. All harkened to the call of the amber.

Several familiar figures appeared among the others. Chispa was there, pausing as he passed through an archway, then making for her, eyes and esse inviting. She leaned down to run her hand across the fox's meadowgrass fur, and he rubbed against her leg. Then he moved on, making for the ring of stones arrayed around the Eteman.

Biqqa, too, had come. Like a wink of gemstone, the hummingbird fluttered around Ketti's head, the emerald of her mossy feathers more vibrant than ever. The Eteman smiled at the spirit beast, though joy failed to reach beyond her lips.

Sarryl went forth as well, leaving his wildsoul's side to join the other beasts, mist swirling off his pearlescent body.

Reaching the edge of the platform, the gathered animals ascended it, then stopped at the ring of stones. A porcupine whose body resembled a pinecone shuffled forward to grasp a jet stone in its small hands. Sniffing it for a moment, it placed it in its mouth, then swallowed. Leiyn sensed the stone entering it, then assimilating, the human esse within becoming one with the animal.

A feeding frenzy followed. Every spirit beast moved forward to claim a stone before turning away. Even Chispa took one, a pearl that he gobbled with conspicuous satisfaction, a shiver running through his grassy fur. Like the others, the silver fox turned and sprang away after his meal, vanishing as he left the perimeter of the living arches.

The affair concluded in minutes. The last of the animals departed the grotto, leaving no stone behind. Ketti stood alone with Biqqa, who still fluttered about her head. The hummingbird dipped her beak into Ketti's hair, then darted off to vanish into the air. Leaving the Eteman alone.

Leiyn remained silent with the others as Ketti walked toward them. Her shoulders sagged, yet she seemed filled with grim satisfaction. She had done her duty to her people. It was one less burden to carry.

Though her guilt would be burden enough.

Ketti stood on the edge of the golden dais for a moment before stepping down. When she spoke, it was with a measure of strength that had been lacking before.

"Some were missing. I did not find Zaki's body, nor Isirat's. Several of the younger ones were also missing."

It should have been a comfort, knowing other Etemans might still be alive. But Leiyn feared she knew their fate.

Batu put her fears into words. "Either they escaped or were captured."

Ketti nodded, minute expressions crossing her face. "They could not have fled Solace without Mehu'Ra's aid, and Ab-Abi spoke nothing of it. If they are prisoners, then we will find them when we find Sharo. If not..." She shook her head. "I can only pray to the spirits for their safety."

Leiyn exchanged a look with Teya. She seemed as much at a loss for what to say as the others.

"Ketti," Ekosa murmured, drawing closer to his beloved's side.

Ketti took the *eesu's* arm, but from how she stood tall, she did not seem to need his comfort.

"Come," she said. "One more matter remains before we leave." Ketti looked to the ruined village above. "It is time you knew the final inheritance of my people. The treachery of the Ta'Ruls."

Ketti turned Ekosa and led the way back up to Solace. Mystified, Leiyn and the others trailed after.

19

BURIED HISTORY

Ketti did not stop until they stood before the castle just beyond the marketplace plaza. While most of it lay in ruin, the two towering doors at its atrium included, the Eteman led them around to the right, where a small, rounded door remained intact. At this portal, she turned back and met their questioning gazes, then turned to Ata.

"I apologize, Atastimina, but you must remain here."

Leiyn caught the dryvan's expression resolving into hard lines. Her face could have been carved from a stump for all the life it showed.

"Why?" Teya asked, the pale red spirals on her cheeks crinkling. "What lies within?"

"Why, little spearmaiden? I can tell you why." The dryvan leaned close to Ketti, moving so quickly that the Eteman flinched back. "She still fears me. Fears that when I tire of assisting mortals and assuaging my guilt, I will kill her. That I am no different from my Kin."

"Some secrets belong to Etemans alone." Ketti looked

small before the skin-walker, but she did not quaver as she defied her.

"To Etemans...and other mortals." Ata rolled her eyes to Leiyn, as if to include her in a jape.

Leiyn saw no room for compromise. Ketti seemed determined to keep their ally out, though Ata had proven her loyalty time and again.

But she grieves.

Leiyn stepped between them, forcing both back a step. "Enough. We have plenty of enemies without making more of each other."

Ata bared her teeth, then turned away with eye-watering speed. Ketti stared at her back, lips pursed and eyes narrowed. Resolute in her demand.

Repressing a sigh, Leiyn gently ushered Ketti forward. "This better be worth it," she muttered.

The Eteman glanced at her but gave no response as she turned to the door. "Come" was all she said as she hauled it open.

Though the door looked heavy and was set in a decrepit wall, it opened smoothly and without a sound. Leiyn spread her mahia within, searching for any lingering danger. When she sensed none, she followed Ketti and her beloved into the darkness. Teya and Batu came behind, the wildsoul convincing his bonded beast to remain behind with Ata.

"Close the door," Ketti commanded, and Teya obliged. Leiyn caught one last glimpse of Ata's glower before the door boomed closed.

The echo filled the room along with an impenetrable gloom. Memories of Osmet in the Qasaar barracks tightened Leiyn's chest. Vision useless, she spread her lifesense around her once again. The only things she sensed were faint traces of esse spiraling down into the ground.

Ketti pulsed her mahia. Gentle white light suffused the room. Leiyn stiffened, staring at its source, a line in the wall a hand thick. It ran down a curving stairwell, illuminating the way. The latent lifeforce within it had expanded to become a lively river.

"*Odisi wangu*... How is this possible?" Ekosa brushed his fingers along the glowing light.

"Bioluminescence." Ketti withdrew her hand from the wall. "Organic light. We instilled the essence of certain algae and insects into nacre, the iridescent lining of mollusk shells." She turned away and set foot on the top stair. "Please follow."

Leiyn kept her eyes on the white band lighting their way down the narrow, steep stairwell. The light it emitted was not wholly white. With mother-of-pearl as its conduit, it had iridescent shimmers, moments where other colors glimmered through. At another time, it would have been mesmerizing, a wonder she would be happy to dissect and discover how it worked.

But danger still loomed over them. Stifling her curiosity, Leiyn kept watch for danger and went deeper below. They went down several flights before it came to an abrupt end.

Leiyn repressed a gasp as she took in the room beyond. The ceiling soared a dozen times her height. Glowing mother-of-pearl lined the walls and banished the shadows. The chamber spread long before them, stretching the length of the ruined castle above.

Shelves occupied most of the floor. Ladders leaned against them to allow retrieval of items dozens of paces up. Through the center of the space, tables and chairs made from ancient wood were scooted close together. The lack of dust suggested this place had not gone unused. There was no musk to it like Itzel's library in Folly, but little scent at all.

A library, it might have appeared in a different context, but these shelves held no books. As the others murmured in awe, Leiyn approached the nearest shelf and peered at its contents. The narrow slots were filled with tablets of various substances. Each tablet shimmered with latent lifeforce.

Artifacts. Hundreds of them. Thousands.

"*Gerinakku*. The annals." Ketti strode forward to stop between the towering shelves. "All the history of our world is chronicled here. That which was not lost, at least." The Eteman turned slowly, her expression solemn. "For aeons, we wrote testaments of our civilization for future generations. We believed they would survive even the destruction of our homeland. Annals such as this were raised to house our knowledge from tens of thousands of seasons. How puissant it seemed before."

Ketti dropped her gaze to the floor. The pain of her people's eradication was written across her diminutive frame. The temptation to ask after the destruction of Etema rose in Leiyn, but she quelled it. Lessons in history could wait for happier times.

And safer ones.

"Why bring us here?" Leiyn swept her gaze across the shelves. "Did you keep weapons down here?"

The Eteman raised her eyes, disdain filling them. The next moment, it was gone. "Knowledge is our most potent weapon. Did you believe I would bring you swords and spears?"

"Knowledge didn't save Solace."

Leiyn stiffened and glanced at Batu. To speak so bluntly was unlike him. Ekosa glared at his friend and moved in front of Ketti. Teya loosed a grunt that might have been a scoff or a laugh. For Ketti's part, she only stared at the wildsoul, lavender eyes like chips of amethyst for all the feeling they showed.

"You are right," she said at last, gaze unwavering. "Knowledge alone will not suffice. But perhaps this shall."

The Eteman glanced at Leiyn, then turned and moved toward the far end of the annals. Leiyn spared Batu a scathing look before following. If he felt any remorse for his comment, he did not show it. His expression remained as hard and hollow-eyed as before.

The shelves shifted as they moved in deeper. In place of the tablets were items encased in glass and quartz. Some seemed little more than rocks until she neared them and saw the bones of creatures depicted upon them.

Fossils.

She fought down the urge to brush a finger across the ridged impressions. At the Lodge, Tadeo had shown her smaller fossils he had discovered in the wilderness. He spoke of them as the testament of creatures long deceased, the only mark they left behind in mineral and mud.

Ketti took some time finding what she searched for. She moved from the central shelves back among the rows, progressing ever outward. Leiyn trailed with the rest of them, wondering at their purpose here. Weariness settled on her in the battle's aftermath. Drawing on her connection to Clouded Fang, who still circled the village above, she buttressed her flagging strength and hoped it would be enough. Raw lifeforce could not perpetually replace rest.

The Eteman reached the far wall and pressed her hand to a panel there. By some trick of the light, a box she had not seen before emerged from the wall. No, not a trick of light—the pulse of mahia as Ketti gripped it was unmistakable. It had been hidden from vision and lifesense alike.

This was a secret never meant to be discovered.

Her throat went dry as Ketti bore her find to a table in the center of the annals. Setting it down, the Eteman stepped back, allowing them to consider it. It was a container made of ivory, a material Leiyn had seen only rarely among Kalgans, who claimed it came from the tusks of mammoths. A carving of a tree, twisted and vital in its depiction, adorned the cover. It was as long as Leiyn's forearm and twice as thick. Whatever it sheltered within was not large.

Ketti had moved with confidence to this point, but now, she flickered her eyes about. Leiyn shared a look with Teya. The former *situal* seemed to come to a similar conclusion as she: this was the reason Ketti had forbade Ata from the entering the annals.

"Come closer," the Eteman murmured. "There is something I must show you."

She produced a tablet a little larger than her hand and placed it on the table beside the ivory box. It looked made of petrified wood, agate and quartz spreading through its center.

At her invitation, Leiyn crowded around it with Teya and Ekosa. Ketti looked up at Batu, her expression hardening. Clearly she had not yet forgiven his words.

"Will you keep watch?" she asked.

Batu shrugged and turned away. Leiyn bit back a sigh. Ekosa was less subtle in his displeasure, frowning at the former plainsrider's broad back.

If Ketti took umbrage to his dismissal, she did not show it. The pearls embedded in her skin pulsed briefly, then she rested her hand on the tablet. "Set your hand upon it. I will guide you through."

Keeping her mahia at the ready, Leiyn pressed her fingers next to the others'.

"This may feel...*qelpu*. Disorienting." Ketti pressed her mahia into the tablet.

At once, there was pressure on her lifeforce. An irresistible summons. It compelled her to join it, similar to the seeing pool, or the panel in the Qasaar barracks wall.

She instinctively resisted. Let the pressure build until it became unbearable.

Come. The word rose unbidden in her mind. *Enter*.

The others had already relented. She felt their spirits settled into the tablet. If it harmed them, she could see no sign of it.

Leiyn sucked in a steadying breath, then dove after them.

20

ECHOES OF MEMORY

Darkness flooded her vision. Flames rose to banish it.

Leiyn meant to stumble back, observe this fresh danger, and escape the choking smoke that filled the air. Instead, her body lurched forward. Foreign thoughts filled her head. An urgency not her own compelled her to action.

Burn them! Burn them all!

Fighting down panic—her own or this other's, she could not tell—Leiyn picked through the assault on her senses. A tree larger than any she had seen rose in silver-limbed majesty. Broad leaves glimmered golden even in the gray haze. Bronze vines twisted around the trunk and through it, pulsating like veins pumping blood.

All of it, burning.

Something flew through the smoke above. Leiyn was not the only one to flinch; whoever's body she occupied did as well, peering up and to glimpse widespread wings and a long, sinuous tail. Then flames belched forward, blue with heat.

An ash dragon. A memory of battle. The burning of a Mothertree.

The Eteman from whose eyes she saw lowered their gaze

and hurried forward. They held a blade, long and curved, in one hand, one forged from titanbone by the dull gleam on its edge. In their other hand, they clutched a talisman similar to those once housed in the Iritu barracks: cylindrical, wooden, and pulsating with latent magic. Her host cast their gaze about them, watchful, fearful. A rabbit hunted by coyotes.

Fear took control as a creature erupted from the empty air to lunge at them.

It could have been a demon of Legion for how it appeared in that smoky darkness. The impression only lasted until it came fully into view. Its limbs were long and graceful, silvered like the tree towering above. The length of its face exaggerated its forlorn expression. Golden eyes, angled and pinched, mirrored the Mothertree's leaves. A lovely tangle of branches tipped with bronze leaves rose from the crown of its head.

An Iritu. As they had once been. As they were meant to be.

A robe was wound about its frame, a length of iridescent fabric that seemed grown of spider silk. It would have been beautiful but for the bunching about its middle. One lithe hand cradled the bundle of cloth as if it held an infant. Ash and amber smudged the fabric, rips telling of the wounds beneath.

For all its delicate appearance, the Iritu blazed with esse. Fury radiated from it like light from a star. Even if it was injured, it still moved as swiftly as death flies from an arrow.

The Eteman from which Leiyn saw did not hesitate. Terror guided their arm as they slashed at their enemy. The Iritu blinked out of existence, then blazed back into their awareness behind.

"Stop!" Leiyn's vessel shouted, their voice male yet high-pitched. The word was in a language she did not know, yet she understood its meaning through his mind. As he shouted, the Eteman stretched the talisman forward and activated it.

Like a spark catching flame on oil-drenched kindling, it erupted with light.

Leiyn struggled to comprehend what followed. Though formed from esse, the impact manifested into a hammer blow as it slammed into the Iritu's back. It did not only bludgeon but contained the cutting edge of an axe. Invisible blades sliced through their lifefire, leaving darkness in their wake.

The skin-walker collapsed, robe and silver back blasted open. Amber ichor drenched the sooty ground. Her host's heart galloped with the uneven gait of a limp horse. Slowly, he approached his victim, blade held before him.

Before he could reach the injured Iritu, a gigantic creature leaped into view. It had roughly the shape of a jaguar but was larger than even the vine titan Leiyn had encountered in the Ofean jungle. Stripes of blonde and black ran through its fur in jagged lines. Power pulsed off it, alternately blinding and chilling.

It did not come alone. Atop its back rode a humanoid figure cast in the same stripes as the beast it rode. They seemed almost a mirage as they gazed down upon them. Yet to Leiyn's vessel, they were distinctly, fearfully real.

Titan caller, trilled through the Eteman's head. The title contained as much terror for him as the Iritu's appearance. *Sun tiger.*

The sun tiger bent its head to the prone Iritu, snuffing it then roaring. Leiyn's vessel stuttered back and fell to his knees.

"Rise, Common!" The voice that came from atop the titan's back was human yet rang with unearthly power. "Make proud your ancestors and slay this wretched creature! Victory is at hand. The final *Ialadt* falls!"

Leiyn found her vessel's head bobbing. "Yes, High Caller. At once, High Caller..."

The titan cast its blazing eyes upon the Eteman before its

Caller commanded it away. They sprang through the smoke, leaving only a bone-jarring roar behind.

Leiyn's vessel peeled himself off the ground before inching toward the fallen Iritu. He held his sword and talisman before him, though his enemy seemed little threat now. Leiyn could not imagine Ata being felled in a single blow, but this Iritu had not the power to recover from it. Their heritage, as Ata called Iritu magic, must have been too feeble to compensate.

The surest course would have been to stab the downed enemy before turning them. But as Leiyn's host stood over the writhing Iritu, he did not strike. Instead, he toed the creature, as if unsure if it still lived.

It lashed at him with a leg, too slow and too weak.

The Eteman easily avoided the strike. With a swift kick, he turned it over, dispelling any notion of mercy. The Iritu screamed as it fell onto its wounded back. Its lovely features were twisted in a mask of agony. Amber bled from its golden eyes. Both arms clutched the robe bunched about its middle like a mother cradling her babe.

A terrible curiosity seized Leiyn, one doubled by the Eteman's desire. Her vessel pocketed the talisman, then reached forward to pull the silken cloth free. The Iritu released one hand to clutch his wrist. Leiyn had felt the strength in dryvans and lyshans, but this grip was weak, no stronger than an ordinary human's.

Mahia pressed into them. The Eteman thrust up his walls, then hesitated. It was not an attack, but an offer of communication. Tentatively, the Eteman accepted, letting their quarry's pleading wash over them.

Please, echoed through the Eteman's soul and into Leiyn. *Please, please...*

Her vessel pried himself free of the weak grip. Roughly, he unwrapped what the Iritu held. His enemy resisted, but their strength was too little. Bit by bit, their prize was unveiled.

Leiyn was uncertain what she beheld at first. Ovular, flat, and smooth, it was roughly the size of a human head. Veins of pale gold and green threaded the opal surface. It could have been a gem but for the pulsation within. The potential of life held at bay.

Her vessel's throat had gone dry. With a trembling hand, he lifted it free and gave voice to Leiyn's suspicions.

"A seed..."

The Iritu's eyes had closed. Their lifeforce ebbed away. Still, they clung to life. They leveled a pleading stare at the Eteman. Her vessel did not flinch from it but clung to the seed in his hand.

The ground trembled, nearly knocking the Eteman from his feet. Clutching the seed close to his chest, he hid it behind his arm and gazed around. The rumbling came closer. A shape, far larger than the sun tiger, loomed from the gloom. Its presence was like a landslide as it pummeled the Eteman's walls.

A hill tortoise marched toward them, heedless of all in its path.

Leiyn's vessel scrambled out of the way, bearing the Mothertree seed with him. Dirt geysered up all around. A quake knocked his legs out from under him. Sprawling to the ground, he curled around the seed and raised his mahia around him, muttering prayers under his breath.

"Protect me, blessed ancestors, sacred spirits! Protect your Common heir, I beg of you..."

One earth-shattering foot stomped near them, so near. Her vessel felt the moment the Iritu's life was snuffed out. He spared them only a thought, too fearful of being the titan's next victim.

A roar sounded through the titan's din. Leiyn's vessel shuddered, waiting for the killing blow that must inevitably fall.

But the hill tortoise paused. Its next rumbling footfall was farther from them, angling away. The next came farther still.

They had survived. But the next trial found them swiftly.

The Eteman commoner felt the beast's descent before he dared to look up. There it was again, winging through the choking smoke and eye-watering ash. There it descended, scales black and gleaming even in the dimness.

The dragon landed on the ground in silence, eyes blazing like forges through the gloom. Esse radiated from it as intensely as heat.

The Eteman cowered once more before the titan, clutching the seed to his chest much like the Iritu had. Through her vessel's visceral terror, Leiyn felt a glimmer of her own response. Something about the dragon stirred feelings within her. She had only ever seen one titan of its kind. Still, she had a nagging feeling that she knew this particular ash dragon.

Clouded Fang?

Conflicted feelings swirled through her before the Eteman's fear swarmed her. The Caller upon the dragon's back leaped free. It was over ten paces to the ground, yet they did not flinch from the fall. Leiyn felt their mahia flare as their feet hit the ground, absorbing the impact and repairing any damage done.

They strode with unwavering intent toward her cowering vessel.

"It is alright. You are safe." The Caller was tall, male, and had every mark of a warrior. Strong of jaw. Eyes set with purpose. Broad of chest and shoulder. His armor was made of overlapping dragon scales that had the same black sheen as his bonded titan. A shield was strapped across his back, but he bore no weapon—though with an ash dragon at his command and his mahia potent, perhaps he had no need of one. Dark hair cascaded in sweaty curls down the back of his neck.

His tread, swift but not rushed, spoke of one swathed in confidence. Yet even amidst a battle, his mien and spirit were of one at peace. Calm. As he glanced at the Iritu who had been crushed by the hill tortoise, his step faltered. Leiyn could not be certain with her vessel's feelings interfering, but she thought it was grief that trembled through the Caller's spirit.

Then the warrior shook his head and raised his gaze to them. Recognition stirred through her vessel at the sight of the approaching man's eyes. Lavender—it was a telling hue, Leiyn sensed from his thoughts. The Common bowed his head, though not as deeply as before, as the Caller stopped before them.

"Caller Ta'Rul. How may I serve?"

Ta'Rul. Leiyn surfaced once more from the Eteman's mind. *A Ta'Rul bonded Clouded Fang?*

As Ketti's ancestor spoke, her vessel's concerns overrode hers. "What is your name, Common?"

Leiyn's host hesitated, but his compulsion to comply overcame whatever reservations he had. "Demesu Gol'Tor, High One."

Gol'Tor. His family name had a ring of familiarity to it, but Leiyn could not rouse enough presence of mind to place it.

"Well met, Demesu Gol'Tor." The Caller held his gaze for a moment, one too long for the destruction surrounding them. It may as well have not existed for all the strange warrior acknowledged it. "And you know who I am."

"Of course, High Caller. All know you, Eshun Ta'Rul."

Eshun tightened his mouth, somehow displeased. Perhaps Demesu's obsequiousness grated on him as it did on Leiyn.

"I know what you hold, Demesu." Leiyn sensed the warrior stretching forth his lifesense to graze the seed, tucked out of sight in her vessel's arm. "You know its import?"

Demesu hesitated. But Leiyn knew from his thoughts that

he would not defy a Caller's will, even this one's. "Yes, Caller Ta'Rul."

"Then you know why we must save it." Eshun turned away, motioning with his head toward the ash dragon, still staring down with its incandescent gaze. "I will bring us to my Hold."

Leiyn waited for her vessel to comply as he had with every other order from a Caller. Instead, he cocked his head, listening to the battle. Hearing it move away from them to another side of the grove, hesitancy took primacy.

"We were told to be wary of you, High One." Every word was tremulous, but Demesu forced them out. "Told to refuse your orders."

Eshun turned back. He smiled, though the corners of his eyes creased in a way that turned it sorrowful.

"They were right to do so, by the way they see the world. But you, Demesu Gol'Tor, can make a different choice."

Her vessel's spirit quavered. Of all the iconoclastic things the Ta'Rul heir had said, this appeared to be the worst of them.

"I am Common, High One. I must obey."

"Will you remain obedient as we exterminate an entire race? Negate even the chance of them bettering themselves?" Eshun walked back toward Leiyn's vessel, but he stopped short to kneel next to the dead Iritu. Leiyn was afforded a glimpse of amber-spattered silver skin before her vessel looked aside, his stomach churning. Demesu coughed and she tasted bile sour on his tongue.

The Ta'Rul heir rose and closed the remaining paces between them. Though Leiyn's vessel flinched back from him, Eshun did not hesitate to clap a gauntleted hand on his shoulder. The Caller's esse pressed against Demesu's, insistent but not domineering.

"Let me show you my conviction, Demesu. Show you why I believe this to be the correct decision. The only decision."

Demesu hesitated, but his habit of submitting to hierarchy seized hold. With a darting look around them, ensuring no more danger had found them, he accepted Eshun's invitation and peered into his esse.

Many images stirred within his lifemark, but only one rose to clarity. A barren landscape devoid of life and esse. Death spread farther than the reach of any sense.

Leiyn's vessel recoiled as if struck. Eshun smiled again with that sad expression.

"I have seen it, Demesu. Seen what became of Etema with my own eyes. The Iritu are not our greatest enemy. We are. We turned our homeland into a place where nothing could live. The violence in our hearts overcame our love for one another."

The Ta'Rul heir's grip tightened, almost enough to be painful. Leiyn felt Demesu's desire to twist away, but he bore it. Stared into those bloodshot lavender eyes as they turned feverishly bright.

"We must be saved from ourselves. And I believe these people, these Iritu, are our best chance of doing so. If you do not believe in preserving them for their sake, let that be enough. We need them, Demesu. Etema needs them."

Even occupying his mind and body, Leiyn could not tell which way Demesu swayed. Conflict ravaged his soul, paralyzing him, torn between loyalties.

Eshun's expression tightened. "I ask much, I know. Let us start with a smaller step: Come with me. Bring the seed to my Hold. If there is trouble, I alone will bear the consequences. Please, Demesu. We must depart while we still can."

The Eteman commoner held out a moment longer, then broke. Leiyn felt what had done it: the unrelenting respect with which Eshun had treated him. Him, a Common, given a choice by a Caller.

"I will bring it to Hold Ta'Rul. I can promise no more."

The Ta'Rul heir smiled. "That is all I ask. Let us be away."

Eshun herded Leiyn's vessel toward the waiting ash dragon. Clouded Fang, if it was him, made no move toward them, content to await their arrival.

A being spun into existence next to them.

Demesu wrenched free of Eshun and fell away with a cry. Terror and despair wracked his mind, freezing him in place. He raised barriers around himself, hiding him as well as the seed he still held. Leiyn railed at his cowardice, but she could not affect him. All of this had already happened. The most she could do was bear witness.

This new Iritu had a more martial appearance. Titanbone armor in shades of blue and purple adorned them from head to foot. The horned helm and war scythe struck deeper fear into Leiyn's vessel.

"It is her!" Demesu babbled. "Laughing Death!"

The Iritu did not seem inclined to laugh then. What little of her silvered face showed through her helm was grave and spattered with red—the red of human blood. She moved forward, silent as a specter. Come to deliver them to their fate.

Laughing Death. Isn't that what they called—?

Eshun spoke, cutting through Leiyn's whirling thoughts. "I could not stop them." Hardness had entered his being, a shell over some raw feeling Leiyn could not glimpse. "I am sorry."

"Sorry?" Laughing Death lived up to her name as she cawed. "My Mother burns, and you are *sorry*?"

"I did all I could. But there is still hope—"

"*There is no hope!*" the Iritu screeched. "I should have cut you down the last time! Slain you as I slew your sister!"

Leiyn's surprise was a match to Demesu's. "Amata Ta'Rul? Then she is—"

"Silence!" For the first time, Eshun appeared as tyrannical as the first Caller had. Some of the dragon with whom he had bonded lurched out as he stared down his fellow Eteman into cowering quietude.

Laughing Death continued forward, her stride lengthening. She seemed to grow before their eyes, towering above them now. Her war scythe raised as she closed the final steps.

"I will correct my error now. If we cannot live, then all mortals must die!"

The Ta'Rul heir grabbed Demesu and shoved him toward the ash dragon. "Run!" he commanded as he slipped his broad shield onto his arm, the same silver hue as the great tree burning behind them. "Do not stop!"

Leiyn's vessel did not question the order. He dashed for the dragon, though it seemed a choice between two kinds of death. By a sliver of lifesense, he felt the Iritu engage Eshun, their lifefires blurring as they reeled in combat. The clacking of scythe against shield and screeches of fury paired with it.

Then the black leviathan roared, drowning out the sounds of combat and staggering Demesu. The Eteman commoner pressed on as an indigo inferno built within the dragon's open mouth.

Down! Leiyn shouted at her vessel.

He needed none of her encouragement, diving for the ground on his own. Heat blasted against his back, so intense it seemed it would sear through clothes and skin. Demesu clutched an arm over his head and kept the tree seed cradled against his chest with his other. Even now, he did not release it.

It seemed an eternity before the conflagration died. Even when it did, Demesu remained where he lay. Prey instinct told him to *hide, hide, hide*.

You cannot hide! Leiyn tried shouting at him. *Run, you* feshtado *fool!*

It took the ground rumbling to rouse him from shock. Demesu lifted his head to confirm what his lifesense already knew: the ash dragon had moved to stand over him. Warmth spread down his crotch and legs. Leiyn recoiled from his shame and terror.

But the need to survive had him stumbling to his feet once more. Moving in a crouch, he ran out from underneath the dragon and approached its leg. As the volcanic titan belched fire once more, Demesu stumbled to a halt and stared up the trunk-like leg before him. He quailed at ascending it.

But the raging Iritu banished the lesser fears.

Plying his mahia, Leiyn's vessel braced his muscles, then leaped. His magic-fueled jump landed him halfway up, where the dragon's leg bent in a crook. With only one hand free, Demesu clung to the creature's rough skin. His strengthened grip was just enough to keep him in place.

Then the ash dragon moved, stepping forward to advance on the Iritu assaulting its master. Fresh urine spread down Demesu's legs as he clung on. His fingers slipped with every thundering footstep.

But he did not fall.

At last, the titan came to a halt. "Up," the Eteman breathed to himself. "Climb up..."

With another burst of lifeforce, he hauled himself up the leg with his free arm, then scrambled up the incline, the soles of his esse-imbued shoes gripping the dragon even as rough hide shifted into slick scales.

Then Demesu was atop it. Atop an ash dragon.

The thought froze him again.

As the titan moved forward, he was sent stumbling off balance to fall hard on his rump. Somehow, he still clasped the Iritu seed.

Eshun Ta'Rul ascended before he could regain his feet. "To me, Demesu!" the Caller ordered, grabbing him with his free hand and hauling the commoner upright.

They moved between the wings erupting from the shoulders of the forelegs, at the base of where the long neck extended forward. Eshun sat Leiyn's vessel down with a forceful shove, then crouched a few paces ahead.

"Rise, Winged Flame!" he shouted, and Leiyn felt the titan responding. Its esse rose, smoldering like a volcano about to erupt.

As the gigantic leathery wings shot out to either side and the tree trunk legs braced to push, Demesu dared to think they might escape.

Laughing Death materialized in the air next to them, war scythe swinging forward.

Eshun intervened before Leiyn's vessel could react. His raised shield caught the curved blade. The force of the blow staggered the Ta'Rul heir, yet he kept his feet.

No—Eshun did more, Leiyn realized. What she had thought was a stumble was a pivot. Rising with strength and speed, the Caller crashed his shield into the Iritu's side.

Laughing Death shrieked as she went flying off the dragon.

"Rise!" Eshun shouted again, and his dragon complied, leaping into the air with a mighty beat of his wings. Demesu clung to the scales and spines, wishing he had both hands free. He debated releasing the Iritu seed to ensure he did but somehow could not seem to prise his arm from it. Part of him refused to release it even now, when the demons it could birth raged at them from below.

"I will kill you, Ta'Rul!" the Iritu howled, her voice just audible over the rushing wind and heaving wings. "Kill you and the rest of your treacherous kin!"

"I am sorry," Leiyn thought she heard Eshun mutter. But with Demesu pressing his head to the dragon's back, she could not be certain he had spoken at all.

They quickly gained altitude. Every flap bore them farther into the air. Farther from the furious shouts of their enemy.

Safe. He would live. Relief flooded through Leiyn's vessel

and infected her. It could not entirely banish her scorn for the Eteman she occupied.

Soon, they were above the golden canopy of the Mothertree. Winged Flame banked, threatening to spill its passengers. Eshun showed no fear of flying. Standing with his shield still in hand, his other hand on one of the dragon's spines, he looked down at the ground.

A sonorous groan, like the very land itself expired, had Demesu raising his head and tremulously peering over the edge. Through the smog, he saw the giant form of the hill tortoise ramming the base of the burning Mothertree.

The tree tilted. An omen of what was to follow.

Another groan filled the clearing, then a thunderous splintering. Roots strained to anchor the Iritu tree to the ground, but it was a battle swiftly being lost. The hill tortoise was implacable, its lifeforce growing with every moment, its determination to uproot the tree more than a match for the Mothertree's fading strength.

Demesu watched as his people won. As the roots pulled free of the ground, broken and flailing like severed limbs. The surfeit of lifeforce that had filled the towering tree died, leaving behind only a smoldering patch of what had been there before.

"I am sorry," Eshun repeated, his gaze lingering on the dead tree. Then the Ta'Rul heir looked back at Demesu. "You still hold the seed?"

Leiyn's vessel nodded, though he feared to move. A single mistake could break his tenuous grip and plummet him to the world far, far below.

"Good." Eshun looked back down at the dying Mothertree. "Then there is hope."

A fresh cloud of smoke drifted over Demesu's vision. Leiyn found herself dispersing among the pall, the wind pulling her apart. Bearing her back to the body she had left behind.

21

THE SEED

Leiyn came back to raised voices echoing through the hallowed annals. Including one that should not have been present.

Wrenching her hand from the box, she blinked away the vestiges of the vision and stared at Ata. Batu had a hand wrapped around the Iritu's wooden arm, though he had no hope of holding her back. Ata scarcely seemed to notice him. Both eyes, white and green, rested on the ivory box on the table.

"What," she breathed, all the tension of a coiled snake in her voice, "do you have there?"

Ata's question echoed through the buried archives. For a moment, no one moved.

Then the dryvan strode forward, dragging Batu in her wake, to stand over the ivory box. They flinched at her approach, but her glare was only for Ketti.

"I ask again, Eteman, and only once more. What hides within this box?"

Leiyn almost reached for her falchions. Ata had proven herself an ally repeatedly, but she had just witnessed the violence within her. *Laughing Death.* All too fitting a name for the vengeful creature she had been centuries before.

"We saw you," Leiyn said, diverting the shapeshifter's attention. She found Ata's hard gaze no less easy to bear, though she tried not to show it. "You and Ketti's ancestor, Eshun Ta'Rul."

Ripples cascaded through Ata's esse. Her glare petrified with the hate it held. "Then he was even more duplicitous than I knew."

"Was he?" Leiyn angled herself between the dryvan and the artifact. "Sounded like you killed his sister, then attacked him. And all he was doing was trying to help."

Leiyn's movements had not been lost on Ata. Yet instead of growing angrier, the hard planes of her face softened. "We were losing the war. Could I have done any less?"

"Yes." Ketti trembled as she stared at the dryvan, but she held firm. "Eshun Ta'Rul was the greatest of my ancestors. Even after what you did, he never lost faith in you. He defied everyone to keep this safe. He left behind the world to shelter it."

"And left it to drown in blood!" Ata laughed, morphing into that bloodthirsty version of herself Leiyn had glimpsed in the vision. It only lasted a moment. "Eshun was no great man, hunter-child. He was a coward, nothing more."

Leiyn held her tongue. That was not the man she had seen in the vision. The only coward had been the man whose memories they experienced, Demesu Gol'Tor, blown on the winds of others' whims. Eshun Ta'Rul had been brave in a way she had rarely seen. Firm in his convictions no matter the world telling him he was wrong. Only in Tadeo and Zuma had she seen such a strength of character before.

And in Isla.

Ata leaned closer, brushing against Leiyn's shoulder as she

did. Leiyn flinched away. The dryvan's lifeforce battered at her boundaries, indiscriminate of friend and enemy.

"Why keep it from me?" the dryvan purred, the sound of it a stark contrast to her militant magic. "How can you not trust me after all I've done for you?"

Thinking of Isla put Leiyn in mind of what her lost friend would have done. Raising her empty hands, Leiyn softened her voice.

"Please, Ata. Give Ketti a chance to explain. We're still allies."

"Allies." The dryvan twisted the word, transforming it. She leaned in closer. Leiyn wondered how easily the sharp teeth Ata bared could tear through her throat. "*Allies* do not lie. Can there be trust with falsehoods paving the path?"

"I have not lied." Ketti held the dryvan's gaze, though the twitching of her eyes made it seem as if she wished to look anywhere else.

"Concealing the truth amounts to the same." Ata straightened to her full height, looming above even Batu. She flicked her hand to the box—casual now, almost disdainful. "Open the casket. Perhaps all can be forgiven."

The Eteman flicked her eyes to Leiyn, imploring. Leiyn sucked on her teeth as she considered. This secret had the potential to fracture their fragile fellowship. They desperately needed Ata. The odds were already stacked too high against them.

Can it survive this?

Rare was the time she recognized such a pivotal moment. The opportunity to bind themselves together, stronger than before. To truly be an alliance.

Or tear them apart.

Once, she would have kept such secrets by reflex. Now, she longed to expose them, bring them all to light. What trust could there be in darkness? Only blind faith.

The Catedrál and their treachery had shown what such faith was worth.

Leiyn returned her gaze to Ketti. "Your ancestor, Eshun, said you need the Iritu to restore Etema. Is that true?"

Ketti hesitated, then shook her head. "We do not know. When I set out with you"—her eyes flickered to Ata, then away—"it is what I sought to discover. But it cannot be our immediate aim. Not now."

Defeating Sharo—Ketti could be resolved to do nothing else. The surest path to that went through the lyshan's sister.

"Open it." Leiyn nodded at the ivory box. "She deserves to know."

The cool composure Ketti had first shown them reappeared. Her esse, however, she failed to disguise the violent tremor through her spirit.

Fear? Or resolve?

Slowly, the Eteman placed her hand on the lid. With a pulse of mahia, a seam appeared around the edge, revealing the lid. It scraped against the edges as Ketti pried it away.

There it was: the same oval seed as in the dream. The brilliance of its silver had dimmed to gray, and the green and gold veins had lost their vivacity. But a glimpse from her lifesense revealed esse to still stir within, hidden by an enchantment in the ivory.

The Iritu Mothertrees had all burned through Eteman attacks. This seed could bring them back.

Leiyn looked up to see Ata transfixed by her people's salvation. If Ketti's soul was hard to read, the dryvan's proved impossible. Only the furor with which it swirled, tempestuous as a storm-riven sea, was familiar enough to know.

Slowly, reverently, she extended her clawed hands to the seed, then gently lifted it.

"*Ialadt*," she whispered, eyes wide as full moons. "Mother."

Oblivious of their stares, the dryvan cradled the seed to her chest. Then Ata opened herself.

Seams appeared between her impression of breasts. A crevice widened in her chest, creating a gap large enough for the seed. The veined oval slotted in as if it had been made to fit there.

The seed within, Ata closed her body around it, as close an embrace as Leiyn had witnessed. Ata let her arms fall to her sides and tilted back her head. Her mismatched eyes fell closed, little more than lines remaining of them.

"It is only safe with me." The dryvan seemed to talk more to herself than them. "I must..."

The silence that followed held all the energy of a tree in a stiff wind, ready to lash back when it ended. Hoping to circumvent it, Leiyn spoke.

"Ata?"

The dryvan's eyes snapped open and bored into Leiyn. "Have you lived without hope, little fox?"

The Wilds Lodge burned behind Leiyn's eyes. "You know I have."

"That was but a glimpse of the despair I have endured these long seasons. And the hope I have now...it is its equal."

Leiyn bowed her head. She had lost nearly everyone she loved and been preyed upon by the Iritu, but her entire race had not faced extinction. What despondency must that have grown within them, dryvan and lyshan alike? It could only have fostered their desire for vengeance. For retribution.

If that horrible despair was removed, would they still yearn for blood? Could even Sharo be converted to peace? Leiyn shivered at the thought.

No. Not him.

Sharo could never know of this. She had seen his nature, glimpsed the abyss behind those cadaverous eyes. He was not the brother Ata remembered. He had become a revenant, a vengeful spirit, the whole of his being bent toward domination.

Weren't you the same once?

She tightened her hands into fists. How could anyone make this terrible choice? To give irredeemable kin one last chance even if it doomed the rest of the world? Or deny them and forever wonder what they would have chosen?

But this choice was not hers to make.

Leiyn raised her head to look at the others. Teya chewed her bottom lip and flexed her hand on her spear. Ekosa wrung his hands before him, eyes flickering about the annals, as if searching for places to hide. Ketti had bowed her head, shoulders weighed down by revelation. Only Batu remained resolute, his esse burning high, his face seeming carved of mahogany.

Leiyn turned back to Ata. "What will you do now that you have a Mothertree seed?"

"You fear I will abandon you?" A hint of Ata's fey humor returned to her undamaged eye. "That I have forgotten the blight my seed-brother has become?"

Leiyn held her gaze and kept her silence. They both knew that was no answer.

Ata grazed a talon along her sternum, then let it fall away. "No, Awakener. I have not forgotten. I must find Sharo—my brother, my failing. I must put an end to this."

"To him." She hardened herself to Ata's plight. Hardened herself to pity. She had accrued enough callouses that it came easily. "You'll put an end to him."

Creases appeared around the dryvan's eyes. Her lips curled open, revealing a glimmer of teeth. Then the expression passed, and she smiled her wide, unsettling grin. "Could it resolve any other way?"

It did not take a politician to detect the evasion. But it was as good as she was wont to get. Leiyn gave her a short nod.

Ata loosed a wild laugh and turned away. "If we are finished with this farce, I believe a decision remains before us. Do not tarry long."

As suddenly as she had appeared, the dryvan parted the fabric of the world and vanished.

Leiyn glanced at the others. Fear, anger, dismay—one and all, they shared her concoction of emotions. Ketti appeared most alarmed, eyes flared as if she wished to hit someone. And the Eteman had never been prone to violence.

Leiyn flinched as Ketti turned her glare on her, but did not look away. If her friend was angry with her, it was best to face it now.

Ketti did not give her the satisfaction. Tearing away her gaze, she stalked past Leiyn and made for the stairwell by which they had entered. Leiyn started after her, but Teya's hand on her shoulder drew her up short.

"Let her be, Redlock," her beloved murmured in her ear.

Reluctantly, Leiyn obeyed. She watched the Eteman make her slow way alone across the archives.

Little more than a mausoleum, now.

She shook her head, wishing it could dislodge the suspicion taking root deep inside her. That, in saving one people, she had damned another.

22

TO BROKEN SHORES

Ata and Ketti awaited the rest of them by the time they surfaced from the annals. Ancient enemies stood facing one another, wary and uncertain, but at peace for the moment. Even Sarryl seemed wary of their standoff, the moon-bear keeping his distance and huffing with discontent.

Repressing a sigh, Leiyn joined their tight circle. When the others had gathered around, the dryvan cast a lazy gaze across them. A taloned hand stroked the vines covering her chest—and the seed buried beneath them.

"Gol'Tor," Ekosa said as they emerged. "That was Deme-su's Hold name, no? Was he Zaki's ancestor?"

Ketti softened before her beloved's question. "Yes. To their shame." A smile flitted across her lips, brief as a summer shower. "We entered the vision together the first time, me and Zaki. They never went near it again." She bowed her head. "They were the bravest of their ancestors."

Leiyn exchanged a pained look with Teya.

"They are, my gem," Ekosa corrected, resting a hand on Ketti's arm. "Not were."

Ketti sighed and nodded.

"And Clouded Fang," Leiyn spoke up, as much to distract the Eteman as to satisfy her curiosity. "Was that him with Eshun? Were they bonded? I thought I recognized him, but in the vision..."

Ketti waved a hand. "I do not know. Only that Winged Flame was the first ash dragon with which my people bonded, and Eshun the first to bond him."

A jealous part of Leiyn hoped it had not been Clouded Fang in the vision, but the greater part wished it to be true. Much as she might wish to be the titan's first and only bonded, it could explain why he had sought her out from the start. It had always seemed more than accidental that he erupted with her overflow of emotions back after that first fateful encounter with Acalan and Zuma. That he had followed her to the Barren and risen to her summons.

Perhaps he had recognized something of his old master in Leiyn. Maybe her Eteman-expanded spirit. Or her quest to bring justice to an unjust world, if titans could comprehend such concepts.

Yet her crusade spread violence far more than Eshun Ta'Rul's had. She wondered if Ketti's ancestor had walked the better path. Could peace ever be bought with blood?

Ata made an impatient noise that approximated the creaking of a tree in a storm, drawing their attention. "Your intention remains to cross the sea, does it not?" The dryvan rolled her eyes until they fell on Leiyn. "To pursue Sharo to the Ancestral Lands?"

Leiyn gave her a tight nod, certain she was not the only one to hear "your" where "our" should have been. "And what's yours?" she shot back, exchanging an arrow for an arrow.

"Oh, the same," Ata replied with a breezy air. "But there are other places I must visit for a time. This seed... You know what it signifies."

"Your abandonment," Batu stated.

The dryvan laughed, jarring in the silence of the ruined village. "Hope, Kinblood! Hope for me. Hope for all Iritu."

She gazed down the street, her features uplifted. Despite what it meant for their party, Leiyn could not help but feel a sliver of her elation. This was the moment for which the Mothertree seed had been preserved.

Hope.

Leiyn tamped down the softer feelings, knowing hard questions remained. "Then you'll no longer help us?" she demanded.

Ata turned wide eyes on her, mocking. "You misunderstand me. I cannot carry you across that ocean, as I have told you before. Too far, too fast! Crossing the continent nearly split you apart. Imagine how you would shatter over thrice that distance!"

Teya crossed her arms. "Then you must have another plan."

"Quite so, spearmaiden. I will bring you to where one may bear you across the sea. Where we have ventured before." Ata turned her gaze upon Ketti.

The Eteman winced, but still complied with an answer. "Breakbay."

"The very same! There, you shall enslave a Vast One to do your bidding." The shapeshifter waved the hand that did not stroke the seed lazily through the air. "That is what you do best, is it not?"

Ekosa hummed in his throat. "A titan may move many times faster than a ship. Wind and weather need not slow it. A trip that would ordinarily take months might only last weeks." He glanced at Ketti, then Leiyn. "Three of us can command titans. We could work in shifts."

"What of the Veil?" Batu challenged. "We do not know how the Qara Gegeen and the first Kalgan settlers pierced it to come to these lands. And if She Who Remains follows—are we to fight the lyshans without you?"

Leiyn had not given much thought to the Veil, the magical barrier said to lie amid the Ocula Ocean, and for which the Veiled Lands had taken their name. Once, it had posed enough of an issue to make passage between the continents impossible. Without knowing how to circumvent it, they might easily be forced to turn back.

"Your people have overcome the Veil many times before," Ata said. "Did a fleet of ships not assail your city? I am certain you are up to the task. As for my wayward kin, that is the genius of this, little wildling: no Iritu would willingly venture into that accursed place, nor swim so far asea." She shuddered, feathers fluttering about her. "I scarcely look forward to returning to that city. Too many Vast Ones with too many tantrums. Besides, why risk it when they can wait?" She smiled sharply. "Time is an Iritu's sharpest weapon."

Leiyn glanced at Ketti, whose expression had returned to stoniness. "Will it work?" she asked. "Could we find a reef whale there or another titan of the sea?"

The Eteman grimaced but nodded. "Many rested there. Yes, we will find one."

Teya chuckled a touch too loud for Leiyn to believe her amused. "Better than a boat, I suppose. All that pitching back and forth… Just fighting on one was enough to make me hurl."

Ekosa loosed a nervous laugh. Leiyn wished she could feel so sanguine. There had been a time when one titan's awakening was enough to overwhelm her. How many would she suffer at Breakbay? Dozens? Hundreds, even?

Ketti endured it. Can you do any less?

"We go to Breakbay," Leiyn said. "Then Ilberia. If we don't find Sharo there, we'll at least take away his toys."

"And draw him out of hiding," Teya affirmed.

Something crossed Ata's expression, but it was too fleeting

for Leiyn to identify. "As fine a plan as any," she said with the same breezy mien as before. "Are we prepared? Or does that monster require a snack first?"

Sarryl growled at the Iritu, only widening her smile. Batu's scowl deepened, but he rested a hand on one of his moonbear's mighty shoulders as if to calm him. "We're ready."

Leiyn looked to Ketti, then followed the Eteman's gaze upward. Among the clouds, Mehu'Ra and Clouded Fang still turned in endless revolutions, shadows against the gray haze. Lightning split across the sky at their looks. The ash dragon answered with a gout of flames, lighting a corresponding fire in Leiyn's chest.

"Ready," she murmured as she released her hold on her titan. She felt Ketti dismiss the tempest hawk as well. Despite this, the titans continued to circle one another. If it was in challenge or camaraderie, Leiyn could not say.

Teya took Leiyn's hand, and she squeezed it back. Ekosa moved closer to Ketti, arms touching. Batu remained close by Sarryl's side.

Ata grinned, manic with delight. "Then gather around, younglings. Let us fly once more!"

Leiyn shot one last look at Solace. The body-strewn plaza was the last thing she saw before the world was torn away.

IV

PART

STREETS OF SALT

23

A DREAM OF BREAKING

The earth rent itself apart.

Tears streamed down Leiyn's face as she fled. Behind, she heard the disembowelment of the world and the beast that feasted upon its innards. Walls cracked and crumbled before its advance. Stones tumbled down around her, debris cutting and choking.

Screams filled the devastated streets. Families, filthy and forlorn, clung to each other as they hustled before her. The ranger in her rebelled at running past. Was she not obligated to protect these people?

Instead, she cuffed her eyes and ran on. There was nothing she could do. Nothing that could stop the pursuing monster.

This is a dream.

The realization only heightened her helplessness. Were this real, she could summon her mahia and meet her hunter. Here, Leiyn had no control over leaving or living. She was powerless.

All she could do was run.

The tumult lessened for a moment. Leiyn risked a glance over her shoulder. Clouds of dust obscured the creature, but its silhouette rose dozens of paces high and many wider. From the main bulk rose a wedged head as large as a temple.

A hill tortoise.

Gray-robed figures moved past her, heading the wrong way. Heading toward the titan. Almost, she seized their sleeves to stop them. But she knew what they were even without her lifesense. Their flaccid expressions told her who they were.

Odiosas, sent to turn back the attack.

Leiyn did not stay to see if they succeeded. Filthy air knifed into her lungs with each stride as she fled.

The buildings fell away to reveal a harbor. Perhaps she could claim a boat? Would the water save her from what came behind? She kept moving, searching for her escape. Sniffing and holding back more useless fears.

Unseen waves buffeted into her, stuttering her to a halt.

As Leiyn watched, the sea bulged upward and took shape. It rose a hundred paces high before condensing. From the water emerged a humped back as large as a small island. A serpentine tail flicked behind it. And above it rose a finned head atop a long neck, all of it crystalline white.

A salt titan?

Despite its cumbersome appearance, the titan moved with staggering speed. Flippers sent waves crashing into the nearest building. The head swayed above, menacing as a viper set to strike.

Leiyn turned in place, staring around her. Everywhere she looked, more titans penned her in. A crowd gathered around her. Flocking like terrified sheep before prowling wolves.

"Let me through!" she shouted, shoving to gain free. A nameless panic clawed in her chest, the need to escape too much to bear. "*Let me out!*"

The rabble did not heed her pleas, nor did the titan. The long, white tail whipped up, then forward. Spray shimmered from it in the scant sunlight above the crowd. Leiyn could not help but watch as she continued her futile struggle.

It descended as a shadow. The crystallized salt shimmered, haunting in its beauty. She stopped when it obscured the sky.

An unsettling silence fell over the crowd at that final moment. The quiet of the damned.

Then came the tempest, and she drowned in it.

24

A TUMULT OF TITANS

Leiyn fell to her knees, choking on spit and fear. Only as the nightmare peeled away did her presence of mind return.

"Rise, Awakener!" crooned Ata, almost jubilant. Pitiless fingers enwrapped Leiyn's arm and yanked her to her feet. "Time to run!"

She swayed and scrubbed her eyes, feeling as if it should be seawater and not sweat there. Her lifesense lay in shambles. Pummeled and pulled and dashed apart, she raised what remained of her walls. It left only her natural senses to comprehend what she beheld.

Ruins rose around her in dilapidated heaps. Stones and rotted timbers piled against each other, the buildings long ago collapsed. The crash of a surf came from nearby. The air was moist and fragrant with seawater.

Then she saw them.

Emerging from the sand in flashes of yellow and white, she knew them for what they were. Saw again the terrified people around her, crushed under the uncaring titans.

Bones. The skeletons of those who had died here remained unburied. Prey to the elements.

Best not join them, Firebrand.

Ata wrenched her arm again, launching her into motion. "Run, little fox!"

Stumbling to catch her balance, Leiyn followed the others as she oriented to the danger. A strange sense of having already lived through this conspired to trick her. The dream, real as it had felt, made her fleeing now surreal.

A crash of lifeforce against her mahia cut through her confusion.

Rising from the bay ahead was the same titan of salt as in her dream. Every bit as tall. Every bit as damning. The only difference now was she and her comrades were farther away. Just out of reach of its head and tail, if they were fortunate.

But it was not the only titan awake. She felt their presence before she saw them: the vibrations underfoot, the rumbling against her lifesense. Even veiled, she could not fully keep out a titan. Certainly not an army of them.

Her horror grew as she picked them out. A hill tortoise rose on pillar legs, a ramshackle building sloughing off its back. A sandstone scorpion, smaller but still large enough to crush any of them, pulled free of the remains of a city wall and scuttled forward. Dust whirled in a twister, foretelling the coming of something like a sand stampede, while nimbi gathered overhead, signaling the coming of a rain mammoth or storm hawk. As mist gathered off the sea, Leiyn wondered if she would discover if "the Winged Death" with which Ranger Gan had once teased her was truly real.

Titans all around—more titans than seemed possible in one place. Enough to destroy a city. Enough to keep anyone with a lick of sense away for decades.

Guess we're all rash now.

Ata had kept her grip on Leiyn's arm, but now released her

and stepped back. As Leiyn twisted around to yell at her to hurry, the dryvan cast her one last look, rife with regret.

Then Ata disappeared.

"*Fesht!*" Leiyn faced forward and broke into a sprint. "Shit on that shapeshifting, feather-plucking—"

Her cursing petered out as air became scarce. All they could do was run. As the titans took shape, they made their implacable way toward them. Perhaps they were merely curious, drawn by their lifeforce in this desolate place. But there was a violence to their tempos and speed. A rage unrelenting in all the years since they felled Breakbay.

"Hurry, Redlock!" Teya grabbed her and pulled her on.

"This way!" Ketti led their party, pearls and coral flashing in the dimming light with her quick steps. Ekosa kept close on her heels. Batu came behind the rest with his moonbear. Sarryl's grunting breaths reeked of protest, but the spirit beast continued lumbering on. Even he had to fear titans.

Through tumbledown backstreets, across buckled pavestones, they wove a path toward the sea. The prey in Leiyn screamed not to venture any nearer to the monstrous salt titan, but she knew as well as any of them that their only hope of survival lay in reaching a reef whale. If one slumbered in the bay or had risen with the rest remained to be seen. With so many titans around, they had not a prayer of finding it by mahia.

They cleared an alley to enter an open plaza. A fountain lay in the center, its sculptures broken and toppled into the basin. Cracked marble spread underfoot, speaking to the wealth once accumulated in Breakbay.

Movement in the corner of her eye brought Leiyn's gaze around.

The giant scorpion had reached them.

It was not as large as some titans, little bigger than a vine jaguar. That was plenty big enough to strike terror through her. Six legs of tawny sandstone ended in spear-sharp points that gouged the pavers as it scurried across the plaza. A pair of clawed forelegs raised before rocky mandibles. A dozen quartz shards scattered across its uneven head like misshapen eyes. And curved above it was the stinger, poised to strike.

Leiyn drew her falchions. Resistance was likely futile; even titanbone could do little against raw stone, much less stone filled with a titan's power. She reached for the thread within her, ever-rooted in her esse, and opened her walls enough to follow it down.

Clouded Fang!

The ash dragon had returned to the ground during their journey through the grottos, but he did not yet slumber. Submitting to his blistering presence, she sent her plea across their bond.

She felt the titan spread his wings and begin to soar across the leagues toward her. But he was too far away. Swift as he flew, it would be several minutes before Clouded Fang reached them.

Blinking her eyes clear, Leiyn skirted away from the approaching giant. The scorpion slowed as their party spread before it, its generous mass shifting back and forth as if deciding on its first prey. The others had drawn their own Iritu weapons. Sarryl roared and rose on his hind legs. Even the moonbear only reached midway up the titan.

Above, the pregnant gray clouds burst downward. A tempest hawk dove through, streaked with blue lightning and trailing the mist of its body. Its screech was like thunder, trembling through Leiyn's ribs.

Mehu'Ra!

But he was too far above. The sandstone scorpion lunged. Leiyn chopped at the leg that fell toward her, chipping at the stone. The rest of it continued forward, bludgeoning her and sending her sprawling.

Leiyn rolled back to her feet, a task made trickier by the rucksack and longbow across her back. Nothing felt broken; even her mahia's walls held up. Clouded Fang came nearer with every moment, and the font of esse he supplied as well. All she needed to do was to hold until he arrived.

The scorpion raised its tail, preparing to strike.

The tempest hawk struck first.

Leiyn stumbled back as the titans clashed. Talons and claws scrabbled against one another; lightning blazed across stony flesh. The greater battle came alive through her lifesense. Even with her walls raised, she felt the tremendous buffets of magic, any enough to kill. The titans fought on, their rage heightening with every moment.

Leiyn glanced at Ketti. The Eteman was pinch-faced and tight-lipped, a hand half-raised toward her bonded titan as if to reach out and assist. As Leiyn's gaze fell on her, Ketti let it fall and motioned them forward. Their companions hurried from the scene, all struggling to keep their feet. Leiyn took up the rear. She winced with every shriek rising behind.

"Hurry!" Ketti called back, her voice faint amid the continued rumbling of other titans. "Mehu'Ra cannot hold against them all!"

Leiyn felt again for Clouded Fang and was relieved to feel him near. Drawing in his lifeforce, she sucked down a dusty breath and moved forward with greater strength. Her mahia's walls thickened, enough to keep the titans at bay.

Only then did she see the shadow falling over them.

"Above!" Leiyn pressed at Ekosa's back, sending him stumbling forward. "Run!"

The *eesu* flung himself flat over the stones before she tore her gaze from him. Teya huddled at Leiyn's side, rare fear flashing in her eyes. The sight of it buried her own fright under fury.

Falchions still drawn, Leiyn raised her gaze to the

descending white tail. The sea monster had gathered water around the massive appendage that glistened in the sparse morning light. The broken edifices rising to either side of them might provide some buffer, but they would not fully protect her. Neither could she avoid it.

They could only weather the blow.

To me! Leiyn urged her bonded titan as she fell to one knee, falchions crossed above her. Teya huddled beside her, spear raised and braced as if to meet an enemy's charge. The dragon's power inundated her, rising like an inferno through her limbs so it seemed flames must rise off her skin.

The tail hit the edge of the buildings. Water, salt, and pebbles sprayed them. A memory of the dream flashed through Leiyn's mind a moment before the impact.

Then came the flood.

She was swept off her feet. Water rushed over her. All became movement and light. Her falchions flailed to either side. Her body flattened. Her head dashed against the pavers, blackening what little remained of her vision. Agony and injury announced itself across every limb.

Then she drifted up. Floating. She had been transported underwater. Detritus swirled around her in dark clouds. Salt crystals glittered like diamonds.

Then the water dispelled, and she was expelled roughly onto the alley floor.

Curling onto her side, Leiyn hurled seawater, then wiped spittle with the back of a gloved hand and panted for breath. Clouded Fang's gaze seared into her from below, fresh waves of esse pulsing into her.

Still alive.

Brushing back wet locks from her face, she cast her gaze about for Teya. The scout lay groaning several paces away. Blood leaked from scrapes on her face and hands, but it was the darker threads through her essence that spasmed worry through Leiyn's gut.

She sheathed her falchions and fell beside Teya. Rallying her borrowed strength, she expelled a glut of lifeforce into her beloved. She could only hope it was enough for Teya to heal.

"Back on your feet, my sky," Leiyn gasped. "No time to rest."

Wrapping her arms around Teya's waist, Leiyn hauled her upright. The former scout hissed and staggered, but she kept her feet.

"Need a *kainox* of my own," Teya muttered as they limped toward where the others waited.

"Plenty around. Why don't you choose a nice one?"

Teya loosed a laugh that ended in a groan. Leiyn could feel the *situal's* wounds mending, the lifeforce Leiyn had provided sufficient to the task. Their pace quickened, enough that the others, faces painted with concern, turned and carried on toward the bay.

But the salt titan had only struck its first blow. Nothing stopped it from leveling another. Leiyn reached for her titan and sent her command to it. The ash dragon responded at once, flapping molten wings and rising through the ground.

They stepped free of the alley in time to see him emerge. A plume of black smoke burst from the line of broken docks. From cinders and ash, Clouded Fang took shape. Pirouetting midair, his wings spread wide and his clawed legs stretched out. He shook his powerful body as if to wake it, from his long neck down to his lashing tail.

The dragon was large, dozens of times longer than Leiyn was tall, but the opponent he ascended toward loomed many times higher. The ocean titan pivoted and raised its glistening tail menacingly. Clouded Fang roared back, the sound of it like a volcano's eruption.

Fire and water clashed.

Leiyn shuddered at their impact. Even as the battle was lost amid hissing clouds, she felt every wallop against her bonded titan. Clouded Fang's molten claws ripped through crystallized flesh. His esse seared through the titan's lifeforce in a blistering column. Where salt met the flames, it hissed into white clouds, leaving behind yellowed and melted hide.

Yet the dragon's opponent was every bit his match. With its long neck, the titan had ample opportunity to bite and bash. Its sinuous tail battered Clouded Fang's wings and long body. Though the dragon was made of ash and smoke, the salt titan's mahia struck as hard as its limbs. And it was a master of the sea. Having suffered enough of the dragon's breath, the salt titan summoned water to rush over it, insulating its hide. When its tail next caught the ash dragon, it was Clouded Fang who caught the worst of the exchange.

Her titan bellowed, equal parts pain and fury.

Leiyn swallowed her terror. She had never had cause to worry about Clouded Fang. Now she wondered if he had met his match.

If she was sending him to his death.

"Go!" Leiyn shoved her companions toward the beach. They had been as transfixed as she by the clash. "We need that whale!"

Ekosa responded, his mahia spreading from his body and into the bay. Leiyn grasped his arm, anchoring and shielding him with her mahia. With titans all around, it was dangerous to leave any gap in one's barriers. Teya flanked his other side and added what little assistance she could.

As she tried holding the elephantine forces at bay, a thought flitted through her mind: *Leash the salt titan.* It would solve two problems at once: freeing Clouded Fang from his battle and negating the need to search for the reef whale, if one remained to be found. And salt could serve as well as coral for a ship.

But as the salt titan battered against her ash dragon, she knew it could not be. Where the reef whale Ketti had leashed had been calm, this one was enraged. Even if it submitted to their will, there was no certainty it would remain so for a trip promising to last weeks.

"More coming!" Batu called over the din.

Leiyn cracked open her eyes. Trying to ignore the damage dealt to her titan, she looked back at the wildsoul and his bear. Three more titanic scorpions clambered across the rooftops. Two were of sandstone like the one Mehu'Ra fought against. The third was formed of veined white marble. Somehow, it made for a yet more terrifying sight.

Leiyn turned from Ekosa when the *eesu* cried out, "I have it!"

"Leash it!" She drew her falchions. "Or we're all dead!"

Leiyn left Teya with Ekosa and hurried to Batu. Barely had she stepped foot beside him before the titans crawled over the final rooftops.

"Can't you transform?" she shot at him.

"Takes too long." He glanced at her. Only their familiarity allowed her to see the fear in his pinched expression.

Then the scorpions were upon them.

Sarryl bellowed as he threw himself at the legs of the marble titan. It was like a cat tangling with a bull. The scorpion's leg buckled for a moment, then surged forth, knocking the moonbear clear. The tail shot forward.

Leiyn did not see if the blow landed as sandstone scorpions charged her and Batu. Channeling esse into strength and speed, Leiyn threw herself forward, chopping into the rocky pillars as she swerved between spindly legs. San Jadiel must have been watching over her; even with her belongings throwing off her balance, she just matched its deadly tarantella. The titan tried to skewer her with spear-sharp feet, but its ponderous bulk helped her stay one moment ahead.

A scream roused her from her frenzied caper.

Leiyn dove free and shot a look toward Batu. The wildsoul had been knocked down. Blood smeared the surrounding debris. Coated his chest.

She froze as memory assaulted her. Isla rose before her eyes, an arrow protruding from her chest. Eyes unmoving. Body dark and devoid of life.

Something crashed into her and sent her flying.

She rolled to her feet as soon as she hit the ground. The awkward landing had knocked her shoulder out of its socket, but a flush of lifeforce set it painfully back into place. Leiyn bared her teeth as she threw herself forward, lashing at the titan that stood between her and her fallen friend.

"Out of my *fucking* way!"

The giant scorpion was impervious to her rage. It lashed its tail, trying to spear her. She narrowly dodged, then chopped her blades against its hide. They had as little effect as before, chipping stone and dimming their latent enchantments. Much more of this, and she worried they would shatter.

A thundering caw split the sky. Lightning flashed. The insides of her nostrils burned.

Leiyn stumbled free as the tempest hawk fell upon the scorpions. The rock titans scuttled aside and abandoned their prey, seeking to escape the predator from above. Mehu'Ra pursued them, besetting them with stormy claws. The air became redolent with petrichor and seared stone.

Trusting Ketti and her titan had the battle in hand, Leiyn spared a moment to glance toward Clouded Fang. Her ash dragon still flew, though his esse had vastly dimmed. He was out of his element. Fire could only burn so long against the might of an ocean.

Hold! she urged him. *You must hold!*

Embroiled in battle, Clouded Fang paid her no heed. He

expelled a fresh glut of lava upon the white hide of the ocean titan, then became lost behind the hissing cloud.

Leiyn pried her focus from the clash and ran to Batu. He lay where she had last seen him, blood saturating his clothes. Life remained in him, but it was corded with injury. His albino animal had limped to his side and moaned over him, white fur turned pink with his injuries.

Hoping Sarryl would not lash out at her approach, she kneeled at Batu's side. He cracked open his eyes to peer at her.

"Held off...a titan," he wheezed with a pink-toothed smile. "A bloody titan."

Relief and terror warred in her chest. "Don't talk," she said, placing her hands around the deepest of the wounds. "Always time to impress me later."

Laughter gurgled in his throat before it gave way to groaning. He did not have long.

Gritting her teeth, she poured esse into him, then guided it to heal his wounds as Xepi had taught her. Periodically, she bolstered his stores, draining every amber bead and imbuing their lifefire into him.

The rampaging of titans rattled against her mahia, reminding her that danger was far from over. Clouded Fang dimmed in her mind, worrisome as a fading pulse.

"Will he live?"

With the worst of the wounds mended, Leiyn pried away her focus to look up at Teya through swimming vision. The *situal* stared at her with a knitted brow, spear held at the ready.

"Seen worse." Batu grunted as he flopped over to rise on hands and knees. The weight of his pack almost collapsed him back to the ground.

"Wait there." Leiyn rose to her feet, then glanced at the ongoing battle between the salt titan and dragon. With their bond dimming, she had to look to be certain Clouded Fang had not yet fallen.

"Ekosa?" she called to the *eesu*.

"He almost has it!" Ketti called from his side.

No sooner had she spoken than the ocean erupted. Amid the other awakened titans, Leiyn failed to note the newcomer until she saw it. The reef whale looked much like the one Ketti had helmed to Southport. The broad hump of its back was rough and uneven from the coral that composed it. This coral was predominantly blue with bursts of green and violet. Fish caught by the titan's surfacing flapped on its back in a surprised frenzy.

"It cannot reach us." Teya studied the coast, eyes pinched with worry. "The shoreline is too shallow. We will have to swim."

"*Fesht.*" Leiyn did not need to look at Batu to know he was in no condition for it. She barely felt she could manage it herself. Only with Ata's aid had they overcome the swell of a sea titan the last time they had been caught in one.

Perhaps in a quiet moment, she could have thought of a way around it. But Mehu'Ra still drove at the scorpions, his thunder rolling across Breakbay. Clouded Fang lost more of himself to his battle with the ocean titan. More titans loomed in the peripheries of her awareness, battering at her mind.

Think, feshtado *fool, think!*

Leiyn pressed the heel of her hand to her forehead. It could not ease the pressure building in her skull. Teya laid a hand on her shoulder, esse extending in comfort.

"We can do this," she murmured.

Leiyn lowered her hand to gesture at the salt titan. "Outswim that?"

Teya shook her head. "You cannot muscle through everything. There is another way."

She was about to object when the answer came to her.

Leiyn almost laughed. Why must she always think to fight first? Doing battle with titans had nearly killed Batu, Clouded Fang, herself.

She did not have to fight them when she could command them.

"I have an idea." Freeing herself from Teya, she sent her esse toward her bonded titan.

Clouded Fang, flee!

Had the ash dragon conveyed human emotion, she might have believed him relieved as he peeled off of the salt titan. Dimmed to wispy black smoke, Clouded Fang looked as if he would not have endured much longer. He spun once midair, then dove back into the ground, making for the rivers of lava that were his haven.

Leiyn focused on the salt titan. Already, it rallied its strength. The weight of its attention set on her as she arrowed into its well of esse. In that moment, it seemed as vast as the bay it occupied, its defenses as impenetrable as the salt of its body.

I yield. She gave of herself to the titan, surrendering her fears and memories along with her esse. *I submit.*

The titan swallowed her offering, then reached for more. She tightened her will, aware of her body sinking to its knees.

You are mine, she told the titan. *As I am yours.*

The salt titan paused. Its long neck swayed as if in consideration of her. It extended her no acceptance, but neither did it reject her.

"Leiyn!"

"I think I calmed it." She cracked open her eyes to stare at Teya, her vision swimming. "We have to go."

Her beloved studied her. "Are you certain you can manage it?"

"I have to."

Ketti hurried from Ekosa's side toward them. Batu

clawed back to his feet and weaved drunkenly across the broken harbor. Sarryl remained at his side, the moonbear unwilling to stray far from his wildsoul. Only Ekosa remained where he was, his lithe frame leaning toward the reef whale. The whole of his will was bent toward keeping it in place.

Leiyn shook her head, trying to clear the daze from it. Now, most of all, she needed to think clearly. "This is our best chance. We have to go."

"Can we make it across the bay?" Teya eyed Batu.

Ketti turned ashen. "I cannot swim."

Frustration grated through Leiyn. She had forgotten that snag. A sudden solution banished it.

"I think I can help. Teya, you take Ekosa. Ketti, you'll hold on to Batu and Sarryl. All you need to do is stay afloat."

Teya narrowed her eyes. "And who will carry you?"

Leiyn smiled thinly. "The titan. No time to explain." She hurried on as the spearmaiden frowned. "Get in the water!"

She attended to her link to the ocean titan as her companions gathered around Ekosa. Teya put an arm over his back and murmured in his ear, conveying the plan. Ketti huddled at Batu's side opposite the moonbear, her bonded titan continuing to harry the scorpions. At Leiyn's word, they shuffled past the rotted wreckage of the docks toward where the sea met the rocky shoreline.

"In!" Leiyn instructed, then reached out to the salt titan to will her desire.

She let the others go before her. Ketti shuddered as she stepped into the cold seawater, waves lapping about her ankles. Batu was riven with injuries and dim in esse, but he remained dogged in pressing forward. Sarryl hesitated at the water's edge and only entered the sea at Batu's request, though not without a low whine. The moonbear panted as he settled in and began paddling, only his snout, his eyes, and the hump of his back cresting the water. Teya lugged at Ekosa, his footsteps stuttering, distracted by his task.

Leiyn stepped in last. The water sucked at her ankles, the current leading her out. But it was only an ordinary swell, far too gentle to bring them out as fast as they needed.

She braced herself, then gave enough esse to the salt titan for her knees to buckle. *More.*

The ocean's tide strengthened, so sudden and fierce it swept Leiyn off her feet. Rocks scraped against her rump and pack. Saltwater charged up her mouth and nose.

The salt titan's current had them now. Spluttering, Leiyn fought to remain above the surface as the ocean thrust them out into its vastness. Fear stuttered through her before she squashed it. She could not allow weakness before this titan. At the first sign of it, she feared it would swallow her.

But her plan was working so far. Her companions' esses trilled with fear, but they stayed above the tumultuous surface. Leiyn caught glimpses of their terrified faces between the waves lapping over her head. Her eyes stung. Her lungs burned. Her soul felt wrung out and dried up.

Hold, Firebrand. You can't lose them!

Like leaves in a river, they were borne toward the waiting reef whale. The raging titans of Breakbay faded to distant threats. Only the salt titan remained, the bulk of the rest of its body becoming more apparent the closer they came. Even with a connection forged between them, it felt like a predator biding its time. Awaiting the right moment to strike.

Hold!

Then her arm scraped against the reef whale's bulk. Leiyn banged her hand as she scrabbled for a handhold. Cursing as blood poured from the wound, she sealed it with a flash of lifefire, then started climbing. Around her, her companions endeavored to do the same.

Subside, she told the salt titan. *Return to your rest.*

The ocean titan remained where it was. Its tide did not diminish. Despair seeped into her. She had reached the limits of her power. Whatever had caused these titans to rampage still infected it. As soon as she released her hold, it would strike again.

"Hold," she wheezed and kept climbing.

She made it atop the titan's back and found an uncomfortable perch amid the coral. It took the entirety of her will to keep the salt titan at bay. When the rest of her comrades finally made it aboard, Leiyn spoke through clenched teeth to Ekosa.

"Take us away."

The *eesu* nodded and pressed his hands deep into the coral. She felt his will spread through the titan. The reef whale creaked beneath them. She wondered if it, too, would try drowning them.

Then its long, powerful tail moved up and down, propelling them forward.

Leiyn clung to her hold on the salt titan for as long as she could. She watched the towering figure of seawater and detritus grow small, the rest of Breakbay fading with it. Only when it disappeared from view did she release it.

Then she collapsed to the coral and let exhaustion have its due.

25

AN EMPTY HORIZON

Evening fell before Leiyn compelled herself to rise.

Paling light prodded into her eyes. Blinking gummed eyelids, she sat up, careful not to snag her clothes on the rough coral. Her pack and longbow, sloughed off in the moments after mounting, remained secure amid the blue branches of coral by her side, if still bedraggled from their swim. She had not yet dared check on the state of her journal, the sketches no doubt smeared and washed off.

The least we could've lost.

The reef whale pulsed esse beneath her, soft and persistent as the ocean waves. Even more than a ship, the titan moved with a gentle undulation that would make a sensitive stomach sick. She lay a gloved hand against the coral and felt the whale's focus draw toward her. Some titans would have been unbearable to be so near, much less to touch. Not so with this one. If anything, she felt safer for its steady fire, comforting as a campfire on a frosty night.

But she did not embrace that comfort yet. Leiyn sent her lifesense deeper, racing along the bond to her titan.

Clouded Fang, she called, though softly, afraid of disturbing his healing rest. *Clouded Fang?*

She felt nothing in response. Only that their bond remained assured her he still lived.

Maybe you can be bonded to a corpse, her doubts mocked.

She shook her head and drew away. A problem for another time. Most likely, the ash dragon only needed to recuperate.

And if he doesn't? If you're alone again?

Belying the thoughts, Leiyn sought the others. She must have fallen unconscious for a time, for she had not noticed where they spread out across the broad back of the whale. Teya, Batu, and Sarryl remained nearby, all finding rest on their outlandish ship. Only the moonbear stirred at her gaze, one heavy-lidded pink eye examining her before closing again. Ekosa and Ketti had strayed toward the front of the coral titan. The Eteman looked to have taken control, for the *eesu* lay prone beside her, esse still with exhaustion.

She knew she should go to her. For a time, she only turned her gaze to the blank horizon. They had seen much that day. Too much sorrow. Too much death. From Qasaar to Solace to Breakbay, now to sailing across the sea on titanback.

But we made it.

Leiyn climbed to her feet, adjusted her weapons belt, and picked her way across the coral. After a moment's consideration, she left the rest of her possessions where they lay. Not only were the highest waves of the sea a dozen paces below, but they were stuck fast amid the coral. On the clear evening, they were unlikely to go anywhere.

Ketti must have sensed her coming, yet she did not turn to greet her. Her gaze cast toward the horizon. Seeing things there that only existed in her mind. Ekosa did not rouse from his rest. Uncomfortable though the coral was, sleep kept its grip on him.

Leiyn sat beside Ketti with a stifled groan. "Fighting titans sure takes it out of you."

Ketti smiled wanly. Her eyes flickered toward Leiyn before returning to the horizon. "They were not so active during my last visit. Nor so aggressive."

"Good thing, or I doubt we would have seen you return." Leiyn looked toward the horizon as well. "The only other titan I've seen so upset was that vine jaguar I told you about. But this wasn't like that, not quite. Then it was like a predator stalking its prey. These titans..." She pursed her lips. "It was like hurt animals lashing out. Like something had riled them up and they took it out on us."

"Perhaps it was me." Ketti barely spoke above a whisper. "My previous visit disturbed them."

"Or Osmet and the other lyshans knew we'd be going that way," Leiyn countered, "and laid a trap. I wouldn't assume it's your fault."

Ketti shrugged, eyes fixed on the watery line in the distance.

Silence curtained over them like the end of a pantomime show. But Leiyn knew she could not give up yet. Clearing her throat, she spoke again.

"How far do you reckon we've traveled?"

The following pause made Leiyn wonder if Ketti would answer. Just as she dredged up another inane thing to say, the Eteman finally spoke.

"I had few opportunities to become proficient at measuring distances in Solace. But the shoreline is beyond my awareness and the ocean deep enough that I would drown. Far, I would say."

Leiyn had not yet tried reaching the limits of her lifesense. The idea of land being so far away made her queasy in a way she did not care for.

"To be fair," Leiyn said with forced cheer, "a puddle could drown you."

Again, the Eteman only gave her the slightest quirk of her lips before her expression turned somber again.

Leiyn sighed and stared toward the sun. The dying light dyed the sparse clouds on the horizon peach and orange. Thoughts of fruit reminded her of her hunger. She quashed it. Ketti needed deeper sustenance. She had to try to provide it.

"I lost almost everyone I knew in the attack on the Wilds Lodge. The other rangers were as good as my family. The lodgemaster and my mentor, Tadeo. Staff I was friendly with. Apprentices that were like little brothers and sisters."

Her throat swelled so she could not continue. She pressed a hand to the fox figurine secured at her waist. Just then, she did not feel Tadeo's ember, but knowing the carving had not fallen out during the battle was a comfort on its own.

Ketti turned her gaze on her. Those lavender eyes were like twin flames, twilight setting them aglow. In contrast, her esse was subdued but for the rivulet that fed into the titan.

Leiyn drew in a shaky breath and pressed on. "But I still had Isla. She shared my pain. She'd known and loved me like a sister since we were children. I wasn't alone. And though it felt like the Lodge was a world of its own, I didn't see the extinction of my people."

Ketti folded in on herself and began shaking. Leiyn tensed, fearing what might come. Even exhausted as she was, she would have preferred fighting a dozen more titans before encountering this.

Breathe, just breathe. Tadeo's voice blew like an ocean breeze through her mind.

Leiyn set a hand on Ketti's shoulder. Like the pebble to break a dam, Ketti began sobbing, trembling under Leiyn's palm.

Leiyn placed her arms around her and drew her in. For a time, they were silent as the Eteman wept for all she had lost.

The sky had turned wine red by the time Ketti pulled away. Sniffing, she wiped at her nose and stared with pink-rimmed eyes up at Leiyn.

"I feel...adrift. A ship without anchor." She gestured at the surrounding sea. "I do not know where I go. What my purpose is. Or perhaps not that—I know what I must do. It is just..." Ketti stared at the scarlet smudged clouds. "*Ama ek ammar*. 'I am all.' A phrase we were taught as children. Even then, safe and isolated in our home, we knew the weight of Etema's legacy. The burden we each bore."

She shook her head and continued in a whisper. "It is too heavy alone, yet I must carry it. For am I not responsible? If I had never left, none of this would have happened. They would all be alive. Mother, Father, Ab-Abi..."

Ketti drew her knees to her chest and pressed her forehead to them.

Leiyn rubbed a hand over Ketti's back. The rough material of the gloves snagged on the silken tunic before releasing.

Rough as a ranger trying to console.

Still, she had to try. "Maybe that's true. Maybe your actions led to this. Or maybe it was mine. But that doesn't mean you killed them. I know—" Leiyn held up her free hand in surrender as Ketti looked up abruptly. "I thought of a dozen things I could've done differently the night the Lodge burned. Maybe you've done the same. But no matter how we failed, it was our enemies who struck the killing blows. Ilberians burned and butchered my people. Lyshans and their pawns stole yours." She squeezed her shoulder tight. "The fault lies with them, not you. Don't take it from them."

Ketti leaned into her as she shook with fresh sobs. Leiyn held her, silent as they watched the bloody light die, then the bruise of dusk spread across its corpse.

26

SEAWORTHY

The others had awoken by the time Leiyn picked her way back to where she had left them. Ketti remained at the front of the titan with Ekosa, who roused as Leiyn left. He would be a better comfort than Leiyn could be. Still, she was reassured thinking she had done some good.

Teya was busy scrounging a cold meal from her pack when Leiyn approached. "No chance of fire," the *situal* said with a regretful smile. "Not while we ride Brine."

"Brine?" Leiyn accepted the hardbread and strip of meat Teya offered.

Her beloved grinned. "A fine name for our titan, no?"

Leiyn was surprised by a chuckle of her own. "I suppose it'll do."

She found a piece of coral approximately shaped like a seat and set to her meal. Batu ate in silence nearby and fed Sarryl more of the meat. Leiyn kept a careful watch on the large animal from the corner of her eye. Though he was a spirit beast and bonded to Batu, the ranger in her struggled to eat in front of a bear.

Best get used to it.

While they ate, Leiyn reached again for Clouded Fang. This time, she felt a glimmer of response along their bond. Not nearly as strong as she was used to, but enough for relief to wash through her.

He'll survive. All of us will.

As if in defiance of her thoughts, Batu spoke up. "Food won't last. We'll need to scavenge."

Teya raised an eyebrow. "In the middle of this watery wasteland?"

"It's not a wasteland." Leiyn spread her lifesense. "You can feel it. There's life all around and below us. Fish, seaweed—other things, perhaps."

She felt the spearmaiden reach out with her mahia. But instead of affirming Leiyn's point, Teya shook her head. "And how will we reach this bounty?"

Leiyn smiled. "Tomorrow, we hunt."

The other two exchanged skeptical looks.

Let them see.

Teya tore off another bite and spoke around it. "I shall leave that to you. What I am wondering is why that city was trying to kill us."

"Wouldn't a Gast know best?" Batu pointed out.

The *situal* eyed him. Leiyn thought it best to intervene. "I can think of two reasons. Ketti and Ata's last visit roused the titans and they haven't slumbered since."

"Raging across three seasons?" Teya shook her head. "Even your tantrums do not last so long."

Leiyn gave her a flat look, to which her beloved grinned.

"Or," Leiyn continued, "someone else riled them up knowing we would go there."

Sarryl growled. Leiyn flinched and drew her food to her chest. At Teya's look, she relaxed and continued eating.

"Sharo," Batu answered for them. "His lyshans, at least."

They chewed on the disquieting thought. How much more

did their enemy anticipate? Did they even now play into Sharo's hands?

She had inadvertently done his bidding many times before. But what could she do but keep trying?

"We survived," Leiyn said at length. "We're coming for him and his empire. That'll have to be enough."

The other two nodded, looking as unconvinced as she felt.

Calling their titanback camp uncomfortable would have been generous. Leiyn's bedroll did little to soften the angular points and uneven surface of the coral. Even where it spread thick enough to lie upon, there were still gaps that her imagination filled with creatures rising through. When sleep finally came, her dreams were plagued by raging titans and taunting lyshans.

It was a relief when dawn approached. Leiyn was up with the gray light and already setting to her plans for gathering food by the time Teya and Batu joined her. At the head of the reef whale, Ekosa had fallen back asleep, while Ketti remained at her vigil.

"Should you take over Brine?" Teya gestured in Ketti's direction as she yawned. "She has been at it all night."

"After this." Leiyn wondered if Ketti did not appreciate the duty as a distraction. And they needed food eventually. Better to know now if this worked rather than while stranded in the middle of the Ocula Ocean.

Batu observed Leiyn's strung bow and nocked arrow, then fetched his own horsebow. She did not stop him. Two bows were better than one.

"Now you are in on this foolishness?" Teya chided him as he returned. "And how do you mean to shoot fish in an ocean? An arrow cannot go deeper than an arm before it planes."

"With heavy arrows, they dive deeper," Leiyn countered. "But that's beside the point. They won't be in the water when we loose."

Leiyn gave no further explanation, sending her mahia diving into the waters below. A school of fish lingered along the belly of the reef whale. To her relief, the titan did nothing to inhibit her magic. It remained as gentle now as it had the day before.

Ignoring Teya's questions, Leiyn eased into the esse of the first fish. It took some moments to understand the composition of its simpler lifeforce, but it was no more difficult than when she had practiced on the woodland creatures of the Titan Wilds. Like with them, she found she could influence the fish, coaxing it to swim around the titan to the surface.

She opened her eyes to find silver scales flashing in the sunlight below them.

Batu started to draw, but Leiyn raised a hand. "Wait. He'll wash away if you shoot now."

Studying the side of the whale, she decided her best course. Moving toward the front of the whale, she called her request to Ketti. The Eteman nodded, then made good on her agreement.

A moment later, Brine raised its flipper underneath the fish, lifting it free of the water.

"Now," Leiyn told Batu.

The plainsrider drew, aimed, and loosed. The arrow cleanly pierced the side of the fish. Leiyn winced as its lifefire went dark.

"Your spirit touches mine," she murmured, the Ranger's Lament coming to her lips.

After a cajoling exchange, Teya relented to clamber down the side of the titan to fetch the skewered fish. She labored back up with it tucked under her arm, her smile brightening.

Brine set its flipper back into the ocean, increasing their pace once more.

"Big one," she admitted as she set it on the coral. It stretched as long as Leiyn's shin and was thick around as her thigh. The stilled eye seemed to stare at Leiyn as blood streamed between its scales from where the arrow pierced it.

"Coral trout," Batu identified.

"If you say so." Teya toed it. "But we will lose time if you raise Brine's flipper for one fish."

"Then we had best get a bigger haul, hadn't we?" Leiyn grinned. "So long as we have someone to gather them."

Teya groaned, then they all laughed. Despite all that had come before, in that moment, the morning seemed bright.

Over the course of the morning, the trio lured, shot, and gathered ten more coral trout, only breaking a single arrow in the process. While they debated how to proceed, Sarryl ambled over and stole a fish for himself. Only Batu's approving smile kept Leiyn from grumbling.

"Do we eat them raw?" Teya asked.

Batu shrugged. "Good enough for Sarryl."

"A *kuit* point," the scout scoffed. "Bears eat rotten meat if it suits them."

He raised an eyebrow. "*Kuit?*"

"'Shit,'" Leiyn translated with a smile. It slipped away as she thought of the raw rats she'd had to eat during her imprisonment in Southport. "Unless we think of another way, we'll just have to bear it."

The plainsrider grinned. "'Bear' it?"

Leiyn and Teya groaned but let off as Ketti and Ekosa approached. Leiyn startled as she noticed the gemstones embedded in the Eteman's skin were drained of esse. The slump in her shoulders and the dimness of her lifefire told the rest of the story.

"String up the trout and leave them in the water for now," Leiyn told her fellow fishers before turning to Ketti. "Let me take over. You need rest."

Ketti opened her mouth, protest alighting in her eyes, but a look from Ekosa silenced her. She sighed and nodded. "Tell me when you are ready."

Leiyn assented and rallied her mahia. Fail here, and they would be stranded leagues away from any shore. Drowning would be the kindest fate they could hope for.

Focus. You've leashed titans before. You won't fail now.

Ketti's gaze turned vague. Leiyn felt as the Eteman released her hold on the reef whale. For a moment, nothing happened. Brine continued swimming forward, as if he were doing as exactly as it meant to all along.

Then he began to sink.

Leiyn drove down with her mahia, saturating him and letting him flow back into her. *I submit. I command.*

There was a moment of resistance, like pressing a hand through mud. Then she burst through.

The titan was hers.

A sigh of relief hissed through her teeth as Brine rose further out of the water. Ekosa wore a knowing smile.

"It tickles the nerves, does it not?"

Leiyn laughed, as much at his odd phrasing as the needling truth. "More than I'd like to admit."

Ketti swayed. Her beloved gripped her arm, keeping her upright.

"Let us rest," he urged her gently.

The Eteman nodded. They moved off toward the middle of the titan's back, where their small camp had been erected.

Leiyn followed them to fetch her weapons, then made for Brine's head to hold her watch. While Batu and Teya hooked the trout onto a line of spare rope, she found a seat and stared out over the sparkling sea. It was an eerie feeling, seeing nothing but water on every horizon. At the moment, no islands even appeared, nor juts of rock. If not for her lifesense, it would have appeared lifeless, ominously so.

Yet she also sensed the ocean from the titan's perspective. How it reveled in the waves lapping against its flanks, pressing water through its porous body. How the schools of fish around its belly tickled as they nibbled its coral, cleaning it of algae and pests and feeding themselves. The sun was not blinding and burning to it, but a soothing warmth. The moist breeze was a balm afterward, refreshing as a cool bath.

For a time, Leiyn sat with the peaceful giant and forgot her worries. For a time, she was content.

The storm came that afternoon.

Leiyn, still guiding the whale, watched with foreboding as the dark clouds gathered above. Day turned almost to night as the sunlight was blotted out. On and on, the thunderheads spread. This promised to be a tempest that would last hours.

A glance at the others showed them to be preparing as best they could. But here on Brine's broad back, there was nowhere to take shelter. The coral was too dense to delve into, and they would not risk harming or offending the titan by carving into its flesh.

When the rain fell, it came in a deluge. Leiyn winced as the sky split and poured over her. The droplets were large and hit like thrown pebbles. Leiyn sunk her hands into the whale's back and gripped hard on the coral. The rising winds stirred the ocean into taller waves. Already, they reached halfway up the whale's back and surged higher with each passing moment.

Lightning brightened the gloom. Thunder rolled with all

the power of a titan's awakening over them. Then a mass of esse welled up in the storm's heart.

Her lifesense knew it for what it was before her mind caught up. Even here, out in the ocean's expanse, titans raged.

The tempest hawk took form behind the clouds. Lightning flashed again, illuminating its silhouette. A deafening cry raised ridges on Leiyn's skin. For a moment, she felt its wild call to her, provoking her to rashness. To fling herself up to join it in the sky.

Snarling, she drove the feeling away with raised walls on her mahia. Only what she needed to maintain her hold over the reef whale did she leave behind. Through the gap, the electrifying presence leaked in, both tantalizing and tormenting.

She twisted around to shout over her shoulder. "Ketti! Drive it away!"

They were too far off and the storm too loud. Stringing together curses worthy of a landlocked sailor, Leiyn pried her hands off the coral and began staggering back to their camp. She had to fight for every step. Though Brine did not pitch like a ship would, it was far from steady footing. A misstep would see her pitched off the side.

But she remained a ranger, and rangers trained for any weather. Timing her movements with the waves, Leiyn made it back to her companions. They huddled beneath their cloaks, hoods pulled up, miserable to the last. Sarryl seemed the worst off among them, moaning with each crash of thunder. She wondered if he could flee into a grotto and chose not to, or if even a spirit beast could not escape in the middle of the ocean.

Driving the thought away, she made for Ketti. The Eteman was the only one without her hood drawn. Face bared to the rain, chin lifted to the sky, she seemed so caught up in the storm that she did not notice the droplets dashing against her unblinking eyes.

"She's in its thrall!" Leiyn moved to shake her arm, to pry her loose of the tempest hawk's intoxicating presence.

Teya intercepted her. "It is Mehu'Ra, Redlock! Can you not feel it?"

Leiyn stared, baffled, until comprehension set in. Tentatively, she lowered her walls to feel for herself. She did not know Solace's protector intimately enough to recognize it by esse alone, but now that she knew, there was a sense of familiarity to the titan in the sky. Ketti's connection to him confirmed the truth.

Mehu'Ra shrieked again, loud enough that Leiyn flinched. The clouds seemed to recoil as well, the squall peeling back from the titan to reveal its body of mist and lightning. Ketti's titan beat his wings, every stroke buffeting the clouds further away.

From beyond emerged clear sky.

Awe filled Leiyn as she watched Ketti and her bonded dismantle the storm. In minutes, the tempest had reduced to wisps. Behind them, the thunderheads regathered to resume their tantrum. They, at least, would be spared its wrath.

Mehu'Ra cawed once more, then shattered out of being with a flash of lightning and dispersal of mist. Leiyn lowered her gaze to the one who had commanded him.

Ketti finally blinked, seeming to come out of her trance, then met their stares with a small smile. "That settles that, as Baltesians say."

"*Odisi wangu*, Ketti!" Ekosa exclaimed. "You command storms?"

"Mehu'Ra commands them," Ketti corrected. "All I do is suggest."

"It amounts to the same." The *eesu* looked to the rest of them, seeking confirmation of his incredulity.

Leiyn crossed her arms. Keeping a straight face, she said flatly, "Very impressive."

Ketti met her stare, looking confused. When Leiyn grinned, a startled giggle escaped Ketti. It was the first glimpse of joy Leiyn had witnessed from her since the destruction of Solace.

Teya sighed and stretched. "Shame for it to leave. Here I was, hoping to test if we were 'seaworthy,' as your outlander sailors say."

Leiyn looked with the others at her. A chortle, pitying at the pale joke, broke free.

Then everyone joined in, and the laughter took on a life of its own. Like the ocean had swelled with the storm, so did their mirth grow and bubble over. Even soaked to the skin and shivering, it warmed them through.

27

INTO THE VEIL

Batu had gathered water from the rainfall with his cloak. They filled their waterskins and drank together, feeling as merry as if brandy filled the skins instead. Afternoon faded to evening, and even in the eeriness of night, hope saturated Leiyn through.

They had withstood a storm. Conquered it. They could survive this sea voyage. What else could stand in their way?

The sense of triumph continued into the next day, even after her nightlong vigil. Leiyn relinquished Brine to Ekosa and slept through the morning, hiding from Omn's punishing glare beneath her cloak. Her skin, fair next to the others, burned worst from the sun, but years spent constantly under its stare insulated her from the worst of it.

When she woke, Leiyn joined Teya and Batu in gathering more fish. As they fretted over how to cook them, Ketti provided a solution, though with obvious reluctance. Etemans maintained a peaceful relationship toward animals, but their need and insistence brought it out of her.

"Stirring *ilis* through flesh can warm it," Ketti said. "Like we grow heat from our bodies."

She looked at Leiyn and Teya, who both nodded. Many was the cold night Leiyn had kept warm by lifeforce alone.

"How does it work?" Leiyn pressed.

"It is simple: push esse into the dead flesh, then..." Ketti made a swirling motion with her hand.

"Stir it," Batu guessed.

She nodded. "Hard and fast."

Teya snorted, but pretended innocence as Leiyn cocked an eyebrow at her.

"And how do you know this?" Leiyn asked Ketti. "It is not as if you ever needed to cook meat."

The Eteman winced. "The annals," she murmured. "They contain many memories. Many unpleasant."

Leiyn remembered the savagery of the titan callers in the memory Ketti had shown them. Etemans had not always been as peaceful as those they met in Solace. Once, they had invaded the Veiled Lands and butchered a people to their final dozens. They had even taken away their Mothertrees, all but the seed now interred in Ata's body. If not for the intervention of Ketti's ancestor, they would have completed their genocide.

Leiyn banished the dark thoughts as she first prepared the fish, then set to practicing Ketti's technique. Moving lifeforce through dead flesh was unsettling, but she bolstered her nerve with thoughts of biting into raw fish. Stirring it faster and faster, she felt the trout heating through with her efforts. Pressing it to its limits, it grew so hot she had to set it down, almost burning her fingertips.

When steam rose off its side, Leiyn cut off a slice and nibbled. Devoid of seasoning, it could hardly be called delicious. But it was edible.

"That'll work." She offered strips to Batu and Teya.

"I would rather eat raw liver," the *situal* complained, but she accepted it with a sour expression.

Batu ate his slice stoically. "Edible," was all he said.

Leiyn glanced back at Ketti. "What will you eat?"

"I have a few ideas." The Eteman peered over the edge of the titan. "Seaweed and kelp become caught on the flanks of the *kainox*. Heated through, they may serve for now."

They spent the rest of the afternoon fetching food Ketti could eat, clambering along the side of the reef whale until they had a tidy pile of greens. Their taste was bitter and slimy, and they still stank of the sea, yet Ketti did not complain. Though her expression grew stiff as she chewed.

Leiyn took a swig from her waterskin. Water. Food. Protection from poor weather. Though a sea voyage had seemed daunting at the start, they had found ways of surviving.

We'll make it, she thought, lowering the skin and staring over the horizon. *We have to.*

On the third morning, she woke to pressure on her lifesense.

Leiyn sat up in her bedroll and stared ahead. She had fretted with the others the night before over whether they still headed in the right direction. The sun and stars could guide them east, but over the entire Ocula Ocean, they might veer far off course.

But there had been one obstacle they could never avoid.

The thing before them was gargantuan, larger than anything she had yet beheld, spreading across the horizon as far as she could see or sense. In the predawn gloom, it was barely more than a gray smudge blotting out the coming light, a bank of fog.

Yet to her mahia, it shimmered with life.

Batu already sat upright and stared at it. Even without mahia, he understood what she sensed.

"The Veil," he murmured.

Leiyn rose. Staying still before the looming wall was impossible. She moved toward the titan's tail to relieve herself, then went to Brine's head where Ketti sat guiding him.

"Did it wake you?" The Eteman glanced at Leiyn before reverting her gaze to the growing Veil. "It is a marvel."

Leiyn crouched beside her, not settled enough to sit. "Do your people say anything of the Veil?"

"'Did' they, I believe you mean." A haggard expression passed over Ketti's face before she continued. "Very little. Etema lies to the west of *Akan'Oala*, your Veiled Lands. To my knowledge, none of my people ventured beyond them." She fell silent, the surf of the ocean filling the void. "It is possible I am the farthest east any Eteman has been."

Leiyn nudged her with an elbow. "Makes you feel brave, doesn't it?"

Ketti captured her gaze, lavender eyes solemn. "Or desperate."

Leiyn twisted her mouth to one side and returned her eyes to the Veil. "No notion how to pass it, then?"

"Not yet. But does it not feel like one of the *kainox*?"

It was not something Leiyn had put words to. "It's larger than any titan I've met," she hedged.

"Or that I have seen in memories or the seeing pool. But much may lie in your Ancestral Lands beyond our knowledge."

"Perhaps." Leiyn lowered her head to pick idly at the coral around her feet. "But ships pass through it. That means we can, too."

"And keep our whale in check?"

"We'll make certain we do." Leiyn stood. "But you should eat and rest. I'll take over."

"As you wish."

After they had transitioned the reef whale from Ketti's control to Leiyn's, the Eteman moved back to join the others at their camp, while Leiyn stood in vigil. The reef whale was a comforting presence pressing against her esse, though it made her yearn again for her own absent titan.

Rest, she thought to Clouded Fang. Just then, their connection felt too thin and stretched for communication, but she pretended otherwise. Consider it too deeply, and she feared despair sweeping her away. *Heal. Become whole.*

A brief warmth, like a passing ray of sunshine, alighted on her lifesense, then subsided. Little enough sign of his regard, but it was as much as she had received in the days since Breakbay. Enough to ward off her deepening dread.

The Veil only continued to expand higher and broader. Fear inevitably crept back in. She had commanded titans and bonded one, greater accomplishments than the mahas of Ilberia, Eyi, or Kalga would ever know. Her past feats only made her more aware of how dwarfed they were by the manifestation of mist and lifeforce before them. It spread to either side as far as she could see or sense. A barrier as impregnable as a fortress wall.

But not impenetrable. The Tricolonies were proof of that. Somehow, the colonists had broken through. And the ships of the Ancestral Lands continued to navigate it.

But how?

As they came within a half-league of the Veil, it took up half the sky and came into starker detail. This was no inert fog bank but contained movement and energy. Specters cavorted and careened along its edges, each just discernible in their imitations.

She started as a great serpent dove in and out of the fog above them, swimming as if through a river. Farther to her right, schooling fish emerged briefly as they leaped free, every movement made in tandem. To her left, the tentacles of a kraken broke out, pawing at the air as if seeking fresh prey.

The wings of seabirds cut out of the top and dove against the ocean's surface before bursting apart.

Every form of marine life appeared present. If this was a titan, it seemed an embodiment of them all.

The manifestations were not illusions. During their brief exhibitions, they contained lifeforce that animated them. Yet they failed to last, the flashes of esse returning to the greater churning whole when their display was through.

Leiyn felt compelled to join them. Falling to a crouch, she clutched the coral to anchor herself in place. Brine gave no sign of concern. The pulsations of his lifeforce almost seemed eager, as if he returned to a place long familiar.

Feeding grounds? she guessed. *Or a place to mate? Do titans do either?*

There was one thing she knew for certain: before her lay an ecosystem unto itself. Life and spirit whirling together with the inevitability of the tides.

They did not belong among it.

As the distance grew ever narrower, the others joined her at the head. Leiyn stood, embarrassed to be caught cowering. If any noticed, they said nothing.

Teya brought Leiyn's weapons and handed them to her. "Any ideas on how to cross it?" her beloved questioned.

Leiyn shook her head as she equipped herself. "Nothing clear."

"We must be like Qara Gegeen." Batu stared at the Veil with a furrowed brow and crossed arms. "Approach it boldly and perceive our way through."

Sarryl made a sound between a grunt and a growl. Somehow, it radiated with the moonbear's approval.

"Is that all?" Teya taunted.

Ketti cut in as Batu glared at the scout. "If it is a titan or something like it, perhaps it can be commanded."

"Leash all of that?" Leiyn gestured down the line of the endless fog.

"No—that would be beyond any of us. But perhaps there is a way to influence a part of it."

"Like moving the limb of a giant." Ekosa took a step beyond the rest of them, his eyes wide so the whites of them were bright against his face.

Ketti grasped his hand. "Do not stray too far."

"I am fine, my gem."

Despite his words, Ekosa did not look back. *He's entranced.* Leiyn felt it in the rhythmic thrum of his esse, a match to the Veil's. Like a titan's awakening, he was succumbing to the greater being.

She grasped Ekosa's shoulder with her free hand and nudged him with her mahia. He looked at her, startled.

"Raise your walls." Leiyn twisted her mouth into a grin. "I'm not fishing you out of the ocean if you decide to jump in."

Ekosa hesitated, then nodded. Only then did she withdraw her hand. As his esse disappeared from her lifesense, the *eesu* sighed, his shoulders slumping.

"Thank you." He included both Leiyn and Ketti with his gaze before returning it to the Veil. "I fear I almost did something foolish."

"Thank the spirits you did not." Ketti drew close to his side. "I do not know how to swim."

He smiled and drew his arm around her.

Loath as she was to interrupt, the looming Veil left Leiyn with scarce choice. "Ketti, you're our best candidate for trying to tame it while I helm the titan. You mind?"

"Of course."

The Eteman drew away from her beloved and stepped forward. Tilting back her head, Ketti spread her arms like a priestess receiving a benediction from Omn.

Then she speared her mahia forward like an arrow, driving into the heart of the Veil.

It stirred in response. A whirlpool formed from the mist before them. Apparitions appeared and vanished too swiftly for Leiyn to catch their forms. The whirlpool seethed, foam frothing up in spirals. There was a violence to it now, a hostility in the shapes it took. They were intruders, unwelcome here.

They should not have come.

Leiyn stepped forward and reached out a hand. "Ketti, wait—"

A tentacle lashed out from the fog—but it did not strike Ketti.

Leiyn threw up her arms as it fell upon her. The blow was not physical, and the mist did little more than kiss her flesh, yet it bludgeoned her esse and drove her to her knees. Her lifeforce shuddered beneath it, writhing and breaching the barriers of her body.

Her hold on the reef whale slipped. Snarling, blinded by pain, Leiyn clawed back for it. Brine shrank from her like a frightened beast. He retreated the only way he knew how.

Brine began to submerge.

Her friends were shouting, but Leiyn blocked them out. *I submit!* she pleaded with the titan. *Let me back in, please!*

The reef whale shuddered to a halt. Hesitantly, he accepted her touch. She was sorely tempted to seize hold of him again, but prudence bade her to remain patient. Far from a simple matter when the Veil loomed over them, the lifeforce within it ablaze.

The titan accepted her command once more. Leiyn blinked her eyes open and raised her head. The Veil was inches before the titan. Even as her vision resolved, its nose entered the space.

The whirlpool before them scattered apart, like a starfish

pulled asunder. The bank of fog parted into a tunnel large enough to admit them, though one shrouded in gloom. Even her lifesense could not perceive its end. Within the mist, the ocean fell eerily calm, the natural currents not able to touch it.

Sarryl growled, low and rumbling. Batu reassured the moonbear with a few murmured words.

"Leiyn?" Teya gripped Leiyn's shoulder, her fingers digging in. "Are we alright?"

"Yes. Sorry." Leiyn clambered back to her feet with her beloved's help. "Just caught me by surprise."

"Us as well." The *situal* stared into the misty tunnel as they passed through its initial arch. "I hope that is our last surprise."

Leiyn quieted her doubts and moved toward Ketti, who still cast her mahia ahead of them. "Are you forming this?" she asked, waving a hand forward. "This tunnel?" She spoke in a hush, the atmosphere too oppressive to speak loudly.

Ketti tilted her head, her gaze distant. "I do not know."

Leiyn furrowed her brow. Before she could ask more, Ekosa shot her a silencing look. She relented, seeing the wisdom in his caution. So long as the Veil remained compliant, they did not need to know more.

Batu moved to stand by Leiyn's shoulder. "What happened back there?" he murmured. "Did you provoke it?"

She raised an eyebrow. "I don't offend everyone I meet."

He chuckled. "Then why do so many act like you do?"

Leiyn decided it was better not to answer that. "Not sure what happened. Ketti reached into it, then it lashed out at me."

Ketti spoke before Batu could. "The *kainox*. Your leashing offended it."

"It took offense?" Teya stared around at the fog, looking as if she could not decide whether to laugh or weep. "What is this thing?"

"Alive." The Eteman whispered, yet in the calm, all could hear her. "It is alive."

No one had a response. With the stillness in the ocean and the fog dampening sound, an eerie silence fell over them. Only the gentle sounds of the reef whale's swimming pierced it.

Leiyn glanced over her shoulder to find the entrance already lost in darkness. They pressed through, not knowing how far this fog extended. Not knowing if this was the safest way through.

Too late for doubt now.

She guided Brine forward into the heart of the Veil.

28

THE CRADLE OF CREATION

Their voyage through the fog stepped outside of time. With the sun blotted out, only a faint gray pall told of the sun still risen. Distance was obscured by shadows. How far they had come, how long they had traveled, were left to speculation.

Leiyn clung to the titan, desperate to not let it slip from her grasp again. She darted her eyes about her, a field mouse stalked by an owl, not knowing from where it watches. She sagged under the weight of the Veil's regard, though she tried not to let it show.

The esse in the mist made it bright to her lifesense, almost dazzling. Almost, it seemed like they swam through. It saturated her being like water would clothes.

A similar disquiet claimed her companions. Only Ketti seemed serene as she forged their way forward. Occasionally, the Eteman looked around, a small smile on her lips. For the first time since Solace, she looked as if she had forgotten her torment.

Leiyn wished she felt half as sanguine. When nothing

appeared to attack them, she hunched down next to Teya and the others. In silent vigil, they watched Brine press forward.

A long while in, Teya finally broke the silence. "How far must we go? I cannot sense its end."

"Nor can I." Leiyn raised her gaze from the placid water, which she had been watching as their passage stirred it into ripples.

"Perhaps we shall never leave." Teya picked off a loose piece of coral and tossed it into the sea. "We have become *lakan*, ghosts held from our next lives, forever floating upon the ocean."

Leiyn elbowed the scout in the ribs. Teya let out a muffled laugh. It drew the stares of the two men, who had huddled together in their own conversation.

"Quiet," Ketti spoke up suddenly. "Look ahead."

They silenced and stood, straining their senses forward. Fresh movement stirred within the Veil's lifeforce. Leiyn tensed as she beheld it.

Another whirlpool.

This one was not only in the mist, but the water. It did not lie directly on their path, but slightly off to the side, just close enough to be visible. At its center gathered...something. She could feel esse layering, a brighter star amid the glittering fog. She perceived matter to it as well, heaping and sinuous.

Seaweed, she realized as they neared it, the briny scent giving it away. *Seaweed and kelp.*

They were almost abreast of it, allowing the others to get a look at it. "What is it?" Ekosa whispered with wide eyes.

Ketti answered, certainty in her voice. "The Veil's creation. Its child."

Leiyn could not look away. Whatever spawn this was, she wanted nothing to do with it. She would have guided the reef whale far out of its way if she dared to leave their misty corridor. All they could do was hope the swell would not pull them in.

Teya gasped and leaned back, looking as if she had been struck. "No. It cannot be..."

"What?" Leiyn combed the scout over with her mahia, fearing the Veil had struck her without Leiyn sensing it. She found no injury. "What happened?"

"I am fine, Leiyn. But that thing... I believe it is a *kainox*. Or it will be."

A titan. Created. It should have been an impossibility. Titans were supposed to be fixtures of the landscape. Neither beast nor spirit, neither land nor element, they were entities that defied comprehension. Ever before, they had seemed old as time itself, existing since Omn formed the world with Its gaze.

But as she beheld the coagulating being, Leiyn could think of no refutation.

Stunned, she resumed her vigil as they came beside the twisters. The water sucked at Brine's fin, but it seemed a gentle eddy, so weak that Leiyn could have outswam it. If this was a titan, it was very early in its formation. She could scarcely discern a shape among the seaweed. Only the esse churning through it and its twitching betrayed what it was. Or would become.

The reef whale carried them past the whirlpool and nascent titan. Leiyn let her gaze linger on it, then faced forward. They might never understand what they had witnessed. Yet it was something she would never forget.

The Veil ended a short time after. Leiyn winced as they emerged from it, eyes grown unaccustomed to the sun's glare. Omn still shone on the other side of the misted barrier. After their time in the gray gloom, It was blinding as the light caught on the crests of the waves rising from the unsettling stillness.

Momentary discomfort, however, was preferable to being caught in that place.

As they left the fog bank behind, everyone turned back to gaze upon it. Phantom creatures appeared from this side as well, awakening in blazes of lifeforce before rejoining their misty mother.

Ketti broke the silence. "We have legends of titans such as these. *Kainox'tlal*—world titans. In them is contained the power of creation. My people say they created all of Etema. The mountains and hills. Rivers and lakes. Plains and valleys. Even some spirits and beasts, their gentler kin."

Leiyn glanced at the Eteman, wondering at the movements in her lifeforce. Was it triumph that flashed through her pearls? Sorrow in how esse churned in her limbs? Contradiction worked up and down her body as she beheld this being that belonged to myth.

Ketti's reaction only heightened Leiyn's awe.

"The creatures of mist," Ekosa said. "I wonder if any of them are real."

"Maybe they're dreams." Batu seemed mesmerized by the Veil still, a hand resting on the broad shoulder of his spirit companion. Sarryl stood in seeming contemplation, the steadiness of his gaze betraying intelligence beyond any ordinary bear.

"Perhaps," Ketti replied. "But dreams mean little until they come true."

She turned and walked away to sit at the fore of the reef whale, arms curled about her legs. Leiyn tarried, wondering if she should go to her. Ekosa moved first, going to sit by her side.

Batu and his bear watched the world titan grow distant. Teya stepped up next to Leiyn and followed her gaze. "Titans like that make you wonder, do they not?"

"Wonder what?"

The scout eyed her sidelong. "Do not tell me you did not contemplate its power. What damage it could wreak upon our enemies."

Leiyn wondered how she had not. Had her sharp edges grown so dull? She grimaced and turned away.

"Doesn't matter," she said over her shoulder. "Titans like that can't be leashed. Too vast. Too powerful. Ketti barely formed a passage through it. Commanding it would take far more than that."

Teya pursued her, leaning close. "But what if there was a way? Not only to awaken it, but bond with it? Sharo could not stand against us."

Leiyn could not say why, but the thought filled her with disquiet. "Maybe. If we survived it. But I have Clouded Fang. He'll be enough."

Her beloved hummed, a sound both teasing and disapproving. "Do not close your mind again, Redlock. We are few enough as it is. To win this war, we may need to achieve the impossible."

When Leiyn did not answer, the scout let out a low, humorless laugh, then wandered down the titan.

Though she had denied the idea to Teya, it filled Leiyn's mind for hours afterward. She glanced over her shoulder until the towering misty wall faded from view. Even then, she could not entirely banish the thought.

Power to kill any lyshan. Power to topple an empire.

She did not yearn for it any longer. But a ranger never discarded a useful arrow. She tucked the thought away, then set her focus on the long, watery road that spread ahead.

29

THE OLD WORLD

In the days after the Veil, their burgeoning routines dug in deep roots. It was all they could do in the face of the monotonous surroundings and unrelenting elements. Thoughts of what lay behind—and ahead—would drive them mad if they let them.

Each found their way of coping. Batu and Sarryl practiced joining, attempting to increase the rate at which they merged into one being. The transformation necessitated a lack of clothes, so the others averted their eyes while they were at it. Yet Leiyn could not help observing through her lifesense, fascinated by the unnatural process.

Over the days, they reduced the process to mere minutes, but Batu expressed frustration that it was still too slow.

"If we're ambushed," he replied when she tried reassuring him, "will we have minutes?"

Teya also set to expanding her capabilities when she was not attempting to bring levity to their dour party. Xepi's words seemed to have burrowed deep within her, for she explored her diminutive mahia with a zeal Leiyn had never witnessed from her. Leiyn did not hold out the same hope for

Teya that the shaman had expressed, but she still encouraged her, even as her beloved ran up against her limits time and again.

Frequently at the end of the day, Leiyn found the scout contemplating the talisman Xepi had given her. By her life-sense, she felt Teya prodding it with her mahia, even plucking at the webbing with a finger. Ignoring Leiyn's warnings, Teya remained determined to understand it through and through.

"Better to make a mistake now than in the thick of a fight," Teya pointed out, forcing Leiyn to relent to her logic.

Ekosa also confronted his limits. Each turn he took commanding Brine left him exhausted and stumbling in a half-dazed stupor. Leiyn tried convincing him to take fewer shifts, but neither she nor Ketti could dissuade him. Yet when Leiyn asked if he still wished to learn the knife, he climbed to his feet and stumbled through the simplest drills she could devise. She could not say he improved, but she hoped something would stick. Perhaps enough to save his life, should she fail to protect him.

You've failed many times before, a part of her taunted. *Bound to happen again.*

Ketti fared better physically but still seemed to suffer the most. For the long periods during which she commanded the reef whale, which could stretch into days at a time, she often sat alone or with Ekosa at Brine's head, gazing upon the hazy horizon. In the long silences and solemn contemplation, Leiyn recognized an echo of her own grief. She and the rest of their companions gave the Eteman the space she needed, only intervening when Ketti missed one too many meals or her vigils extended past prudence.

For Leiyn's part, when she was not guiding Brine and teaching Ekosa, she fretted over the many things out of her control. Seeking to escape her thoughts, she once extracted her journal and graphite pens only to despair at their bedraggled state. Her drawings were as she feared: smudged beyond recovery. She would have to reproduce all of them.

The least this war has stolen from me.

She made some half-hearted attempts to draw the marine animals that flocked around Brine's flanks and even tried depicting Feral as she had last seen the mare. But with the pages crinkled and the graphite uneven in application, she knew it to be futile. Artistic indulgences would have to wait for more peaceful times—should they ever come.

The one daily ritual that stuck was plying at her bond to Clouded Fang. She hummed the thread with esse and waited to see if the ash dragon would respond. Occasionally, she felt his regard turn on her, burning eyes staring across the watery leagues. Most often, he gave no response. She could not tell if he recovered from his battle against Breakbay's salt titan. That alone was cause for worry.

She had fought lyshans without him before. Khamo would have slain her if not for Clouded Fang. If he left her or perished, they had no hope for victory.

Unless you bond with another.

The thorny idea cut her to consider, but she held it gingerly, as she would a porcupine. She had bonded once with a titan; could she not do it again? Distasteful as it might be, she had to win this war. She would do whatever she must to see those she loved through it alive.

Those few who remained.

Seventeen days had passed since the Veil when something interrupted the horizon.

"Come look!" called Ekosa from where he helmed Brine at the titan's head.

Leiyn hurried with the others to join him. The golden light

preceding sunset streamed through the sky, casting shadows over the seascape and confusing the eyes. Yet as Leiyn squinted toward where the *eesu* pointed, she drew the same conclusion.

"Land." She shared a smile with the others.

The elements and strange form of travel had worn on them all. Even esse-infused clothes could not keep them from crusting with salt from numerable dips into the sea. Brine always reeked of fish and seaweed. Leiyn's hair hung heavy in its braid, stiff and greasy. Her teeth felt filmed with grime.

But the anticipation of landlocked liberties was short-lived. Ashore, their enemies awaited them along with their bloody duty. Their reprieve was drawing to an end. If the lyshans proved as persistent as they had been in the Veiled Lands, they would see little rest in the days to come.

Even more concerning, they could not be certain they had reached their destination. They had tried to navigate true to the Ancestral Lands, but the constellations had grown unfamiliar the farther they roamed, and mahia could only stretch so far. None of them knew what distant shores they approached. They might be mere leagues away from Vasara or across the continent.

This first landmass appeared to be an island. Flickers of esse told of its occupation before the lighthouse came into view. At Leiyn's urging, Ekosa directed the reef whale to give it a wide berth.

But their presence had not gone unnoticed. Their touch was light, their lifesense thin as mist, but Leiyn had advanced too far in her mahia to be eluded. Calming her esse so as not to alert their watcher, she tentatively stretched toward the structure to detect its source. It was as she feared: a maha resided among the people. Of what origin remained to be seen.

"I feel him, too," Ketti murmured.

"Feel who?" Batu demanded. "Someone with magic?"

"Yes." Leiyn gestured toward the structure. "That's Kalgan design, isn't it?"

Batu studied it for a moment. "Yes," he said at last. "See the flying eaves?"

"*Fesht.*" She kept her curse soft, but the others tensed at it, sensitive to shifts in their party's mood. "We're far off course," she explained. "There are islands near the northern and southern borders. Even if we're fortunate and in the north—"

"—the Eyin Empire lies between it and Ilberia." Ekosa grimaced as he finished her thought.

Batu scowled at the island, as if it were to blame for their quandary. "Then we're a hundred leagues off course."

"At best," Teya amended.

Batu laughed, harsh and hard-edged. Sarryl rumbled and shouldered him. His wildsoul reached down to curl his fingers into the moonbear's fur, his scowl lessening a touch.

Leiyn swallowed her disappointment. "It's not all bad news. We reached the Ancestral Lands atop a titan in a fraction of the time it would have taken otherwise. And we have a rough idea of where we are and the direction we need to go." She pointed north, easily established with the sun low behind them. "Maybe we take a week longer than we hoped. But we'll be at Vasara soon enough."

The dejection of the others lightened. Teya nodded. The furrow in Batu's brow lessened. Only Ketti seemed untouched, her features as haggard as before.

"Ship," Ekosa announced, pointing around the northern edge of the island. "Coming our way."

Leiyn focused her lifesense in its direction. "With two more mahas," she said. "Or wisdoms, rather."

"We do not need conflict." Ketti stepped up next to Ekosa, resting a hand gently on his narrow shoulder. "Take us up the coastline. We should be able to outrun them."

The *eesu* nodded and closed his eyes—his habit when

sending commands to the titan. Brine proved compliant, shifting their course to the left. The sway of the titan's swimming grew more pronounced as they picked up speed.

Esse flashed into Leiyn's lifesense. Before she could make sense of it, Ekosa keeled over as if struck.

"Ekosa!" Ketti kneeled over the fallen *eesu*, her mahia diving into him. Leiyn felt the dark rifts that had been driven through him. Brine rumbled below them, then began to submerge.

The huntress awoke within her.

"Shield him!" Leiyn snapped at Ketti, then glanced at Teya and Batu. "Ready for an attack. I'll helm Brine."

Both nodded. They had drawn their weapons already, but Batu now replaced his and bent toward Sarryl. Whatever he murmured made the moonbear turn toward him, huffing a breath.

"Your clothes," Leiyn reminded as she turned away, intuiting his intentions.

"Right."

Cloth swished as Batu stripped off his garb. Leiyn spared her companions no more attention, sending her mahia diving into the titan beneath them.

Submit, she commanded Brine. *As I submit.*

Though not bonded, they had grown familiar over their weeks together. The reef whale did not resist as she leashed him to her will. With a thought, Brine resumed his quickened pace and rose higher out of the water, stabilizing their journey.

She had only just settled when the first blow came. It lacked the power to injure her but hit hard enough to smart. Snarling, Leiyn raised her mahia's walls. They would not be impregnable so long as she commanded a titan, but any wisdom of average ability would be too feeble to break through.

The scream from behind had her spinning back with her

falchion raised. She had feared that, with her walls raised, the wisdoms sought easier prey in Teya and Batu.

A far worse sight greeted her.

This attacker was a monster of flesh and scale. Tentacles, each as thick around as Leiyn's thigh, whipped like flails at her friends. Batu had not had time to complete the joining with Sarryl, so he fought shirtless with the moonbear at his side. Already, bruises and scarlet streaks decorated his bared skin.

Other tentacles found purchase in Brine's coral, dragging a bulbous body up behind. The bulk of the creature was more incomprehensible still. A shark's head rested above the scaled torso from which the tentacles extended like a grotesque lion's mane. Finned feet tipped with sharp claws dug into the titan's tender flesh. Brine's pain coursed through Leiyn's mind.

She might have still believed it was a strange beast risen from the deep but for its esse. Cracking open her walls, she glimpsed hundreds of damned souls writhing within, all battling for supremacy.

Only one creature embraced such perversion.

"Lyshan!" Leiyn roared, then charged with blades leading.

30

MONSTERS FROM THE DEEP

Forged titanbone caught the dying light as Leiyn drove her falchions toward the nearest tentacle.

The lyshan was not negligent of her attack. Even as four tentacles swatted at Batu and Teya, two slid around Leiyn's blades to attack her. Curses slipped past her lips as she evaded the first silver limb.

The second battered into her ribs and sent her sprawling.

She hit Brine's back and rolled to her feet. The strength of the blow had her coughing for breath. But for her Iritu armor, her ribs would have shattered. Drawing in esse from several amber beads, Leiyn fueled her limbs with strength and speed, then drove back at her enemy.

Brine shifted, nearly sending her rolling down the whale's precipitous side as she lost her balance. A titan's emotions were not like a human's, but Leiyn had spent enough time with Brine to sense his disturbance. She sent calming thoughts through their connection even as she resumed her charge.

The titan's shudder had disrupted the others as well. The lyshan had slipped farther down Brine's side but quickly regained its perch. Batu and Sarryl stood with axe and claws at the ready. Teya sported an ugly red mark down one side of her face, but her esse still shone brightly and her expression was determined. She had Xepi's webbed artifact in her hand, her intentions clear.

Alarm fanned into rage. Rangers were not supposed to vent their emotions and warn of their attack, but Leiyn could not contain the shriek that ripped free of her throat. Reflexes quickened, she evaded a tentacle's lash, then sliced both blades forward. She chose her placement well; the lyshan could not avoid both of them.

Amber ichor sprayed as the shorter falchion sliced through the tentacle.

The shark mouth gaped wide, then the lyshan rushed up the side of the reef whale. Batu went flying from a lashing silver tentacle; her lifesense showed him to be injured but alive farther down Brine's back. Lacking protection on his upper body, he was lucky to have survived.

Teya ducked another blow and drove her titanbone speartip into the scaled flesh but could not close in to use the talisman. Sarryl bellowed and launched his massive bulk forward, the moonbear a force to be reckoned with, even without being joined to Batu. His hooked claws and sharp teeth tore through the writhing appendages. Golden blood sprayed, joining the red spotting the coral at their feet.

Fear drove her as much as fury now. Her companions were too frail, too vulnerable.

End it, Firebrand!

Leiyn wove through the lashing limbs, dealing slight cuts as she went and advancing on the lyshan. Blows rained down on her, but reinforced with enchanted armor and overflowing lifeforce, she weathered them.

Yet she could not find a path through. The tentacles were still too many and too thickly crowded together. A thicket of scales and flesh spread between her and the enemy.

So she began hacking her way through.

The lyshan moved quickly, but it could not evade her. Again and again, her falchions found its flesh and carved through it. Ichor saturated her clothes and spurted against her face. She spat as some found its way into her mouth, cloying and earthy as half-rotted meat.

Finally battered into retreat, Leiyn withdrew and took stock. Bruises layered her body and her muscles ached, but the monstrous lyshan had lost three more tentacles. Only two remained harrying its mortal combatants, while two still anchored the lyshan against the side of the ocean titan. The stumps of the other four writhed around like headless serpents not yet embracing death.

She had rallied to press forward again when an unusual sensation against her lifesense gave her pause. The severed tentacles were not entirely necrotic; esse churned up their lengths to seethe against the exposed ends. Leiyn watched in dismay as amber-smeared tips pressed free of the pale meat. In moments, they protruded a foot long, rapidly replacing what had been lost.

The wide mouth of the shark yawned, taunting as a smile, dagger teeth gnashing together.

"Keep back!" Leiyn shouted to the others.

She sent fresh esse to her wounds, healing and bolstering them, then drew recklessly from the rest in her pouch. A bloated feeling filled her even as she channeled it into all the energy her muscles could handle. Never before had she felt stretched so thin.

Head throbbing, heart galloping, she drove forward. Her foot slipped on coral slick with blood. A fortunate happenstance—a pubescent tentacle swung through the air overhead, strong enough to decapitate.

Leiyn gained her feet and resumed her charge. Her falchions danced among the limbs. Like scythes through grass, she cut through them. Tentacles not yet regrown were shaved even shorter. The last two received their own injuries.

Even severed, the tentacles could kill. The lyshan bashed them into her from every angle, her blades unable to keep them at bay. Her clothes lost their glow as the enchantments in them died. Only the brimming esse in her body kept her bones from breaking.

Then she was through the labyrinth of limbs and soaring toward the silver monster beyond them. The lyshan gaped its wide mouth soundlessly at her. A scream? A plea for mercy?

She drove the twin fangs of titanbone deep into her enemy's chest.

For a disorienting moment, she thought she had missed. Then she realized the truth. The lyshan, still glowing feverishly with life, had let go of the titan.

Plummeting them both toward the ocean.

Leiyn worked her legs between them, placed her boots on its broad chest, then kicked, trying to pull the blades free. Before she could, half a dozen appendages wrapped around her, crushing her to its chest.

They hit the surface of the water and plunged through.

The shock of the cold froze her, but the impact jolted her free of the lyshan's weakening grip. Saltwater spilled across her vision; the briny taste of it flooded her mouth. Choking, robbed of air, Leiyn still clung to her falchions. She worked a boot against her adversary and tugged at the blades again. They pulled loose in clouds of shimmering ichor, a sight strangely beautiful.

Her eyes stung as she paddled away. With the blades leaving its body, the lyshan whipped back into motion. Already, the darkness through its lifeforce began receding as the corrupted Iritu repaired the damage she had done. Even with mangled tentacles, it had adapted to thrive here. She could not match the speed with which it undulated through the water with any amount of esse.

Leiyn thrashed, kicking for the surface. But she could not swim fast enough.

It hit with the impact of a galloping horse. A hundred knives drove into her flesh, gnawing and rending. Dark clouds of her blood washed over her face into her mouth.

Spitting, drowning, Leiyn bolstered her flagging strength. Though each movement tore her flesh more, she reared back, then drove the falchions into the lyshan's head.

Her enemy went stiff. She had pierced where the brain would lie on an ordinary creature, but the Iritu did not operate the same as mortal beings. It was not enough to kill it. Yet it seemed stunned, and the jaws making mincemeat of her midriff ceased to gnaw.

Keeping hold of her weapons, Leiyn writhed free and stemmed the worst of the bleeding with a flood of esse. Faint-headed, she barely clung to consciousness. Her heart raced too fast; her lungs strained for air. If she did not reach the surface soon, she would drown. But release her enemy and the lyshan would attack again. The result would be the same.

She saw but one choice: swim. Reaching for what little strength remained to her, Leiyn kicked for the surface with the lyshan in tow. Her falchions shifted in the flesh, but they did not pull free. The lyshan twitched, expiring.

But her enemy was dead weight, and she was too far gone. No matter how she kicked, she could not gain an inch, much less reach the surface. Darkness spotted her vision as she stared up at the fading light.

Let go, Firebrand, came a distant thought. So distant it almost seemed not to come from herself.

For a moment, she considered letting go of her burdens and simply floating in the ocean. Allowing the sea to sweep all her concerns away. But as her grip loosened on the falchions, she understood.

Let go.

She loosened her grip on the Iritu weapons. The hilts slipped free of her hands.

As the falchions sank with the lyshan, Leiyn swam for the surface.

31

LANDFALL

Even the two dozen paces to the surface felt beyond Leiyn, but thoughts of her friends kept her swimming. Her heartbeat hammered in her ears. Her lungs screamed. She kicked and paddled and reached with all her tattered will.

At last, the ocean released her.

Breaking the surface, Leiyn coughed and heaved up saltwater, then choked down air. For several moments, it was all she could do to float.

Fear of the approaching giant put life back in her.

Her lifesense had dimmed like her other senses, but she could scarcely avoid noticing a titan. Leiyn tried swimming aside, but she could do little more than tread water as she watched Brine surge through the sea, waves rising in his wake. Stranded below, the reef whale loomed larger than he ever had while atop his back.

She flinched, bracing for impact.

But Brine turned aside and slowed. A wave sloshed over her head. Coming up spluttering, she watched with tired relief as one massive forefin halted next to her.

A lithe figure dove from atop Brine's back. They plunged into the sea a dozen feet away, then emerged beside her.

"Leiyn!" Teya paddled the final strokes to her, terror rampant in her expression. "Are you hurt?"

Leiyn could not muster the energy to answer. Her heart pattered with the uneven rhythm of the gravely ill.

The *situal* must have seen it in her face, for she asked no more questions. Wrapping an arm around Leiyn's middle, Teya flinched at the feel of the torn clothes and ragged flesh, then started kicking for the whale. Leiyn helped as much as she could, though it amounted to little more than keeping herself afloat.

The fin, as wide as the training yard back at the Wilds Lodge, waited in the water for them. As the coral came beneath their feet, they staggered up the slick incline to the whale's side.

"Can you climb?" Teya asked between breaths.

Though far from certain, Leiyn nodded. She set her hands to Brine's flank and began laboring up. Teya came behind, covering her movements and steadying Leiyn with a hand when her grip failed or she missed a foothold.

Somehow, they made it to the top. Leiyn lay down, careful not to jostle her tender flesh. Her wounds no longer bled, but they were recent enough that they would open at the slightest provocation.

The others gathered around her. Batu crouched at her side, bloodied and beaten as well, but his lifefire burned high.

"You alright?" he asked.

Leiyn coughed up more seawater before croaking an answer. "Never better."

That won undeserved laughter from her friends. Ketti moved in with assurances of healing. Leiyn winced as her hands pressed lifeforce into her injuries. First came the burn, then the balm of mending. When the Eteman pulled away, Leiyn breathed easily once more.

Teya kneeled next to her, passing a scrutinizing eye over her. "You may need a change of clothes."

A glance down confirmed her assessment. The lyshan had chewed through both her jerkin and tunic, leaving them in rags and as devoid of esse as ordinary fabric.

"Not the Eteman set," she moaned.

Teya grinned. "I am afraid so."

Even Ketti smiled at that, though it proved fleeting.

"What happened to the Kalgans and their ship?" Leiyn looked around them, reaching out her lifesense as she did. Nothing was immediately around them, but she thought she sensed the lifefires of the wisdom and sailors leagues behind.

Teya shrugged. "They did not pursue. I would guess they did not wish to fight both a titan and a *sach'aan*."

"Guess wisdoms are wise." Leiyn donned a bland smile.

Her beloved rolled her eyes.

"Your swords," Ekosa spoke up. "Where have they gone?" He had the pinched look he always got when he took command of Brine.

Smile evaporating, Leiyn jerked her head toward the sea. "Sank with our new friend."

"Better them than you." Teya gripped Leiyn's hand, tight as if afraid she might slip away.

Ketti turned forward. "We may be out of danger for the moment, but we will not remain so. On the sea, we remain vulnerable."

Leiyn nodded, fearing what came next, but seeing no way around it. "So we make landfall."

"And walk the rest of the way to the Union?" Batu scowled toward the growing continent, as if it were to blame.

Ketti turned back to him, resolute. "On land, we may take refuge in grottos. Atop a reef whale, that is not possible."

They had considered the prospect in earlier discussions and discounted it. To enter grottos with a bonded titan was one thing; it was altogether another to do so with a wild titan. Out on the ocean, they had not wished to risk it, and Leiyn found little desire to try it now.

A wish for Feral to be there ambushed her. Not only would the mare make the trip north speedier, but she longed for her mount's unruly behavior.

To think I'd ever miss that old nag.

Leiyn roused from her thoughts to speak. "Besides, Ata is joining us. Sooner or later, she'll find us. From there, it's a step and a skip to where we need to go."

She did not mention the prospect that Ata would not come. That was not a scenario she wished to consider. Yet doubt glimmered in the others' eyes. She could not deny a similar anxiety stirring in her chest.

"Our only safe way forward is on land," Leiyn continued. "Without my swords, without Clouded Fang...I cannot protect you as I should."

Fear choked her. She coughed to cover it and looked toward the shore, now spread across the horizon. She pretended to study it for a place to land.

"Redlock." Teya brushed Leiyn's arm.

She did not pull away, though part of her wanted to. "Are we agreed?" Leiyn asked without looking around.

They murmured their assents, as soft as the sea.

The light had dwindled to gray by the time they found a suitable stretch of shoreline. Ketti took command of Brine to move him so close to the rocky beach that the titan looked as if he might become stranded. Then they tarried at the reef whale's head, reluctant to leave the titan who had provided them both passage and home for weeks on end.

Leiyn kneeled and pressed a hand to the rough, cornflower blue coral. Felt the thrum of life spreading below her.

"Thank you," she murmured, pressing her feelings into a pulse of esse.

Though Ketti still commanded him, she felt the whale's regard. Almost, she thought her warmth mirrored as lifeforce tickled up through her feet.

Leiyn rose, knowing they should delay no longer than they must, and shouldered her pack and bow. Though the falchions had been lost to the sea, she still wore their scabbards on her hips next to her remaining anelace and the Eteman dagger she had claimed from Solace. They did not impinge her climb down the side of the titan to its broad flapper but seemed to move too freely without the blades.

How will you kill lyshans now, Firebrand?

Beyond the fin lay a shallow swim to shore. Leiyn lingered after the others, watching most for Ketti's progress. Ekosa assisted her and seemed to be trying to teach her to swim, though the rising tide did most of the work pressing her toward shallower waters. Batu and Sarryl went next, remaining close behind their companions in case they needed assistance. Teya waited for Leiyn. Together, they leaped in. The seawater was shockingly cold before her esse warmed her limbs.

It was a gradual slope to the rocky shore. Soon, they were plodding through the shallows rather than swimming. Moving beyond the surf, Leiyn reached Ketti and turned back with her to the reef whale. The Eteman pressed her hand to her forehead and bowed. Leiyn felt her emit a matching pulse of esse as she released control.

"*Burumu etak akki, basamu ersu akki,*" Ketti murmured.

Ekosa translated. "'The skies watch over you, the lands cradle you.'"

With the leash severed, the titan moved away. Brine shifted his bulk with mighty strokes of his flippers and tail. The sea groaned as he turned around. In minutes, he was moving back out toward deeper waters. Back to Breakbay, his home, Leiyn could only assume.

"Come," Batu called from closer to shore. "We must take shelter."

The encroaching darkness hurried them along. Though their surroundings were illuminated to Leiyn's lifesense, lyshans could hide from mahia. She needed her eyes as much as her hidden sense to guard against unwanted visitors.

The beach was composed largely of gray stones, many of them as big as their boots, while a few were bloated into boulders. They clambered over them to a rise atop which a stunted meadow spread. On the other side of it lay more tufted grass in a marsh that smelled of salt and moldering mud.

"We should be beyond the tide here," Ekosa said, gazing about them. "And it looks unlikely to be better farther on."

"Then this is our camp," Teya said with faux cheer. "Ketti?"

At a motion from the Eteman, they gathered around her and braced themselves. Ketti shifted them into a grotto without fanfare. Though the transition went easily, Leiyn exhaled as it completed. Even having grown adept at handling it, she wondered if she would ever truly grow used to it. As before, Sarryl's appearance transformed, his edges misting and his heavy body seeming likely to waft away in a strong wind.

They set up camp. With her Iritu outfit in shreds, Leiyn reluctantly changed into her extra set of clothes, the Eteman garb given to her by Ketti's mother. Though they fit just as well, she could never grow used to the garish colors, the aqua and violet bright even in the gloom.

By the time they lay on their bedrolls, still damp from their dip in the sea, only the light of the moons and stars remained.

To Leiyn, though, the latent magic of grottos made the air shimmer like starlight danced among them.

She closed her eyes and let her lifesense drift with the sparks.

A wave lapped against her cheek, warm and wet. A pleasant greeting of the ocean.

But I'm not on the sea.

Leiyn bolted upright, staring at the creature that darted back from her. In the moments before her mind came fully awake, she wondered if she was still dreaming. What she saw was surely impossible. The creature had the shape of a small, sleek dog, but in place of fur, lustrous grass rustled in the breeze coming off the sea.

Then familiar ochre eyes locked onto hers, and she grinned. "Chispa! What are you doing here?"

She held out a hand, palm up. Startled by her abrupt awakening, the silver fox was slow to meet her invitation. Chispa sniffed as he approached, eyes never leaving her. Only after he took a proper smell did he consent to nuzzle her. She ran a hand along his snout, and he pressed harder into her.

Though she enjoyed the attention of the fox, suspicion intruded on the moment. "Is she here?" she murmured. "Did you help her find us?"

Chispa sat up and locked eyes with her again. The orange hues shifted to become mismatched: one white, the other a vibrant green.

Leiyn sighed, ruffled his head, and rose to wake the others. All were quick to rouse, the nerves of the day before not yet dissipated. With wary looks at Chispa, they repacked camp, then huddled together with their belongings held close.

Hesitating, Ketti triggered the transition. The grotto stripped away around them, returning them to the world.

A figure, blazing with lifefire, stood not two paces away.

"At last, the mortals awake." Ata rose from the ground with languid grace and a vaguely mocking smile. "Not a restful sleep, by your appearance. Did sea travel not suit you?"

"Atastimina," Ketti greeted her stiffly. Chispa was cheerier in his welcome, bounding over and rubbing against the dryvan's leg.

Leiyn narrowed her eyes at Ata. There seemed something different to the dryvan, subtle but distinct. As her gaze drifted across the tangle of vines and flowers that was her hair, she saw it: her pointed ears had elongated and sprouted into green feathers.

"Ah, you noticed, did you?" Ata brushed her talons through the tips. "Another wished to take passage with me. But oh, you've grown impatient, haven't you?"

Ata bowed her head and cupped her hands over her ears, like a child might when they were scared. Leiyn took a step back as her esse writhed, undulating through her head. Ketti gasped, and Ekosa and Teya flinched as well. Batu, not possessing lifesense, grew uneasy from their reactions, his esse stirring faster. Sarryl growled.

But the dryvan only scooped her hands to her mouth, then cast out her hands like she spread petals at a wedding. From them emerged a small flying creature, one instantly familiar.

"Biqqa." Ketti stepped forward, and the emerald hummingbird darted around her head, almost too fast to follow. The Eteman smiled at her old friend, though there seemed a touch of discomfort in her eyes.

"Touching reunions all around." Gone were Ata's feathery ears, replaced by the pointed wooden ones from before. Her deriding smile, though, remained the same. "But perhaps we have more pressing matters to be about. I'm afraid my brother will not be so happy to see you about. I have already avoided two of my Kin while awaiting your arrival."

"We ran into one as well," Leiyn said, lips quirking. "Seemed happy to see us."

The dryvan raised her mossy brows. "Did you? And did they survive the encounter?"

"No. But it took something of mine with it." She brushed her hand across the empty scabbards.

Ata hummed in her throat, much as Eld once had, and looked toward the shore. "My people rarely visited this land during the height of our civilization. We saw little need of it, with our Mothertrees across the sea. We'll find no storehouses here to supplement your arsenal." Green and white eyes traveled back to Leiyn's waist. "That Eteman dagger will cut but not infect. You must rely upon your arrows and titan, yes?"

"I suppose." She knew every bit how difficult it was to shoot a lyshan in possession of their faculties, especially if they went armored, as many of them now did. But it seemed she had little choice in the matter.

You marked Man'nah with an arrow. Khamo, too. What's a few more?

"But these are matters best discussed in safer environs." Ata swept her gaze over their party, her amusement heightened as her eyes rested on the moonbear. "Still loyal to your wildsoul, are you? Very well. You may come along."

Without a second warning, Leiyn felt them shift back into a grotto. Instinct had her bracing for it so her balance barely wobbled.

"Now," Ata said, ignorant of the others still adjusting to the transition, "we should set our sights on our next steps. You have spoken of the seat of Ilberian power at Vasara, have you not?"

Leiyn raised a hand. "Hold for a moment. What were you

up to? The Mothertree seed." She jabbed a finger toward Ata's middle. "Is it still inside you?"

The dryvan went still, her smugness vanishing. "That is not your concern."

Warning bells rang in Leiyn's head, but she pressed on. Saints knew she ignored danger often enough. "It took you away from our mission. We could have used your help at Breakbay. The titans there almost killed us, you know that? And on the passage across the sea—"

"They did not kill you," Ata cut her off. "Nor did my Kin on the sea. And yes, the seed changes all. But I have told you before: my mission remains the same. There can be no peace for any of us while Sharo continues his plans."

Will you kill him? she wanted to shout at the dryvan. But she knew a direct question would only draw out Ata's ire. Teya's warning look had her turning aside instead, attempting to tame her frustration.

"Looking forward, then," Teya said, diverting the conversation. "We planned on walking north, but I trust that is no longer necessary."

The dryvan squawked a laugh that had Leiyn hunching her shoulders. "Such banal forms of travel your kind must take!" Ata still grinned as her mirth subsided. "We can reach anywhere in these so-called Ancestral Lands in moments now that we no longer have an ocean to cross. As for our destination, I have a proposal."

"A proposal." Leiyn kept her tone flat, afraid that the sharp edges of irritation were creeping in. "And what would that be?"

Esse glimmered in Ata's unblinded eye. "A location that might prove advantageous to our mission."

Ekosa cleared his throat. "Should we not, ah, gather supplies? I do not mean to complain, but barely palatable fish and tepid seaweed have not made for the most appetizing fare.

A properly cooked meal would seem in order. Perhaps there is a town nearby where you might negotiate for us?" He looked at Batu.

Ata stared at the *eesu* with obvious impatience. Batu answered with more equanimity.

"I'm as eager for food as you are, Ekosa, but even if we found someone who took Tricolonies currency, we have little coin. And I don't think Sarryl would like me leaving him behind." He placed a hand between his bear's shoulders, fingers disappearing into the pale mist of his grotto form.

Ekosa looked torn by indecision. Leiyn decided to lay the matter to rest.

"Batu's right—it's too great a risk. But you'll still get a proper meal." She nodded at Batu and Teya. "We have three hunters among us. Move to an unpopulated area and we'll be able to provide for ourselves."

The *eesu* sighed and tossed up his hands. "At least the meat will be seared."

Ata's amusement waned with each passing moment. "If that is settled, might you be interested in where we are going?"

It grated on Leiyn, how the dryvan assumed they would go along with a plan she had yet to divulge. Once more, she stuffed down the feelings.

"Please," Leiyn said drily. "Enlighten us,"

Ata grinned, ferocity twisting her features. "There is an ally only a little ways outside the city we seek. One who possesses knowledge of this land and our enemy. One whom my little Kinblood might be particularly interested in."

Batu frowned at her. "Who?"

"I would not wish to spoil the surprise!" The dryvan swept her gaze across them until her disparate eyes settled on Leiyn. "Shall we pay them a visit?"

Already, she had reached the end of her tolerance of the dryvan's antics. There was a manic energy about her that had been absent since her fellow dryvans had been slaughtered at Sharo's orders. The Mothertree seed—or the promise of it—had changed her.

But Ata had yet to betray them. Swallowing a sigh, Leiyn found the others looking to her.

My decision, then.

"Like my father always said, better to do a thing than live in the fear of it." She gave Ata a tight nod. "Let's go."

The dryvan issued another shrieking laugh, then ripped away the thin veil separating them from the world.

PART V

A BIRTHRIGHT IN BLOOD

32

A DREAM OF GLASS

While trekking through the wilderness, there came moments of suspense, transitions before you knew what lay beyond. Like pressing aside thick brush that leads to a clearing or peering inside the depths of a cave. Wondering what lies beneath the rushing waters at a river crossing.

As she was torn across the land, Leiyn hung in just such a moment. Reality shattered over her again and again as if she burst through countless panes of glass. The shards did not scatter but drove into her eyes. On each was etched a cutting memory.

Isla, her face bloodless and still.

Tadeo, his body gory with wounds, sprawled among the corpses of the Suncoats he had slain.

The Etemans, doomed for having helped her escape the lyshans.

She wept tears of blood, but they did not blind her to the flashing scenes. Her ears filled with the screams of the dying. Over and over, all the deaths she had witnessed, all she had committed, burrowed into her mind and soul.

Most of all, she saw her victims. The Suncoats. The odiosas. The animals. Her poor dog, Licky, loyal even as she accidentally drained him of life.

As she felt she could endure no more, another figure emerged from the scarlet river, alive but no less unwelcome.

Sharo.

This could not be a memory, for even with his back turned, she noticed his differences. Though tall, there had always been a shriveled look to the lyshan, a senescence set in over long centuries. Now, even beneath his robe, she could tell the frailty had vanished. His shoulders were broader, his neck thicker. The skin on the back of his bared head seemed less the charred wood of a tree after a forest fire and more the smooth gray of river stone.

Sharo turned, and his eyes captured her. No mere pits existed there, their depths lit by esse, but gray, fleshy orbs dotted with black pupils. Like the prepubescence of spawning eyes.

Leiyn tried running, but she was caught in the dream's current. Sharo was not so confined. With a slow, deliberate stride, he walked toward her, unperturbed by the red water swirling around them.

Leave me be! She tried to scream the words, but there was no air in her lungs. Her limbs moved, but the lyshan only ever drew nearer.

As he came within her reach, Leiyn struck. It was like an infant striking an adult for all the strength she could muster. Sharo smiled as he caught her wrists. His lips were not mere lines, but ridges as supple as Ata's.

He leaned in as if for a kiss. Leiyn shrieked and struggled, but it was no use.

Let me go, let me go, let me go—

Sharo did not kiss her. No kiss could be so defiling, so greedy. He wormed down into her and grasped at her lifefire.

This was a parasite's bite, a stinger sucking blood. A violation of her body's barriers. She was powerless in his grip, helpless to escape.

Then something grabbed her ankle. Fearing a second enemy, Leiyn kicked, trying to dislodge its hold. But the pull was irresistible.

Ripped free of Sharo's probing, Leiyn was dragged through the scarlet pool. The lyshan's laughter followed her down.

33

BOORISH BEHAVIOR

Leiyn opened her eyes to find them wet.

Frantic, she scrubbed at them, fearing the worst. Moisture came away, but not blood. Tears beaded on the knuckles of her gloves.

She bowed her head and sucked in a breath. Crisp air greeted her. For a moment, all she could do was breathe and rub at her eyes. She flinched as she remembered the crunching glass that had filled them moments before.

Just a vision. A delusion.

Yet what she had seen of Sharo—had that, too, been mere fantasy? She had seen the changes wrought upon her enemy so vividly. His moldering touch had been tactile on her skin, his magic unguent against her soul.

Breathe, just breathe.

"Leiyn!" Teya hissed. "Get up!"

The urgency in her beloved's voice galvanized her. Leiyn blinked away the last of the tears and raised her head. By the dim morning glow, she saw her companions standing around her while she still kneeled. They laid hands on their weapons, though none yet drew them. Sarryl bared his teeth, a growl rumbling in his chest.

Only Ata stood at ease. As her eyes flickered to Leiyn, a knowing smile perched on her chestnut lips.

Just like her brother's smile.

She flinched and followed her friends' gazes. Before a toppled log and a banked campfire crouched a man and a hairy beast. Or so she thought—but as she watched, the two figures were becoming one. It was incomprehensible to her eyes, bodies distorting in ways mortals should never be capable of. Only by her mahia could she make sense of it.

Wildsoul.

Leiyn staggered to her feet and set a hand to her anelace, wishing she still had her falchions. "What's going on? Who is that?"

"A potential ally," Ata said without looking over, "if he would but listen." She addressed the transforming man, calm but exasperated. "Heed me, wildsoul. I have said we mean you no harm."

"Go away!" came the responding roar. "Leave here now!" The words came out garbled, the rage of a beast behind them.

Leiyn cursed Ata under her breath as she tried to rouse her sluggish brain. Before she could think of a way to calm the wildsoul, Batu and Sarryl stepped forward. The moonbear had ceased to growl, though he looked tense and ready to brawl, shoulders hunched and eyes focused.

Batu raised his empty hands. "I know you're angry. I'd be the same if you took me by surprise. But I think I could learn from you. That we could." He placed a hand on his bear's shoulder.

The wildsoul's joining halted. Fern-green eyes peered out from a grotesquely morphed face. The beast he was bonded with emerged halfway from his chest. Mud-brown, its back hooves pawed the ground urgently. A short, tufted tail flicked madly.

A boar?

"What do you want?" The man's voice remained roughened, but some of the rage had dropped from it. "Why have you come here? And how—?"

"Questions we would be delighted to answer," Ata interrupted. "But first, you must give us the chance."

The bright eyes shifted under the broad brow. "You. You're one of them."

"Them?" The revelation roused Leiyn from her malaise. "You've seen Iritu before?"

The boar-man turned his eyes on her. She tried not to flinch. As he appeared just then, there was something terrible to that gaze. A violence barely contained.

If he understood what she said, he gave no sign of it. The wildsoul turned his ferocious stare back on the dryvan. "Their kind cannot be trusted."

"Most can't. But she can." Leiyn jerked her head toward Ata.

"I am honored to hear it." The dryvan sketched a mocking bow.

"I'm Batu." Batu placed a hand on his chest, then patted his moonbear on the shoulder. "This is Sarryl."

The wildsoul stared at the pair. "Rhun," he rumbled. "And Bristle."

"Well met, both of you." Batu kneeled, coming eye-level with the half-joined man. "Please, Rhun, Bristle. If you cannot trust her, trust me. We won't hurt either of you."

Rhun glanced around once more. Then, with a groan, the wildsoul reversed the joining.

Already queasy, Leiyn looked away until the boar had fully emerged from the man's chest. Bristle backed away, tossing his massive head and snorting. Rhun was poorly clothed, his shirt torn up the front where his chest and neck had broadened. He did not seem to notice it.

"We shall see," the wildsoul said, his voice baritone still, but human once more.

As he gained his feet, Leiyn took him in. Even devoid of the boar, he had a savage appearance. Greasy locks of chestnut hair hung in tangled curls to his shoulders and fell over his face. His generous beard, tinged more red than his hair, was even wilder and looked to have never been trimmed. His face was leathery and deeply tanned, telling of a life spent outdoors, as was the skin visible through his torn clothing. Some of the color may have been from dirt—it was smeared across his forehead as if he had been rolling around in mud. Even before they had been ripped, his garments looked worn far past when Leiyn would have cast them aside. To call them patched would have been a disservice to seamstresses the world over.

Despite his barbaric appearance, his eyes remained striking and clear, betraying intelligence belying his squalid conditions. They also remained wary, promising swift retribution for betrayal.

He's been hunted. And has hunted himself.

Predator and prey—she recognized that caustic combination. The same as catalyzed within herself.

The boar snorted and nudged his human's side. He was larger than any Leiyn had seen before, longer than she was tall and weighing at least thrice as much. Yellowed tusks emerged from a broad face. His brown eyes, comparatively small, peered at her and her companions with more intelligence than she would have expected of such a brutish creature.

"I ask again," Rhun said, turning his shadowed eyes from Batu to Ata, "why are you here? What do you want with us?"

Batu opened his mouth but paused as Chispa and Biqqa moved forward. Leiyn wanted to call out a warning to the silver fox but stopped short. He usually fled at the first sign of danger. That he would approach this pair spoke volumes.

Bristle snorted and sauntered forth. They spent several moments sniffing one another, the emerald hummingbird darting about their heads. Then Chispa rolled over and yipped, playful and easy. The hog responded with a high-pitched squeal of his own and a shaking of his rump. Biqqa flew circles around them both, as excited as Leiyn had ever seen her.

Rhun laughed. "You making friends there, you silly beast?"

Bristle cocked his substantial head to look at his wildsoul. Seeing Rhun's smile, he turned back with a hop and a fresh squeal.

Postures relaxed. Leiyn found her own shoulders dropping. But as Ata propped a hand on her narrow hip and smiled, Leiyn tensed again.

"We wish you to join our cause," the dryvan announced.

The wildsoul let nothing show of what he thought of that. "What cause is that?"

Ata spread her arms wide. "To topple an empire!"

Leiyn stiffened her jaw. The animals might enjoy one another, but that did not mean they could be sure of Rhun. But like Isla, Batu had always been quicker to trust.

"To kill one like her." The plainsrider gestured to Ata. "He has done harm to us and our homes. Murdered those we love."

Batu bowed his head, a battle waged across his expression. A mirror of that war started up in Leiyn. Isla flashed through her mind, still vivid from the waking dream. Memories cut once more.

Preoccupied as she was, she almost missed the spasm in Rhun's esse.

"You've seen her kind before." She leveled a hard stare at the wildsoul. "You've met an Iritu, haven't you?"

Rhun met her gaze without flinching. "Yes."

"What was their name?" Batu asked. His moonbear tilted his head, betraying his curiosity.

"Don't know." The backwoodsman shook his head. "He never said."

"But it was male?" Leiyn pressed.

"Seemed so."

Ata chuckled and strode around the clearing. Leiyn tensed along with Rhun, watching the dryvan circle them. The animals, sensing the shifting mood, broke apart. Bristle moved so he faced wherever Ata paced, small eyes tracking her.

"We know who it is, little mortals," she said, voice singsong as she swayed with exaggerated strides. "Sharo would not ignore a Kinblood in this land. Though it seems you have landed yourself in his bad graces." She cast him a sidelong look. "Defied his will, if I must indulge in conjecture. You have a stubborn look about you."

Leiyn looked to Rhun, worrying he might take offense, but he showed no more emotion than before. The hog let out a grunt and shuffled toward her in an aggressive stance that told much.

"Bristle," Rhun grunted, gripping the coarse hair of his boar and bodily hauling him back. He cast Batu a somewhat sheepish look. "He's the stubborn one of us."

"I know the feeling." Batu smiled. Sarryl cast what seemed a disapproving glare at both wildsouls. That drew out Rhun's smile as well.

Leiyn didn't allow herself to be drawn into the good humor. "What did Sharo want? Why did he approach you?"

Rhun's smile slipped. "He didn't. Had a run-in with his soldiers in some ruins. Came within our territory." He mussed Bristle's head with rough fondness. "Went into the ruins to drive them out, and the one like her was there." He nodded toward Ata, still pacing around them. "He spoke with us. Seemed interested in our joining. But mostly, he warned us not to mess with what he had caged in the pit below."

"Caged?" Teya asked. "What was caged?"

Rhun glanced her way but answered Batu. "A titan. Wouldn't blame you if you don't believe me. But I know what I saw. Resembled a big cat, but all shadow and light. The not-man called it a sun tiger."

Not-man? And a titan caged? She might have thought it impossible once. But she had seen titans being excavated, had ridden upon one for weeks on end. The Iritu had forged weapons from their bones. Even such colossal creatures could be tamed, captured, and killed.

But here in the Ancestral Lands?

The titans of the Veiled Lands were the primary reason it was viewed as a barbaric and dangerous wilderness. Leiyn had always assumed that meant there were no titans back here in the old world. But titans existed here as they did everywhere else—or they had once.

Were they all caged? Killed? Driven away?

She had never encountered a maha of the Ancestral Lands that was stronger than her or Ketti, but Ekosa had opened her eyes to the expansive capabilities of their mahia. The *eesuwé* of Eyi were skilled in magical architecture; they had even built pillars similar to those used around Qasaar to keep away stray titans. Ilberia, too, had to have some sophistication in its use of mahia, even if it was implemented through subjugated odiosas.

Perhaps they had discovered ways of enslaving titans.

Rhun spoke again. "Bristle here wouldn't let things lie, though. After the man left, we took care of the soldiers, then freed the big cat." He chuckled. "Thought it would kill us, but it seemed grateful, if those things are capable of it. This great lump was certainly happy."

He nudged the boar with his hip, who huffed in protest.

Leiyn found her wariness waning. Strangers surrounded

Rhun, yet he did not hide his fondness for his hog. Ata had thought him valuable enough to seek, and Batu was no poor judge of character.

Swallowing a sigh, she stepped forward and extended an arm. "I'm sorry for mistrusting you. And for our companion thrusting us on you like this."

Bristle tensed at her approach, and Rhun eyed her outstretched arm mistrustfully. Just as she was about to withdraw, he moved to accept it, his calloused hand enveloping her forearm.

"Not the worst surprise we've had in the morn." The man grinned, revealing a mouthful of yellowed teeth.

Glad as she was for the warm greeting, Leiyn was just as happy to withdraw. The man's odor was every bit the match for his boar, and his breath was none too fair, either.

And you smell like a rose?

Rhun's smile faded as he looked around at Ata. "Can't promise to join your hunt. Have Bristle to think of, and my life, too. But you can join our camp." He jerked his head toward Batu and Sarryl. "Think I'll speak with those two."

Ata halted to face him. "That shall do for now. Enjoy your chat, Kinblood. The rest of us will otherwise occupy ourselves. Baths, perhaps, are in order?"

As the dryvan grinned at her, Leiyn grimaced and looked aside. Her gaze traveled to Teya, who shrugged. *Could do worse*, the scout seemed to say.

Leiyn turned to Rhun. "Point us to the nearest river and I'll be content."

34

WISDOM OF THE WILDS

While Batu and Ata stayed behind at Rhun's camp with the spirit beasts, Leiyn and the rest of their companions sought baths a month overdue. They left with Ata's assurances that she would hide them from the lyshans.

"So long as you do not stray too far," the dryvan said with a mocking smile.

Leiyn had been skeptical of the backwoodsman pointing them to a proper place to bathe with his own lack of hygiene, but the stream was as deep as her waist and ran cold and clear. Not sensing humans for several leagues upstream who might taint the water, she drank of it and found it tasted as sweet as it looked.

Once they washed the layers of salt and grime from their skin, Leiyn and Teya split off to hunt for meat, while Ketti and Ekosa foraged from the surrounding forest. After their near encounter with a lyshan the day before, she was reluctant to further split their party, but Ata's heritage still tingled across her awareness. She had to trust that the Iritu would not fail them.

She did not like using her mahia to hunt, but Leiyn opted for expediency. Discovering the lone stag took moments; tracking and lulling him into complacency for their arrows a little while longer. Its antlers spread wider and flatter than the deer of the Veiled Lands, almost resembling a moose, though they remained sharp-tipped. Had they not been hurrying, she would have drawn them for later comparison to the deer she knew. Perhaps, if there was idle time at camp, she would sketch them still.

With their quarry in tow, they trekked back to the wildsoul's camp. Batu offered to assist them upon their return, but they turned him away, leaving him to continue conversing with their host. While she helped Teya prepare the deer, Leiyn let her lifesense wander back to Rhun. Though it was prying without an explicit invitation, she peered into his lifemark.

Never stopped me before.

Wildsoul he might be, but he had no guard against her mahia. It was as simple as looking for the images to present themselves, one at a time. They began with a copse of trees much like the ones surrounding them. If she concentrated hard enough, she could pick up the gentle noises of a peaceful forest.

Where he feels at home.

The second image was more dynamic, depicting his boar rolling about in a mucky pond. An innocent, playful picture oozing with as much love as mud.

The other half of his soul.

The third ripped through with the fury of a wildfire. Leiyn flinched as cinders blasted against her lifesense, bright and painful. More burst out as timbers caved into a swath of houses. Humble abodes all, they were burning. Dark shapes strewn between the destruction told of people and animals recently slaughtered.

All he has lost.

Leiyn withdrew with her brow furrowed. Rhun longed for peace, but hatred burned deeper. The third image of the life-mark was often the most telling.

She wondered how that wrath would manifest. It could burn them as easily as whoever his enemy was.

They finished skinning the stag by the time Ekosa and Ketti returned with their finds. Berries, still somewhat green from the earliness of the season, roots, and wild onions made up most of it.

Leaving Teya to prepare the deer's organs, Leiyn washed her hands and went to where Ata stood staring out to the south. The dryvan did not look over as Leiyn joined her. Chispa came with her, rubbing against Leiyn's leg, then Ata's.

"You know," Leiyn said, "you could warn us before throwing us into danger."

Ata smiled, languid as after a night of drinking. "But wouldn't that be less amusing?"

They lapsed back into silence. Leiyn listened to the forest, observing the unfamiliar songs of the birds and humming of the bugs. Even after traveling many foreign lands, she never grew used to being out of her element. Chispa wandered toward the tree line, stopping several paces away to sit on his hindquarters and stare into the wilderness.

"What lies that way?" she asked at length.

The dryvan slid her eyes over to her. "Vasara. Can you not feel the city's stirring?"

Leiyn reached her lifesense out far, but wherever the city lay was beyond her reach. "Not yet."

"Hm. You have some way to develop yet, little fox."

She ignored the slight. "Then we are in Ilberia."

"Of course. Did I not say we would be?"

Leiyn held her tongue. As unreliable as Ata was, provoking the dryvan would only make her more so.

"The Devilwoods, some call this place." Ata smiled sidelong at her, sharp teeth peeking between her lips. "Appropriate, would you not say?"

Leiyn snorted a laugh. "As much as I'd like to flatter you, I doubt it was for your people."

"Perhaps not. Though those with Iritu blood are a different matter." She nodded toward the far side of the camp where the wildsouls bent their heads together. "I trust they are responsible for its reputation."

Curiosity nipped at her. Almost, she asked how wildsouls came to be in Ilberia at all. But evoking that dark past came with risks. Besides, Leiyn could hazard a guess. Even if the Iritu had not colonized the Ancestral Lands, they had certainly visited them since the last Mothertree burned. The same atrocities as they had inflicted upon the Gasts could have easily taken place here as well.

Some matters, however, could not remain untouched.

"On our way here, I saw something. A dream of sorts." Leiyn hesitated, the memories cutting anew.

Ata rolled her eyes. "All mortals believe their dreams to be remarkable when they're mere delusion. But if you must speak of it, do tell me about this *dream*."

Leiyn stifled her irritation. "Call it a vision, then. It felt real enough. I saw Sharo in it. He looked different. Haler. Like he was healing. Or...regenerating."

The dryvan's amusement drained away, leaving only the hard planes of a weatherworn tree. "He must be feasting, and feasting well."

"Feasting?"

Leiyn could guess what she meant, but needed it confirmed. Ata seemed to see it in her eyes.

"Yes," she murmured. "On mortal lifeforce. It must be the same for Osmet. The esse fuels their heritage to greater heights, ones from which they had fallen."

"Greater heights?"

Ata stared into the forest gloom, her gaze growing distant. "Stronger. More adaptable. Harder to kill." She blinked once, slow and deliberate, before shifting her eyes back to Leiyn. "We cannot know until we meet them. But meet them, we must."

Leiyn gave her a wry smile. "Didn't sail across the world just to turn back."

"No. Nor should you." The dryvan turned to face her. "You are like the Eteman warriors of old, Leiyn. Any of them were a match for my Kin." She returned Leiyn's smile with a sharp-toothed one of her own. "And you have me."

"Glad for it." Leiyn glanced at Chispa, barely shifted from where he had seated himself, then stared beyond into the forest. She tried to disguise her expression along with the flutter through her lifeforce. Her doubts were enough burden without encumbering her allies with them.

Ata had not been at Sharo's mercy. He had not ravaged Ata's being. Even if it had been a dream, even if it had not been him reaching into Leiyn, it had left a wound. One mahia could not heal.

You've scars aplenty, Firebrand. What's one more?

She spoke, hoping it would quiet her thoughts. "What do you hope to gain from Rhun?"

"Only what it does not cost him to share." Ata peeked at her through the cracked lid of her good eye. "Knowledge. A wildsoul knows this land as few others would. He may tell us all that we would not even know to ask. You would not wish to charge blindly at our enemies once more, would you, *Firebrand?*"

"We've taken too long reaching here as it is," Leiyn retorted. "Every delay gives Sharo more time to enact his plans."

Ata waved a hand through the air. "It shall not take long to convince the Kinblood. Once he realizes his and his beast's survival aligns with our goals, I'm certain we'll find him compliant."

"You knew Sharo contacted him."

"I suspected," Ata corrected. "My brother could not have failed to notice him, and he would have considered him both a threat and an opportunity. The better for us that Sharo menaced him. Rhun sees his position as irreconcilable now—or he will once we convince him."

Manipulating a man to assist in our murderous mission. Yet Leiyn did not speak against it. Though she hunted for vengeance as much as justice, it did not change the heart of the matter. Sharo was a danger to all, Rhun and Bristle included.

She just hoped their assistance would not cost the pair their lives.

"Look at them," Teya murmured, bloody knife tilting down as she glanced up. "It is like he is reunited with a lost uncle, even if they look nothing alike."

Leiyn looked aside from carving the stag into steaks to follow Teya's gaze. Even as the afternoon waned into evening, Batu still spoke with Rhun. They had only paused their discussions to take care of necessities, after which they resumed as if without interruption.

It gladdened her to see it. After all Batu had suffered, it was good for him to belong again.

She also felt a strange affinity to the backwoodsman. Something about his features—his reddish hair, his bright eyes—made him seem familiar. Only as one spark roused in her esse did she understand what that connection might be.

Mother.

Leiyn would have touched her lock of auburn hair had her

hands not been filthy. While she had inherited much of her father's darker coloring, that tress was the color of her mother's hair. Her eyes, too, had been inherited from her mother. *Bright as the sky,* as her father had once said, wistful and full of longing.

She looked away. A coincidence, nothing more. While red hair was uncommon in Baltesia, it was not unknown. She was "painting from wind," as Tadeo would have termed it.

Her stare did not go unnoticed.

"Leiyn," Rhun called. "Might we speak?"

Leiyn looked up. Though she felt hesitant, not knowing where their conversation might lead, they could not afford to slight a potential ally.

"Go on," Teya murmured. "I know my way around deer."

Nodding, Leiyn washed off her hands in a basin Rhun had supplied, turning its water pink, and walked toward them. Ketti and Ekosa's stares followed her from where they kneeled by the campfire cooking gathered roots into a palatable state. Chispa and Biqqa congregated near them as if interested in the fibrous stew. Ata was nowhere to be seen, having strode off into the trees some time before. Only the prickling of her heritage protecting them reassured Leiyn that she remained nearby.

Reaching the pair of wildsouls and their beasts, Leiyn tarried, seeing no place to sit. Batu noticed her searching gaze and stood, moving aside for her to take his seat.

"Need to stretch my legs," he said, flashing a smile at the older Ilberian before he and Sarryl moved off toward the woods.

Leiyn sat and tried not to stare at the boar beside Rhun. Bristle had lain down, but there was an energy to his presence that spoke of constant vigilance. Rhun, on the other hand, had a stolid calmness to him that reminded her of Tadeo.

Though Tadeo was cleaner.

"You wanted to speak?" she said into the gathering silence.

The backwoodsmen stared at her for a long moment, then nodded toward the campfire. "Why's she have stones in her skin?"

Leiyn followed his gaze to Ketti. "Tradition."

Rhun's gaze lingered, then he shrugged and looked back at Leiyn. "You were born in the Veiled Lands?"

"Yes." Leiyn gestured to the rest of her companions. "We all were."

He scanned the others, then returned his gaze to her, eyes flickering to her forehead. No, she realized—to her russet tress, pulled back with the rest of her hair into a braid.

He leaned in close. "You were born there. But your blood —that comes from my people."

Leiyn lifted her brows. "I think I'd know if I was a wildsoul."

His tangled locks swung like vines as he shook his head. "Not that. I mean being Asraichean. Didn't you know?"

"What is that, Asraichean?" The word was unfamiliar and formed differently from the Ilberian sounds she was used to. Yet recognition stirred in her, spreading through her chest like warm honey.

Mother? She quested after her mother's spark. *Why do you awaken?*

As ever, the fleck of lifeforce gave no answer, but only continued to pulse gentle heat, subtle as a star seen from the corner of your eye.

Rhun ran a rough hand through his jungly beard. "Was it your mother or father?"

"What do you mean?"

"The one with red hair." He held up one of his own locks, the grime filming them only partially dampening the fiery color. "Which was it?"

An innocuous enough question, but all it implied blockaded the air in her throat.

"My mother."

The wildsoul nodded, hand falling back to his leg. "The trait runs strong in us. In Asraicheans."

"Asraichean..." Leiyn pried the lock free of her braid to stare at it. A piece of her mother made manifest. She let it fall across her cheek as she looked up. "This is why you think we share blood?"

"Not only that. Your name—didn't you wonder about it? Doesn't sound like any Ilberian name I know."

Leiyn shrugged. During her childhood, she had been teased for it, but children picked at anything that stood out. And it had been her mother's name. She had thought little beyond that.

"And your eyes." Rhun leaned down to peer into them. "A blue for the heavens."

She looked away, tucking the loose lock behind her ear. To her horror, a blush crept across her cheeks.

"You haven't told me what that means," she said, as much to distract as out of curiosity.

"Asraichean?" Rhun straightened and spread an arm. "Our people were the first to live here. 'Farst and laest,' as my mother used to say. Though looks like we won't last that long."

"The first," Leiyn repeated as she followed his gesture to the forest. "The first inhabitants of Ilberia?"

"Aye—and Kalga and Eyi once, so the stories say. 'The Flames of the Hills,' we were once known, and not only for our hair." Rhun grinned, every stained tooth on display. "We made sure the invaders from the east burned, but they were too many and too strong. We Asraicheans faded to embers—yet embers still smolder, no?"

She shared a fleeting smile with him, but the revelation was too strong upon her to sustain. "Ilberians were colonists here. This isn't their native land, no more than the Veiled Lands."

"Long ago, aye." Rhun shrugged. "They have made it theirs now."

Just as Baltesians have made the Veiled Lands their home.

She closed her eyes, thoughts spinning in the darkness. Over and over, innocents were invaded, displaced, winnowed. Time and again, warmongers laid claim to what did not belong to them. In her veins ran the blood of both conquerors and the conquered. Colonist and native. Victim and aggressor.

You've always been a contradiction, a part of her whispered. *That hasn't changed.*

Yet it seemed the world had shifted, like the transition to a grotto. Only this change took place within.

Opening her eyes, Leiyn met Rhun's lingering gaze. His green eyes, as bright and vibrant as hers.

"Thank you," she murmured. "For all of this."

She stood and turned away while he remained seated.

"Should you wish to know more," he spoke to her back, "I am here."

Leiyn moved to help Teya with the deer, eager to busy her hands. Perhaps then she might sift through all that swirled through her head.

35

TO KILL A KING

By sunset, Leiyn and Teya had carved the deer into strips and begun smoking them over a separate banked fire. Over the original campfire, they cooked steaks to share with the others. Only Ketti refused, remaining herbivorous in her people's way. Without time to cure and salt to flavor, it made for a tough, gamey meal.

Better than fish, she reminded herself as she ripped off a fresh bite.

Ata returned as they finished eating, striding into the camp without greeting or acknowledgment of her absence. Moving to stand next to Leiyn, she leveled her gaze at Rhun.

"I have given you time to consider, Kinblood. Will you aid our injudicious quest?"

Rhun glanced at Batu, who sat next to him once more on the fallen tree. "Yes," he said at last. "If only to keep little brother alive. Too few remain in our pack."

The backwoodsman gripped Batu's shoulder with a fond shake. Bristle snorted and bumped against the younger wildsoul's knee. Batu smiled at them both, one hand resting on

Sarryl. The moonbear nuzzled his chest, looking as relaxed as Leiyn had ever seen him.

Melancholy wafted through Leiyn, cold and poignant. *A single day, yet he found a home here.* Had they no other choice but to leave, she might have been happier at the thought.

"But not just for him," Rhun continued, removing his hand and shifting his gaze to Ata. "This Sharo has made life difficult. If all you've said is true, Bristle won't be safe until the notman's gone."

Ata lifted her chin. "I have not lied, wildsoul, nor will I. My brother is every bit the threat you believe him."

Rhun lowered his head. Leiyn observed how he clenched his hands into fists.

"And I wouldn't mind paying the Caelrey a visit," he murmured, the words almost hidden under a crackle from the campfire.

Before any could respond, Rhun raised his head, almost seeming to emerge from a trance. "If Vasara is our aim, we should make for it now. A festival begins in three days. The Careta Desfíl; the Procession of Masks."

She had to delve back into memories of the year she had spent in Southport to recall the festival. The capital of Baltesia had held their own celebration modeled after the Procession of Masks, but the talk had always been of the grander version held in the Union capital. It celebrated Omn's inauguration of spring, with the populace wearing masks of animals to represent the world's reawakening.

Rhun laughed, the sound as rough as old leather. "Fitting this should come now. This *holy day*—it was taken from us, from Asraicheans, by the first Baltesar, that cursed king who formed their Union. It celebrates more than spring—it's connection and shared love. But that is not what they've made it. Theirs is a garish celebration, masks worn for novelty. Their

Union knows nothing of unity. Their Catedrál pisses on its intent!"

His voice rose steadily through his pronouncement to end in a roar. They flinched while he mastered himself and turned his head aside. Leiyn tensed and strained her senses to pick up any sign of danger. How far did the sound spread from their camp?

More unsettling was the danger this wildsoul posed. Not only to their enemies, but to themselves.

"They've stolen from all of us," Leiyn said with forced calm. "And I'm as angry as you. But we cannot allow that to make us lose control. Recklessness gets people killed."

The irony was not lost on her companions. Teya raised an eyebrow her way, and Batu's gaze spoke as much. But Leiyn had heard the advice often enough to know when it applied. Even if part of her still wished to charge in, consequences be damned.

And she had more than herself to live for. Isla remained alive in her—not as a spark, but in memory. Getting herself killed would be a poor way to honor her sacrifice.

Teya turned back to Rhun. "You know it's getting out of hand if she's saying that."

Ata laughed, a touch louder than appropriate. "Quite true, quite true! But passion is something to be harnessed, not stifled. Keep your hatred, Kinblood. Stoke it. When the time comes, we shall show them how they have wronged us."

Leiyn disliked the words and the effect they had on Rhun. The wildsoul grinned, a feral aspect to his face.

"Aye," he growled. "We will."

Bristle snorted and pawed the ground as he tossed his head, every motion reeking of challenge.

"This procession," Ketti interrupted. "How can this help in reaching the World King?"

Rhun shook his head, greasy locks waving about his face.

"The Caelrey takes part in it, as does the Altacura. They're supposed to be the highlight of the festival. Taking credit for spring, no doubt," he ended in an angry mutter.

"And will they be lightly guarded?" the Eteman pressed.

The wildsoul laughed. "Not likely. Better than his palace or the Basilica Sóveran, though."

Leiyn had not heard often of the Basilica Sóveran, but every Omnist knew of it. The home of the Altacura, it was the seat of Catedrál power.

"On that point, he is correct," Ata cut in. "The World King's castle has protections similar to those my Kin and I once wove over Qasaar. Not as strong, perhaps, but resilient enough that I would be slow to penetrate them. I imagine the same to be true of the Altacura's stronghold."

"So you cannot bring us inside," Teya surmised.

The dryvan waved a hand, talons clicking against each other. "In so many words. Claiming this man in the open would be far easier."

Ekosa cleared his throat, drawing their attention. "All I have heard of Ilberian magic confirms this. While not as sophisticated as Eyin architecture, it has been rumored odiosas were used for more than hunting those with *idan*."

"Then the castle's out." Leiyn leveled her gaze at Rhun. "Do you know where we should lay our ambush?"

Rhun grinned. "Do we look like city folk to you?" He clapped a hand on Bristle's shoulder. The boar turned one beady eye reproachfully on him and huffed. "No," the wildsoul continued. "Got to find that out when we get there."

Leiyn's stomach sank. They were like ranger apprentices wandering the forest without a map or rucksack. Lost. It would make avoiding rashness all the more difficult.

"We'll reconnoiter beforehand." Leiyn hardened her voice to leave no room for argument. "Me, Teya, Ekosa, and Batu. The rest of you will draw too much attention to bring with."

Batu shifted, drawing Leiyn's eye. He seemed reluctant as he met her gaze.

"I'm sorry, Leiyn," he murmured. "But I won't leave Sarryl behind. And I don't think a bear would pass unnoticed in Vasara."

She clenched her jaw, biting back words she might regret. Though she was bonded with Clouded Fang, and mysteriously tied to Chispa, and inexplicably fond of Feral, the relationship between a wildsoul and their beast went beyond any of those. Frustrating and inconvenient as it sometimes proved, she had to accept Batu's pronouncement.

"Fine," she said, sharper than she meant to. "Then it'll be us three." Hoping her irritation was not apparent, Leiyn looked at Ata. "You can take us in tomorrow?"

The Iritu smiled. "Nothing would delight me more."

Most of the others looked thoughtful and nodded along with the burgeoning plan. Ketti was the exception. Her expression placid, she stared at Ata.

"When we reach the Ilberian leaders," she said, "what do you intend with them, Iritu?"

Ata's smile morphed as she turned it on the Eteman. So cutting that Leiyn wondered if she would leap at her enemy of old. Then the moment passed, and the dryvan appeared at her ease again.

"Mortals are always dying." Ata flicked her hand through the air. "What is one more?"

She means to kill him.

Ice coursed through her veins. She had been so focused on reaching the World King she had not thought about how they should deal with him. But what else could they do? Openly abducting a king could hardly end in a civil discussion.

"Truly?" Ekosa leaned onto his knees, eyes flitting across their party. "Is this our aim? We are not assassins. Can we not take them hostage?"

The dryvan waved a hand. "Perhaps, if there is the opportunity. But we have this sole chance. We cannot allow mercy to spoil it."

Leiyn grimaced, then spoke what she knew she must. "This could never be bloodless. People will die. We can try to spare the king and priestess, puppets that they are, but the guards and soldiers will still suffer."

"Precisely." Ata shared a triumphant smile with Leiyn, one she did not return. The dryvan scarcely seemed to notice as she turned back to the others. "Why should we preserve one life when the slaves suffer?"

Teya raised her chin and drew back her shoulders. Her voice was taut as a fishing line. "They are not slaves. They serve by their choice."

Leiyn glanced sidelong at the scout. It was not so difficult to guess at the reasons for her reaction. Teya had been in a similar role as the Suncoats for the Many Tribes. Perhaps denying their agency denied her own.

Or maybe she needs them to be guilty to kill them.

The Iritu shrugged, feathers fluttering. "The fly lands on excrement. Are they any less filthy for acting in their nature?"

Ketti crossed her arms. "I will not be a murderer."

Again, you mean? The words almost pressed out of Leiyn, but she caged them behind her teeth. The violence the Eteman had been forced into—that Leiyn had made her party to—had left enough of a mark without Leiyn driving the dagger in deeper.

Ata whirled on her, striding around the fire to loom over the slight woman. "Will you not? Your ancestors had no such compunction!" She jabbed a talon at Ketti's face, halting it mere inches away. "Sharo slaughtered your people. Butchered them all. Do you not burn for vengeance? Should his puppets suffer any less?"

Leiyn found her hand had fallen to her anelace, thumb

tracing the fox Tadeo had carved into the pommel. She forced it back to her side.

Ata won't hurt her. She'd never.

The others remained tense. Only Ketti looked placid before the dryvan's outrage.

"I wish that upon Sharo," she replied. "Him, and the Iritu who follow him. No others need suffer beyond that."

"I think you will find that to be far from true, hunter-child." Her wooden face twisted, Ata whirled away and strode to the opposite side of the fire.

Silence gathered over their camp. Their party stared into the flames. Loath as Leiyn was to break it, she knew questions remained to be answered.

"If we succeed," she said, careful in her wording, "what then? Removing the World King and the Altacura doesn't take away Sharo's hold on the Union. He might replace them with puppets even more loyal to him."

Ata turned to her, esse gathering in her good eye so it shone to her lifesense. "Of course he will! But that shall take time, Awakener, and significant effort. Mortals are difficult to corral in the direction you desire."

Do you corral us? she wanted to ask. Again, she kept the thought silent.

"We shall not afford him either," the dryvan continued with a wide smile. "While he scrambles to keep hold of his empire, that is the moment we shall strike."

Leiyn lowered her head, staring at the ground. She felt her companions' stares on her, looking to her to confirm the dryvan's bloody intentions.

How many will we kill to reach Sharo?

She had no answer. Yet what other choice did they have? They had no way of finding Sharo. They had to bring him to them. Taking away his tools was their best chance of doing that.

But it had been easier to conceive of before. Before it came time to commit the crimes.

We must. I must.

Leiyn clenched her hands into fists. This was not for petty vengeance. This was about survival, the survival of all humanity, and their freedom. And the future of the Iritu as well.

She could not hesitate to claim justice. Even justice bought with blood.

Leiyn raised her head and met their stares. "Then we go," she spoke, her throat raw. "To the king and the Altacura."

Rhun rose, Bristle huffing as he followed suit. "Three days. We must leave at dawn tomorrow. Unless you have swifter means of travel." His eyes flitted to Ata.

"As you saw upon our arrival, Kinblood, we do." Ata turned her sharp gaze on Leiyn, then continued to their companions. "Take your rest this night. Tomorrow, you shall be in Vasara."

Leiyn huddled into Teya, drawing on her esse to banish the chill settled into her bones. The *situal* stroked her hair, fingertips brushing her scalp.

"Can we do this?" Teya murmured, her voice vibrating in her chest against Leiyn's cheek. "Can we kill this king and high priestess in cold blood?"

Retorts and rationalizations ran through Leiyn's mind. Like a hunter behind a herd, she drove them away.

"Do we have a choice?"

Silence settled over them, heavy as their duty. Her beloved's hand settled on the back of Leiyn's neck. Leiyn might have thought Teya had drifted to sleep but for the wakefulness of her lifefire.

When Teya spoke, it was in a whisper. "We must keep watch over Rhun."

"I know. He has a temper." Leiyn raised her head to glance up at her through the gloom. "Nothing I'm not familiar with."

The scout gave her a fleeting smile. "There is more. I overheard part of what he told Batu. He used to live with others like them. An entire village of wildsouls. But Suncoats came and wiped them out."

The pieces slotted into place. Leiyn exhaled, long and slow. Rhun's story sounded eerily similar to her own. And judging by the anger he had expressed, the same drum of vengeance beat in his breast that had thrummed in hers.

She shifted to rest her chin on Teya's sternum, meeting the *situal's* shrouded eyes. "We'll watch him. Keep him from doing something foolish. But we cannot leave him behind. He's proven his worth. Might be he has more to offer."

Teya rested back her head, a sigh gusting from her lips. "We shall see."

36

CITY OF SAINTS

Leiyn had always traveled lightly. But even for a ranger of the Wilds Lodge, her belongings felt too minimal.

As she stood prepared for Ata to whisk them across Ilberia, she shuffled in place, feeling the absence of her longbow and quivers. Forbidden within the city's walls, the same as all martial weapons not borne by guards, they would be too difficult to hide for the two days she, Teya, and Ekosa were to spend in Vasara. Teya betrayed a similar discomfort, deprived of her spear and bow. Only Ekosa did not have to discard items, his only weapon beyond mahia being an Eteman knife that was easily hidden.

One thing comforted her that morning. Once more, Leiyn had reached for Clouded Fang, as she had done a dozen times across the sea. Instead of being greeted by a vague presence, the ash dragon had burned brightly in her mind. Elation trilled through her as she beheld his vital spirit. He was not fully recovered, but he was here with her. Across an entire ocean, he had followed her.

Perhaps she meant more to him than she knew. Perhaps he

truly wished to protect her. She had smiled into the gloom at the thought.

Though it was just past dawn, those not accompanying them had already packed, though they did not carry their rucksacks yet. Ata was to bring the three of them inside the city before returning to move the rest to a camp closer to Vasara. Batu seemed nearly as uncomfortable as she, failing to meet her gaze. Ashamed, she did not doubt, that he was not going with them. But his bond was evidently more powerful. He made no move to join them but remained at his moonbear's side.

Ketti took her exclusion better. Quiet since their conversation the night before, she watched placidly as Leiyn and the others moved to the opposite side of the campfire. Ekosa had given her a tender kiss farewell, but even that she scarcely returned.

"Are you prepared?" Ata came strutting out of the woods, as unburdened as ever. "You must use the little time we have if we are to succeed."

Leiyn tensed, remembering what had happened the last time Ata whisked them across the countryside. But if waking dreams of Sharo were to find her again, there was little she could do about it. "Yes."

Teya and Ekosa echoed her reply with equally flaccid enthusiasm.

"Then we go." Ata lolled her head back toward Ketti and the wildsouls. "Be good while I'm gone."

Batu finally met Leiyn's gaze, still lingering on him. His honey-brown eyes were the last thing she saw before the world tore away.

She suffered no dreams during this leap. Though the scene that greeted her eyes had the trappings of a nightmare.

Brown, shadowed stone replaced where Batu had stood, the walls of an alley that extended in either direction. Relief at escaping Sharo's torment lasted only until the alley's smell hit her. The caustic combination was the same as in other metropolises: offal and urine, rotting food and unwashed bodies.

Saints, I hate cities.

Leiyn took stock as a vigilant ranger ought to. Teya and Ekosa had made it there with her. Ata was absent; wisely, the dryvan had only remained for as long as necessary. Ata had also chosen as good a spot as she could have given the distance they traveled. The fragrant backstreet was largely unoccupied, the refuse lining its corners and coating the ground a likely reason for it. The alley extended for thirty paces in either direction before ending in the squalid wall of a hut or a shop of little renown.

But their appearance had not gone entirely unnoticed. Three youths, their faces dirty and their clothes a step above rags, stared at them from a far end of the alleyway, slack-jawed and wide-eyed. They seemed unable to believe they were truly there, for no sense of common decency compelled them to look aside.

Leiyn bared her teeth at them, halfway between a smile and a snarl. That awoke their sense of preservation. The trio scurried away, darting glances over their shoulders as they disappeared around a corner.

"Well, we made it." Teya was still looking up and down the empty alley, a hand resting on the pommel of her Eteman knife. "What now?"

"Now, we survey." Leiyn tested her Eteman dagger and ranger anelace to ensure they would not stick in their sheaths. Then she paced to the right, peering down the way. Though she had spoken decisively, she had yet to figure out their next move.

"We might begin with locating the route along which the procession will take place," Ekosa suggested, coming up beside Leiyn. "Then determining the ideal location to waylay your World King."

"He's not mine." Her retort lacked rancor as her attention moved to the problem before them. She spread her lifesense around, enduring the clamorous wave as she observed where people were positioned. Some occupied the buildings to either side; many more flowed down a street parallel to them that promised to be much wider—and cleaner, should San Hugo favor them.

But fortune was not to be theirs. As her lifesense brushed against one passerby, they reached back.

"Odiosa!" she hissed.

Leiyn withdrew to her body and hid her lifefire. Her heart hammered, imagining the odiosa sending their seeking tendrils after them. Had they noticed the disappearance of her life-force? Would they see if the others hid as well? But she had always preferred action to hoping.

"Raise your walls," she said to the other two, who watched with alarm. Though she could no longer sense it, she assumed they complied by their grimaces.

"Did they catch you?" Teya pressed.

Leiyn shook her head. "Don't know. But we shouldn't stay here to find out."

Beckoning them to follow, she led the others away from the odiosa toward where the youths had disappeared. As they emerged into the adjoining alley, this one narrower than the first, the din of the crowds washed over them. Leiyn was almost glad her lifesense was veiled; it would have only added to her growing discomfort.

She stepped out of the shadows and blinked, dazzled by

daylight. Vasara was known as the City of Saints, and from the view of this promenade, she could see why. The bustling street was wide, perhaps two score paces across—more a plaza than a street. The buildings, constructed from an ancient dark wood and worn black basalt, did not loom, but only rose two or three stories, allowing the sun to knife against the bright stone pavers. The air was fragrant with human sweat, but complicated with the scents of food: spices, fish, onions, and garlic prominent among them. The accents of the shouting vendors and conversing pedestrians turned their shared language into one almost exotic. Lifting over the bustle were the strains of music—a vihuela, by its plaintive strings.

The scene felt both foreign and achingly familiar. Many streets in Southport were not so different from this.

To think I'd miss any city.

"This way," Leiyn called over her shoulder, turning them east toward the rising sun. Towers loomed ahead, but backlit as they were, she could only guess at their identities. Teya and Ekosa kept close on her heels as she pressed into the crowd. There were not only pedestrians present, but animals as well—livestock, on the whole. A lane for carriages proceeded down the middle, those on foot darting before the prancing hooves of the fine steeds pulling them. This also seemed to be a market street of some kind. Vendors hawking their wares stood before stalls with bright awnings, like male birds seeking scarce females.

Passing the stands, Leiyn pressed through the crush of the crowd. She resented each brush against her skin, the offender's lifeforce jabbing against her walls. The stink of humanity already felt as if it coated her nose. Her only solace was that here, she would not be lauded as the "Tideraiser." Anonymity had always been preferable to notoriety.

Especially when they had bloody business to be about.

Yet they did not go unobserved. Many a pedestrian stared

at Teya and Ekosa. Though there were others of Eyin origin around, they were infrequent, and no other Gast or native of the Veiled Lands was to be seen. Teya's foreign hair and fierce facial tattoos made her stand out nearly as much as Ketti would have.

"Hoods up," Leiyn muttered over her shoulder, drawing up her own as she did. Teya and Ekosa complied at once, no doubt noticing the stares as well.

Leiyn faced forward when she saw sunlight catch on steel. She flinched. Helmed soldiers moved among the vendors. Suncoats, or city guards at least, patrolled the street.

Cursing under her breath, Leiyn and her friends gave the soldiers a wide berth. For once, she was grateful to be in a crowd. The guards did not notice them, preoccupied with tense conversations held with some vendors.

After a sweltering period of pushing through the crowd and avoiding more pairs of Suncoats, Leiyn nodded toward a break that appeared between stalls. Her companions following, she led them into the relative solace of the shadowed walls. The stink of waste drifted from it as it had from previous ones, but at that moment, it was a preferable exchange.

"Should be far enough." Leiyn wiped a hand across her brow as she peered at the other two. "Where to now?"

Ekosa cleared his throat. Despite the risk of discovery and the onrush of the crowd, he remained unruffled. A life spent in the capital of Ore-Ofe had prepared him far better than Leiyn for their surrounds, despite Ilberia being her purported motherland.

"We require information," the *eesu* said. "First, to discover where we are. Then to locate the route along which the procession will proceed."

Teya crossed her arms. "And how do you suggest gathering this information?" Like Leiyn, the *situal* was out of her element. Though she tried hiding it, Leiyn knew Teya too well to miss her fretting.

Ekosa shrugged. "Either we find someplace high or we ask around."

Leiyn glanced back the way they had come. "Pretty flat across the city. And I doubt any temples, manors, or guard towers will be happy to let us up."

"We could use *semah*," Teya pointed out. "Blind them to our passage, sneak past."

"Or we might pay to learn what we require." Ekosa withdrew a hand from his cloak, revealing a violet silk pouch, its mouth cinched together with gold string. The contents clinked as he held it up. "I am certain there are merchants who would be happy to supply our location should we be generous in our purchases."

Leiyn stared at the pouch. "Where you'd get that?"

He smiled and hid it under his cloak again. "Do you not remember? I grew up a thief. In crowds such as this, it is a simple matter to cut a purse loose."

"But you used mahia back then. Don't tell me you used it now."

His wince spoke the truth. Leiyn furrowed her brow but sighed away her frustration.

"Best to not risk it again," she said. "Not unless we must. But the coin should come in useful."

Ekosa relaxed his shoulders. "Of course. My apologies. I admit, I acted on instinct, though it has been years since I stole."

"Don't worry about it." Leiyn nodded back toward the boulevard, still churning with as thick of crowds as before. "We'd best find our loose lips."

They settled on a food stand whose shopkeeper, a man with an affable smile and a patched brimmed hat, had skewers of spiced fish on display. Leiyn had little concept of Ilberian prices, but it seemed extortion when the man asked for six bronze. At her protest, he grinned through a dark beard and shrugged.

"Festival prices, lass. Blame the World King, not me!"

After a look from Teya, Leiyn subsided, and Ekosa paid for their meal. As he pressed the coins into the vendor's hand, the *eesu* did not fully relinquish them, but asked his questions while holding the man there.

"We are new to Vasara and quite lost. Can you tell us where the Procession of Masks will go through?"

The Ilberian's eyes caught a greedy gleam. "Might be I can," he hedged. "But with the parade interrupting business and all—"

"Looks like it's helping more than hurting," Leiyn cut in.

The man glared at her. "You'd do better to learn a sweet tongue, girl, if you're wanting something."

"Leiyn." Teya's hand was tight on her shoulder. "Leave this to Ekosa."

She wanted to point out the blatant injustice before her, but knew it was no use. Teya was right. Ekosa knew this business better than she, and the discomfort of the crowds drove up the temperature of her temper more than she liked to admit.

Her intervention did not doom the affair, fortunately. After several more coins exchanged hands—only tin and copper, Leiyn was relieved to see—Ekosa obtained their answers. They took their scant meal back to the alleyway where they had recently found shelter in and removed their hoods in the relative safety of the shadows.

The *eesu* muttered a curse in his own tongue before speaking in Ilberian. "He cheated us, but at least we know."

Leiyn propped a hand on her hip. "Know what?"

Ekosa gestured at the broad street. "This is the Promenada Palacia, the main street of Vasara. As you might surmise from its name, it leads directly to the Caelrey's palace."

Teya laughed and shook her head. "Meaning this is the route for the procession."

"Precisely."

Leiyn quelled her vexation and focused on what was important. "Do we know where we are?"

"Yes. He was not stingy in that, at least." Ekosa looked around, as if gazing upon their surrounds anew. "This is the Ciudad Interna, which is separated from the Ciudad Abultado by a wall."

"Not unlike Southport," Leiyn noted.

"Yes. And like many cities with two walls, the richer residents primarily occupy these areas. Though not all, as we have seen."

"And the kings, too." Teya chewed on her fish, then grimaced and spat. "Left the bones in, *egreshti* bastard."

Leiyn eyed the fish she held with fresh distaste. Though it was greasy against her fingers and she was hungry enough for it to look appetizing, she held off against tearing into it. "We need to walk the Promenada Palacia, then. Find the best location for an ambush."

"And what, pray, would such a lovely trio be wishing to ambush on this bright and beautiful day?"

Leiyn whirled toward the voice, her free hand diving under her cloak for a knife. Vigilant as she had been toward the street, her walled-off lifesense had left her blind to the alleyway, and Ekosa had failed to warn them.

The man before them posed little obvious threat. Shorter by a head and with a cadaverous frame, his decrepit clothes looked to have more life in them than he, though he moved with enough energy to buoy the impression. He wore a fraying hood that pooled about narrow shoulders and had no accompanying cloak. A gap-toothed grin projected out from a face blemished by years of rough living. Burst blood vessels across his nose and cheeks told of a proclivity for liquor. Thin graying hair and sallow skin foreshadowed him having few years left to enjoy it.

"No business of yours." Leiyn sharpened her voice to be as pointed as an arrowhead. "Leave us be."

"Oh-ho, but business shared is business doubled!" The rogue, delighted with his own words, widened his grin. Leiyn wondered if she looked close enough if she would glimpse maggots already crawling through his gums.

"Perhaps we would not like this affair doubled." Teya seemed more amused than threatened as she stood with her head cocked and her lips twisted up in a corner. Her hands, however, remained close to her knives.

"Halved it is, then! You have but to speak the word, and Halftooth Hector shall supply your wish."

If he was a benevolent spirit like the tales told around firesides, Halftooth Hector had the foulest look Leiyn had seen. *And the foulest smell*, she thought, trying not to wrinkle her nose at the stench arising from his proximity.

"We need nothing from you." Rather than increase her hostility, Leiyn restrained it. "Please. I wouldn't wish to have any trouble."

"Trouble?" The drunkard tottered a step closer with a wheezing laugh. "This I can half, yes I can! Speak your wish and it shall be done. A place to sleep? To slake? To ascend? A word, and its location is yours!"

"The lady has told you to leave." Ekosa had more iron in his voice than Leiyn usually heard from him. "I would advise you to listen."

"The lady?" Hector squinted at Leiyn, then Teya, before looking back at Leiyn. "And here I thought I was speaking to a legend! Eh, Tideraiser?"

A shiver ran through her. Blindsided, Leiyn could not help darting a look around her, betraying the truth. The look of delight in the rogue's eyes told it had been as much a guess as an accusation.

Clever, Firebrand. Outsmarted by a drunk.

She leaned in, ignoring his bitter breath. "What makes you think I'm this Tideraiser?"

Hector's smile dimmed, a glimpse of her hard intent breaking through his addlement. "Everyone in Vasara—nay, all Ilberia—knows of you, Lady Tideraiser. The Witch of the Wilds, butchering good Unionmen. The one who broke the Armada, the mightiest fleet ever seen. The songs speak of the thread of fire through your hair—there," he said, pointing with an unsteady finger.

Leiyn straightened, wishing she had kept her hood up. Teya was quicker with a reply.

"If she is this Lady Tideraiser"—a quirk of her beloved's lips betrayed barely repressed amusement—"is nettling her not a poor idea? What is to keep her from butchering you, little man?"

The rogue shuffled back a few steps, tripping on the discarded remains of a basket and nearly falling flat on his back. "P-pardons, Lady Tideraiser and friends," he spluttered, darting looks behind him as he backed away. "Forget old Hector—nay, this old fool! I'll say nary a word, nary a whisper. Not a *sound* till you wish it!"

He did not leave Leiyn time to issue further threats but darted back down the passage. Leiyn saw him slip and almost fall flat before he turned the corner and out of sight.

With his disappearance, the last of her thin amusement fell into tatters. "They know," she hissed to Teya. "How are we supposed to learn anything now?"

The scout reached over to tug Leiyn's hood back over her head. "That will be a start. Do not fear, Redlock. Hundreds have not recognized you. None will know you by your face alone."

"Masks," Ekosa said. "Once the festival begins, everyone hides their faces, no? We will be few among thousands then."

Leiyn nodded, already irritated at her hood obscuring her vision. With her lifesense veiled, she felt too blind and vulnerable.

A drunk caught you by surprise, a part of her mocked. *How will you fare against soldiers and lyshans?*

"Come on," she muttered, speaking as much to silence the voice as from the necessity of moving. "Best discover what else we can."

Feeling much like the fox Tadeo had always seen in her, Leiyn darted a look either way down the street, then led her comrades back into the crowd.

37

FOR THE LOST

The trio continued to wander the Promenada Palacia for the rest of the day. The noise, the constant press of esse, the stenches and shoving and glare off of the bright stone—all of it conspired to make Leiyn's head ache. If not for her mahia easing the pain, she would have devolved into one of her fouler moods.

Fear and watchfulness also kept her in check. In addition to avoiding the city guards, Suncoats, and occasional odiosas that patrolled the prominent street, she took to avoiding those with too-sly of looks in their eyes. Those trafficking in information, like Halftooth Hector, might be looking for just such an opportunity as she provided. She could risk no further recognitions.

She fretted the drunkard would betray her to the king, but Teya waved away her worries. "Who would listen to that fool? They will laugh and turn him away."

"It matters not," Ekosa interjected. "Sharo knows we are in the Ancestral Lands. He may guess our intentions to reach the Caelrey. If he does, then they already know."

That had her pulling her hood down further, never mind

the sun beating down. Leiyn felt she had sweated every drop of water in her body by the time Omn fell below the sea beyond the city harbors. With Ekosa leading, they located an abandoned alley off the Promenada that was like the one they had started their day in—and just as smelly. From all they could tell, it was outside the city guard's nightly patrols and as safe a location as they were wont to get.

There, they huddled in their bedrolls under a fresh drizzle. Leiyn kept watch for more than half the night. Unable to stand the darkness, which was barely remitted by the glow from the surrounding homes, she opened her lifesense. Relief flooded in as the city came alive to her mahia. She restricted herself to their alley, wary of anyone seeking to surprise them while they slept.

The night passed uneventfully. As soon as light edged into the sky, Teya, who had taken the second watch, shook Leiyn and Ekosa awake. Groggy and footsore, Leiyn leashed her temper as they made their way back to the Promenada Palacia, hoping their efforts that day would prove more fruitful. They had this one day to settle the plan. To succeed in their ambush or doom their rebellion.

No pressure.

The day promised to be even more difficult than the one before. Leiyn recoiled from her first glimpse of the promenade. The wide street was swarming not only with Suncoats and city guards, but palace guards as well. She guessed they must be the royal guard by their armor. Clad in full-plate with conical helms and tall shields and spears, they were gilded along the rims and emblazoned with the Caelrey's rising sun. Even more than Suncoats, these men and women spoke with unflinching authority.

Before their coming, the bustling promenade was quickly vacated. Those vendors who had risen before the dawn argued with guards who seemed to tell them to pack up. Within minutes of watching, Leiyn burned while a Suncoat backhanded an Eyin man who was selling an assortment of brightly dyed clothes and hats. The man, who had been arguing moments before, groveled on the pavers before the soldier until they kicked him up. Not long afterward, he disbanded his stall and limped it away.

Not every merchant was forced to leave. Ekosa was the first to identify the reasoning behind it. "They drive away the foreigners," he said with a grimace. "All Kalgans and Eyins."

"The Many Tribes would be among them if my people had the misfortune of being here." Teya crossed her arms and scowled at the proceedings.

"Don't draw attention." Leiyn waved them down a side street. "There might be an opportunity here."

She led her companions to the next opening in the promenade and scanned the scattering vendors from beneath her hood. It took only minutes for her to find her quarry.

"There," she murmured, gesturing toward the woman with a nod.

Teya looked where Leiyn indicated. "Her? She is no foreigner. Why is she being forced away?"

"She's Asraichean. See the red hair? The bright eyes? They're treated as well as foreigners here."

Leiyn motioned them back toward the shadows when a guard glanced their way, just keeping the woman in sight.

"Is every person with red hair Asraichean, then?" Ekosa wondered.

Leiyn shrugged. "I know as much as you do. But if I'm right, she'll be even more aggrieved against the Union."

They waited, listening to the woman's shouted protests. Concentrating, Leiyn could just make out what she was saying.

"It's the day before the Procession! Can you not see I'm

selling masks? Where do you think people are going to come to buy them?"

Leiyn did not catch the city guard's answer, but she saw his reaction. With a grin at his companion, they toppled the cart full of the woman's wares. Masks sparkling with metal dust skidded across the bright pavers. A passerby trampled one, then blanched and scurried on.

Just like the man they had seen backhanded, this woman knew when she was beaten. Her shouts silenced as she kneeled to reclaim her wares. Not quickly enough—one guard kneed her in the back and sent her sprawling. Both laughing, they issued a final muted word to the Asraichean, then moved on to their next victim.

Leiyn watched as the woman picked herself slowly up off the white stones and brushed back the locks of her curly hair, fallen in front of her face. She stood unsteadily, then tried to right her cart. The abuse must have injured her, for she struggled to lift it.

The smolder in Leiyn's chest warned of her intentions a moment before she strode from the shadows toward the Asraichean.

"Wait!" Teya hissed at her back.

Leiyn did not pause. Keeping her hood up, she watched for nearby patrols. A pair of Suncoats stood just across the way, but they were preoccupied with harassing another of the vendors, this one a Kalgan woman.

She only saw the odiosa with them once she stood over the upturned cart.

Leiyn ducked down, hoping the odiosa had not seen her. With her walls up, her esse would be hidden, but that brought other problems; no odiosa could miss the meaning of a person with veiled esse. Beside her, the Asraichean woman stared at her, teeth showing between parted lips. A lined brow and crow's feet around her light gray eyes told of encroaching middle age. Though Leiyn had called the woman's hair red, it tended more toward auburn, though memories of ruddier hues lingered among the locks.

"Now's not a good time," the mask seller said after a beat. "If you want a mask, follow me off the Promenade. I can sell to you there."

"Sure," Leiyn answered. "Let me lend you a hand."

As she reached for the nearest mask, a blue one with the crest of a jay, the woman snapped, "Don't touch the merchandise."

Leiyn withdrew her hand and bit back a caustic reply. Instead, she rose and cast a wary glance toward where the odiosa had been. She had evidently gone unnoticed, for the witch hunter had drifted along after his Suncoat escorts. Reassured, Leiyn set her hands on the overturned cart and brought it back upright.

The woman rose, arms laden with masks, her wariness dimmed but lingering. "Thanks," she muttered as she deposited her load, then kneeled to fetch the others.

Teya and Ekosa drifted out from the alley, drawing the Asraichean's stare. "My companions," Leiyn explained, keeping her tone pleasant. "Also looking for masks."

"Follow me." The woman's gaze lingered on Teya, then returned to Leiyn. Was it her imagination, or did a flicker of comprehension cross her eyes?

Do they know of Gasts here? Or is my reputation enough?

If she knew who they were, the mask seller spoke nothing of it. Shifting her cart to align the large wooden wheel on its axle, she heaved on the handles and started pushing it down the Promenada Palacia. With a glance at her companions, Leiyn followed.

She fought the temptation to look at every guard and odiosa they passed. Though the expulsion continued and the day was still early, the promenade had already filled with crowds again, hiding them from immediate notice. The Asraichean vendor glanced at these passersby with the forlorn look of an opportunity missed, but she did not stop to sell her masks, only called for people to move out of her way.

When they finally turned off the promenade, Leiyn sighed and glanced over her shoulder. A shiver ran through her at seeing the gray robes of an odiosa standing not ten paces away. With their back turned to them, though, they remained unaware of their passage.

Her look was not lost on the mask seller. As Leiyn faced forward, the auburn woman shifted her gaze away and continued pushing.

"I'll set up over here," she called over her shoulder. "Decent traffic at Carmen's Crossing."

They followed her to a three-way intersection where a small plaza boasted a marble statue of San Carmen. The Saint's foot was mounted on the head of her famed executioner's axe, reputed by Omnist scripture to have been used to behead many a heathen dissident. The Asraichean parked her cart under the Saint's outstretched hand and, with a grimace, turned her back on her.

Not much of an Omnist, then.

"You want masks," the vendor said, gesturing to the overflowing bed, "here they are. One otero each."

"Silver?" Even from her limited experience of prices in Vasara, it seemed blatant extortion. Still, after discontented contemplation, Leiyn gestured to Ekosa, who produced the coins from his stolen pouch without protest.

The three rifled through the masks. Leiyn thought of her best approach as she selected hers, unable to help selecting an orange fox. Ekosa picked up one depicting a gray bullish creature with a horn projecting from its nose; a rhinoceros, he identified it, a creature native to the primary island of the Eyin Empire that lay in the east. Teya took an eagle, gold-headed rather than the red species of the Titan Wilds after which her tribe was named.

With masks in hand, the vendor stared at them expectantly. Still, Leiyn wavered, knowing the longer the moment drew out, the stranger their behavior would seem. Though with what she had to ask, an awkward pause would be the least of their worries.

"Back at the Promenada Palacia," Leiyn started, "why did the guards drive you away?"

Anger flashed in the woman's eyes. She stifled it the next moment. "Why do you think?"

"You're Asraichean."

"What of it?" the vendor snapped. "Have to make a living, don't I? Better one of us profits off our stolen traditions than one of them."

Once, such snippy remarks would have set off Leiyn's own temper. Now, she saw enough of herself in the woman to realize what was behind it. The Asraichean felt she betrayed her people in selling these masks. Though she only did what was necessary for survival, she still had to reckon with her guilt.

"I didn't mean to criticize you." Leiyn brushed back her hood to reveal her auburn tress. "Only that we share that heritage."

The mask seller's eyes lingered on her lock. "A touch more in me than you."

"I'll grant that."

"But you can pass, can't you? You're not known as a Red at a glance." Bitterness seethed in the woman's voice.

A Red. That they were discriminated against was plain. Leiyn had not thought it went so far.

Did Ilberians treat Gasts any differently? Or even those from other Ancestral Lands?

"You could wear a hood or a hat," Leiyn suggested. "Hide it."

The vendor narrowed her eyes, so light a gray they verged toward white. Freckles peppered skin burned and tanned from constant sun exposure. "They would know. And I'm not one to hide."

Leiyn smiled. "I'm cut from the same cloth. But circumstances change every beast's behavior."

The vendor shrugged, then looked past Leiyn, eyes scanning the roads behind her.

Growing impatient and looking for more customers. The pleasantries had carried on too long. Leiyn leaned in closer. "What's your name?"

The Asraichean woman looked back at her. "Nava," she answered after a pause.

"Nava. It's good to meet you."

"And yours?" Nava cut in before Leiyn could continue.

Leiyn glanced back at Teya and Ekosa. Teya shrugged. The decision was hers. She turned back to find the mask seller watching her every movement.

"Isla," she said. "I'm Isla." A lump rose in her throat, catching her by surprise. She swallowed.

Nava narrowed her eyes. "Isla it is."

She knows. The signs had been accumulating, the looks too knowing. Yet she had not called out her lie. Perhaps she was only afraid of Leiyn hurting her. She could imagine the stories that had spread here of her savagery. But Nava was not on good terms with the city guard. It was unlikely she would run to them for help.

She decided to see how far she could push.

"The Procession of Masks," Leiyn said. "It's coming down the Promenada tomorrow?"

The Asraichean woman gave her a curt nod. "As it does every year."

"I hear World King Baltesar is in it. Where would be the best place to view him?"

Nava stiffened. Even without her lifesense, Leiyn could tell an epiphany had fallen on her. The mask seller looked down and started fretting with her wares, arranging them so the animals could be seen to full effect. "I think it's best you go now. Don't want customers to think I'm too busy for them."

Nava was slipping from her grasp. Leiyn wanted to look back at her companions, but her connection to the Asraichean was hers alone. This was her mess to clean up.

Leiyn leaned on the cart, making it creak and bringing Nava's eyes back up to hers. "Look. I think you know more about me than you want to admit. If my accent didn't give me away as being from the Veiled Lands, then my clothes and companions did. And I think this isn't the first you've heard of a woman with a lock of red hair."

It spoke much of the woman's fierce spirit that she did not look away. "Yes," Nava said, quiet but firm. "I know you, Tideraiser."

Even though she had all but known it, hearing the admittance sent a trill of fear through Leiyn. She quelled it. It was too late for uncertainty.

"Whatever you've heard of me, know this: I mean you no harm, nor to any innocents. I've only come because I must."

"To kill the Caelrey?"

Leiyn hesitated. It was as good as an admittance faced with such a question. Only the truth could redeem her now.

"Not if we can avoid it." Leiyn tightened her hand on the edge of the cart so it groaned. She realized she had channeled a sliver of esse into strength and threatened to crack the wood under her grip. With effort, she loosened it.

Nava had already noticed, silver eyes wide.

"I think it's best if you go." The Asraichean woman looked

aside, a curl of red hair falling before her face, hiding her eyes from view.

Leiyn straightened. "If you wish us to, we will. But as I understand it, Asraicheans have as much reason to want the Union broken as any colonist."

"Please." Nava did not meet her eye.

She wavered, wondering if she needed to push further, then sighed. If anyone who knew her identity saw their interaction, she might have already implicated Nava in their plot. The woman had a hard enough life without them adding to her troubles.

"Thank you for the masks." Leiyn pushed away from the cart, but before turning, she added, "A word of advice: don't attend the parade tomorrow."

She avoided her companions' gazes as she turned and started walking away. Failure again, and it could only be set on her shoulders.

"Wait."

Nava's call was quiet, but Leiyn stopped at it. Turning back, she found the Asraichean woman chewing her lip and staring with dilated pupils.

Fear. How well she knew that look. How it shone from the eyes of the Suncoats she had slaughtered.

Nava spoke, drawing Leiyn from the dark memories. "The Procession is protected like never before," the vendor said. "Soldiers. Guards. Odiosas. Like they're expecting trouble."

Leiyn looked at Teya and Ekosa, her worries mirrored in their eyes. Unwelcome news, but it was better to hear it now.

To know Sharo prepared for them.

"If you still must go..." The mask seller grimaced, seeming at odds with herself. "Go to Plaza dil Jadiel." She gestured back at the promenade toward the palace. "Farther east. Wide area with a fountain and statue of the Saint. You cannot miss it. With masks and the usual crowds, even you three might blend in."

Leiyn nodded. "Thank you, Nava. We're in your debt."

It would have been wise to turn and walk away then. But she had always had a need to understand.

"Why?" she asked Nava. "Why help us?"

The Asraichean woman hesitated. Then the fear vanished, replaced by harder emotion. "For all we've lost."

Leiyn held her gaze for a moment, then nodded and turned away. For Nava's sake, she hoped it would be the last they saw of one another.

38

OF MASKS & MONARCHS

"Leiyn. It is time."

Leiyn was slow to rouse to Ekosa's hand on her shoulder. Rain had fallen during the night, soaking her to the skin and making her shiver before she drew on esse for warmth. Nodding acknowledgment to the *eesu*, she extracted herself from the sodden blankets and squeezed what liquid she could from it.

Wet clothes, she could live with. It was the lack of restful sleep that was catching up to her. Drawing from an amber bead, she banished the aches of the night. Even then, she felt disconnected from her body, unmoored and drifting.

Teya, who had slept the night through, seemed better rested than she, though the braids hanging down the unshaven side of the scout's head looked as bedraggled as she felt. "Are you prepared, Redlock?" she murmured, brushing a finger across her cheek.

Leiyn drew her beloved in to press their foreheads together. "Ready as ever."

Clouds gathered thick in the sky, but the night's storm had broken, allowing the gray dawn to peek through. They were three shadows against the bright stones with their hoods drawn up and cloaks bundled around them. In the damp morning, they were not out of place; already, the Promenada Palacia was filling with spectators for the parade, all angling to get the best spots.

Teya led the way to Plaza dil Jadiel. Having surveyed it the night before, they found their way across the wide square and drew as close as they could to the fountain at its center. The statue of the handsome Saint of Grace and Beauty was positioned with an arm lifted in the air, a palm upturned as if in offering to the heavens. Around him were the woodland creatures he was said to have summoned from the forest to feed his starving people. Water spewed from the tips of a deer's antlers, the ears of a rabbit, and the mouth of a beaver.

A crowd, five people thick, stood between them and the armed men and women who formed a perimeter along the route. For now, it would do—her being recognized or Teya being accosted before the World King arrived would be disastrous.

As more people arrived with masks already in place, Leiyn, Teya, and Ekosa all donned theirs. With her companions' features hidden by the aspects of the hawk and rhinoceros, she found they became truly hidden among the crowd. Even an alert odiosa would have difficulty picking them out with their veiled lifeforce. Anonymity was even worth her vision being restricted by the narrow openings in her fox mask.

Even without her lifesense, she remained a ranger, and a ranger was always vigilant for threats. As she scanned the tops of the buildings, she picked out the archers in the brief moments their heads bobbed above the parapets and beyond the eaves. Four were positioned near, posing a risk, though were few enough to be little trouble. It was the possibility of others she had not yet seen that worried her.

The morning dragged on. The crowd around them thickened, as did the noise. As the start of the parade drew nearer, one of them would have to expose themselves by lowering their walls in order for Ata to find them. Chispa, if he had joined with the dryvan, could likely get her close nonetheless, the silver fox's uncanny ability to find Leiyn undiminished. But they had to be certain. Teya insisted on assuming the risky duty first, though only after Leiyn extracted the promise that she would let her take over before long.

Worries gnawed at Leiyn as they stood in the crowd waiting. Could Ata time her appearance well enough? Would the people around her be hurt when a dryvan and two transformed wildsouls charged through? And her companions—could she keep them safe? Without her falchions, close-quarters combat would be even more dangerous.

Faced worse odds, Firebrand.

Yet Leiyn could not help darting glances around her. Waiting had never been her strong suit; waiting in a city crowd even less so. Behind every mask might lie an odiosa or a covert agent of Sharo's. She had missed Halftooth Hector coming upon them in the alley. With a hood and a mask obscuring her vision, her lifesense veiled, and the crowd hiding the noise of an approach, would she see the knife before it stabbed her in the back?

Breathe, just breathe.

She fretted away the morning, turning through her worries until they grew frayed and thin. Her Eteman clothes dried quickly, a slight alleviation for her discomfort. But as the sun burned away the gloom and ever more people packed in behind them, the heat grew unbearable. Leiyn clutched Tadeo's fox figurine, gaining comfort from the dim spark within it, and toyed with the hilt of the knife she still carried from the Wilds Lodge. It would be her reserve blade, the Eteman dagger far more resilient than ordinary steel, but a part of her always preferred her first weapon.

If only our bows would arrive. Even with few armor-piercing arrows remaining, it would make for a far more effective weapon in the congested environment.

A sudden roar rose from the crowd, issuing in a wave down the promenade from the palace. Even before she heard the distant trumpets floating over the tumult, she knew what it must signify.

The parade had begun.

Leiyn turned back to Teya. "I'll take my turn!" she shouted over the tumult. She lowered her walls to emphasize what she meant.

The scout raised her eyebrows but complied by raising her own walls. "Be careful!"

Leiyn smiled briefly and turned away. They both knew how futile a warning that was.

Even blinded by the conflagration of thousands of lifefires, it was a relief to have her lifesense open. Leiyn kept it tucked in close, not stretching her senses beyond the knot of masked Ilberians surrounding them. It would not warn her of odiosas or enemies from afar, but any assassins that tried creeping up on them would be met with a sharp surprise.

Reassured, Leiyn focused back on the festivities. Despite the fanfare cascading down the Promenada Palacia, the parade had not yet reached them.

It took at least a quarter hour more before the first act appeared—then they came on with riveting speed. Leiyn's breath caught as a rider bucked up and down atop a kicking, spinning bull. He was a massive specimen, black-coated and spitting as he tossed his great horned head and tried to dislodge his passenger. The rider clung with only one hand, the other flying above his head. A tricorn hat pressed low over his face and impossibly remained on. His tasseled jacket, dyed a rich scarlet, flapped with every bucking motion like a flag in a squall.

There was not just one rider: four more came behind, all in brightly colored jackets with their triangular black hats, clinging to their own wildly bucking bulls. As Leiyn wondered what kept the enraged beasts from charging into the crowd, she noticed the horses trotting behind. Masked riders in nondescript black guided them, but it was those riding behind that struck icy fear through Leiyn: odiosas, four in total and clad in their usual gray robes. She looked away, worried she would draw their attention, but they passed without glancing to either side.

The bull riders were only the first spectacle. Next came a calmer, but no less captivating, performance. Four horses drew a platform atop which spun half a dozen women in silver dresses that caught the light. Star dancers—even in Baltesia, they were renowned. Called the "Jewels of the Heavens," they were part of a royal retinue that only performed at the Caelrey's behest. Leiyn had heard they only danced after dark, but the sight before her contradicted that rumor.

Despite the peril and their deadly mission, the performance drew Leiyn in. The women swayed and spun, jewels or glass in their ruffled dresses sparking like waves in sunlight. Almost, it seemed a trick of mahia in how they transfixed her. Their hands and arms were as expressive as their hips, sinuous as snakes as they cavorted and clicked wooden castanets that kept time with the movements of their feet.

They danced to more than their handheld percussion. A rondalla of musicians, a dozen in all, came behind on the wheeled stage. Half strummed the six-stringed vihuelas; others piped on wooden flutes or rattled tambourines with gusto.

As the troupe gave way to fire breathers expelling gouts of flame into the sky, then acrobats flipping and vaulting over the pavers, Leiyn almost missed the people behind her shifting. She would have assumed it was someone trying to push their way to the front but for the absence of esse that came into the gap.

Someone approached with their lifeforce veiled.

Leiyn whirled, her knife drawn and concealed, and stared at the intruder. No assassin greeted her eyes, but a far more welcome sight.

"Ketti." Leiyn breathed a sigh as she replaced her knife in its sheath.

The people around them muttered and shifted, disturbed by Leiyn's abrupt movements. She ignored them as she and her companions huddled close around the Eteman.

"I am glad you are safe, my gem," Ekosa said, cupping the back of his beloved's neck.

Ketti smiled at him. "I worried for you." The smile slipped away as her bright lavender eyes moved across Teya and Leiyn. "But we must move swiftly. The king—he has not appeared yet?"

"No." Leiyn jerked her head toward the palace. "Still coming."

"Good. Here—I brought you these."

Ketti raised her hands, revealing them to be burdened with weapons. Teya and Leiyn gave their packs over to Ketti and Ekosa, then took their equipment and secured them. Quivers once more on her hip and across her back, Leiyn accepted her longbow and strung it, bracing the lower limb against her leg and bending it to loop the bowstring over the upper tip.

"We only use these as a last measure," Leiyn cautioned. "Ketti, you can bring Mehu'Ra here?"

Understanding alit in the Eteman's eyes. "You wish to drive them away with titans."

Leiyn nodded. "If we can. Wait for my mark."

The stirring of the crowd drew her attention. Their weapons had not gone unnoticed. Like animals starting at smoke in a dry forest, alarm spread among those surrounding them. A quick glance told Leiyn ignoring them would not quell the panic. Cause too much commotion and they risked losing this one opportunity.

She closed her eyes and expanded her mahia, reaching into the esses of the Ilberians.

Calm. Peace. All is well.

She communicated not with words, but gentle influence, soothing with an influx of lifeforce that would feel pleasant to its recipients. Humans were animals at their core and could be manipulated the same, though it required more skill. Leiyn had finally gained that finesse after seasons of practice.

When the angry muttering had died down and the cheery noises resumed, Leiyn withdrew her mahia and opened her eyes. She had not drawn the attention of odiosas that she could tell, but it had been more mahia than she could count on being ignored. Scanning their surroundings, she searched for any offending odiosas. If they looked at her, she did not see them.

Ketti leaned in close to murmur in her ear. A glimmer of her esse peeked through, her walls fractionally open. "That was well done."

Leiyn shrugged. "Think we got away with it?"

"I will cover you if they notice. You have more pressing concerns."

Following Ketti's gesture, Leiyn looked back to the parade to see a contingent of thirty palace guards marching down the open lane. These were even more impressively adorned than the previous royal guards she had seen, yellow plumes erupting from their helms and golden capes cascading from gilded pauldrons. Their strides were perfectly matched, their discipline impeccable. None looked to either side, but faced straight ahead, set on their path like the wind-up toys Leiyn had once seen a merchant's child play with.

It was what came after the guards that set her heart racing. Pulled by proud white stallions that jingled with the bells in their manes, the palanquin was as ornate as any she had seen. Aubergine velvet draped across it like moss over the entrance to a cave. Gold lined the fabric and edged the roof and floor. The decor within the shadowed interior was no less opulent, nor was the figure who reclined on the gilded throne.

World King Baltesar of House Vasa, Fourth of His Name. The Caelrey of Ilberia. Her onetime monarch.

Their quarry.

Leiyn absorbed her first look. Baltesar's likeness was fashioned upon Ilberian currency, yet that familiarity only made him seem the stranger to see with her own eyes. He had an even more foppish appearance than Mauricio, though it lacked the nonchalance of the consul's fashion. A waterfall of tight black curls spilled down the white lace adorning the monarch's shoulders. His prominent mustache was perfectly groomed, oiled and curled into points. His skin stood in stark contrast to his hair, so sallow and pale that Leiyn wondered if he had ever stepped foot in the sun. More likely, he powdered it, though she could not see why he would bother.

The sovereign was not shy in displaying his wealth. Rubies and diamonds bejeweled the golden crown on his brow. His coat—a cloak, almost, though cropped short—was a match to the deep violet of the curtains and possessed a velvet sheen. Frivolous patterns were inlaid in gold across the lapels and diminutive sleeves that fell no farther than pauldrons. The vest she glimpsed underneath seemed much the same as the coat, as were the pantaloons. His undershirt was of cloth-of-silver, silken and shimmering like the dresses of the star dancers. More white lace curled around his cuffs. Rings adorned his fingers, every kind of precious metal and gemstone flashing upon them. His most modest ornament was the gold medallion emerging beneath a ruby broach. Leiyn had seen similar pendants worn by priestesses, if forged of simpler metals, and knew the five-point sun of Omn to be emblazoned upon it.

Heat flared in her like a wildfire on a dry day. This pompous fool sat upon his silken pillows in his glittering finery, yet he had the gall to appear blasé to it all. But for a glimmer of white in his eyes, she might have thought him dozing, leaning as he did against the arm of his chair, head propped on a hand.

Perhaps he was a fool, a hedonist unconcerned with all that occurred outside his palace walls. Perhaps he only served Sharo out of fear and the threat of violence. Yet he could not be wholly ignorant of the death he had commanded over her land and her people. Not unless he wished to be.

Does he care at all?

Leiyn resented Mauricio's frivolity, but she held a grudging respect for the Consul Elect, as did the people who had elected him. This king was chosen by no one—none but Omn Itself, if the Catedrál was to be believed. And that was not an endorsement she was inclined to heed.

He was not her king. In her heart, he never had been.

She fed that inner fire with every repulsive detail, stoking the flames higher. She would need her hatred burning hot if she meant to seize this opportunity.

And she had to. They would have no better chance of achieving their aims.

To topple an empire.

The cheers rose to thunderous volume as the Caelrey's palanquin drew abreast. Leiyn's throat had gone dry, while her palms sweat out what little moisture remained to her.

Teya leaned in close but still had to shout to be heard. "Where is the Altacura?"

Leiyn looked beyond the royal palanquin for another. Reason stood that Gran Ayda's entrance would be every bit as extravagant as Baltesar's. But any sign of her or the Holy Catedrál was absent.

"Either she's farther back," Leiyn shouted back, "or someone warned her not to show."

Teya frowned, still searching. "Why her and not the king?"

Leiyn cuffed her forehead and wiped her eyes clean. Her best guess was that Sharo had refrained from risking both of his pawns and sought to draw them out by sacrificing the lesser one. They could be playing into his hands.

"Doesn't matter." Leiyn ripped off her mask and let it fall to the ground. "He's here now."

She met Teya's gaze to see her beloved grimace. Teya had already strung her bow and nocked an arrow. Following Leiyn's lead, she removed her hawk mask and faced their quarry.

Your time, Firebrand.

Leiyn nocked one of her few remaining bodkin arrows, designed to pierce armor, then turned to Ketti. The Eteman met her gaze with a nod. As one, they extended their mahia to their titans—Ketti to the sky, Leiyn deep below.

Clouded Fang. Rise.

The ash dragon set his searing gaze upon her, acknowledging her call. But he did nothing but stare. Panic struck through her. Why did he not come? Had she been too commanding? Did all the clustered humans make him hesitant, like many beasts would be to enter a city? Did he still recuperate from his battle with the salt titan of Breakbay?

Protect, she beseeched him. *Protect us.*

Intensifying shouts turned Leiyn's gaze upward. Dark clouds swirled together, blotting out the bright day that had reigned just moments before. The fearful mutterings from the surrounding crowd were drowned out by the sky rumbling. Light and esse flashed, harbingers of the coming storm.

Leiyn flitted her lifesense once more to her bonded titan, then let her mahia bloom. Her magic expanded over the plaza. The dancing lifefires of the crowd swayed together as all beheld the tempest, come far too sudden to be natural. Even insulated in their metropolis, they seemed to suspect what it portended.

A screech reverberated in Leiyn's chest just before lightning crawled across the sky.

Mehu'Ra tore through the thunderstorm, the tempest hawk wreathed in blue lightning. Feathers formed from clouds gave shape to his vast wingspan, his hooked beak, his wicked claws. The essence of life, raw and unbridled, sparked across Leiyn's senses. Her hair stood on end from his nearness and power. Even knowing he meant her no harm, she flinched at his coming.

Bridled fear broke into pandemonium. Screams arose as the frantic shoving began. The masked crowd retreated as rapidly as they could, leaving only Leiyn and her friends behind. It afforded them open space to move—and left them exposed.

But even the Ilberian soldiers appeared overwrought. As Mehu'Ra swooped low overhead, armored men and women cowered and covered their heads. Fear swept through their spirits like wind across meadowgrass. A few even fled with the crowd, heedless to their superiors shouting after them.

Still standing tall with her comrades, Leiyn shut out the tumult and turmoil. All that remained was their mission. Their quarry.

The Caelrey still curled up in his ornate chair upon the palanquin. Mouth agape, he peered hesitantly around the curtained roof to catch sight of the titan terrorizing his city. With Mehu'Ra's spread of fear, it did not seem to occur to him or his protectors how exposed he was.

Leiyn started to lift her bow. How easy it would be to take his life. Was he not responsible for the deaths of thousands of Baltesians? The torment of tens of thousands? Would death not be the justice he deserved?

Are you then an assassin? spoke a voice in her mind, one unsettlingly like Isla's. *Both judge and executioner? The monster they believe you to be?*

Leiyn pried her hand from the bowstring to rub the back of her neck. Uncertainty gripped her when only purpose should have filled her mind. *"Fesht!"* she hissed under her breath. But even with her frustration mounting, she could not decide.

"Leiyn!"

She looked up to find Teya watching her with wide-eyed bafflement. The scout did not hesitate but nodded at the clear path before them.

"We must take him," her beloved continued. "Now!"

It was all the prompting she needed. Returning her hand to her bowstring, Leiyn snuffed out her doubts. They would keep the World King alive if they could.

And kill him if they could not.

Nodding at her companions, she surged forward to lead the charge.

39

DEATH BY DAYLIGHT

Her feet pounded the pavers as Leiyn sprinted toward the Caelrey.

Plaza dil Jadiel lay open around them. As Mehu'Ra swooped in low once more, those few remaining civilians threw themselves to the ground, while the city and palace guards raised shields and arms overhead. Beyond, a servant clad in velvet livery had reclaimed enough presence of mind to clamber onto the palanquin and urge his monarch away. Inexplicably, Baltesar seemed to be resisting, pulling away from his manservant's intrusive touches.

When he saw them charging toward them, she knew his stubbornness would not last.

Drawing in the lifeforce from one of her amber beads, Leiyn channeled a burst of speed and pulled ahead of her companions. Seize the Caelrey, and any soldiers prone to defiance would be forced to back away. The World King was the key to ending this day without spilling blood. Though Ilberians shared Sharo's guilt for all they had done to the peoples of the Veiled Lands, she did not wish to kill them for it.

Not unless she must.

Cowed Union warriors lined the palanquin before them. As they finally noticed their approach, some attempted to rally their courage and form into ranks. Steel hissed from scabbards as Suncoats stood upright. Behind the initial line, palace guards righted themselves as well.

So much for a bloodless day.

Leiyn skidded to a halt a dozen paces shy of their lines and raised her bow. Without Clouded Fang, she had little chance of breaking through. Even as she drew back the nocked arrow and aimed, she sent a fresh plea down her bond.

Please, Clouded Fang, come to me!

One titan still aided their assault. Mehu'Ra shrieked with all of his stormborn fury as he dove at the assembled soldiers. Men and women screamed as lightning licked over their armor. Their agony lashed at Leiyn's lifesense, dark wounds appearing across their souls. A few of the foremost Suncoats fell from the attack, though none succumbed to it. Yet even as they cowered, too many remained in her way to reach the Caelrey.

There would be no abducting the World King. Only one path remained to them. One narrow opportunity.

Leiyn took aim at the pale monarch. Baltesar gaped at her from his seat, seeming unable to comprehend that she threatened to kill him. His manservant was not so sanguine. Tugging on Baltesar again, he made the World King stagger and tumble from the palanquin—and out of her line of sight.

Fesht!

The Suncoats before her were recovering from Mehu'Ra's latest pass. None could miss her nocked arrow or where she aimed.

"Assassins!" one cried. "Protect the king!"

The shout was echoed up and down the lines. An arrow flew forward to silence one of them, and it had not been Leiyn to loose. Darkness spread through their esse, striking icy tendrils through Leiyn's soul. From the corner of her eye, Leiyn saw Teya nocking a second arrow with calm precision, untroubled by the life she took. Her aim was plain: to take vengeance for all the wrongs visited upon the Gasts and other native peoples.

Leiyn tried to embrace a similar rage as she shifted her aim. They would need to fight their way through now. She would not survive if her heart bled for every soldier she slew.

She needed to be the huntress. Only the killer in her could keep those she loved alive.

Deadening herself to what she would sow, Leiyn loosed her arrow. The palace guard she sighted rocked back as her arrow tore through his jaw.

Fresh cries of alarm spread at two of their number falling. Suncoats, city watch, and palace guards bubbled out from their line toward them. Only Mehu'Ra's dive halted their advance. This time, the tempest hawk flew in low enough to knock his cloudy talons into them. Lightning coursed down the claws to blacken the armor of a dozen Baltesians. The acrid smell of burnt flesh wafted into Leiyn's nostrils as the titan soared upward, leaving a swath of corpses in his wake.

Heart thundering at the near danger, Leiyn ignored their enemy's halted advance and nocked another bodkin arrow. With her lifesense open, she easily tracked the marksmen still positioned atop the surrounding roofs. Mehu'Ra had held them off, but the terror he spread already seemed to be lifting.

As one emerged and aimed a loaded crossbow, she loosed. Her arrow caught him across his exposed head. The crossbowman disappeared from view again. She had hoped for a killing blow, but her lifesense showed it to be no more than a glancing one. The best she could hope for was that he would be stunned for a time.

Other marksmen marshaled their courage and loosed upon them. Leiyn jerked away from one bolt while the rest flew wide of her. Teya grunted as one caught her in the shoulder, but her enchanted clothes repelled it, preventing any more injury than a bruise.

The palace guards and Suncoats rallied once more and pressed forward. Leiyn stole a moment to loose a third arrow, catching a crossbowman in the neck as he came into view at the edge of the plaza.

Mahia blew against her lifesense, warning of a different brand of impending attack.

Leiyn looked for the offending odiosa even as she nocked another arrow. Yet the magical blow never landed. As a veil of shimmering lifeforce fell over her, she understood why. Ketti faced the direction of the enslaved maha, lifeforce sparking with her bonded titan's power, then retaliated with a blast invisible except to lifesense. The odiosa crumpled at once. Few were a match for the Eteman.

A more tangible threat closed in as soldiers advanced across the plaza. Already, they were a few paces away.

Two options remained before her: advance or retreat. For once, Leiyn chose the wiser path.

"Fall back!" she bellowed.

The others were already backing away, self-preservation winning out before the surging line of armored foes. Risking a glimpse over her shoulder, she saw the fountain at the center of the plaza lay just a few paces away.

"Behind the fountain!"

She leaped onto the lip of the stone and raised her bow. Nocking one arrow, she tucked two others against the stave of the bow. It was not a technique she opted for often, but faced with a sea of enemies, speed mattered as much as precision.

With moments to spare, she loosed.

Once, twice, thrice, arrows flew from her longbow. Three soldiers fell; only one was dead, but the others were gravely injured. Faced with so many foes and at such close range, she could scarcely miss.

More crossbow bolts spat toward her. All missed to ping against the stone animals and Saint behind. Dust and shards spat over Leiyn as she withdrew three more arrows, broadheads as she spent her bodkins. Her companions had mounted the fountain with her, Ketti and Ekosa standing in the water. The *eesu's* eyes were wide as they faced down the impossible odds, while the Eteman wore an unsettlingly calm expression. Leiyn felt how she brimmed with the power of her bonded titan. Mehu'Ra banked toward them once more, promising a nearing reprieve.

Once more, Leiyn yearned for Clouded Fang's aid. But still, the ash dragon did not rise but only continued to stare up at her. Content to let her fight on her own.

All around, armed Ilberians swarmed the plaza, blades drawn and kite shields held high. Beyond, the royal palanquin lay empty, World King Baltesar long since escorted away. Their opportunity was slipping away if it had not already. Even survival seemed a more distant prospect with each passing moment.

Ata, Batu, where the hells are you?

Leiyn loosed another shot at the armored men before the first stroke of a sword swept up. Had she her falchions, she could have cut through them all. With only knives at her hips and only one of them enchanted for durability, that was a much more difficult prospect.

But strength and speed were not the only ways her mahia granted her an edge.

Sucking down two amber beads, Leiyn released the built-up esse in a burst. As the wave hit the soldiers in an invisible assault, they staggered, defenseless before it. Leiyn loosed two more arrows before they could rally for another charge. As they tried charging again, she unleashed another blast.

"It's the Wilds Witch!" one of them groaned, seeming unable to rise from where he kneeled on the pavers. "That Tideraiser bitch!"

"Poetic," she snarled as she silenced him with an arrow.

A trio of city guards sought to take advantage of her distraction, jabbing their spears at her. Leiyn dodged one and knocked aside the other with her longbow, but the slick stone conspired to make her foot slip.

The third spear drove into her sternum.

It would have been a killing blow but for her protection. Her shirt and vest darkened, but the imbued esse prevented the speartip from piercing the cloth.

Leiyn sent the guards reeling again with her mahia, then sent off another three quick shots. Moments later, arrows bristled from their helms, the men wearing them collapsing.

Even as the icy grip of their deaths tried to freeze her in place, fresh pain ratcheted through her skull.

She came to gurgling water. Darkness spotted her vision. She heard Teya yelling, but it seemed to come from a great distance. By her lifesense, she detected the injury that had been dealt to her head.

A devil-damned crossbow!

Sending esse to the wound, Leiyn sloshed in the fountain until she found her feet. Whipping her head around and gasping for air, she looked for more assailants.

She almost missed the sword chopping at her head.

A soldier had gained the lip of the fountain. Leiyn raised her longbow in time to block his falling blade. Chips flew off the stave as the steel gouged into it.

Fury burned through the malaise.

"Bastard!" Funneling strength through her legs, she kicked the soldier in the chest. Steel crumpled beneath her shoe. The man sailed off the fountain to crash into a pair of his comrades. By the darkening of his lifeforce, he would not rise again soon.

Leiyn whirled, blinked her vision free of the sparks dotting it, and fitted another arrow to her bowstring. A quick scan of her lifesense showed three crossbowmen remained, all reloading. She gritted her teeth and waited for them to emerge, pulsing her mahia to keep the soldiers around the fountain at bay. Ignore the marksmen again and she risked another shot to the head. One for which there was no guarantee she would survive.

Mehu'Ra screeched as he swept down once more. Another swath of Ilberians died in the pass, their armor amplifying the lightning rather than protecting against it. Yet as the tempest hawk lifted back into the sky, the plaza and promenade still swarmed with soldiers. They were surrounded on all sides by sharp steel and hard gazes. Ilberian frustration and humiliation at losing the war was now harnessed toward this sole goal: putting down the Wilds Witch and her Legion-born friends. By all Leiyn could see, they would soon achieve that aim.

Then, the ground rumbled.

Her breath held, Leiyn risked turning her lifesense downward. She peered beneath the tunnels and sewers of the city to delve into the molten stone far below.

There, a scourge rose. A monster in their enemies' eyes. One Leiyn had never been more overjoyed to feel.

At last, Clouded Fang rose.

Relief flooded her along with his potent lifeforce. The ash dragon's power saturated her, revitalizing sluggish limbs and banishing the lingering effects of injuries.

He had not abandoned her.

She could feel why it had taken him so long to answer her summons. Though he burned with all the might of a volcano set to erupt, his esse shone dimmer than ever before. As she had feared, he continued to recuperate from the last battle.

But he remained a titan. Mere mortals could not stand in their way.

Leiyn loosed the arrows she held, then leaped forward into the gap the fallen soldiers left. As her feet touched the ground, the ash dragon arose all around her, filtering through the gaps in the pavestones. Smoke rushed down her throat. Far from choking, she reveled in the bitter taste, the burn in her lungs. It like fire truly blazed within her, and she had but to exhale to loose it upon her enemies.

The Ilberians had held their ground before one titan. Before two, their bravery broke.

"Titan!" one soldier cried as he turned tail. "*Dragon!*"

She grinned at their backs as more followed, then remembered herself. With the path clear, their original aim had once more become attainable.

"I'm going after the king!" she shouted over her shoulder as she took off at a dash.

She did not wait to see if her companions heard. With their enemies' ranks broken, they would survive her departure. Leaping over bodies, avoiding masks and food discarded in the wake of the crowd's escape, Leiyn made for the royal palanquin. The Ilberians fled before her, then ran faster as she commanded Clouded Fang to fly low overhead. The ash dragon circled just above the reach of the rooftops. Shingles flew off with each of his revolutions.

Reaching the palanquin, Leiyn circumvented it to the far side where she had seen the World King dismount. Baltesar was long gone, but she hoped her training as a ranger might show her where to seek him. Yet the scene was too chaotic for her to make sense of it. Footsteps in dust, the best she could hope for, would have long since blown away under the beat of titanic wings.

Leiyn sent her lifesense out instead. It would have been easier to find a flea in a field. She did not know the king's esse, not having had a chance to observe it before the battle began, so all those running away appeared much the same to her. She would have to lay eyes on him to be certain.

But as she reasoned through it, the direction Baltesar took promised to be the same as his Suncoats and guards: east down the promenade toward the palace. It was the only place he could hope to hide from mahas commanding titans. With the enchantments woven into its stones, defenses that guarded it from dryvans, it would be difficult for Leiyn to siege even with an ash dragon at her back. But if she was swift, she might still catch them before they reached safety.

"Then we run," she muttered as she set back into a sprint, Clouded Fang turning after her.

She did not go far. Leiyn had only reached the far end of Plaza dil Jadiel when half a dozen new combatants blazed into being behind her. Leiyn whirled back, her bow raised, one of her few Iritu arrows nocked. The blinding esses betrayed who they were even before she set eyes on them.

The lyshans had arrived.

Not all who had appeared were lyshans, though. Ata, Batu, and Rhun looked to be fighting three of the antagonistic Iritu. The reason for their delay was clear now; wounds already layered over their bodies and spirits telling of a battle long since engaged. The wildsouls looked to be suffering the worst of the exchange. Batu, transformed by his joining with Sarryl, sported coarse white hair dyed pink with his blood. Rhun, shaggy and covered in Bristle's brown fur, limped as he circled their enemies, his fury undiminished as he bellowed.

Ata gleamed with gold ichor, but most of it looked to have originated from her enemies. Though Leiyn had not seen her carrying her gear, she was clad now in her devilish armor of violet and aqua. In her hands, she clutched the titanbone war scythe, its curved blade dripping with her kin's lifeblood. Her esse blazed like a full moon over a cloudless field. As Leiyn watched, she moved with blinding speed through a grotto to reappear at a lyshan's back and slash across it.

Her victim bellowed, the sound reverberating through Leiyn's bones. It was the same bullish lyshan that had waylaid them in Solace; Ram'bal, Ata had called him. Neither hide nor armor could keep off the dryvan's attacks. Wounds delved through him, both in body and spirit, and his lifeforce had dimmed to an ember glow.

His corrupted comrades fared better. Leiyn recognized Osmet even as she transformed into a bat to elude Rhun's tearing claws. Batu circled the last lyshan, this one new to Leiyn. Tall and lithe, a pair of moth-like wings sprouted from its back, while a crown of horns resembling an elder buck's sprouted from its brow. Pine green armor layered the rest of its body, textured like the hide of Clouded Fang's underbelly. She guessed it had come from the skin of a dragon or a creature much like it. In its clawed hands, it held two sickle-shaped swords that dripped with scarlet.

Fear for her friends vied with her purpose. They had come to hunt the Caelrey. She needed to pry Baltesar from Sharo's grasp.

But if they die like Isla?

It was no choice at all. Abandoning her pursuit, Leiyn raised her bow, drew back the bowstring, and loosed.

The antlered lyshan did not look her way as it dodged, blinking in and out of existence to come around Batu's back. As it swiped the sickles, Leiyn felt its lifesense touch upon her in contemplation of this new threat, then dismissing her. Batu roared with pain as he spun, swatting at his opponent. The lyshan only leaped into the air to slash from above, mothy wings holding it aloft until it touched down safely out of reach.

Though she burned at being ignored, the lyshan's underestimation gave her a keen advantage. Leiyn shut out Batu's pain and nocked another arrow. As she did, she sent a command to her titan.

Clouded Fang circled back overhead, then folded in his smoky wings for a dive. An inferno stirred in his belly, brightening the black haze.

"Batu!" she shouted.

As her friend looked around, shaggy countenance dazed and bloodied, she loosed. The antlered lyshan dodged, as she had known he would.

But it could not dodge both her attack and her titan's.

Clouded Fang unleashed his breath upon the shapeshifter. The flames hit the green lyshan with earth-shattering force. Pavers buckled and blackened. Leiyn fought to keep her feet as she nocked another Iritu arrow and tried tracking her prey. To her relief, Batu had heeded her warning and stumbled free. The conflagration had interrupted the other bouts, though only briefly. Even as she looked toward them, they resumed with equal ferocity as before.

The lyshan reemerged from the grotto in which it had sheltered, its wings shriveled to skeletons and its dragonhide armor scorched. But its esse shone as brightly as before. Even as she watched, it shed its old wings and new ones budded like spring blooms from the nubs.

"*Egreshti* devil!"

She sent her mahia surging forth with her next arrow and ordered Clouded Fang into another dive. She just needed to corner it for a moment, distract it long enough for her titan to seize hold. Then there would be no escaping his teeth.

But this lyshan was more slippery than the one they had killed in Solace. Relying on speed and slyness, it evaded her arrow, deflected her magic, and struck at Batu even while dodging Clouded Fang's lunge. The ash dragon vanished underground where he circled back, unseen but for his esse.

If only he could hide.

But ash dragons did not have that capability, not unless they slumbered. There would be no missing Clouded Fang's charge even from below.

"Leiyn! Where has the king gone?"

Leiyn looked up to see Teya, Ekosa, and Ketti running toward her. Mehu'Ra banked to follow his bonded caller, leaving off harrying those soldiers brave or foolish enough to linger at the periphery of the plaza. Relief that they were alive and largely unharmed lasted only a moment.

Leiyn jerked her head to the road behind them as she nocked another arrow. "Saw him and his retinue headed for the castle. Might be there by now."

"Should we not pursue?" Teya pressed. She held her spear at the ready, fearless even as lyshans battered their companions with strikes that could kill.

"Not while we're fighting lyshans." Leiyn ignored their protests and raised her bow for another shot. She was already halfway through her Iritu arrows, but that was a concern for afterward. Only survival mattered.

Though she longed to help Batu, this time, she sent the arrow flying at Ram'bal. Caught by surprise and less nimble than his brethren, the arrow lodged in his left shoulder. At once, the sorcery imbued in it began eating at his lifeforce, a dozen souls lost in seconds.

The lyshan roared and swatted at the arrow, but though he broke off the shaft, he only drove the pointed tip in deeper. His distraction cost him further. Ata was on him at once, her scythe cutting across his neck. Ram'bal tipped over, his great horned head falling back. Even as he slumped to the ground, esse diminished, Ata shrieked and slashed into him, again and again. Golden droplets glittered in the gray light as they coated the white stones.

All life faded from his corpse.

Osmet only laughed at her kin's demise and vanished from Rhun's path. A grunt erupted from the boar-man, but he recovered quickly to spin around on all fours, searching for where the lyshan had gone. His beady gaze raised to see Leiyn raising her bow, their companions beside her.

Roaring with outrage, the transformed Rhun charged up the street, heading straight for them.

"Move!" Leiyn followed her own advice and, abandoning her shot, sprinted out of the wildsoul's way. She felt her companions following.

But instead of tearing past them, Rhun skidded to a halt. "Where is he?" he bellowed, the words mangled by his transformation. "The king! Where's the king?"

Leiyn held firm before the maddened wildsoul, jerking her head up the promenade. "The palace."

Rhun snarled, darkened eyes narrowing. Leiyn tensed and raised her bow, halfway expecting him to attack.

Instead, he turned and tore down the road, heading for the Caelrey's castle.

Teya pushed her after him. "Follow him, Leiyn! Make sure he only kills who he should."

Leiyn wanted to shout protests back. Batu held his own for the moment, but he had taken too many wounds, lost too much blood. Every lurch from the willowy lyshan's blades showed how her friend's reflexes had slowed and his strength dimmed.

But it had to be her. Only she and Ketti had the power of titans, and that would be needed to catch up to Rhun and the World King. And with Leiyn's ranger training, she had a better chance of survival on her own.

She met Teya's gaze. "Don't let him die."

"I would never." Giving her a grim nod, the *situal* hefted her spear, lifted her voice in a Gast war cry, and charged back into the fray.

Leiyn watched them for a moment, then turned to Ketti and Ekosa. "Keep them safe."

Without waiting for an answer, she turned and sprinted after Rhun.

40

TEARS OF GOLD

Pulse thrumming in her veins, her panting filling her ears, Leiyn ran hard in pursuit of the wildsoul. Still, Rhun sped ahead of her, his bellowing breaths growing fainter with each loping stride. The buildings lining the Promenada Palacia flew by, smeared like paint spread over canvas. Fearful faces filled the windows, their esses quivering against Leiyn's lifesense among the homes and alleys. She ignored them, set on her quarry and the mass of people moving ahead of him.

Clouded Fang!

She beseeched her titan and felt a pulse back from where he flew below. At her unspoken command, Clouded Fang sped ahead, his blistering esse warning of his approach.

Fresh screams filled the air. The promenade proceeded up an incline, obscuring the road ahead. Replacing her arrow with a broadhead without breaking stride, she strained to see what awaited her.

Her lifesense told her when Rhun began his butchery.

Leiyn ascended the rise and slowed at the sight of which her lifesense had warned her. Ilberians, both soldiers and servants, amassed before the palace gate. They seemed to have been hampered from entering by the gates themselves, for the stream of people pushing within was thin. Outside of them, the rest of those gathered schooled together like fish.

Rhun was the shark in their midst. Looming several heads above the Ilberians, the wildsoul was saturated with scarlet, much of it not his own. With each swipe of his bulky arms and toss of his tusked head, he claimed yet more victims. They had killed many Ilberians this day, the wildsoul savaged those people uncaring of whether they were armed or innocent. Brutal beyond any justification.

Yet the battle was not entirely one-sided. Spears and arrows emerged from Rhun's hide, many of them snapped halfway down. His lifefire dimmed with each wound taken, though none were yet enough to stop him.

"King!" the transfigured man shrieked over and over. "*King!*"

She could not see the Caelrey, but she knew he must be just beyond the gate. Swallowing, Leiyn sent a command to Clouded Fang, then continued her approach within fifty paces. Though she could not condone Rhun's actions, he remained aligned in their ultimate purpose. They had to break through.

She sent an arrow flying.

A broadhead not designed for piercing armor, her first arrow pinged off the helm of a guardsman. It was only sufficient to draw his glance, a pause before he thrust his spear at the wildsoul again.

Leiyn snarled and continued forward. Drawing her Eteman dagger in her right hand, she kept her bow in her left to use as a stave. Her blade a mere two-hands long and her enchanted clothes severely dimmed, she was ill-equipped to be taking on armed men.

But her mahia remained strong and her reflexes quick.

Quick enough, perhaps, to move within range of spears and swords before they skewered her.

But only if she gained an advantage.

Clouded Fang! she sent along their bond. *Rise!*

The ash dragon complied. Cries of surprise and pain filled the air as black smoke billowed over them from beyond the gate. A titan's ascent often brought deleterious effects—Clouded Fang was no different. Like blistering volcanic winds, his esse blinded and burned as it fell upon the soldiers. The thin stream of people heading into the palace scattered throughout the inner courtyard, fleeing before the rising titan.

Leiyn took advantage of the confusion as she waded into the melee. The first Suncoat barely saw her coming before Leiyn drove her reinforced dagger through the gap in her helm. A city guardsman appeared next, shock shifting to rage as he turned his spear on her. Leiyn knocked the tip aside with a sweep of her bow, then closed the distance between them in a lunge, knife leading. Though imbued with esse, the dagger was not titanbone and did not cut through the steel but only gouged it. Still, she hit with enough force to stun and stagger the man, gaining her precious moments.

Palace guards closed around her, the terror of the titan easing. Four in all, their armor appeared impenetrable and the reach of their swords long. Leiyn snarled and pulsed out her mahia, dazzling their senses before lashing at the one on her left. A bash of her bow and a stab of her knife had him on the ground, his gashed chin spewing scarlet.

From nearby, Rhun issued a fresh roar, and the armored bodies around Leiyn shifted away. Leiyn jabbed her knife under the lip of one's helm, then tore it free as she shoved the palace guard away, red droplets spraying. Leiyn whirled to face her next opponents and saw them backing away. The Ilberians saw who she was then. She read it on their lips, glimpsed it in their wide eyes.

"Witch!" one hissed, then flinched from her glare.

Rhun grunted, then charged into the sudden gap in the gate. Leiyn moved after him, and the cowed men and women shifted out of her way. She did not kill more of them. They only did their duty, as she did hers. Any lives she spared was one less mark on her soul.

Clouded Fang hovered before the palace, blocking off any escape. With every buffet of his wings, he flooded the courtyard with yet more smoke. All was obscured but his burning eyes and the smoldering fire in his belly. Only by her lifesense did she see the massive draconic form at the heart of the umber cloud.

Leiyn shifted her attention to the wildsoul. Rhun charged wildly into the smog. He could not have seen or smelled anything beyond the smoke, and if he was anything like Batu, he possessed no lifesense. But his hearing must have been keen, for he headed with unerring accuracy toward the biggest knot of people, huddled amid a copse of trees to the right.

The Caelrey.

Leiyn ran after him. Eyes stinging with smoke, she strained to catch sight of their quarry. They emerged first as silhouettes, dwarfed by the hulking figure of Rhun. The wildsoul had already reached them. He slowed, seeking his prey, then surged forth.

"Rhun!" she wheezed. "Wait!"

He was beyond hearing. "Do not touch me!" she heard a man screech. Then dark tears dragged across her lifesense like a monster's jagged claws.

Leiyn staggered forward when something rolled into her foot and clinked to the pavers. Pausing, she saw it to be a shimmering circle of metal, dimmed by dark flecks.

The crown.

A figure brimming with lifeforce appeared beside Leiyn.

She drove her knife around toward them until she recognized Ata and pulled her blow.

The dryvan ignored her error. "We must flee, little fox! My Kin come." Ata looked to Rhun. "The king?"

Leiyn was glad for the smoke as she looked toward the wildsoul. The wet, heavy blows of Rhun savaging a body continued even now that the pained cries had fallen silent. No esse remained in that body. Those surrounding them had fled, leaving the wildsoul alone to sate his vengeance.

The Caelrey lay dead.

Leiyn gave Ata a nod, bile pressing up her throat.

"Then he has what he wanted." Ata gripped Leiyn's arm. "We go."

Leiyn ripped free. "We cannot leave him!"

"There's no time! Or do you wish to fight those who come?"

What if Sharo's among them? But it was a vain thought. He would send his brethren first to ensure they were weakened before revealing himself. And if the changes she had seen upon him were true, she needed to face him when she had the advantage.

Still, she stepped toward the wildsoul, tarrying a dozen strides away. "Rhun!" she called across the smoke-strewn courtyard. "Come with us!"

The wildsoul never paused his ravaging. The cries issuing from his brutish lips seemed sobs now, as full of sorrow as anger.

"Rhun, please—"

Four figures, their esses as powerful as Ata's, appeared around them. In the gloom, Leiyn only recognized the hunched, deformed figure of Osmet. The others appeared more formidable than her.

One loomed above the others, larger even than the bullish

lyshan. What seemed to be a blade of some kind—or perhaps a horn—thrust up from his head into the murky sky.

Another spread on all fours across the ground. Not as large as the other, there seemed a predatory stance to the way it crouched. Its tail swished behind it, stirring the filthy air. Luminous eyes caught enough light to gleam through the smoke.

The last was willowy almost to the point of fragile, like a blighted tree deformed in harsh conditions. And like a tree, too many limbs thrust out from its body. The branching arms clutched what she could only assume to be weapons.

All of them stood between her and Rhun.

The wildsoul finally paused in his carnage to behold these newcomers. She felt wariness filter through the cracks of his rage. Fear followed a moment after.

"Sister, Sister!" Osmet cackled. "How well you have done clearing the way for our brother. The Wilds Witch has slain the king. Now, where shall they look for a savior? Perhaps to a devil, eh, eh?"

Ata spared no words for her Kin. Grabbing Leiyn's shoulder tightly enough for her claws to pierce the Eteman clothes, she draped her heritage over her.

The mad lyshan's laughter followed them through the void.

The abruptness of their departure staggered Leiyn as they reappeared at Plaza dil Jadiel. The bright stones were smeared with ichor and blood and blackened where Clouded Fang had unleashed his breath. Bodies were strewn among the wreckage. The arm had broken off the statue of San Jadiel amid the fountain, and water sprayed from the stump as if in a feeble attempt to clear away the scene of death.

Her companions knotted nearby, gathered around someone kneeling amid them.

Batu.

Dark tears through his lifeforce told of grievous wounds, but none seemed fatal. They were all alive. For now, it was enough.

You made your choice, Rhun.

At Leiyn and Ata's appearance, her friends looked up.

"Did you find him?" Teya demanded. "The Caelrey?"

Leiyn nodded. Batu raised his head. Still joined with his moonbear, his eyes were tinged pink, but as they locked onto hers, she glimpsed the man beneath.

"Rhun," he rumbled. "Where is he?"

Ata wrenched Leiyn forward and spoke first. "No time—we must depart. Prepare yourselves, younglings!"

Knowing she had but a moment, Leiyn reached out to Clouded Fang. The ash dragon had retreated from the lyshans; even one such as he feared lyshans when gathered in number.

Go, she told him. *Sleep.*

As the titan descended back into the ground, Leiyn felt her hold on him slip. The last she saw was a discarded mask, broken in two and stained with blood.

Then all faded into a formless fog.

PART VI

ISLE OF REVERIE

41

A DREAM OF MASKS

Six masked men stepped free of the fog to flank her. Leiyn raised her dagger and bow only to find she held neither. The weight of the anelace on her hip was also absent, and she no longer felt the hidden knife kept at her ankle. But the sight of her hands captured her. Her fingerless gloves were saturated and stained, blood crusting under her nails.

She tore her gaze away and looked beyond. The men were closing within striking distance. Leiyn reached for her mahia, but she felt nothing of it. A void greeted her where her life-sense should have been.

Fear hemmed her back as the masked men advanced. Their masks were of beasts too familiar to be coincidence. A silver fox. A white bear. An emerald hummingbird. A gray rhinoceros. But the one at their fore did not wear the aspect of an animal, but a laughing demon, red-faced and horned.

Worthless. Weak. You will die alone! You deserve *to die alone!*

Did they speak? Or were those her thoughts? The voices seemed to come from within her mind.

Is all of this in my head?

As one, the men surged across the final paces. Leiyn dodged back and raised her arms protectively. Without being able to draw on esse, she felt slow and frail.

Blades sliced her skin.

Gasping, blood pouring down her arms, she staggered back. Only as she looked down did she realize she did not wear her imbued Eteman clothes, but a garb such as she would have worn back at the Wilds Lodge. Simple, undyed wool without a scrap of magic to it. Now it was being dyed scarlet with her blood.

A dream, just a dream.

But could dreams hurt like this? Should she smell the sweat of her assailants, feel the fear fluttering in the veins in her neck? Like the previous visions, it felt too real to dismiss.

Get out, Firebrand!

As the masked men lunged at her again, Leiyn did something she rarely had in the waking world:

She ran.

Daggers cut across her back, lines of fire awakening across her back. She put on a burst of speed, outpacing them, knowing the full extent of the damage would make itself known before long. She fled into the gray wasteland, never knowing if she made any progress. There were no trees, no plants of any kind, nor any kind of landmark. She was alone but for the men trying to kill her.

"This isn't real," she panted between gasping breaths. "None of this is real!"

Leiyn darted a look over her shoulder. Even without mahia, she remained a swift runner, and soon left her pursuers behind in the gray fog. When the last had long disappeared amidst the gray world, she slowed to catch her breath.

Where can I go?

She turned in a circle, looking for any sign of an escape, a break in the monotony. None of her senses detected a way out. She was trapped in this colorless world, trapped with men who sought to do her harm.

When a break in the mist came, it was with a shudder of recognition.

Her pursuers had found her.

A second joined the first, then a third. Within moments, she was surrounded, the men with their bloody knives penning her in.

Terror such as she had never known gripped her, conspiring to send her to her knees. Stubbornness and the will to survive kept her standing.

"What do you want?" The question came out in a screeching plea. "Leave me alone!"

The men, if they were truly men behind their masks, gave no answer. They closed the distance between her and them, then braced to strike as one.

Leiyn held up her arms in a protective stance. She was unlikely to outbrawl six armed men.

But she would still fight like all the hells.

Once more, her foes lunged. As they did, a light burned through the fog—a light that came from below. The masked men tumbled forward, their knives falling short. As Leiyn watched, they fell through the floor that had been there a moment before, tumbling down toward the light.

Leiyn stared at it. An orb shone below. It was longer than it was wide, and in its center lay a round, black abyss.

An eye.

Her stomach lurched. Without warning, she was falling, tumbling into the eye. A scream built in her throat, but the speed of her descent trapped it there, choking her. She stared into the shining eye and prayed aloud as she fell.

"Mercy, Omn Almighty! *Mercy!*"

As futile an attempt as before. The chasm of the eye swallowed the sound, the same as it did the masked men. The same as she was about to be.

The light shone all around her. Darkness grew below. Leiyn closed her eyes and stopped fighting. Surrendered.

She had done all she could. She was ready to die.

As she hit the bottom, the cradle of unrelenting ground almost came as a relief.

42

REFUGE

Water rushed up her nose.

Leiyn spluttered and jerked upright, coughing, and wiped her eyes clear. Other people littered the beach on which she found herself, each reacting as she had as the surf rushed over them. Her companions—as she recognized them, relief saturated her as thoroughly as saltwater.

Another wave rushed over her, unpleasantly cold, shocking her into action. She scrambled to her feet, brushed herself free of sand, and took stock of the situation. Somehow, she had kept hold of her longbow and weapons. Her pack remained with Ekosa, whom she had given it to before the ambush. She felt up and down her body, but neither touch nor lifesense revealed any lingering wounds.

As she straightened her jerkin, her sleeve pulled up. The skin beneath caught her eye. Leiyn stared at the pink lines crisscrossing her forearm. Too faint to be called wounds and barely leaving an impression on her lifesense, yet the sight of them sent chills through her.

The masked men. The eye.

It had been a dream, only a dream—yet their knives had

cut. If that was real, was the rest of it? The gigantic eye that swallowed her—what was that supposed to be? Who had those men been? And Sharo before—had all she had seen of him been real as well?

She lowered her arm and looked up. Travel by grotto typically only took a moment, but the sunlight was already golden with oncoming sunset. For reasons she could only guess at, they had lost hours in that single leap—or days, if this was no longer the same evening.

"Leiyn?"

Leiyn looked around, relief swelling in her breast. Teya tottered toward her, the rest of their companions straggling behind. Batu had separated from Sarryl and pulled on trousers, but he had not yet put on the shirt bunched in his hand, revealing the horrid wounds across his body. His moonbear bore the same cuts and moved ponderously next to him. Ketti and Ekosa appeared unharmed, and Teya's injuries were shallow. Ata was nowhere to be seen.

"Leiyn!" Batu hurried past the others, staggering as he slipped and almost fell to the sand. His moonbear moaned and butted his side, urging him back up. The wildsoul did not spare him a look, casting his desperate gaze upon Leiyn. "Where are they? Rhun and Bristle—didn't they make it?"

Her face must have betrayed the truth, for his eyes widened. Leiyn grasped for excuses.

"I'm sorry, Batu. He was beyond Ata's reach."

"Beyond her reach?" Fear morphed into fury. "She took all of us—she could have taken him! But she never meant to, did she?" Batu rose to his full height, heedless of how his wounds pulled and wept fresh blood down his chest and whipped his head around. "Where is she?"

"Gone." Leiyn had suspected the truth as soon as she noticed her absence. "I think we're on our own."

"Not this time, younglings."

Leiyn startled as the lyshan unveiled her lifeforce while descending the slope before them. Her talons easily found purchase in the sand, and her languid lope never shifted. Nor had her knowing smile. Just then, Leiyn found it particularly irritating.

Batu must have seen worse in it. He started toward her, face twisted into a snarl. Leiyn and Teya moved between them, Leiyn pressing a hand to Batu's chest where it was free of injury. She held firm as he tried pushing past her.

"Calm down," she snapped, her own temper barely bridled. "We've fought enough."

He stopped resisting, but she could feel the roil of his esse against her own. His glare as unabated, as was the hardness of his words. "You abandoned them. Left them to die!"

Ata stopped several paces up the slope and stared coolly back. "I did as I must. Rhun and Bristle slaked their thirst for vengeance rather than fled. They seemed to enjoy brutalizing that king's body, did they not, Leiyn?"

Leiyn grimaced and looked away. She was glad Clouded Fang had hidden most of the carnage from view. The sluicing of blood and meat as Rhun tore into the corpse still echoed in her ears.

Batu rounded his shoulders. "You could have saved them."

She recognized the beginning of a sob behind those words. A lump formed in Leiyn's throat.

"Not with four of my Kin between us." With a brisk air, Ata looked aside and cast her gaze over the beach. "We have more pressing matters. I have brought us to as near the Catedrál as I was able, but I was foiled here at the beach. Something about this place..." She trailed off, frowning up at the mountain rising above.

Leiyn followed her gaze. "This is Refugio?"

For all she had heard of the Hallowed Isle, she had never tried to picture it. This place seemed more rugged than she had expected. The mountain at which the dryvan stared appeared the dominant feature to it; Monte Ardiente, she dredged up its name from the dim recesses of her brief Catedrál education. The rest of the landscape sloped around it. Ridges, undulating and stony, cascaded down its sides and rose to either side of their beach, hemming them into a valley that appeared difficult to escape. Mastic trees and a tangled underbrush spread across the basin, promising a strenuous hike through.

Most worrying was how her lifesense perceived it. Leiyn shared the disquiet Ata felt. It was like being in a grotto or the presence of a titan, though tolerable and far less intrusive. In every moment, she felt the island pressing against her lifesense, a pulsation almost like a heartbeat thrumming from below.

What are you?

Ketti broke the silence. "Our *semah*—it will not work here?"

The dryvan roused back to herself, a smile stretching her wooden lips wide. "Your power, I would not fear for. Perhaps you shall experience discomfort, but little more. I will not risk mine unless we must. Moving through grottos may come with...unintended consequences."

Yet another complication. Leiyn stiffened her jaw. "We'll figure out a way into the Catedrál. But we have to find our way there first."

"Actually," Ekosa cut in, "we should first tend to our wounds and rest. And perhaps discuss what our plans are?"

Racing ahead as usual, Firebrand.

"We find shelter, then." Leiyn glanced at Ata. "Don't suppose you already found some?"

The dryvan quirked her mossy eyebrows. "Possibly. Though the requirements of you frail mortals still eludes me." She turned and bounded up the slope, not waiting to ascertain if they would follow.

Leiyn had drained her amber beads of lifeforce, but her esse still burned high. Drawing on it for strength, she moved to Batu's side, placed a hand to his arm, and pressed more lifeforce into him.

"Can you walk?" She spoke gently as she could manage, though discomfited and wary as she was, it veered toward abrupt.

Batu bobbed his head. He did not meet her eyes, but moved past at a plodding pace. Sarryl cast her a reproachful gaze before ambling after him.

Leiyn swallowed a sigh. As Ekosa passed by, she took back her pack from him, then fell back to the rear of their party. Touching her bond to Clouded Fang for reassurance, she nocked an arrow and kept watch as they made their way up.

The trek through the valley was every bit as pleasant as she had anticipated. The trail led ever upward, at times steep enough that they climbed with both hands and feet. The bugs added to their difficulties as soon as they entered the forest. Leiyn wiped the sweat from her brow and banished the pestering midges with intermittent blasts of esse, but they always came back, buzzing in her ears and before her eyes. The muttered exclamations of her companions and slaps at their skin told they suffered as much as she did. Only Batu and Ata seemed immune, the wildsoul too mired in misery to mind such minor irritations.

Ata led them out of the forest and up the ridge. A path lay unseen up the eastern edge, though it promised a fatal fall should they slip from the narrow ledge. They all followed in determined silence. Leiyn kept a careful watch on Batu and his moonbear, worrying over them. From the extent of their wounds, they could easily be unbalanced. But both remained steady-footed, even as ocean winds conspired to blow at inopportune moments. As if the island itself wished them to slip.

The hike ended in a shallow cavern. Little more than an indentation in the ridge, it promised marginal shelter from rain. The wind, at least, was blocked by the continued ridgeline, which rose and fell in a semblance of waves above. Putting away her arrow, Leiyn set down her pack and bow, then moved to Batu and Sarryl where they slumped against the cavern wall. Both spirit beast and wildsoul looked up with the same baleful look as she approached, but neither voiced complaint as she squatted next to them.

"May I?" she murmured.

Batu nodded, so Leiyn set her hands on him, closed her eyes, and began healing his wounds. Ketti soon joined them to do the same for Sarryl, who tolerated the Eteman's touch better than Leiyn's. One after another, they coaxed the cuts closed and eradicated the infection already taking root.

When the last had sealed shut, Leiyn staggered to her feet, then sought a perch next to Teya. The scout cast her a sympathetic smile and handed her a strip of smoked venison. Leiyn accepted it and, hungry as she was, ate it without relish. Ketti found her way to Leiyn's other side, her footing steadier than Leiyn's. The precious stones embedded in her skin had dimmed of lifeforce, telling whence her stores of energy came.

The Eteman opened her rucksack and ate from the nuts and unripe berries she had collected. "Perhaps we had best seek shelter in a grotto," she said around a mouthful.

"I would not." Ata did not turn around as she spoke. "Not here."

Leiyn narrowed her eyes at the dryvan's feathery back. "Why not here?"

Ata looked over her shoulder, head lolling at an impossible angle. "My heritage is...stunted. It would be more perilous to use our power than not."

"Stunted?" Dread slithered through Leiyn, eating at her like maggots would dead wood. She shared a look with Teya and saw her fears reflected in her beloved's eyes. "What does that mean?"

Ata only laughed and faced the sea.

Leiyn turned to Ketti. The Eteman seemed to think the same as she: that perhaps they ought to make the attempt themselves. But things were dire if Ata declared something dangerous. Leiyn shook her head, and Ketti subsided, gems folding into her wrinkled brow.

Ekosa shifted in his seat against the shallow cavern before hesitantly breaking the silence. "If we are staying put, perhaps we ought to discuss what comes next."

Ata laughed again. Stomach sinking, Leiyn faced the dryvan.

"Is it not evident?" the dryvan said over a feathered shoulder. "We go to the high priestess and take her from my brother, the same as we did his king."

"There would not happen to be a parade soon?" Teya muttered.

Ata turned back, mismatched eyes shadowed from the setting sun. "She would not attend if there were. No, spear-maiden. There is only one route to this Altacura. Inevitabilities are best faced with your senses open."

The *situal* shrugged. "I prefer to see if they can be avoided first."

"How many more?" Batu broke in, drawing everyone's eyes. He stared at Ata, a baleful look in his eyes. "How many more," he repeated, "of your Kin must we kill?"

Ata smiled. Myriad emotions flitted through her essence, too many and quick for Leiyn to track.

"Well," the dryvan said, holding up a hand, "you've met the effervescent Osmet. And there's Enthil, that winged wretch wearing dragonhide." She counted each on her claws.

"He escaped, but I killed Ram'bal, and you took care of Shu'eil in Solace and Nabo on the water. That leaves Urta, Azarah, Ish'tar...and my brother." She closed her hand into a fist and let it fall.

"Only six?" Leiyn's chest loosened, breath coming more easily. "The rest are dead?" she pressed, scarcely daring to hope.

"They are." Ata did not sound pleased by the revelation. She stroked a finger across her chest—caressing the Mothertree seed within, Leiyn knew. "Only seven Iritu remain."

"For now."

It was Ketti who said this, to Leiyn's surprise. Their companions seemed to share that bafflement. The Eteman only bowed her head and held her silence.

Leiyn tried wrapping her mind around it. Perhaps the shift was not so different from her own pivot in perspective regarding Gasts. A realization that the crimes of a few did not dictate the guilt of all. That every people deserved hope. And redemption was always possible.

She reached for Teya's hand and gripped it tightly. Teya squeezed hers back.

"Then it's almost done." Batu did not reflect the peaceful intent Ketti had shared. His eyes were shadowed as he stared at the stone between their party. "We've almost won."

The dryvan narrowed her eyes. Leiyn thought it best to intervene, lest an argument be coming.

"Best not get ahead of ourselves. We barely survived the last fight." She hesitated, then continued without mention of Rhun and Bristle. His absence was conspicuous enough without her evoking it.

"First thing is we reconnoiter. Scout out the area and see what we can learn of the Catedrál compound itself." She dredged up maps of the Ancestral Lands from her memory.

"There's a port near the Catedrál called Bayo Sol. I'll head there, learn what I can from the locals."

"And be recognized again?" Teya snorted a laugh. "If they knew you in Vasara, they will know you there. Better careful than dead, Redlock. I will go in your stead."

Leiyn reined in her temper. "A Gast will appear more out of place. I'll have my hood up—no one will get a good look."

Batu opened his mouth as if to speak, then shut it. Leiyn was glad he did not volunteer. Though he had known Rhun and Bristle but a few days, she knew how much he had valued their companionship. Now, like Isla, they had been ripped away. He needed time to mourn.

Though he'll have too little as it is.

"Ekosa and I will remain behind," Ketti said. "I would draw more eyes than either of you and we must forage if we are to stay here any length of time."

"And find clean water," Ekosa added. "Summoning Mehu'Ra here would be unwise, I think."

Leiyn nodded, glad for her acumen. None should have remained alone, Batu least of all. "Good. We leave at dawn."

"And here I was, hoping to sleep in." Teya smiled teasingly.

"I must conduct my own explorations." Ata turned back to them but cast her gaze on high to the mountain again. "There is much I must understand here."

The dryvan wasted no more time on words. Heedless of the hour of day or the need for rest, she strode off to the opposite ridge and climbed up it with implacable strides. Where shoes would have slipped, her talons found sure footing.

Leiyn watched until she disappeared. "Sure," she muttered around a mouthful of tough meat. "You go do that."

Teya gave her a pitying look. "*Sach'aan* do as they please. Perhaps she is our ally, but I would not call her our friend."

She called me seed-sister. Swore to aid us. Said she owed me a debt that could not be repaid.

Leiyn stifled the pitiable thoughts. Much had occurred since Leiyn had saved Ata's life. They had both changed. She could only hope the dryvan would hold true to her word.

"We killed the World King." Batu's words fell between them. His gaze was as ponderous as he lifted it to stare at the rest of them. "Or Rhun did, rather," he added, his eyes dropping back to the ground.

"Doesn't matter who struck the final blow," Leiyn said. "We're all regicides in the eyes of the Union. We'll all be hunted."

"Your people will see it differently," Teya offered. "Perhaps mine as well. To kill the outlander king—it is a thing the Many Tribes did not dream possible."

Ekosa wiped a hand over his face, his jade ring flashing in the wan sunlight. "I do not see my exile changing. Ore-Ofe remains with Eyi, and the Eyin Empire as Ilberia's ally."

Ketti and Batu remained silent. There was no changing either of their situations as well. Leiyn wondered if she even wanted Mauricio's forgiveness.

And where but Baltesia can you call home?

She drove the thought away. That was for after their war was finished. After Sharo lay dead, and all his lyshans with him.

Plenty of time after, she thought, her amusement dark as cold coals.

"There's something else," Leiyn said, a fragmented conversation resurfacing. "She Who Remains, Osmet—she appeared with three other lyshans after Rhun and Bristle caught the king."

Batu stared at her, drawing Leiyn's gaze. "Is that why?" he croaked. "Why you left him?"

Leiyn repressed a wince and nodded. "We didn't have much of a choice."

"Did she speak?" Ketti's question was edged sharp as titan-bone. "That *gallu*, Osmet—what did she say?"

Leiyn shrugged, trying to piece her memories together. "That we've helped Sharo rather than hurt him. In removing the Caelrey, we may have created a way for Sharo to take direct control of the Union. And that fear of us will drive Ilberians into accepting his reign."

"A *sach'aan* as king?" Teya shook her head. "I cannot believe it."

"Why not?" Ekosa leaned onto his knees. "We Ofeans believe our queens to be divine. Would Ilberia not come to accept their king as eternal?"

Leiyn scowled at the stone at her feet. *Sharo's changing. Maybe enough to pass for human, if he wishes.* But those were thoughts best kept private.

"We won't give him a chance," she said, trying to sound more certain than she felt. "We take away the Catedrál, send the Union into chaos, and draw him out of hiding. Him and the rest of the lyshans."

"One at a time, if the ancestors are merciful," Teya said with a wan smile.

Leiyn returned it. They both knew they would not be so fortunate.

43

SCARS

The eye filled her mind as she awoke.

Leiyn sat up slowly, trying to claw back the fragmented dream. Was it a vast eye she had seen, or just the sense of being watched? When she thought it over, she pieced together not an eye, but rocks studded with gemstones shot through with twisted roots.

Roots red as veins.

Even so, it had not been so different from the dream she'd had while traveling to Qasaar. An Isle of Death...so it had seemed then. Had that been Refugio she had seen? Had part of her known, even then, that she must come here?

Had she chosen to come here, or had something else drawn her?

She shook her head and extracted herself from her bedroll. The morning air had a lingering whiff of winter, and the stone beneath them had left her bruised and uncomfortable all the night through. They were nothing a burst of esse could not banish.

Ketti, the least injured among them, had kept watch

through the night. She nodded at Leiyn upon her rousing, which Leiyn returned.

Before she went anywhere, Leiyn refilled one of her amber beads, as she had throughout the previous evening. Only five swirled with lifeforce. It would be enough to last her in an emergency—enough until Clouded Fang came to her call.

She touched on their bond once more. Only after she felt the ash dragon's burning gaze did she let him lapse back into slumber.

Teya was up moments after her. Soon, they had readied for the long trek across the island. Though they would bring packs with food and water and keep their knives on their belts, their bows and Teya's spear had to remain behind, no doubt forbidden at the foot of the Holy Catedrál as they had been in Vasara.

Though it posed a risk to travel without full armaments, more concerning to Leiyn was Ata's absence. The dryvan had not reappeared since the night before, and when Leiyn tried seeking her out, she failed to do so. Either Ata was veiled, or, like Iritu magic, Leiyn's mahia found its limits on this island.

Much as she might hope it was true, it was a thin hope to hang her companions' lives on. Yet with little other choice, Leiyn swallowed her fears and pretended all would be well, a charade she was beginning to master. Even if the fear remained.

As they made their farewells, Batu bade them, "Be careful."

Leiyn flashed a wry smile. "When am I not?"

He rolled his eyes.

They skirted down the ledge by which they had first arrived at their camp, then moved west across the valley to the opposing ridge. Scaling that cliff only brought them marginally closer to their destination. If Leiyn stretched forth her life-sense, she could feel the town of Bayo Sol leagues afar—three or four, at a guess, though distance was always difficult to estimate by mahia. Over such difficult terrain, it would not be an easy hike to accomplish in a single day.

No harder than many in the Titan Wilds, she reminded herself.

Beyond the western ridge, however, lay tamer wilderness. Teya found a game trail to follow, trafficked enough that the grass had been stamped to dirt, and their pace increased. Until then, they had traveled in wary silence, but with the easy walking, conversation blossomed again.

When Teya spoke, her topic of choice was one Leiyn would have rather avoided.

"You must trust us, Redlock." The *situal* spoke over her shoulder, the narrowness of the trail necessitating they travel in single file. "Trust me."

Leiyn scowled off into the wilderness, glad her beloved could not see her. "I do trust you."

As Teya shot a look back, Leiyn carefully smoothed her expression. By the scout's frown, Teya had not missed it.

"You have a strange way of showing it," she said as she faced forward. "Back in Vasara, you were supposed to go after the Caelrey, but you stayed back. You do not think we can take care of ourselves."

"It's not that, Teya. It's..." If Teya did not already understand after all they had been through, how could Leiyn hope to explain? But for Teya's sake, she had to try. "It's what happened with Isla."

Teya sighed. "Of course it is to do with Isla. You are afraid if you turn away from us for a moment, you will lose us." The *situal* looked back again. "That will not happen, Redlock."

"You cannot promise that," Leiyn hissed. "Don't act like you can."

In the stillness that followed, shame swelled within her. When she grew too swollen with it, Leiyn set aside her pride.

"Look. I know I made a mistake. I should have gone after Baltesar." Leiyn studied her feet, though the ground was even enough she did not have to watch where she walked. "But I might have saved Batu's life by staying behind. If it comes to losing one of you or losing this war, you cannot ask me to make a different choice."

"I can," Teya murmured, just audible over their crunching footsteps. "And I will."

Silence threatened them once more. Leiyn had tired of its song. "I won't lose you."

Teya sighed. "I am a warrior, Leiyn, the same as you. We both knew we could lose our lives when we joined this fight." She glanced back again. "Fear may kill us the same as the lack of it. Your fear may have cost Rhun his life. It may cost me mine, or you yours, if you let it."

"Rhun got himself killed, not me. And what am I supposed to do, stop caring about you?" Leiyn wanted to bowl over a tree, rip it from its roots and toss it down the slope to the sea. "Just accept that I'll watch you die? That you'll be gone before I even notice?"

"If we lose the war, you will lose all of us," Teya countered. "Only by dedicating ourselves to the mission and not flattering our fear can we hope to succeed." The scout sighed. "You must move past this, Redlock, and soon. For all our sakes."

Leiyn turned away. She did not promise she would try. Even that much was beyond the truth.

They carried on in silence, giving Leiyn the opportunity to observe their surroundings in greater detail. The sea yawned to their left, visible through gaps in the trees. Upon the horizon, the main continent of the Ancestral Lands was barely visible. The occasional ship sailed by. She knew little of seacraft, but enough to know these were no fisher vessels. The Catedrál patrolled its waters. She hoped their camp would not be visible and that the others knew to remain wary.

To their right loomed Refugio's central mountain, Monte Ardiente. From this angle, they could observe it better than from the beach where they had washed up. Two stone slabs thrust into a peak from the rocky hills splayed at its feet. Even if she did not know it had once been a volcano from the stories of San Inhoa's first miracle, the black basalt rife down the cliffs and sides would have told her. A hole in the peak's side told of a caldera, one long since dormant. Rock flowed from the opening like a river of calcified tears.

The giant eye of her visions flashed into her mind. Leiyn blinked and pushed it away. Now was not the moment to consider what it might mean. More practical considerations lay before them.

Cage it, lion cub.

Facing forward, Leiyn broke the silence as if their conversation had never ceased. "I won't endanger you, Teya. I won't let my fears get in the way, I swear it."

She felt her beloved's stare on her, but did not turn back to meet it. Afraid she would see all she had omitted in the oath reflected in her skeptical eyes.

Teya sighed. "For now, that must do. Put it from your mind. All will be well. Only six lyshans remain, no?"

Leiyn nodded, then increased their pace. She hoped Teya was right. Hoped the war was drawing to a close as it appeared, as their enemies' ranks narrowed.

Her fears whispered a darker tale. And she could not help but listen.

44

THE GOLDEN PORT

They set a swift pace across the island, so it was barely past noon when they drew close to Bayo Sol.

As civilization reasserted itself, buildings emerged along their widening trail. "What are they?" Teya whispered, eyeing the first of them.

"Chapels, I suppose. For meditation."

Most of the chapels were little more than round gazebos set amid a clearing. Idols to the Sacred Saints and Omn sheltered within, wooden and stone ones that carried little material value.

Even had she still believed in the Catedrál's creed, Leiyn doubted she would have sought such places for worship. The greatest holiness she had felt was while lost in the wilderness, not within walls shaped by mortal hands.

The chapels lay unoccupied until within a half-league of the town, where some had one or two people within. None possessed mahia that Leiyn could tell. Still, she and Teya gave them a wide berth, venturing among the tangled brush and traveling in near silence as only rangers and *situali* could.

As the town came into view, they hid their mahia. Though

it was unlikely odiosas watched all those around town, it paid to be cautious. Here at the heart of Catedrál power, news of the Caelrey's death may well have reached them.

Even with their magic veiled, Leiyn knew they would stick out like diseased branches on a blossoming tree. The hike had done little to improve their bedraggled state. Having not spared the time to launder their clothes, Leiyn worried they had missed a spot of blood on the Eteman clothing.

Her efforts were not in vain. Bayo Sol was a paragon for any town. As clean as Premier Itzel kept Folly, this port sparkled in the sunlight. White stone and stucco adorned its streets and structures. Terracotta roofs and golden banners were welcome splashes of color. Gardens, too, were not infrequent, cropping up in plazas where glittering fountains shot water through the air. Statues adorned most intersections.

Above it all rose the campus of the Holy Catedrál. Approaching Bayo Sol from a higher vantage, Leiyn considered the compound. Many times the size of Mauricio's enclosure back in Southport, it was on a scale to rival any king's palace. Like the town below, the buildings were formed of shimmering white stone, and dozens of them crowded within its walls. Among them was a cathedral of at least thrice the breadth of the First Temple of Baltesia and twice its height. Beyond lay an even more impressive sight: the Basilica Sóveran. A palace of glowing stone and glittering windows that was home to the Altacura herself.

As beautiful and impressive as the campus was, it made for a formidable fortress. Guards watched at regular intervals from the crenelations. Odiosas were present as well, and though fewer in number, Leiyn counted a handful from their vantage.

It would be no simple matter to win their way inside.

"Won't accomplish anything standing up here," Leiyn muttered.

At Teya's nod, Leiyn led the way down into the port. The defenses of Bayo Sol were far more relaxed than how the Catedrál appeared. No guards accosted them before allowing entry, nor were there gates or walls to speak of. Those few guards they saw looked relaxed and almost bored as they leaned on their pikes and chatted in pairs. The populace, too, appeared haler and happier than in most towns Leiyn had visited. Vagrants and paupers often made up a majority of crowds back in Baltesia, but here, Leiyn espied nothing but respectable people.

She cursed the fortune of the villagers. Moving through the town cloaked and unkempt would be made all the more difficult for it.

"Let's keep to the alleys," Leiyn muttered, moving for the closest one as a guard looked over with a frown.

The *situal* nodded. "Stole the words from my lips."

Only once they were out of sight among the shadowed walls did Leiyn breathe a sigh of relief. Even there, the town defied expectations. Excrement had plainly been dumped there before by the faint odor, but it seemed a distant memory. Narrow canals running alongside the buildings told the rest of the tale: aboveground sewers bore their waste into the sea.

"Where to now?" Teya glanced along the alley. "Where can we go where we will not stand out?"

Leiyn doubted that place existed. But they had not come all this way only to turn back.

"We'll try this way," she said, gesturing toward the alley.

They turned the corner, following the alley out to a plaza. Crystalline water shimmered in the air as it sprayed from marble statues of the five Sacred Saints. They stood upon a vast plain orb, the typical representation of Omn. Around the fountain, people gathered. Some children splashed in the water, while those filling ewers and buckets shooed them away from it. Other adults sat at its edge, conversing as if they had no other business to be about in the middle of the day. A few glanced over at Leiyn and Teya's appearance, but though their brows creased, any suspicion lasted but a moment before they returned to their tasks.

"A strange place," Teya murmured. "I cannot understand it."

"Nor can I." Leiyn nodded toward the broad staircase leading up to the Catedrál proper. "Let's get closer."

They spent the afternoon moving through the streets of Bayo Sol, weaving around the walls separating the town from the campus. Other subtle barriers became obvious the more time they spent there. Priestesses in their gold-and-white robes, the sun and stars of the Catedrál emblazoned upon their chests, moved about the town like royalty. The city watch also deferred to their Omnist counterparts: paladins, Leiyn had heard them named. Their armor was of a metal so white it was blinding to behold. Omn's symbol was etched in gold on their breastplates, and white plumage rose from their helms fashioned like lion's maws. As decorative as their armor appeared, however, it also seemed fully functional and difficult to contend with. Her falchions would have cut through them.

If only I'd held onto them.

They attempted to gather information by means other than their own senses. Lacking Ilberian coin, they forewent the risks of robbery and attempted to speak to vendors and rely upon their generosity. To Leiyn's surprise, many were happy to stand and chat, even when Leiyn and Teya stood in the way of customers.

"Newcomers," one jolly pot-bellied man said, beaming at them as a woman ambled up to his fruit stand. "Can you imagine? Two young ladies come here! And just arrived, by the looks of them."

The woman was less welcoming. Sniffing in their direction, she selected a handful of figs, then hurried away.

"Don't mind Vega," the fruit seller said with a dismissive wave. "She's like that with everyone. Now, what were you wondering?"

From the peddler, who named himself Yavin, Leiyn and Teya learned about how the town was run. The big man made it out to be as affluent as it first struck them. "All blessings flow from the Catedrál," he said with a respectful nod toward the campus, signing the sun across his chest. "We would not lead our lives without following their example."

There was only one exception to this prosperity: the vagrants. "They come from all over," Yavin said, sweeping an arm to the distant shores just visible from his stand. "Pilgrims come for the First Altar on the Ardiente—like yourselves, 'less I'm mistaken. Others just looking for a bit of generosity in lives scant of it." He shook his head with pious pity. "Every person deserves a kind turn, don't they?"

Leiyn agreed, trying not to let her distraction show. If they resembled pilgrims, they might not stick out as much as she feared. A disguise worth exploring, at least while in town. She doubted it could win them passage within the Catedrál walls; they could not veil their esse and walk openly before priestesses and odiosas.

"Of course," Teya agreed with a glance at Leiyn. "I am glad they are taken care of."

Leiyn bobbed her head, then cast a meaningful look up at the compound. "So we present ourselves at the gate?"

Yavin grinned, assured his guess was accurate. "That you do. Acolytes there will show you to the altars. Most like to burn an offering or article of someone who passed for each of the Saints, then sit and think on Unknowable Omn." He held up his hands. "But you know your business better than I. Fruit is all I know, from my *abuelo* to my *padre* down to me!"

Leiyn obliged him a smile. Despite his thoughtless faith, she enjoyed his affability. "Thanks, Yavin."

"Of course, young ladies, of course." His good humor dimmed as his gaze lingered on Teya's face. "Say, if you don't mind me asking, where are you two from? Don't recognize your accents, and I know them from the world over."

She should have expected the question, but the fruit seller's easy manner had lulled her into complacency. Pulse fluttering, Leiyn hid her agitation with a shrug. "A nowhere village. Folks always say we speak funny there."

"Ah, that must be it."

Despite his words, as they spoke their farewells and crossed the plaza away from Yavin, Leiyn felt his gaze lingering.

"Think he will say anything?" Teya murmured when they had retreated to the safety of the alley.

"Don't know. And I don't like not knowing." Leiyn looked either way down the alley, then set off from the plaza. "Let's see if we cannot find these pilgrims Yavin mentioned. Maybe there's a way we can sneak in with them."

"With our mahia veiled?"

"I know, I know. But there might be some advantage we're not seeing."

The *situal* relented, so they made their way around the edge of town up closer to the Catedrál campus. The paladins and guards increased in number as the walls and shining buildings loomed on the hill above. Leiyn had to tell herself not to hunch as they passed them, nor look aside as they cast hard gazes at each of them under their hoods.

"Hold!"

Leiyn stiffened through the shoulders as a man's authoritative voice rang down the street after them. She kept walking. Teya barely broke stride as well, intuiting Leiyn's plan.

"You two," the male guard repeated, armor rattling as he set after them, "stop right there!"

"Cover me," Leiyn hissed, then lowered her walls. Bayo

Sol came into dazzling awareness as she stretched out her lifesense. She did not let it slow her, nor Teya's own mahia extending over her to hide her from prying eyes. She had to work swiftly if they had any hope of this succeeding.

She felt the guards approaching behind them, lifeforce swirling with suspicion. Leiyn infiltrated their bodies with ease and pressed in different thoughts.

Innocent. Unimportant. Ignore, ignore.

The man and his comrade—a woman—stuttered to a halt. Confusion battled them into a standstill, allowing Leiyn and Teya to widen their lead. She heard them mutter, but they were too far to distinguish their words. But as suspicion proliferated across their lifefires, she could guess what had triggered it.

It had always been too much to hope Catedrál guards were not trained against mahia.

Casting aside subtlety, Leiyn sent a wave of esse into the pursuing guards, staggering both. The male fell to one knee with a rattle while the female stayed upright, her lifeforce betraying the effort her resistance required. By the time they recovered, Leiyn and Teya had already turned the far corner and were clearing away. Ducking into the closest alley, they turned at the far corner, then waited.

Any relief was short lived. With her lifesense still open, Leiyn felt the guards still hard in pursuit. But they moved past the alley to continue down to the harbor.

"We should head east," Teya whispered.

Leiyn nodded. Having been driven to the western side of town, they had to cross back to return to where their companions camped.

"The central plaza," Leiyn said at length. "It's far from the Catedrál. We can hide among the other people."

"And if they are watching for us?" Teya shook her head. "Never mind. I know we have few options."

With Leiyn scanning their path before them and Teya covering her, they evaded paladins and guards until they reached the plaza. It was more sparsely occupied than Leiyn had hoped; some vendors were packing up for the day, and fewer customers streamed between the stands. The Catedrál's warriors, however, were in ample supply. A dozen combed the rubble, peering at every bystander they passed.

"They're searching for us," Leiyn muttered.

"But not everywhere." Teya nodded toward the broad stairs that led up to the white campus. "I think we found our beggars."

Leiyn followed her gaze to the broad stairs leading up to the white campus of the Catedrál. A motley crowd had gathered at the base of them. In contrast to the local populace, their clothes were in various states of disrepair and patched from hood to shoe. Some were bowed with injury; others could barely stand at all, leaning heavily on weathered canes. Of those with bared head, Leiyn spotted graying among half. The others seemed young, many barely old enough to qualify as adults.

Several stairs above them, a priestess in white and gold robes waited with her hands clasped before her. Her long hair was a dark curtain down her back. A sash of silver silk cinched the robe around her waist, flattering her figure. As the woman cast her bright gaze over the crowd, a suspicion crept up on her. Knowing it to be foolish, she stretched forth her lifesense to examine the priestess. She had but to brush her esse to recognize it.

Adelina.

Here was the same woman who had overseen the First Temple of Baltesia. The one who had lured Leiyn into the bowels of the temple, ambushed her, then had her thrown in a hidden dungeon for six days without food or water. A tremor worked through her at the memory. She felt the gristle of raw rat meat between her teeth, tasted warm blood on her tongue.

Leiyn fought down a gag and withdrew her mahia. Hatred was all she should have felt for the priestess. Yet despite herself, despite Teya standing beside her, she felt the allure of the shapely woman once more.

Fool, she chastised herself, drowning the pathetic attraction.

She had stared too long. Sister Adelina raised her gaze in their direction. Leiyn ducked back around the corner before she could think better of it, Teya following.

"What is it?" the scout whispered. "Do you know that woman?"

Leiyn hesitated, then explained who it was. Her beloved's expression darkened with each word.

"*Egreshti itsk.*" Teya looked back around the corner, her scowl apparent even within her shadowed hood. "I would like to show the sly bitch how pleasant imprisonment is."

Exasperated but warmed through, Leiyn pulled the *situal* back out of sight. "Don't be a fool. The best thing we can do is avoid her. If anyone recognizes me here, it's her."

Teya still wore a mutinous expression, but she nodded. "I will behave myself, then. For now."

Pressing reassurances on Leiyn, the scout looked around the corner once more. "She is overseeing the giving of food to the crowd," Teya reported. "Two younger women with her are passing it out from heavy baskets."

Leiyn risked a look herself. It was as Teya said: acolytes moved among the vagrants, handing out bread and fruit. For all their shabby appearance, the paupers were respectful and orderly as they accepted their fare. They held back from devouring it at once but merely clasped it while seeming to await something.

The acolytes returned to Adelina's side as the priestess

raised her hands over the assemblage. "May the Sacred Saints bless each one of you this day," she called, loud enough to be heard even across the plaza. "May Omn watch over and protect you. By the example of those who came before us, we shall strive each day to shine brighter than the one before. We are the Light cast upon the world."

"We strive to drive out the Darkness," the vagrants spoke back with eerie coordination.

Adelina smiled, seemingly full of benevolence, and raised her arms. Voluminous sleeves trailed from her wrists. In her pristine robe, they seemed like the wings of an angel. "Go and be at peace."

With that, the crowd dispersed and consumed their fare, the reticence of the moments before vanished before their hunger. The guards about the plaza moved toward them, seeing an opportunity to search for their quarry. It left the walk across only monitored by two guards, both of whom were looking toward Adelina as she walked back up the stairs toward the Catedrál. Leiyn fought not to follow their gaze. She had enough to worry about without an attraction to her former captor.

"Let's go," she said to Teya. "While they're distracted."

The scout nodded and, with a furtive look either way, set off across the plaza. Leiyn followed, but as one among the vagrants turned to her, she came stuttering to a halt.

A familiar face stared back at her. His hair was longer and darker than the blonde she had known it to be. His face was gaunter, and there was a hollowness to his eyes and his cheeks. He cradled an arm to his chest, the sleeve tied over the end of the stump.

Even had she not recognized his injury, Leiyn could not easily forget Arias di Carille.

Leiyn ducked her head, as much from the danger of the moment as shame. He could easily recognize her as she had him. And considering the state he found himself in, she doubted he would harbor much gratitude for her saving his life. Not after she had been the one to lop off his arm.

And doom him to this existence.

"Come!" Teya hissed back at her, rousing Leiyn from her stupor. She hurried after the scout, waiting for the shout to follow. But if Arias knew her, he said nothing. The guards, preoccupied with ogling the priestess, missed them passing by entirely.

They reached the far end of the plaza and set for the way out of town. Yet Leiyn could not help feeling ghostly gazes upon her back. All she could do was shrug them away and focus on the perils before them.

She knew better than to hope she could escape the past.

45

FAITH & FIENDS

Darkness had long since fallen by the time Leiyn and Teya ascended the ridge to their camp. The last league they had navigated by lifesense alone, the cloud-covered sky casting little illumination upon their uncertain path. Much of the journey passed in silence, Leiyn too preoccupied with her thoughts to sustain conversation.

Their companions eagerly awaited them. "What did you find?" Batu asked, standing at their approach. Sarryl was absent for the moment, likely hunting for his meal.

Together, they explained all they could. The others looked discomfited as they finished.

"That is not enough information," Ketti said, the pearls upon her brow bunching. "We must discover more."

"But you two cannot return." Batu crossed his arms. "I will go."

"As will I," Ekosa said. Though he smiled at Leiyn's glance, his eyes told a different story. Seeing her read his fear, he added, "None will suspect us."

"Unless rumors have spread about the Wilds Witch's

companions," Leiyn protested. "I have mahia. I can get out of situations that would trap both of you."

"Even with *semah*, we were almost caught." Teya shook her head. "You should not return, Redlock. I forbid it."

"Do you, now?" Leiyn cast her a scathing look, softened by a smile.

The scout crossed her arms and cocked her eyebrows. "You know it is for the best."

Leiyn repressed a grimace. She had been thrashed enough times on the Wilds Lodge training yard to know when she had lost.

"You're right," she said. "You stand a better chance than I do. But I'm accompanying you to the edge of town."

Teya sighed, while Batu smiled.

"Sarryl could use the company." He stared into the shrouded forest. "Wouldn't want him to wait alone."

"If you insist," Ekosa said, "I would welcome you that far." He glanced at Ketti. "So long as you are not needed here."

Leiyn read into that look. "Teya, you should stay behind to protect our camp." As Teya nodded, she continued, "When we reach town tomorrow, Batu, Ekosa, you should find Arias. You remember him, Batu?"

The wildsoul frowned. "The soldier with one arm. The one we captured before he escaped."

"The same. We saw him among a group of beggars. Find him, and he might tell us what we need to know."

Batu's confusion only seemed to grow. "Why would he speak to us? You cut off his arm, took him prisoner. He should hate us."

The muscles along her stomach tightened. "We can make him talk."

The others shared looks. Leiyn carefully avoided them, staring into the dim glow of their banked campfire. Bad enough for her to contemplate such dark methods; she did not want to see them reflected in their eyes.

"Ata," she spoke up, seeking to divert the conversation. "Has she been back?"

Ketti shook her head. "Not since she left yesterday."

Where are you, you fickle feshtado *tree?*

"She'll return," Leiyn said. "We'll do what we can in the meantime."

Batu faced out toward the sea. As he spoke, she felt his words were meant for all. "And if she doesn't?"

Leiyn pretended not to hear as she readied for bed. None of the others answered.

They set out at dawn, the same as Leiyn and Teya had the day before. The trek was made easier by Leiyn knowing the way, but Ekosa slowed them, lacking the trained resiliency of rangers and plainsriders. Bayo Sol came into view just past noon once more.

As agreed, at half a league away, Leiyn remained with Sarryl in a clearing atop a forested hill while Batu and Ekosa pressed on. The wilderness, still thick around town, soon hid them from view, but she could not help following them with her lifesense. Only when the danger of detection grew too great did she withdraw.

The moonbear huffed and wandered into the nearby forest, where he pressed his back against a tree and rubbed against it. Restlessness gnawed at Leiyn. She paced the sparse clearing, then ventured into the surrounding woods, knowing they would not return for some hours still. Yet she could not stand straying far, even with her lifesense keeping her aware of anyone that came into the vicinity.

Once Sarryl had his fill of scratching, he wandered the nearby woods. If he searched for food, he found scant fortune. Soon, the moonbear tired of the futile hunt and returned to the clearing, where he folded onto the ground and fell asleep.

Leiyn circled the glade, unable to keep still and unwilling to stray far. Thinking to make use of her surplus of energy, she filled her amber beads with lifeforce, though careful to leave plenty if they needed to run or fight. When she had filled just over half of them, she began drawing esse from the surrounding trees, always careful never to draw too much to debilitate or kill. She had caused enough needless death without adding more.

When the beads were full, she looked at Sarryl and thought of Chispa, wondering where he was now. Did he wander with Ata? Or venture on his own?

Worrying over an etaro *fox,* she chastised herself. *He can take care of himself.*

With her mind filled with fretting, time distended. It seemed to take all afternoon and evening before her companions returned, though she doubted more than a couple of hours had passed. A drizzle had started up, and though it was uncomfortable to stand in, she was glad for the excuse it gave Batu and Ekosa to have their hoods pulled up.

The rain continued even when they came into sight. Tentatively, Leiyn confirmed their identities with her lifesense, then looked to the third person with them, all misery forgotten.

Arias had come—and willingly, if his walking on his own was any tell.

Leiyn returned to the clearing to await them. Sarryl must have sensed his wildsoul's return, for he roused and shook off the vestiges of sleep as they came into view. She held herself in watchful expectation as they crossed the last few strides and entered the clearing.

"Arias," she said, her tone reserved. "I didn't think you'd come."

The young soldier—or former soldier, she had to assume—returned her wariness. His recent misfortunes played out across his person. He did not wear a cloak, and judging by the state of his clothes, she doubted he owned one. Patches dotted his threadbare coat, his trousers were stained and in need of washing, and his boots had sprouted holes.

Despite his privations, he lacked the hunch of the beaten mongrel. He held his severed arm to his chest, but the rest of his bearing was prideful and upright. His suffering had not bent or broken him; some hidden source of strength straightened his spine.

Arias started to answer, then startled, only just seeming to notice Sarryl. "What's that...?" His eyes flickered to Leiyn, the fear in them plain.

Leiyn shook her head. She could guess what he assumed. Why would the Wilds Witch also not be a beastfolk, after all?

"Not I," she said. "Though you're not far wrong."

The former Suncoat sidestepped from the men he had ventured with. His gaze flickered from Batu to Ekosa. His line of thought was plain: that the man he had not met before would be the more likely wildsoul. Batu answered the unspoken question, however, when he approached the moonbear and gave him a sound scratching behind the ears.

"It's me," he said over his shoulder, voice flat. "But that's not why you're here."

"No, it's not." Arias sucked down a breath, then let it out shakily. He reclaimed some of his composure and met Leiyn's eyes. "Though I'm not yet certain of the reason."

Leiyn considered enlightening him, but remembered words of Tadeo cautioned her against it. *The hunter who ties the snare too tight may find their prey slipping it,* he had said as they laid snares for hares. At the time, she had taken it as another way of his to say *Don't be rash* without saying the words.

Though he was right on both counts.

Ignoring Arias's question, she asked him one of her own. "How did you come to be in Bayo Sol?"

The youth had always seemed intelligent, even when it had been buried beneath blind patriotism. The brief narrowing of his eyes told of her evasion not being lost on him.

"By faith," he answered at last. "And nowhere else to go."

"Faith?" Batu asked, his tone gentler than Leiyn's.

Arias nodded, inclining his head toward the plainsrider. "Those remaining of my detachment withdrew after the Armada's loss at Southport. Upon my return to Vasara, I was discharged from the army." A scowl flitted across his face, an echo of the pain of that time, yet he smoothed his expression with admirable grace. "I returned to my family home in Carille for a time, but nothing remained for me there—only shame and pity. I would be a burden to my parents unless I found employment, and few had use for a man with one arm."

Leiyn looked aside. The memory of that moment flashed through her mind. The ease with which she lopped off his arm. The swollen sense of power infecting her.

No wonder they think me a monster.

Arias continued, heedless of her thoughts. "I returned to Vasara and begged my captain to find me any place among their ranks. He refused me, saying, 'The World King has no use for half a soldier.'" A smile flitted across his lips. "'Had' no use, now, I suppose I should say."

She started. *He knows.* Word of the Caelrey's death must have spread since she and Teya visited the day before. Batu and Ekosa were fortunate not to have been accosted themselves.

"What did you hear?" Leiyn asked.

"Only what the sailors said at the docks. That the Wilds

Witch slaughtered World King Baltesar during the Procession of Masks, in broad daylight before all his subjects. That she called down titans and monsters to kill good Union soldiers." The young man screwed up his eyes at her. "Is any of it true?"

Leiyn weighed the benefits of lying, then shrugged. "Enough of it."

A wide, fierce smile spread over his face. "Good."

Batu and Ekosa exchanged a glance behind the former Suncoat's back. Leiyn shared their surprise, though she endeavored to keep it from her face.

Arias saw through it. His smile faded, though his joy still shone from his bloodshot eyes. "The Caelrey was a rot in our Union. It was his command that had us soldiers consorting with devils. Already, I wondered what worth the World King had for Ilberia. What divine right he could claim when he dabbled in darkness." He shook his head. "Any loyalty I held for him died the day his captain turned me away. After I gave my arm and prospects to serve him, and he could not be bothered to let me work."

Leiyn fought hard not to look aside. Her shame endeavored to draw her gaze to her feet. "What happened?" she asked, tentative despite her intentions to remain cold. "After they turned you away?"

The youth's fervor dimmed. "I couldn't bear returning to Carille, so I made my home on the capital's streets. There were many hungry nights. Cold nights. I would have died there. But San Inhoa showed me her mercy.

"I went to a temple for alms, as I often did, when a priestess looked into me. 'Go to the Hallowed Isle, its Golden Harbor,' she told me. 'There, you will find your purpose.' Giving me a loaf of bread and coin for the passage, I went away with my faith renewed and my purpose clear. I made for Refugio as she bade."

With each word, Leiyn felt her hopes sinking. She recognized that look in his eyes. Knew now the hidden well from which he drew strength.

Blind devotion.

Religiosity had not been common at the Wilds Lodge, but there had been some devoted Omnists—Yolant, their intermittent musician, foremost among them. When they spoke of their beliefs, their minds seemed to freeze over, blocking any attempts of reason to breach.

And were you any different, part of her mocked, *in your beliefs of Gasts?*

Somehow, the thought tamed her fears. "And when you arrived here," she prompted him, "what then?"

Arias's gaze hardened. "It seemed a beautiful place to start. The priestesses were generous, always providing for those of us cursed with misfortune. I was able to do small tasks for the local populace, and they began to trust me. Enough that they whispered of what was truly happening."

"Truly happening?" Ekosa queried. "What do you mean?"

Arias eyed the *eesu* warily. Leiyn worried he would not answer him, but he continued after a moment's scrutiny. "People were disappearing. At first, it was just the odiosas. No one complained about that, nor noticed it much; even here, people don't care for witch hunters. But when half as many walked the town as before, it became difficult to avoid seeing it.

"People blamed it on the war, claiming the odiosas died to *ferino* witches. And the Wilds Witch," he added with a glance Leiyn's way. "But then others without a home went missing. A few disappeared at first, enough that people noticed. Especially when it wasn't those most likely to die, the old and infirm, but those young and hale."

The former Suncoat paused, his gaze falling to the ground. "I worried I would be taken, too. Then people stopped going missing. At least, we thought so...until some priestesses stopped appearing for service."

Leiyn had gone still as prey spotted by a predator. The conclusion stared her down, every bit as perilous. She did not dare accept it but waited in breathless anticipation.

Arias scowled as he met her eyes. "After what I'd seen while conscripted, I knew what was happening. Devils had come. They'd corrupted even the heart of the Holy Catedrál."

Sharo. Leiyn hissed out a sigh between her teeth. She had suspected the truth, but proof of his presence made their conclusions firm. It would not be one of his henchmen responsible—had her vision not shown him changing, becoming more vital? Had she not suspected those visions were less than dreams, but all too real?

This is how. He's evolving. Growing. Seizing more power with each mortal soul.

What was he capable of now? Had he attained Man'nah's raw power and paired it with his cunning? Inherited his former master's madness, too many spirits going to war against each other?

She had come for answers and only found more questions. But the prospect of knowledge lay before her.

She knew what they had to do.

Arias watched her process this news. His eyes were hard as he repeated his first question.

"Why did you come here, Leiyn?"

Leiyn held his gaze. This was the reason he had come. This was the test he wished to press upon her. And since she had no intention of killing him, she knew she had best pass it. The young man's fervid faith ensured he would betray their presence otherwise.

"We've come to kill your devils."

Arias weighed her with his gaze, eyes shifting between hers. "Did you not call them upon us? Upon the dead king?"

"No." Even if he considered Ata a devil, which he might, that much was true; what control had Leiyn ever had over the dryvan? "Those who control Ilberia and the Catedrál are our enemies," she continued, venturing away from treacherous waters. "We would have you freed."

He stared a moment longer, then smiled, savage as a lyshan out for blood. "Good. Their desecration cannot go unpunished."

Leiyn nodded, unwilling to say more. Letting slip how little she cared for desecration upon his faith might compromise their tenuous agreement.

"You will find them within the campus, I'm certain of it," the young man continued. With their aims assured, he began to speak rapidly, eager to be of assistance. "The priestesses have a secret way of entering the Catedrál, or so it is said. I don't know where it lies, but if you can find it, perhaps you can reach these devils without bloodshed."

"We want nothing more." Though she would call none innocent who served the Union or Catedrál, she had no desire to take their lives. Enough of the dead haunted her nights without adding to them.

You believe this will be bloodless? part of her taunted. *Foolish as well as rash, Firebrand.*

"Thank you, Arias," she spoke over her doubts. "If we had any coin to give—"

He cut her off with a vehement shake of his head. "I wouldn't take it. I live by the grace of the Saints and shall continue to do so, Omn willing. It's enough to do my part in ridding its entity of evil."

Leiyn contented herself with a nod. It would do neither of them favors to tell him how torturous routing an infection could be.

"We'd best be going." She looked at Batu and Ekosa. Both men moved toward her. Sarryl left the shadows, his pink-eyed gaze lingering on the young man they left behind.

Arias stood, undeterred by the beast's gaze, and raised his hand in farewell. "May San Carmen bless your undertaking!" he called. "Go with her righteousness upon you!"

Leiyn did not turn back. Suspecting his blessing would be of little service.

46

TO BURN STONE

Teya and Ketti eagerly awaited their news.

"Well?" the *situal* demanded upon their return, following Leiyn as she set down her pack. "Did you learn what we need?"

"Most of it."

She told the pair of what they discovered while swallowing what little food remained to them. Their supplies had been scant even before coming here; if they stayed much longer, they would need to hunt and forage to replenish them.

A good thing we won't be staying.

As she finished, Leiyn glanced around the ridge. A futile gesture—her lifesense already told her it was devoid of anything more than birds and insects. "Ata still hasn't returned?"

"No," Ketti replied, voice hushed.

Leiyn swallowed a sigh. "Then we'll have to assume she's not coming."

Everyone fell quiet at the prospect, but they had stared into the face of despair often enough of late to not blanch before it now.

"How do we discover this entrance?" Ekosa queried. "If it is known only to priestesses?"

"And what traps await us if we do find it?" Batu murmured. "The lyshans took the artifacts of Qasaar. Surely, they will use them."

Leiyn frowned at the wildsoul. "That, I cannot answer. But as for how to enter, I have an idea."

"Do you?" Teya elbowed Leiyn in the ribs. "Do tell, Redlock."

Playfully shoving the *situal*, Leiyn divulged her plan.

Though she was still humming from their discussions, Leiyn could not talk Teya out of taking the first watch. She lay down in her bedroll, expecting to stare at the constellations and recite their stories long into the night, yet she had only recalled one before her eyelids slipped closed.

Leiyn opened her eyes to darkness.

Sitting up, she found herself at the entrance to a cave. Though it did not appear to be deep, shadows pooled within it like water in a well. Fear thrummed through her as she crawled to her feet. No sense of hers could pierce that darkness.

Then wide eyes gleamed out from it—or what seemed like eyes. There were dozens of them, all devoid of pupils and silver-limned as if by moonlight, peering at her without emotion, without blinking.

"A question, little mortal, a question," crowed a familiar voice. "Care to dare a reply?"

"Osmet." Leiyn inched her hand toward her Eteman knife, but it was no longer belted at her hip. She was weaponless, but she refused to let panic in. Lose her head now and she stood no chance of survival. "She Who Remains."

"The latter, child, the latter—have I not told you, hm, hm?" The lyshan's eyes came closer, but nothing of her body was revealed from the darkness. Almost, she seemed formed of that darkness, her shapeshifting expanding beyond the bounds of reason. "Listen closer to this question: What remains after a scream?"

Only part of Leiyn paid Osmet's words heed. From the corner of her eye, she searched for where she had left her weapons and pack but saw no sign of their shapes at her feet. She did not even see her bedroll, though she had only just risen from it.

A dream?

If it was, the thought did not dispel it. She feared only one end would.

"Are you listening, little one? Do you ignore me?" The eyes crept closer, grew larger. Each silver orb loomed as large as saucers now. "A perilous price might be paid for that."

"I'm listening." Leiyn inched back. Her heels bumped against stone. Feeling backward revealed more stone stretching behind her.

It must be a dream. Must be...

"An echo," she answered, fearing the stretching silence. As if in mockery of her answer, she heard her words repeated back to her in the cave before her, growing fainter with each reverberation.

"Echo!" The mad lyshan cackled. "Echo, echo! But it does not remain long, does it? I ask again, child: What remains after a scream?"

Leiyn slid across the wall to the right, hoping that direction would not also abruptly end. The moonlight had to come from somewhere; even if she had to climb out, she would make the attempt.

As the answer occurred to her, she came to a stop.

"Nothing." She saw Isla, pierced by the arrow, face still, lying motionless on the ship's deck. "Nothing remains."

The silver eyes stared at her in silence. "Yes. That is correct. Nothing."

They snapped shut.

Leiyn ran for it, a mad dash for somewhere, anywhere, but in the darkness with that monster. The inky dark tangled in her limbs like spider silk, sticky and clinging. A shriek lacerated her throat, filling the cave with echoes—

"Leiyn, peace, peace! You are safe! You must awake!"

She blinked and stared around her. The world was still dark, but not in the unnatural way of Osmet's cave. And it was not an obsidian web that entrapped her, but her bedroll.

I'm awake.

"Sorry," she muttered, letting her arms fall. "I'm sorry."

Teya crouched over her, concern still creasing her face and deepening its shadows. "You were dreaming." Her beloved brushed a hand over Leiyn's hair, smoothing it, then cradling the back of her neck. "Screaming."

What remains after a scream?

Leiyn bowed her head, pressing her forehead against Teya's. "Just a nightmare. Sorry to wake you."

"I was keeping watch, Redlock. But I doubt anyone could have slept through that." Teya hesitated, fingers working through tresses of Leiyn's unbound hair. "Do you wish to speak of it?"

Leiyn drew back as she shook her head. Seeing Teya's expression, she tried for a reassuring smile.

"I'm fine. I can take the watch if you want to catch some sleep."

The *situal* seemed unconvinced, but she nodded and rose to her feet. "Watch well."

"Always do."

Leiyn fastened on her weapons belt and strung her bow, then moved over to the edge of the camp. The others, woken by her shouts, soon settled back in their blankets. She watched their esses calm as they slumbered once more.

While her senses kept watch, her mind turned inward. The dream had been no ordinary one; of that, she was certain. It more resembled the visions she experienced when traveling by grotto. Those, she had reason to believe, were glimpses into true things. Perhaps this one was as well. Perhaps Osmet had truly communed with her, mind and soul. But when Ata could not fully access her heritage, how could any lyshan?

She stared into the darkness, toward the few distant lights still burning from Bayo Sol, barely visible through the dense wilderness. Crickets sang. From a distant tree, an owl hooted. Without the thoughts clouding her mind, it would have been peaceful.

Evolution—the lyshan had spoken of it at their first encounter. Did the answer lay there? Had she—and Sharo—broken free of their boundaries? Unlocked unforeseen potential? The mere thought of it raised her skin into gooseflesh.

What remains after a scream?

Strange as the dream had been, stranger still though the ideas it evoked in her, she could ignore neither. Leiyn turned her gaze from the forest to the sea. Both moons were out that night, casting enough light to see the island off the shore. Its three pointed spires reached toward the starry sky, like a buried beast trying to claw it down.

She reached into the pouch at her belt and fished out Tadeo's fox figurine. As she worked her fingers over the worn wood, the wisdom of the late lodgemaster washed through her.

Better to be prepared and disappointed.

Incomprehensible as it seemed, she had to understand this dream. To survive their coming encounter, she had to be prepared for anything.

Leiyn ghosted back to the camp and rifled softly through her belongings. It was rash, what she intended, but it was a thing best done in solitude. She doubted Teya or the others would approve.

It did not take long to find what she sought. Leiyn drew out the small pouch and pulled open its ties. The must of Xepi's mushroom and cactus concoction coated the inside of her nostrils. Even a sniff of it made her unsteady.

Cinching it closed, she shook her head free of the wooziness and crept back to where she had kept watch. She did not want to take the time to steep water for tea such as the shaman had given her. Urgency crept through her. Even now, she felt Osmet's many eyes staring, goading.

She had to understand.

Leiyn pried open the pouch once more and fished out a few caps of *nacatl*, then added in some of the dust from the *peyotl* crowns. Grimacing at them in the gloom, she decided it was better not to see them.

Time for a little rashness, Firebrand.

Still, she hesitated, thinking of how Isla would have reacted to what she did now. Probably, she would have thrown Tadeo's words at her and listed all the reasons it was a foolish idea, then offered a sensible alternative.

But she's not here.

Leiyn put the mixture into her mouth and chewed. It tasted worse than the scent, dirt and body odor and bitter all at once. Leiyn gagged but kept from spitting them up. She uncapped her waterskin and drank them down.

The effect was instantaneous. Her hold on her mahia loosened. Her lifesense, usually leashed and only attending to what she commanded, ran wild like a hound let off its leash. Every mote of life, every insect and spot of moss on the rocks, drew her attention. She felt herself melting into it, becoming part of it.

Then she felt it below.

As her mind left her body, she became aware of it gazing into her. The island, the entire island, seemed to consider her expanding self. She regarded it in turn. There was something unfathomable to it. A latent presence undimmed by time or circumstance.

Eternal.

Tentatively, Leiyn reached into the Hallowed Isle. Like the whispers of Qasaar, it felt all-encompassing. But those had been a thousand lingering souls speaking in concert. This was whole unto itself, a being within which entire worlds existed.

A world titan?

She moved her lifesense through the land, exploring its nooks and crannies, seeing if the presence shifted. It inundated it all: the rocks, the trees, everything that lived in or on it. Yet as she pressed upward into Monte Ardiente, there was a change. Like an increase in temperature, a greater energy stirred in the peak. Knowledge seeped into her like water into cloth.

It lived once.

Images flickered through her mind. The bright glow of lava flow. The deep black of settled stone. Steam rising where molten rock met ocean water.

Then the great eye beheld her.

She flinched away. It appeared much the same as in her visions, only now it burned with unrelenting fire like Clouded Fang's eyes. An inferno blazed within, magma churning around a black stone pupil.

Leiyn froze. The eye pulled at her, sucking her in toward it, the current like a river flowing toward a waterfall. It was a journey she could not hope to survive.

Neither could she resist.

Moment by moment, she drew closer to it. The outer

layers of her being burned away, exposing the sensitive soul beneath. She flinched at the pain, then welcomed it. This was a cleansing fire. One that would purify her as Omn's gaze never could.

A shadow of smoke rose before it and spread its wings, blocking her from the fiery gaze.

Leiyn jerked forward, gasping. She stood again on the ridge, the dark night chill on her sweaty skin. The fiery eye had dissipated, leaving only Clouded Fang in her mind. Almost, she imagined the ash dragon looked upon her with reproach.

A low laugh rose in her throat. "Don't say you're jealous," she whispered to the darkness.

"Jealousy better fits mortals, I think."

Leiyn whirled. She tried to nock an arrow to her longbow, but the lingering influence of the mushrooms conspired against her. As the visitor unveiled their esse, though, Leiyn abandoned the attempt with a sigh.

"*Fesht*, Ata! What if I had shot you?"

The shapeshifter let out a low laugh. "You would have had to fit an arrow to your string first, little fox."

Leiyn shook her head, lamenting her debilitation. This moment felt as if she needed all her wits about her. "Where have you been?"

Ata tilted her head far to one side. "Investigating the island. As you have."

She did not let herself be diverted. "You left us again. What if your Kin had found us?"

What if they already did?

She shook her head again. Seeing Osmet in a dream did not qualify. Even if it had been, in some way, real.

Ata smiled, but it was not altogether mocking. "Shall I assist you?"

Before Leiyn could answer, the dryvan stood close before

her and reached out with her hands. Leiyn almost jerked away from those clawed fingers but relented after a moment's consideration.

Ata gently placed the tips of her talons against Leiyn's temples. The mushrooms had Leiyn's lifesense diving deep into the dryvan with the contact, tumbling through the layers of her soul. Images flashed through her mind, too many and swift to catch more than impressions. But there was violence there, and flames. Humans and dryvans dying. Trees burning.

Then the dryvan hummed deep in her chest. A matching resonance vibrated through Leiyn. Swiftly, she was expelled from Ata's essence, then found herself staunchly back within the confines of her body.

Leiyn fell back against the stone ledge, blinking. It took her several moments to adjust to her lifesense being back within her control.

"Thanks," she mumbled.

"A risk to take those while keeping watch." The dryvan raised one mossy eyebrow, though a quirk of her wooden lips betrayed her bemusement. "Fortunate that I have kept watch from afar."

"Have you?"

"Did you think I would leave you unprotected? My heritage is not so fallible as that."

"Just enough that you cannot form grottos."

Leiyn regretted the words as soon as they left her lips. Yet she only raised her chin and kept her silence. Even if Ata had done her a favor by ridding her of the mushrooms' effects, had she not been driven to it by the dryvan's absence?

Ata's smile morphed, becoming too wide and full of teeth. "Precisely what necessitated my departure. But I have returned, have I not?" The dryvan raised one clawed hand to tap a talon to Leiyn's chest. "Tell me, then—what have I missed? Other than your usual foolhardiness, of course."

Leiyn fought down the urge to sweep away her jabbing finger, irritating as it was. "Come dawn, we go to the Catedrál."

"At dawn?" Ata lowered her claw, her wooden features smoothing. "Are we prepared for this?"

"As much as we can be. Once we make our next move, we have to press our advantage. Word's spread of Baltesar's death and who's behind it. If Sharo didn't already tell the Altacura of the danger she's in, she knows now. And too many might have recognized me here already."

"Is that so?" The dryvan's esse shimmered with her amusement. "Has someone grown careless? Dare I say *rash*?"

Leiyn huffed a laugh. "Not this time."

"No, perhaps not." Ata peered at her, her gaze keen. As if it pierced her flesh to sift her soul.

As well she might.

"The island," Leiyn said. "Do you know why it has interfered with your magic?"

"Oh, yes." Her smile turned mocking, though it did not seem directed at Leiyn. "It is the simplest explanation. One I should have known all along." Ata kneeled to spread her talons along the stone, almost loving in her gentleness. "We call them Vast Mothers."

Leiyn understood at once. "*Kainox'tlal,* Ketti called them," she murmured. "World titans."

"Like titans, yes, but far, far greater." Ata rose, claws lingering on the stone, stirring dust into a cloud as her hand lifted away. "The Kin contended with these beings long, long ago, but it has been aeons since we came near one. To think one existed here all along..." The dryvan bowed her head, eyelids drifting closed.

"We came across another," Leiyn said. "In the middle of the Ocula Ocean, what we call the Veil, seemed a world titan like this island. We saw it birthing titans, dreaming them..." She shook her head, unable to make sense of it. But her questions remained. "But this one doesn't feel alive like that one did. It feels more...dormant. Dead, even, if that's possible."

"Oh, it is quite possible. You do not think we took bone from Vast Ones still alive, do you?" Her intact eye shimmered with a sheen of esse. "Every living thing ends. Even the Vast Mothers."

"Then what are we feeling if it's dead? How can it interfere with your magic and ours? Why does it still seem so alive? I communed with it just before you came here—or thought I did. But if it is dead..."

Ata walked next to Leiyn to lean her lithe frame on the stone, staring out over the ocean—to the trio of spires off the coast, Leiyn thought.

Claws? she wondered. *Could they possibly be?*

"Not all alive is confined to a physical form," the dryvan said. "Some are caught in between. Restless. Not quite living, but not quite dead."

"Like titans?" Leiyn suggested.

"In a way." Ata tilted her head. "Though it is a more mercurial thing than that. I speak of what you would call spirits, like those who whisper in the walls of my people's ruins—in Qasaar, in Solace—but free of the stones."

"Phantoms." Leiyn scowled out at the claws. "Ghosts."

"So mortals might say. But these are no human spirits, nor even of the Kin. The revenants I speak of are from an older race, one long departed from this world. One who refuses to yield their claim to it."

Unbidden chills raised Leiyn's skin into bumps. She ran her hands over her arms, trying to coax the standing hairs down.

"Why are you telling me this?" she asked, her voice catching.

Ata looked at her, eyes crinkled with amusement. "To give you nightmares."

"Ata."

The Iritu laughed and shrugged her feathery shoulders. "As an example and a warning. You mortals believe you have dominated this world, but you scuttle upon its surface, ants with no knowledge of what lies beneath the crust. Arrogance was the downfall of the Iritu civilization; from all I have seen of your kind, it will be yours as well." Ata turned to face Leiyn. Drawn to her full height, she loomed a head over Leiyn. "I doubt Vast Mothers may truly ever die. Like a dormant volcano, what is to say that, one day, they will not be reborn?"

Reborn, a part of Leiyn whispered. *Or reawakened.*

She recoiled from the thought. Even if she could rouse this world titan from its torpor, would she? It would likely kill everyone atop this island, herself included. Even if she could save herself and her companions, who could say how long it would rampage before it stopped? How many innocents would die in Ilberia if it made its way south?

The bloodshed ends here.

"I had a dream," Leiyn said. Realizing it must seem a disjointed thought at Ata's quizzical look, Leiyn continued. "Not of Sharo, but Osmet."

"Osmet?" The dryvan's gaze sharpened. "When? This night?"

Leiyn nodded. "Before I took over the watch. It was like the visions when we travel by grotto, Ata. Too real to be a dream. She taunted me with a riddle. Herded me against a wall. I was trapped, but before she could catch me, I woke up."

What remains after a scream?

"And the vision I had when coming here..." Leiyn rolled up her sleeves and squinted at her forearms. The thin lacerations had disappeared, her mahia erasing even the slightest injuries. "I woke with cuts on my arms," she continued, pulling her sleeves back down. "Gone now, but I saw them. They were there."

The dryvan stared at her, pinning her with all the intensity of an eagle. Then she bared her teeth and looked over the ocean.

"I do not understand!" Ata seethed. "It should not be possible."

Hope had always held fear at bay, even as evidence of their enemies' power mounted against them. Now, that hope drowned in fear. Leiyn buffeted back shivers by plying her esse, burning it high within her. The dryvan must notice it, but Leiyn was beyond caring.

"They're changing, Ata. Evolving, like Osmet said back in Solace." Leiyn hesitated, still reluctant to believe what Arias had reported. But denial was a poor replacement for truth. "A person in town told us there have been disappearances. First odiosas, then beggars, then townspeople and priestesses. It's Sharo, isn't it? Sharo and the others. They're...what, absorbing their souls?"

"Their beings," Ata murmured, speaking as if with a bitten tongue. "Their essence. Yes, what you call a soul. He consumes them as Man'nah once did."

Leiyn gripped the stone, trying to ground her thoughts. *He'll be more powerful than he was before. Maybe as powerful as Man'nah.* She had only beaten the lyshan lord because half of him had wanted to die. Sharo as she had last seen him was united in his purpose. Paired with his slyness, and even with all the skill and strength she had gained, even with her allies by her side, did they stand a chance?

"It doesn't change what we must do," Leiyn spoke aloud. "And it all but confirms one thing: he's here or comes here often. Which makes it the more likely we can lure him out of hiding by taking the Catedrál away."

Ata nodded. "And cut away his ready supply. Yes, Leiyn,

you are correct. Our aims remain the same." A pensive look twisted her features. "But if we find him, what shall we discover, I wonder? What new shape has he adopted? What new power does he hold?"

Leiyn flinched. The vision of Sharo ravaging her soul flashed through her mind.

"It doesn't matter," she rasped. "He'll die all the same."

The dryvan glanced over, mossy eyebrows quirked. "Flames alone cannot consume stone, Awakener. Determination cannot kill. We shall go, as you say, but we must claim every advantage we can."

Leiyn leaned toward her, the warnings washing over her like rain over eroded fields. "What's lava? If the fire's hot enough, it can even melt rock."

As the Iritu rolled her eyes, Leiyn touched on her connection to Clouded Fang. The ash dragon remained after rising to defend her from the island. He leveled his burning gaze at her from below.

Ata speaking drew her out of her contemplation. "I have seen how you have grown, Leiyn. Embraced the scattered parts of yourself and forged them together. It has made you strong. Stronger than before. Powerful enough to threaten even those Iritu who remain, with all their tricks and pawns and deceit." She paused, wooden lips puckered with thought. "But loss can break as well as bind. Take care that it does not guide your actions."

Leiyn turned away, her chest aching. When had loss not guided her hand? From birth, she had felt its keen edge. Her mother's absence. Her father's anger and anguish, then his death after. Losing her home each time she gained a new one. The Wilds Lodge and all the family she had found in it.

Isla.

She did not know who she was without her sorrow. All she

knew was to paddle hard above it. To not drink it in with more than sips. To not let it drown her.

"Before we go," Leiyn spoke to the darkness, "there's something I must ask of you. Something you must swear to do." She forced herself to meet the dryvan's gaze. "Please."

Was it pity that gathered in those alien eyes? Leiyn tensed her muscles, trying to numb herself to it.

"Speak, little fox," Ata murmured. "I will listen."

PART VII

HEART OF SANCTITY

47

A DREAM OF FATE

Leiyn slunk through the wilderness.

The surrounding forest looked to be the same as that which spread across Refugio, but her view of it now was from low to the ground. Her senses, too, had transformed, her keener nose cataloguing a bouquet of scents. Every sound, however slight, was caught by her generous ears. She twitched them, listening for signs of danger, of which there were multitudes in this perilous world.

Another presence brushed against her, a soul soft and welcoming. Only with that touch did Leiyn recognize whose body she occupied.

Chispa.

The silver fox pulsed, pleased by her acknowledgment. If he found it alarming that she shared his body, he gave no indication of it. Inquisitiveness snuffed at her with all the friendliness of his moist nose.

She did not push him away but observed herself through his perception. She remained a predator yet had become part of his skulk. The guardian of beasts small and large. A Master of the Vast Ones who ruled the sprawling wilderness and the fires deep below.

Yet he perceived how her thoughts ever turned to the cold caverns within. He saw the hollows in her soul that had never been filled in but only covered over. Willfully forgotten.

When seen through his eyes, Leiyn could not ignore the scars that death had scored upon her.

Yet such dark musings did not touch Chispa for long. Hunger turned the fox's attention back to his task at hand. He was on the prowl for prey, it seemed—and swiftly closing in.

Leiyn caught the scent of vermin somewhere in the undergrowth ahead. Chispa slowed, creeping forward at a glacial pace. His eyes stared unblinking into the gloom. As sensitive as they were, they still struggled to pierce the veil of the night.

Movement among the leaves came mere steps away. Chispa burst into motion, leaping into the air and coming down on the vegetation. He snapped his jaws, attempting to snag the tiny creature. His innate sorcery, unhindered by the island, lashed out to stun and confuse.

The rodent made a valiant effort to escape, but the silver fox was too much for it. As Chispa captured it in his jaws, it went limp, resigned to its fate.

Leiyn grimaced at the feeling of rat between Chispa's teeth. Memories rose of her time in captivity, when rats and their meager sustenance had been all that kept her alive.

Chispa stilled. Attuned to her thoughts, he hesitated to finish the kill. Only as she quelled her own revulsion did he bite down.

Blood, salty and warm, flooded their mouth.

Leiyn tried to experience it as the fox did. It was a relief to abandon her own feelings on the matter. How much easier it would be to live as Chispa did, moving from one meal to the next. Trouble only came when he involved himself in human affairs.

I'm glad you came, she thought to him. *But look after yourself, my little friend.*

She felt his understanding. Foxes were sometimes predators but were often prey. He smelled and recognized the fear fragrant in her thoughts.

The rodent still in his mouth, Chispa fled. Racing through the forest, he dove into a bush and vanished. And as swiftly as they had come together, they parted. The fox had entered a grotto and moved beyond her reach.

Leiyn wished she could flee with him. Instead, she let her spirit drift back to her body.

Back to the fate that awaited her.

48

SHROUDED DAWN

Leiyn opened her eyes to a gray dawn. Though she had stolen only a few hours of sleep, nervous energy buzzed through her.

Today. Today it would all be settled. The Altacura would be cast down. If they were fortunate, Sharo would be as well.

What would tomorrow bring?

She shook the thoughts free. Tomorrow could take care of itself. She needed all her wits about her if they were going to make it there. All of them alive.

Don't let them die, Firebrand.

She let her gaze wander over their party. Each of them had been strangers not so long ago. Batu. Teya. Ekosa and Ketti.

Now, she held them closest in the world. Feared most for their safety.

Yet you still throw them into the fire.

She knew she had little choice in the matter. If she snuck off, she might keep them out of this, but she was not so foolish as to do that. She needed them. Needed them, even when she only wanted to keep them safe.

This was the price for peace. Much as she resented it.

Seeing Teya sitting at the far end, staring out over the sea as she broke her morning fast, Leiyn pushed the brooding thoughts away. She had her contingency, had done all she could to protect them. Now, the best thing she could do for her friends was stay focused.

Leiyn pulled out a strip of seared venison, still in supply from their time at Rhun's camp, and chewed through the tough meat. It was not long before her jaw ached from the effort.

"This might be the toughest thing we face all day," she grumbled as she swallowed.

Teya laughed and glanced at her. "We can hope."

They fell silent as they watched the sun feebly try to peek beyond the mass of clouds. It failed as it soared above it, leaving gloom to amass over Refugio.

Teya broke the silence. "Remember what I said? Back in the forest on our way to Bayo Sol for the first time?"

Leiyn stifled a grimace. "I remember."

"What did your father say? 'Cage your fear.' Have you done so?"

"Yes, my sky. I have."

The lie flowed smoothly from her lips. Too smoothly, perhaps. The scout narrowed her eyes at her. As she took another bite of her meal, she turned away.

"The final day," Teya murmured. "It is hard to believe."

"Had to come sometime."

"And none too soon." Finishing her food, her beloved stood and offered her hand. "Ready to meet it?"

Leiyn took it and stood beside her. "Ready as ever."

49

SIN COME CALLING

Leiyn drew her hood farther down before walking the final stretch to Bayo Sol.

She walked alone. The absence of her companions ached all the more keenly for her walls being raised. The island felt empty and barren even as trees pressed in close and the brush hid her from view. Life was meant to be embraced, not kept out, as she had done for too many years.

A glint of reflected light betrayed the position of the waiting guards.

Leiyn ducked, then slowly came upright. The soldiers watched the main entrance into town. The street petered out halfway up the incline, turning from white stone to dirt with little fanfare. At the present angle of the land, she could only see the top of their helms. They could not see her in return.

Leiyn backed away until the gleaming helms disappeared from view. Moving farther up the slope, away from any straightforward path into town, she sought viable routes between the properties. If she chose her moment well, she might yet escape prying eyes.

The forest ended several dozen strides short of the port.

Leiyn paused at the tree line. As the hour grew late, most of Bayo Sol's residents were bound to be at their dinner tables, taking their evening meal before seeking their beds. With a look both ways to ensure no one remained in view, Leiyn sprinted for the nearest stucco wall. A gap no more than a couple feet wide awaited her between the two-story homes. For the moment, the rear doors to the adjoining houses remained closed.

She slipped into the narrow alley sideways. A waft of stenches hit her, ordure and rotten food chief among them. Fighting down a gag, Leiyn did not look down at her squelching shoes, but hurried toward the band of light on the other side.

Stepping free, the air turned cool and fresh. Sucking down a breath, she did not notice the people staring at her from their porch until they spoke.

"Oi! What're you doing back there?" A man with tightly curled gray hair and a balding pate glared at her from behind a cloud of pipe smoke. A woman with tired eyes and the four children next to him stiffened. Leiyn could imagine the sight she made: a strange, hooded woman appearing from such a narrow alley.

"Apologies," Leiyn muttered as she turned and strode away.

The older man shouted at her back. Shoulders tight, she hurried away until his voice grew distant, then quieted as she turned the corner.

A diligent guard might check on the cause of the ruckus in the quiet town, but out of sight of the witnesses, Leiyn knew it was better to walk at a brisk, even pace. A woman with places to be, but not desperate to arrive. With a whiff of fortune, it might be enough to avoid unwanted attention.

Though Saints know we've had little luck.

She walked the upper white streets until her shoes stopped

leaving tracks, then doubled back around to find her way to the central plaza. The passersby were fewer than her previous visit. Something had changed in Bayo Sol.

If they knew the Caelrey to be dead, the city watch remained remarkably unaware. The handful of guards stationed at the plaza were gathered in a knot, heads bent close in hushed conversation. Only one stood apart by the broad stairs leading up to the Catedrál campus, staring wistfully at his fellow guards. A dozen vendors remained about the peripheries of the plaza, though most were well into packing up their stalls. She noticed the fruit seller from two days before, Yavin. Bent over his wares as he arranged them in his cart, he did not see her in return.

Leiyn turned away, letting her hood obscure her features. She looked toward the stairs and waited.

She had timed her approach well. The gathering began nearly as soon as she arrived. They emerged from the alleys, leaving muddy tracks in their wake. Old and young, male and female—only the shabbiness of their clothes united them.

A glimpse of a truncated arm told of Arias's presence before she caught sight of his face. The former soldier was turned away from her, facing the stairs with the others as they awaited their evening meal. For most, it looked to be their only meal for the day, skeletal frames apparent through their accumulated rags. It promised to not be long before the young man looked any different.

Tonight, she would change their futures. For better or worse remained to be seen.

Leiyn pretended to fuss with the hem of her cloak as she waited for the priestess and her acolytes to appear. Her hopes proved well-founded: the evening alms were Adelina's assignment, and the comely priestess had returned once more for the duty.

White-robed acolytes handed out bread and fruit, taking

no longer than necessary. Leiyn had long since picked out the stitches of the hem she had worked on, the string hanging frayed along the tattered edge.

Isla could have fixed it in minutes.

She looked up to see Adelina ascending the stairs, the acolytes flanking her. With a covert glance either way, Leiyn set across the plaza toward the dispersing crowd. She chose her approach with care, taking a trajectory that placed beggars between her and Arias. An unnecessary precaution: the young man seemed to notice little beyond his meal, dirty blonde locks falling over his eyes as he ate.

Leiyn moved past them, breathing shallowly at the rank odor rising from the vagrants, and pressed up the stairs. She kept behind at a reasonable distance, a dozen strides between her and the servants of the Catedrál. A man of Batu's size, hooded and cloaked, might have looked threatening following them, but she hoped her smaller frame would let her pass unnoticed. Leiyn hunched her shoulders and tried to make herself seem small and unimposing.

Either fortune or stratagem worked in her favor, for none of the white-robed women seemed to make note of her. The one acolyte who looked back passed her gaze over Leiyn without interest.

An oversight she would make them rue.

As they continued up the stairs, Leiyn worried she had misjudged their path, that all would return to the Catedrál for the night. She slowed, not wishing to come closer to the paladins at the gates than need bade.

The two acolytes headed through the gate, bearing away their empty baskets. But Adelina turned to the right—the very direction Leiyn had anticipated.

Turning back down the stairs, affecting a woman who had forgotten something left behind by throwing up her hands, Leiyn hurried around the curving street below. It was the long way around, as she knew from walking the street earlier that day, but it would lead to Adelina's most likely destination.

She came around the last bend to see Adelina entering the chapel doors. A smile flitted across Leiyn's lips before she quashed it. Plenty could go wrong still. The most crucial parts of their plan still lay ahead.

Steadying her breath, Leiyn crossed the street and pressed through the heavy maple door. The hinges squealed. She flinched, peering within to see if anyone observed her entrance. The chapel was sparsely occupied. Only one person glanced her way: a citizen by their dress. Adelina did not turn back.

Arrogant as ever.

Leiyn slipped inside and carefully closed the door. It took her eyes a moment to adjust to the gloomy interior. The chapel was smaller than the First Temple of Baltesia, but no less grand. It had the same configuration as any Omnist temple. An orb representing Omn the Unknown lay at its center, a podium set at its base. Like the orb were a droplet in a puddle, concentric pews rippled out from it. Six wings branched out from the center chamber. Five ended in candlelit altars to the Sacred Saints. The sixth led to a door.

Seven people occupied the temple, most in quiet contemplation of the Saints. A middle-aged man sat on a pew, head bowed, his bearing and dress that of a scholarly type. A frumpy acolyte swept her broom with inefficient strokes across the immaculate marble tiles. At San Inhoa's altar, a woman clad in black with a veil lit a candle and set it amid those already burning.

Adelina had paused by San Carmen's altar to speak with another visitor. Seeing the comeliness of the supplicant and the warmth of the priestess's smile, it was easy to guess Adelina's motivations.

Not so innocent as you pretend.

The dark-haired priestess placed a hand on the woman's arm, touch lingering, then turned and made for the back doorway. Leiyn tarried a moment to stare at the severe, molded features of the Saint of Justice before setting after her. The light from the tall stained-glass windows painted a collage of color over the nave. She pretended to admire them as she walked, playing the part of the pilgrim. It was not difficult to pretend. Even with her dark purpose, the atmosphere and art made it easy to appreciate.

Art paid for in blood.

The pretty woman looked up and smiled as Leiyn passed. Leiyn smoothed away her inadvertent scowl. Too late; with a slight startle, the woman looked away from her.

Leiyn hunched her shoulders and moved swiftly past, hoping her body odor was not as pungent as she imagined.

She waited for the acolyte to turn away in her slow sweeping before Leiyn approached the sixth alcove. With a glance over her shoulder to ensure no one looked her way, she pressed through the door. These hinges proved well-oiled; to prevent an embarrassing entrance mid-service, Leiyn imagined.

The corridor beyond was even more darkly cast than the chapel nave. Leiyn closed the door and waited, looking for any sign of danger. Adelina had already ambushed and bested her once. She had no intention of letting it happen again.

Satisfied she was alone, Leiyn crept forward, placing each foot so it fell silently on the stone. The hallway was sparse, though the walls and floor remained as ornate and immaculate as the chamber without. Leiyn moved around the bend in the corridor, then retreated a step.

Adelina stood a score of paces beyond, bent over a door. The clinking of metal told of her turning a key in a lock.

An office? A closet of holy supplies?

She had to move swiftly lest the priestess locked herself in her room all night. Leiyn ghosted around the bend and down the corridor to where Adelina fiddled with the door.

"Legion-cursed lock," she muttered, just audible. "Why won't you open...?"

The anelace whispered from its sheath. Leiyn grabbed the priestess around the waist and rested the steel against Adelina's throat.

"Don't move."

Adelina stiffened. But she had not surrendered.

The priestess lashed with mahia against Leiyn's walls. Their bodies touching made it more difficult to resist her attacks.

But Leiyn had grown since their last encounter. Her walls held true. She pressed the blade in until the skin broke. Adelina whimpered and ceased her invisible attack.

Leiyn squashed her guilt. "Won't work this time," she hissed in her ear. "Come quietly and that'll be the only injury you take."

"How are you here?" Adelina's voice had risen, growing shrill. "Have you come to haunt me?"

"Quiet!" Leiyn was sorely tempted to bring her own mahia to bear, but there was too much risk in exposing herself. She had to hope Adelina's own writhing lifeforce went unnoticed. "I'm no ghost, Adelina. Feel the knife? I'm here, flesh and blood. And you're not getting away until I let you."

Like a toddler after a tantrum, the priestess sagged against Leiyn, defeated and overcome. "You're going to kill me."

Leiyn had to filter esse into strength to hold Adelina's weight. The way she whispered in her ear might have been intimate but for the blood beading down the anelace. "I won't have to if you obey. Walk."

Leiyn pushed her deeper into the hall, away from the office she had struggled to open and the chapel nave toward a door a short way farther. She held the knife so she did not accidentally slice into Adelina's jugular. It helped that the threat of it had become unnecessary, the priestess having turned fully compliant. Her fragile mind could not tolerate this upending of power.

Or she's faking. Fooled you once, didn't she?

Had her lifesense not been veiled, Leiyn might have been able to tell from the state of Adelina's esse. As things stood, she expected the worst.

"Open it," Leiyn ordered as they reached the door. "Slowly."

The tremble in Adelina's hands did not seem fabricated as she fumbled for the latch. Sliding it free, she gingerly pulled on the handle. The heavy door groaned as it opened onto a back street.

Two men waited in a shadowed alcove before them.

"Out." Leiyn shoved her captive toward the men, switching her hold as she did to grip Adelina by her arm while moving the knife to press against her back. Not as clean a way to kill with clothes slowing the entry of the blade, but even a priestess of questionable morality was unlikely to know the finer points of murder.

Batu and Ekosa stepped forth. The wildsoul grabbed Adelina's other arm, his broad hand enveloping it. The *eesu* looked troubled, but he only hesitated a moment before looking either way down the alley, then moving ahead and motioning them after him.

"The way is clear," he whispered. "For now."

Leiyn and Batu guided Adelina after him, heading for more occluded alleys. The roads were empty, ensured by Ata's subtle manipulation. Even with her mahia's walls raised, Leiyn could feel the dryvan's heritage driving unwanted eyes away. *Flee*, the Iritu magic whispered. *Turn away*.

Still, Leiyn sent a brief prayer for further fortune to San

Jadiel. Though after kidnapping one of his priestesses, she could hardly expect him to extend his favor.

They turned a corner and entered an alley too narrow for all three of them to stand abreast. Batu moved ahead, leaving Leiyn to keep hold of the priestess. Teya awaited them at the entrance. The *situal* turned sideways to allow them past, her spear in hand and her expression grim. Her dark eyes swept over Adelina before landing on Leiyn.

"She is the one who seduced you?" she asked with a raised brow. "I thought you had finer taste."

Leiyn gave her a sharp look as she pushed Adelina past. The scout's smile did not shift. Little seemed capable of dampening Gast humor.

Ketti and Ata waited at the alley's end. As the priestess caught sight of the dryvan, a squeal escaped her. Leiyn could hardly blame her. Once more, the dryvan wore her titanbone armor and carried the long war scythe. Where she kept them, Leiyn had never weaseled out. A perplexing question when Ata could not even access grottos at the moment.

Prey instinct told Leiyn to flee at the fearsome sight, but rationality kept hold. Leiyn jabbed her knife in deep enough to pierce Adelina's robes and graze her flesh.

"Not another sound," she warned.

Adelina fell silent, though she resisted Leiyn's efforts to move her closer to Ata. "It's one of them," she whispered. "One of the devils."

Leiyn turned the priestess around so she could see her face. "So you've met them."

Those piercing emerald eyes met hers, their charm dampened by terror. Even in such a state, though, she seemed to recognize her error, for she held her tongue.

Leiyn shoved so the priestess stumbled backward. "Fine," she muttered. "The hard way it is."

"Please." Adelina fell to her knees, heedless of the grime

besmirching her bright garments. "I have served the Saints, followed their example. My soul must—"

"Your soul will be fine. Move."

"I suppose we can come to you." Ata grinned as she sauntered forward with an exaggerated sway. "Hello, little bird."

"Ata," Ketti murmured. "Allow me." Without waiting for permission, the Eteman squeezed past the dryvan to kneel before the priestess.

Adelina regarded Ketti with almost equal wariness to what she afforded Ata. Leiyn watched her eyes take in the precious gems embedded in her flesh.

"What *ferino* savagery is this?" the priestess whispered.

"Manners," Leiyn tutted, but did not punish the insult. Enough fear filled Adelina as it was. Push too hard, and terror might break her mind beyond use. Leiyn did not know how much torture she could stomach inflicting. Even with her lifesense closed off, each injury cut into her conscience.

Did she take pity on you? On all those Baltesians who died in their war?

Batu slid past them, making for the entrance to the alley. Leiyn looked after him with eyes narrowed.

"Where are you going?"

The plainsrider glanced over his shoulder. "Sarryl. We must begin our joining."

"Right. Meet us at the compound. And be careful."

Batu nodded and stalked away.

Listening to his receding footsteps, Leiyn turned back to their quarry. Ata had moved to loom behind the priestess. Adelina trembled and wrapped her arms around herself.

"This cannot be," the priestess breathed, barely audible. "None of this can be..."

"Denial will not help you," Ketti said, gentle still. "Only the truth. Tell us what you know of the Catedrál. Where are the Altacura's quarters?"

Adelina gave no answer. After repeating the question twice, the Eteman looked up, torn with indecision.

Leiyn struggled. "She's beyond reason. We'll have to find the answers ourselves."

Ketti flinched, but otherwise she maintained her composure. Lowering her lavender eyes to the priestess again, she reached forward to grip her hands.

Adelina yanked free and scooted back across the filthy alley. "Get away from me, *ferino* witch!" she hissed.

Ata tutted as she leaned down. "That is no way to speak, little bird. Even I am not so uncouth as to utter such vulgarities."

Leiyn swallowed a sigh and pressed Ata away. "Cover us. Wouldn't want anyone to see this."

The dryvan's mismatched eyes bored into her. "I could ravage her mind."

"And leave her broken," Leiyn countered. "Please, Ata."

"Very well." Puckering her lips in a pout, the Iritu closed her eyes. Leiyn waited the tingle of her heritage against her walls before lowering them.

She kneeled behind Adelina and gripped her firmly by the shoulders, then pressed her mahia into the priestess.

Her walls were flimsy things, paper shields that folded at the first assault. Adelina struggled, but it was as feeble a contest as Leiyn against Sharo in her vision. Leiyn held down Adelina's walls but penetrated no further.

Still, she glimpsed the first image of Adelina's esse. A white dove fluttered in a pristine bird bath preening its feathers. It did not take an Omnist scholar to understand its meaning. Adelina saw herself as clean of sin. As pure and blameless as a beautiful bird.

Of course she does.

"Ketti," she murmured.

Through her lifesense, she felt the Eteman nod, then take

Adelina's hands once more. The priestess no longer possessed the wits or strength to pull away. Ketti pressed her mahia inside, then began rifling through her, mind and soul.

Leiyn held her walls down with far more vigor than such scant resistance called for. The reverberations of Ketti's delving echoed through her lifesense. Adelina instinctively fought them, but Leiyn turned away every attack before it could harm Ketti. Still, they were uncomfortable to endure. With every strike rebuffed, she felt more like an accomplice to a crime.

At last, Ketti withdrew and leaned back. "I have learned all I can."

Leiyn released her hold on Adelina, allowing the priestess to slump to the ground. "The Altacura?"

"In her chambers or audience hall. I know where both are, or almost. Reading the maps we keep in our minds is difficult. They are colored by perspective, purpose, feeling..."

"That'll do," Leiyn interjected. "And their defenses?"

Ketti frowned. "It is strange. Beyond guards and odiosas, I cannot say that there are any."

"There must be," Ekosa spoke from the alley entrance. "They know we come for the Altacura, no? How could they fail to prepare?"

Ata chuckled. "They have my Kin. What more protection do they need?"

"Protection from your kind," Leiyn retorted.

The dryvan's smile widened. "If they are wise!"

Ketti remained untouched by amusement, her mouth set in a thin line. "Titans are unlikely as well. They stay away from this place."

"As they would," Ata said, sobering. "A Vast Mother would deter all but the most desperate. Or those compelled."

The other two nodded. Leiyn had recounted most of her

and Ata's conversation the night before on the walk over, so they knew what the Hallowed Isle likely was.

"And the secret entrance Arias spoke of," Leiyn said. "Does it exist?"

"It does," Ketti replied. "It requires a token to access: her amulet."

Leiyn nodded and reached around the priestess. As her finger settled on the whitewood amulet hanging from her neck, Adelina jerked, almost throwing her off balance.

"Enough of that," Leiyn grunted as she quelled the rebellious priestess by both physical and magical means. When Adelina was once more subdued, she yanked the amulet free by breaking its chain. The ruptured metal links pattered to the ground.

"Stop..." Adelina sagged onto her side, glossy hair matted with sweat and filth. "Please..."

Leiyn looked away. The best way to cover their tracks now was to kill the priestess. After all Adelina had subjected her to under the First Temple, after all she had done to promote the foul work of the Holy Catedrál, she should have felt more willing.

The Ranger's Oath sounded in her head, spoken with Tadeo's voice. *Perceive. Preserve. Protect.*

She sheathed her knife and looked at Ata. "Can you keep her unconscious while we're gone? Just long enough for us to get away."

"You mean to spare her life?" Ata smiled, sharp teeth peeking through. "If it is a matter of guilt, I would be happy to shoulder the burden."

Leiyn shook her head. "We'll spill enough blood as it is."

"As you wish."

The dryvan bent over and covered Adelina's entire head with a taloned hand. A scream started issuing from the priestess but cut off before it became more than a high-pitched gurgle. Leiyn felt the Iritu sweep through Adelina's esse like she had before cut through Suncoats with her scythe. The woman's life-force dimmed as she slumped down to the ground, unconscious.

"So feeble." Ata stretched up to her full height, all the more intimidating when clad in her armor. Her gaze lingered on the priestess before rising to Leiyn's stare. "Still, it would be best if we move swiftly. She should remain unconscious for the night, but even my heritage may have unpredictable results."

Already, Leiyn regretted her mercy. But it was likely her last chance for it.

50

KNIVES AMONG SHADOWS

Ketti led them along the eastern side of the Catedrál campus. Sentries were posted at regular intervals along the wall, but an ordinary human posed no trouble to a dryvan's heritage. Like Zuma had once blinded a Suncoat, so Ata did to all those they passed. No number of onlookers seemed beyond the reach of her power.

Still, when the sentries swept their gazes over their company, Leiyn flinched, expecting them to sound the alarm. Yet soon, the guards looked away, none the wiser for their passage.

Odiosas and priestesses might have posed more trouble, but none guarded the walls that night. If that was a fortunate turn or an ominous sign remained to be seen.

The stretch of white wall Ketti led them to looked no different from the rest. Only a social trail, worn by many feet passing this way, betrayed the location of the hidden door. Leiyn handed over Adelina's amulet to Ketti, who pressed it to one of the white stones. With Ata veiling their party, Leiyn had her lifesense open to witness esse glowing within the stones. The whitewood circle came alive as well as it activated the unseen mechanisms. Seams appeared as the false section swung inward with a groan.

Leiyn followed the others in, examining the portal as she went. The enchantments were impressive, akin to those made by Eteman or Iritu design. A feat that should have been beyond the Catedrál.

What other surprises awaited them?

A courtyard sheltered by low walls lay beyond the entrances; to hide the comings and goings of the priestesses, Leiyn guessed. Teya came through last but hesitated at the opening.

"Batu?" she whispered. "Should we wait for him?"

Leiyn started to answer when an enormous figure loomed from the dark forest on the ridge above. Her gut tightened even as she realized who it was.

"There's your answer," Leiyn muttered back.

Like their passage, Batu's descent went unnoticed by the guards on the walls. Leiyn winced at his heavy footsteps and panting, unavoidable while joined with the moonbear. She wondered how long even Ata could hide them.

"Let us tarry no longer." Ata did not lower her voice as she faced the grand building. "Our quarry awaits."

The Iritu strode off, undeterred as she stepped into plain view beyond the squat walls.

"*Fesht.*" Leiyn hurried after her, nocking an arrow as she went. She scanned the broad courtyard for any sign of alarm and saw none. The others followed, Batu and Sarryl only just able fit under the low doorway. Teya closed the door behind them.

Ata led the way across the broad court. Tinkling fountains, ornate statues, and flourishing gardens sprouted among the bright pavestones. Paladins stood at regular intervals, but were ignorant of their passage.

Only one twitched as they passed not three feet from him.

Confusion flashed across his expression. Leiyn tensed, readying to loose upon him. Her lifesense told of a marginal potential for mahia in him, undeveloped and untested. But when Ata's heritage waxed and his expression smoothed over, Leiyn exhaled, eased the tension on her bowstring, and went past.

"There," Ketti said when they had moved out of earshot, pointing at the palatial building ahead. "Gran Ayda takes residence within."

Leiyn took in the Basilica Sóveran as they approached it. Like every good Omnist, she had heard tell of the beauty and sanctity of the Altacura's residence and the heart of the Holy Catedrál. The tales had not exaggerated it; rather, they still fell short of capturing the sight. Columns as broad as Leiyn could spread her arms lay interspersed across the expansive portico. A pediment shaded it and boasted depictions of the first three Sacred Saints. The basilica preceded the Ascension of San Luciana and San Hugo, for it had been built well over three centuries prior, from what she remembered of her brief temple lessons. Grand doors waited beneath, still open despite the late hour.

She grimaced, picturing the white stone stained red. They had avoided blood thus far, but with lyshans involved, it would not be long before their luck ran out.

Swiftly, they ascended the broad stairs. Leiyn kept glancing back, fearing Ata's magic would not shield them from any looking across the courtyard, but none stirred with alarm. Continuing forward, they stepped through the open entrance.

Scant sunlight illuminated the interior. More columns lined the way, stained glass windows appearing between them. Carpet ran down the center of the white stone, scarlet adorned with gold thread.

Ata spared none of it a look but continued straight down the carpeted corridor. Muttering fresh curses under her breath, Leiyn followed. She turned back often to watch their rear. The sight of the hulking Batu, transformed with white fur and distorted features and lumbering nearly three paces tall, filled her with instinctual fear every time she laid eyes on him, even when she knew he was on her side.

Let me never fight a wildsoul, she prayed, ignoring the irony of appealing to the Saints.

The corridor ended in a second grand hallway. It spread in either direction and was guarded by two more paladins. Statues of important scenes and figures in Catedrál history lined the walls, explanatory placards at their base.

"Her quarters lay this way," Ketti whispered before turning them to the left. Leiyn followed with the others, though not without a wary look at the oblivious guards.

They went to the end of the hall, then up a spiral staircase into which Batu struggled to fit. Grunting and heaving, he pushed his broadened shoulders through with a growl that echoed through the empty halls. Leiyn winced but spoke no reprimand. She knew he was being as quiet as a joined wildsoul could.

Still, when the upper corridor came into view, Leiyn flinched. Two paladins stood astride a rounded ornate door. Paintings of past Altacuras hung along the wall, further identifying where they were.

They had found Gran Ayda's rooms.

Leiyn mulled over how to proceed. Ata made the choice for them. Without breaking stride, the dryvan ambled up to the pair of paladins, then tapped a talon to each of their heads. Leiyn felt her mahia lash forward—not the blunt force of a whip, but the unleashing of a snare.

The men crumpled in a cacophony of metal.

Leiyn hissed a curse and raised her bow back the way they had come. Batu turned with her, long teeth bared.

No more paladins appeared, nor did Leiyn sense any. She waited for several moments before relaxing her bow.

"Ata!" Leiyn hissed back. "What are you doing?"

The dryvan ignored her. By her lifesense, she felt the Iritu move closer to the door, press against it, then bend down. A glance over her shoulder showed the dryvan inserting a talon in the lock. Ata's esse twisted as she shifted the form along the finger. The next moment, the latch slipped, and she pressed the door open.

"A clever trick," Teya muttered to Leiyn, holding her spear at the ready. "Though she might have exercised more caution before."

Leiyn only shook her head and kept watch.

Ata entered the room with Ketti and Ekosa. Moments later, they reappeared with the dryvan leading.

"Not home." The Iritu slithered between them to take the lead. "Shall we check the audience chamber?"

With little choice, Leiyn turned with the others back to the staircase, leaving the bedchamber door open and unlatched. The collapsed guards would already be clue enough to what had occurred. Attempting to hide them when anyone with lifesense would detect them would be a waste of precious time.

You could kill them.

She hurried after the others, glad no one else had suggested it.

Their order reversed, Batu loomed ahead of her, his broad head moving from side to side. As they exited the stairs and headed back the way they had come, only walls and closed doors flanked them. Leiyn felt the same prickle of unease between her shoulders. The basilica was too empty, their passage through it unchallenged. Where were the odiosas? The priestesses? It lacked even servants or acolytes scuttling about that must keep the palatial edifice in immaculate condition.

Unless their foes were foolhardy or incompetent—and she doubted one with power such as the head of the Catedrál commanded would be either—there was only one conclusion:

They were expected.

Reaching the split in the corridors, they headed forward. A grander atrium awaited, gilded and with marble columns rising throughout it. At the end of it lay two wooden doors rising to twice her height. Leiyn cast her gaze around. She looked up at the frescoes above, thinking of all the shapes she had seen lyshans take. Yet none hung from the high ceiling nor waited in the shadowed alcoves. The room was as empty as those before.

Reaching the door, Ketti paused and looked back, her brow furrowed. "We are here. The audience chamber."

The Eteman no doubt sensed what Leiyn had: esse shifted within the wood. Leiyn backed away, wondering what enchantment awaited them. A protective barrier? A hex for unwelcome visitors? The chamber beyond lay dark and lifeless. Devoid of occupants.

Or hidden from mahia.

Ata moved to the handles, heedless of potential danger. Before Leiyn could do more than choke out a warning, the dryvan shoved against the doors. They were not locked, and the mighty push sent them soaring open. Thunder filled the room to the high ceiling as they shuddered to a halt.

Leiyn hissed a violent oath and raised her bow. Braziers and chandeliers illuminated every corner and cranny of the chamber. They revealed it not to be empty, but a room brimming with people, spread over the layered daises at the far end. Paladins, swords drawn and shields held before them. Odiosas, expressions vague and gray robes drab. Priestesses, faces hard and their white-and-gold robes glowing in the luminescence.

Four of the paladins snagged her attention, their clothes garish and foreign in their fit. As she beheld the yellowed heads of the greataxes they cradled in their arms, Leiyn understood. The Catedrál's soldiers had been given Iritu artifacts of their own.

At their center, sitting upon the ornate golden throne, was a woman. Her garb was unremarkable, a plain white gown halfway to a nightshift. Her head was shaved bare, highlighting the slimness of her neck, the petiteness of her head. Beneath a sheer veil, her skin was smooth and a sallow tan, telling of one infrequently in the sun. Stark tendons and shallow wrinkles betrayed her age was beyond Leiyn's initial estimation, the tells of a woman who aged well. Or a woman kept young by unnatural means.

Had her throne not been indication enough of her identity, had Leiyn not recognized her visage from the carvings in many temples, had her potent mahia that eclipsed any maha in the room but Leiyn and Ketti, she would have known her by her poise alone.

This was Gran Ayda di Inhoa. The Altacura. Mother of Mercy.

Their quarry. Sharo's puppet.

But it was not Sharo who claimed Ayda then. A different lyshan crouched atop the back of her throne. One whose visage alone made Leiyn blanch.

Osmet cackled as she dropped the veil over those gathered. Many of the paladins flinched at the sound, and a few priestesses cried out in surprise. Her appearance before would have inspired fear in the stoutest of hearts, but now the Iritu had shifted her aspect to be more horrifying still. Eyes, unsettlingly humanoid, had multiplied across a face erupting with mandibles. Slavering teeth appeared amidst them, needle-sharp and many-rowed. Legs lined with spiny black hairs curled over the back of the throne, holding the lyshan in place. A bulbous body hung out of sight behind that Leiyn knew was there by lifesense. That Osmet could spin silk was obvious;

signs of webbing accumulated in the corners of the ceiling. It gave the impression that this was no audience chamber, but a long-abandoned attic.

Into the fading echoes of Osmet's laughter, the Altacura spoke.

"Be welcome in the Basilica Sóveran, my children." Gran Ayda's voice was high and ringing as it filled the audience chamber. "Please, enter and be at ease. You are guests in the home of the Saints. I am eager to meet you."

51

HOLY MOTHER

The last place Leiyn wished to enter was that audience chamber. But as Ata strode forth without hesitation, she gritted her teeth and followed.

As she walked, Leiyn reached for Clouded Fang. The ash dragon roused to her touch and turned his bright gaze upon her. She did not yet call him. First, she wanted the full measure of their adversaries. A ranger did not loose at the first target but waited to find the weakest point.

"Leiyn!" Teya hissed, keeping pace next to her. "What are we doing? We must flee!"

Leiyn shook her head, never breaking stride. "Not this time."

The *situal* seized her arm, dragging her to a halt. Her eyes were frenzied, darting back toward the array of enemies awaiting them. "Do you mean to let us die?"

Teya knew where to strike. Leiyn pushed down the compulsion to rub her chest where an ache had sprouted. A glance at the others behind showed similar fear spread across their features. Even Batu, towering and fearsome as he had become, hunched his shoulders before the collected enemies.

She hardened herself to it. Clung to the plan and its contingencies.

Cage it.

"No," Leiyn hissed. "You're not dying today."

"Leiyn, please—"

Leiyn already turned away, hurrying to catch up to Ata.

The dryvan had not slowed. Only when she stood ten strides from the throne and its dais did she stop.

"Osmet," she said, looking at the lyshan and ignoring the humans. "Summon my brother. I have a proposal."

The lyshan clacked her mandibles together and twisted around so she peered at them nearly upside down. "Am I your pigeon to sing your messages to him? Come, lost little sister—speak to me your secret desire!"

Ata stared at the twisted Iritu in silence. Leiyn stepped up on Ata's left and glanced up at the dryvan, seeing her wooden face remained placid and smooth. Only the turbulence in her esse betrayed her irritation.

Osmet cackled again and rotated on the throne so her head emerged off the side of the chair, looming over the Altacura's shoulder. The high priestess flinched, but remarkably, Ayda maintained her composure.

"Have we grown shy, Atastimina? Mute and mum and dumb? Silent as a mortal monk, silent as the dead?"

The singsong manner of the lyshan's speech put Leiyn in mind of her nightmare. She clenched her jaw, wondering why the vision filled her with more fear than all the enemies before her.

What remains after a scream?

Leiyn aimed her words at the Altacura. "You greeted us as if expecting us. As if you wish to speak."

Gran Ayda started. She had not expected to be addressed, Leiyn saw now. The aura about her had dimmed since their entrance, but her esse brightened as she gazed upon Leiyn.

Even overshadowed by immortal shapeshifters, she remained the Altacura, a beacon of power in her own right.

"You are Leiyn of Orille, are you not?" Ayda asked with that same ringing quality in her voice. "The one they call the Tideraiser? The Wilds Witch? Once a ranger who patrolled the wilderness of the Veiled Lands?"

Leiyn raised an eyebrow. "You know the answer. No more games, Ayda. Enough are being played." She motioned with her bow toward the lyshan clinging to the back of her throne.

The paladins scowled and the priestesses shifted at Leiyn's blatant disrespect. Leiyn wondered if anyone had ever addressed the Altacura without her title. Ayda seemed inordinately pleased, her features lifting in a smile.

"You are everything they claim and more. It pleases me to behold. The Sacred Five often utilize unorthodox tools. Omn works in mysterious ways, does It not?"

"Tools like your devils?" Leiyn cast a meaningful glance at Osmet, who appeared content to watch, her many eyes blinking, one after the other. "We didn't come to debate theology. Omn and the Saints aren't your masters any longer."

There—it manifested as a mere flicker in Ayda's eyes, but a roil in her esse. *She chafes at her chains.* Leiyn doubted it was enough to pit her enemies against one another. But they needed any advantage, however slight.

"Sacrilege," a middle-aged priestess hissed, her cowl pressed tightly across her broad forehead. "Holy Mother, allow us to silence the infidel!"

Ayda held up a hand. "Peace, Sister Martina. Does San Hugo not counsel vigorous debate before taking up arms? Do the scriptures not condone violence only as a final recourse?"

"She spits upon tradition!" Sister Martina objected. "She holds the Office of the Altacura in contempt! She is a witch, a murderer, a *ferino* whore. What discussion can be had that does not end in blood?"

Teya hissed at the slur, but the Altacura spoke before the *situal* could.

"Hold your tongue, child."

Ayda only raised her voice marginally, but the priestess stiffened as if lashed, then bowed her head. "Apologies, Holy Mother," Martina muttered.

The Altacura maintained her stare on the pigheaded priestess for a long moment, then looked up at Leiyn. "If you did not visit for theology, why then did you come, Tideraiser? Or do you prefer Leiyn?"

Leiyn ignored the invitation. To be familiar with your enemy was to dull your blade. She had lost too much of her edge to risk losing more.

"Why serve him?" She wondered if her paladins and priestesses knew their true master. If they had always known and accepted him as Ayda did. "What do you stand to gain? You sit at the head of one of the most powerful institutions in Unera. You're praised and worshipped across the oceans. What more do you need?"

Again, that almost imperceptible flutter shot through her soul.

"I serve no profane power," Ayda said, "but the Light Above. In Its light, all sin shall burn away."

The lyshan's laugh behind her undermined the words. Leiyn watched as once more, the leader of the Catedrál seethed.

Now to rattle those chains.

"You know they lack their full power here, don't you?" Leiyn gestured at Osmet as the lyshan's laughter sputtered away. "The island stifles it."

She did not get the reaction she expected. Instead of intrigued or frightened, something else passed through Ayda's soul. Something haughtier. Self-assured.

"All servants have their limitations," Ayda said. "Refugio is a holy place."

Leiyn fought down a grimace. There was only one way she could uncover the truth of whatever was going on here. Even if it meant shooting blindly into the dark.

"It's the world titan, isn't it? The one buried beneath the island. It keeps the Iritu in check."

Again, that smug reaction passed through Ayda. Like she knew secrets Leiyn only glimpsed.

"Even titans fear the power of the Unknowable," the Altacura said. "In death, there is power. Power eternal. We did not kill the titan. But we have ensured its death did not go to waste."

So it is dead.

Before Leiyn could think of another angle of attack, Ata spoke, ignoring all but her fellow Iritu.

"Are you content with this, Osmet?" The dryvan spread her arms. "To be his servant? To grovel at his feet, disguise yourself as a horrendous beast to frighten mortals? Once, he cherished you above all others. Above me." The dryvan laughed and let her arms fall to her side. "Now look at you. How he must despise you now! Do you not remember how my brother loves beauty? And you...perhaps you have survived longest among your rotten kind. You have adapted as none of us could. But nothing of beauty remains. Nothing he could love."

The lyshan had gone still—the stillness of a predator set to strike. Leiyn raised her bow and tensed the bowstring, aiming at the spiderlike Iritu. The paladins shouted and raised their shields, swords rising as well. Leiyn felt the priestesses and odiosas gather their mahia, ready to dazzle her and her companions.

Osmet did not spring. She scuttled forward, hooked feet pressing onto the Altacura as well as the throne. The head of the Catedrál gasped as a foot pressed into her, folding over a scarlet blossom that appeared on the white garment over her leg. Leiyn felt the movement of her mahia as she healed the wound.

The lyshan scarcely seemed to notice. Her morphed features twisted as she raised herself before Ata. Only now that the whole of her bulbous body was unveiled did Leiyn see she was larger than the last time they had encountered her. Far larger than Ata, if more vulnerable without armor or titanbone weapons.

"You wish to speak with him?" she hissed. "I am all you shall get! Tell me why you are here, lonely Atastimina, lest I assume we have nothing left to discuss."

Ata did not flinch away from the lyshan, though she seemed a sparrow staring down a hawk. "Tell him I bring hope."

"Hope. *Hope!*" Osmet threw back her head, loosing a caw like a diving eagle's. "Then it is true—you have nothing."

Leiyn looked at Ata. The truth tussled in her chest with respect for the dryvan's wishes.

They called one another friend and ally. Sister, even. But this opportunity might come only once.

She could not lose it.

"Ata," Leiyn said. "Tell her."

Ata whipped toward Leiyn, her gaze cutting. "Leave this to me."

Osmet turned her dozen eyes on Leiyn. Though it felt foolish to the point of reckless to let a lyshan out of her sight, Leiyn kept track of her by her lifesense and held Ata's gaze.

"This might be our only chance. Tell her or I will."

Ata stretched taller, her wooden body creaking as she leaned forward. Leiyn tensed, half-expecting the dryvan to strike her.

Then the dryvan shrank. If not for her armor, Leiyn felt

she might have curled into herself, a petal left too long in the sun.

"Tell Sharo..." Within her shadowed helm, Ata closed her eyes. When she opened them, fresh resolve shone from them. "Tell him I found a seed. An *Ialadt* seed."

Osmet skittered toward Ata so swiftly Leiyn had drawn and almost loosed upon her before stopping herself. Her grotesque head leaned over Ata, her many-eyed gaze fixed on her fellow Iritu. Sounds flowed from her mouth, but Leiyn could not make sense of them. Only one word did she recognize of their tongue: "*Ialadta*."

"Yes." Ata stared, defiant, into the lyshan's gaze. "But I won't say more unless you bring him here."

She raised her war scythe. Osmet scampered back. The curved point dipped toward the lyshan in a challenge. A taunt.

"Bring him or I'll kill you," Ata continued. "You and the rest of our Kin. I won't stop until he comes."

Osmet hissed, spittle flying from between her mandibles. It hit the marble tiles and acrid smoke rose in a puff, the bright stone withering away. Leiyn grimaced. Her spit made for a potent acid—yet another weapon to watch for.

Before the lyshan could respond, a blinding presence took form next to her.

Leiyn whirled toward this newcomer, heart drumming. She knew them to be a second lyshan, for only an Iritu could appear from thin air. But how could they defy the island when it limited Ata's heritage?

Still, she did not expect it to be *him*.

"Sharo!" Leiyn snarled, sharpening the name to dagger-point.

Sharo smiled at her and spread his arms wide. Scarlet robes, silken and every bit as rich as the last time she had seen him, fell away from his wrists in voluminous sleeves. Jewelry, studded with organic gems and glimmering with esse, clanked on his wrists, fingers, and neck. Sandals, oiled and ornate with filagree, lashed about his feet to disappear beneath the gold-threaded hem. A circlet of birch sat upon his brow, pearls adorning the whitewood.

But his clothing was the most constant part about him. Every change she had witnessed in her dreams was real. No longer was he the charred, shriveled thing he had been upon their first meeting, but instead was robust and vital. His skin had smoothed and grown as supple as a newborn tree. His eyes were no longer pits, but a lively silver, shifting in luminance like storm clouds borne upon a violent gust. Hair grew from the once-bare scalp, tufted and fibrous as fiddleheads. Beneath his robes, his body had broadened, thickened, strengthened.

No longer was he starved and thin, but a monster who had sated his every hunger. Every bit the lyshan lord Man'nah had once been.

"You called, Sister," Sharo said to Ata. "So we have answered. Have you come all this way for a purpose or only a reunion?"

So quickly he dismissed her. Leiyn did not let fury throw off her aim as she drew the bowstring to her cheek. Anchored her hand on her jaw.

She took her shot.

52

ASCENSION

The arrow flew—and went wide of its target.

As it cracked a stained glass window behind, Leiyn repressed a snarl and glared at Ata. At the moment of release, the dryvan had pushed aside her bow.

Ata only met her eyes for a moment, her eyes hard and purposeful.

Around them, the room erupted with posturing. Osmet clacked her mandibles, acidic spit peppering the floor. Paladins rattled their armaments. Odiosas and priestesses bubbled over with mahia. Batu roared, the bestial sound striking instinctive fear through even Leiyn. Teya held up her spear as if preparing to charge. Ekosa and Ketti matched their esse to the opposing mahas.

But neither side attacked. Leiyn returned her gaze to Ata.

"What are you doing?" she hissed. "This is our chance!"

The dryvan did not answer but only faced her transformed brother. Emotions moved through Ata's stratified lifeforce so swiftly Leiyn could scarcely follow. Was this treachery? Familial loyalty? Could she remain loyal to her brother after all Sharo had done?

Leiyn nocked a second Iritu arrow, but did not draw. It was one of the few she had. Until she had the full measure of the situation, she would not loose again.

Then Sharo would die.

The lyshan lord had not shifted. If he feared Leiyn's arrow, no part of him showed it. A smile curled lips as supple as his sister's. His too-lively eyes flitted between Leiyn and Ata.

Sharo lowered his arms. "Is it true, Sister, what you have said? Have you found what we sought all these long years?"

Ata met his gaze with a raised chin. "That depends. Who do I speak to? Does my brother remain? Or has Sharo lost his way like Man'nah before him?"

The lyshan lord flicked his hand, dismissive. "Dispense with the philosophy, my dear Ata. You asked for us because you trust us. We have come. And as ever, we shall come to an accord."

We. Us. He spoke like Man'nah. His esse brimmed with multitudes of souls, far more chaotic than before. But unlike his late master, his essence was ordered. It formed like a pyramid, one layer atop another, all heeling to the apex.

He's still in control. Just.

Ata did not reciprocate her brother's warmth. Tense and ready, her wooden limbs knotted like the roots of a gnarled willow.

"I want to trust you, Sharo. Trust you as I did before. But after all you've done, how can I?"

The lyshan lord moved forward, every step so smooth he seemed to glide over the tiles. His eyes never left his sister.

"Because we remain as we have ever been," he murmured, gentle. Like a father speaking to his daughter. She could almost imagine him brushing a hand softly through her hair.

Sharo, gentle?

The thought snagged like clothes snagged on thorns. Leiyn

shook her head, trying to free herself of the vision. Only then did she notice the subtle heritage Sharo exuded.

Glamour.

"Careful," Leiyn called over her shoulder as she tensed her bowstring. "He's trying to charm us!"

Her companions shook themselves, slackened expressions recovering their edge. Leiyn looked to Ata to see if Sharo's magic had reached his sister, but the dryvan appeared the same as she had before, just as tense and wary.

Ketti roused first. "Where are they, *gallu*?" she shouted at him, as close to losing control as Leiyn had seen her. "Where have you taken my people?"

Sharo smiled. "Come with us, hunter-child," he murmured, though his voice somehow carried through the audience chamber. "Perhaps we shall show you."

The Eteman started to snarl a reply, but Ekosa took her arm, quieting her with words Leiyn could not hear.

Ata moved, drawing back Leiyn's attention. The dryvan's coiled limbs slackened. Her height diminished so she rose barely taller than Leiyn. She shrank both in body and presence.

"Come to the ashes of our Mother, Sharo," Ata said softly. "Come alone. Rid yourselves of this rot you burden yourself with. Only then we might plant our future. Together."

Leiyn's throat squeezed shut. She stared her accusations at the dryvan. Ata did not look her way. Not once did her gaze waver from her brother.

Is this it? Is this how she betrays us?

"Ata—" she started.

The dryvan's good eye slid over to pin her. "Please, Leiyn. Allow me this."

Her tone was guileless, pleading. No glamour rode upon the request. If Ata manipulated her, it was only by words.

Leiyn tensed her jaw, wavering. Then gave a curt nod. Apart, they had no hope of taking down Sharo. She had to trust Ata had a plan.

Ata faced forward. "Well, Brother? Will you abandon your vengeance? Will you look to a better future with me?"

At Sharo's shoulder, Osmet twitched and tilted her monstrous head. Her dozen eyes flickered between Sharo and Ata. Uncertain—the mad lyshan did not believe in her leader.

The lyshan lord lowered his head. His shoulders shook, robe quivering with the motion. Leiyn's ears perked as the sound he issued rose in volume.

Laughter.

"Yes, we shall join you at our Mother's ashes, Atastimina. But you are mistaken in what you call rot." He raised one long, sharp finger to point at Leiyn. "We Iritu shall never be safe so long as mortals know of our birthplace. It shall only be a matter of time before they burn the *Ialadta* again. Is that not so?" he asked, turning his gray eyes on Leiyn.

"No," she answered flatly. "It's not."

A too-wide grin split his face. "Do you hear a shred of veracity to her words, Sister? They lie to protect themselves, as they ever have! But if you peer into their beings, you shall know the truth. Violence is the seed of their souls. All they are grows from it."

Ata returned her brother's smile. But where madness was the root of his, Leiyn saw only sorrow in the dryvan's.

"No, Sharo. I don't see that in them. But you... You've bathed in hatred for so long you can see nothing else."

She crossed the distance between them, a hand pressed to her chest. To the *Ialadt* seed resting there, Leiyn realized. She had not hidden it like Leiyn had suspected. Like any mother, Ata could not bear to be parted from her child.

"But I believe the one I love remains within," she said, her voice softening as she neared him. "Prove me right, Brother. Come to where our Mother's boughs once stretched high and her roots drank deep. Come alone. Bring her back with me."

Sharo moved forward to meet her. Leiyn could draw only shallow breaths. Would he kill her? Steal away their most potent ally? Rip the seed from her chest and claim it as his own, stealing any leverage they hoped to have?

She longed to speak against the foolish action. But Ata had asked for her trust. Had the dryvan not done enough to earn it?

And if it costs our lives and cause?

As they reached one another, Sharo extended a hand. Ata placed hers in his. She faced away from Leiyn now, but her esse told more than her expression could have. Emotions tangled together in her soul, powerful and opposing. Conflicted.

"We wish for nothing more," Sharo murmured. "*I* wish that. But Ata, my sister, my precious, can you not see the necessity of what we propose? They nearly extinguished our people. Will you allow them to complete their crusade?"

The war waged on within Ata. Leiyn looked to Ketti and saw her alarm mirrored in the Eteman's face. Teya and Ekosa also looked to Leiyn, fear leaching their courage. Even Batu, infected with rage, betrayed uncertainty in his lifeforce.

Trust had anchored their party, but Leiyn could not sacrifice those she loved for it.

She lowered her bow and raised her gaze to the Altacura, still seated upon her throne. "Listen to him, Holy Mother. Do you not hear his words? Sharo would kill and enslave us all. Do you believe yourself exempt?" Leiyn forced a laugh. "As soon as you have served your purpose, he'll discard you as he discards any tool. That's all mortals are to him: tools. Our lives mean nothing to him." She swept her gaze over the rest of the gathered Ilberians. "He and his kind are Legion returned!"

Like a gust blowing through treetops, her words spurred uncertainty in their souls. She watched it spread and grow among the paladins and priestesses. Logic alone had not birthed it; the sight of those they served was far more responsible. The cinder only needed air to fan it into flames.

Their faith was in the Catedrál, the Altacura, the Saints and Omn. Not in devils wearing flesh.

Sharo drew her gaze as he spoke. "Ah, Oldsoul. Your resolve remains undimmed." He smiled. The fondness in it reminded her of Tadeo smiling at the ranger apprentices.

He's twisting your memories. Don't let him!

"If we are as you say," he continued, "if we revile humankind, then why have we adopted this form?" He withdrew his hand from Ata and swept it down his figure. "The Kin have long despised mortals. We have resisted our nature, adopted the bodies of simple beasts and plants to distance ourselves from you. In our resentment, we ignored how our bodies mirrored yours."

He spread his arms once more, and Leiyn saw how he gloried in his body. How their dread was the reflection by which he reveled. "We were meant to be like this. Be like humans. But more, far more."

Ata retreated a step from her brother. The war within her seemed to have resolved.

"What have you done?" the dryvan whispered, then spoke louder. "Is this why you are here? Harvesting humans like their kind butchers beasts?"

Sharo lowered his arms, the smile smoothing away. "We have evolved, Sister, as we all must. As you must. Yes, we absorbed the essence of those touched by the world. Again and again, we have come close to their magic, their mahia, similar but separate from our Inheritance. Now, we have transcended. We are many, but we have not lost our way as Man'nah did. Not even the Vast Mothers can quell us!"

Ata retreated further, her chest contracting beneath the curtain of ivy as if to clutch at the Mothertree seed within. Relieved the dryvan remained on their side, Leiyn still worried about Sharo's claims.

Transcended...

The presence of a world titan did not dampen his heritage —he had shown that through his sudden appearance. How much more was he capable of?

Leiyn looked again to the Altacura, but instead of Sharo's words encouraging rebellion, they seemed to have dampened it. Terror had its claws in Ayda and her followers. Leiyn doubted any words could reach her now.

She had no other choice but to try.

"Gran Ayda." Leiyn let her desperation fill her voice. "Please, listen to me. Fight with us. Throw him off. We needn't be enemies."

Osmet, who had largely been silent, clacked her mandibles and spewed laughter along with spit. "Hear this, Sister, dear Sister? We needn't fight, not at all!" The lyshan slithered up to Sharo and nestled her head against his shoulder like a hound in heat. "We can be together once more, yes, yes. Perhaps I shall even share!"

Ata stepped forward, essence writhing at Osmet's words. She halted as Sharo held up a hand.

"She Who Remains, that is enough. You displease us."

The rebuke was paired with a lash of magic. The lyshan stumbled away, her dozen eyes unfocused as if dazed. She did not speak against the rough treatment, but accepted it, though Leiyn saw her seething spread through her many souls.

Ata smiled, hard and sharp.

Not everyone was so pleased. The adherents to the Catedrál shifted, their fear making their lifefires bright and trembling. How much more should they fear one who cowed even his fellow devils?

Though Leiyn tried to deny it, their terror echoed within her. Sharo was truly first among the lyshans. A lord every bit as tyrannical as Man'nah. She ground her hand into the grip of her bow.

I'll kill him just the same.

"Please, Ayda," Leiyn started again. "Just listen to me—"

"It is too late for that, Oldsoul," Sharo interrupted, his voice grown thunderous and drowning out hers. "Ayda, we have discussed enough."

The Altacura paled beneath her veil. Leiyn stared at her, imploring. She could not tell from either expression or esse if she had swayed Ayda.

The mature woman reached down to her side. When she raised her hand, it revealed a strange device that resembled a Kalgan hourglass in shape, two chambers connected by a narrow funnel, and appeared made entirely of glass, though of an impure and murky variety. Something sloshed within the dual chambers, a viscous liquid that clung to the glass and coated it. Esse shimmered within it, adding to the amber hue. The same color gold as the glass.

The same hue as Iritu blood.

Ayda held the artifact upright, then began tilting it. The room shifted; imperceptible at first but steadily becoming more apparent. Leiyn fought to keep her balance. It was as if the floor had become sand beneath her feet and sloughed away even as she stood. The walls dripped, stone becoming liquid, turning the same direction as the artifact.

"Stop her!" Leiyn raised her bow and aimed at the Altacura. She loosed her arrow, but the wavering materiality conspired against her aim. One of her last Iritu arrows went soaring past the throne.

The head of the Catedrál flinched, then continued her slow revolution of the hourglass.

Teya and Batu started a drunken charge, only to be met by

equally unsteady paladins. Osmet, too, skittered forward, harsh laughter filling the shimmering air. The priestesses clung together, their lifeforce surging as they fought for balance. Ekosa and Ketti did much the same. The odiosas remained where they were, uncaring as reality dripped away.

Not wishing to waste more of her enchanted arrows, Leiyn nocked an ordinary broadhead and aimed it. Ata's shout made her hesitate.

"Sharo, don't!"

In her peripheral vision, Leiyn saw Ata lunge for her brother, snapping forward with speed only an Iritu could attain. Sharo met her charge with an embrace. Leiyn could not tell if he crushed her or held her close in loving reunion.

Cursing, Leiyn loosed again. This time, she struck true. The Altacura cried out as she fell back against her throne, the arrow lodged in her shoulder.

As the hourglass shook, the world split. Leiyn felt the air stick in her lungs as she peered into two opposing Uneras. Underfoot remained the bright marble tiles of the basilica, the bases of the thick columns and bottoms of the stained glass windows diving into it.

Midway up, they disintegrated into gloomy, smoky air. A gray pall loomed above, flecks of orange like fireflies among it. No, not fireflies—embers not yet extinguished. The stench of rotted eggs rode on a torrid breeze, gusting through the remnants of the audience chamber.

Her stomach kicked, unsettled by the shift. Vertigo made her vision spin and dance. Leiyn sucked at the odorous air and nocked a third arrow. She raised her bow and tried to aim. Her lifesense, just as disrupted as her eyes, still showed that the missile had not struck anything vital.

But pain could be disruptive. Enough, she had to hope, to stop whatever spell the Altacura wove.

But though Ayda remained seated, she held the hourglass

up once more. Face twisted with pain and determination, the high priestess spun the artifact the last quarter turn in one swift motion. The liquid sloshed through it, shiningly bright as the sun.

The world ripped away—and Leiyn spilled into the hells.

53

THE FIRST HELL

Leiyn pitched to the ground and rolled to her feet. Sparks danced before her eyes, born from more than imagination. Like the glimpse during the transition, this place shimmered with flecks of lifeforce and embers. Heat and esse rose in equal measures, both blistering to her senses.

She fought to remain standing and took in her surroundings. Gone was the basilica; gone were the Altacura and her throne. A fire-ravaged landscape spread in their stead. Branching rivers of lava flowed down the looming mountain, spilling from a crevasse near the peak. Black rock, uneven and pitted with cavities, spread under her shoes. Plumes of putrid smoke spilled into the sky, obscuring it. Sulfur coated her tongue and mouth, the taste of it foul. Ashes danced upon a fiery breeze that blew down the slope and set her cloak to dancing.

As far as she had imagined the black hells, this was as close as they came.

But she was not so superstitious as to believe that. *A grotto —has to be.* The artifact Ayda had held was of Iritu make, designed to transfer those in its web to a grotto.

And, unless she was mistaken, trap them.

Her cloak rose on her neck, choking her. Leiyn loosed her hand from the bowstring to unclasp it and send it flying away. Squinting against the gloom, she took stock of those with her. The transition had disrupted the burgeoning battle, but as its combatants adjusted, survival instincts overrode panic and confusion. Her friends had all been sent with her—or almost all. Ata had disappeared with Sharo and the Altacura. She wondered if the brother and sister still reeled in their uncertain embrace. Wondered if they fought or if Ata capitulated to Sharo's invitation.

Batu recovered his wits first. The white fur along his bulky frame the brightest thing in the dismal surroundings, he reared on his hind legs and bellowed a challenge that reverberated through Leiyn's bones. Teya was up after him, spear raised as she stood by his side. The *situal* glanced back at Leiyn with a beseeching look before she faced forward again.

Behind them stood Ekosa and Ketti. Ekosa formed his mahia into a wall, readying for attacks of magical origin. Ketti ignored any assault for the moment as she reached into the sky. Thunder rumbled beyond the veil of black smoke. Storm clouds gathered, portents of Mehu'Ra's descent.

Clouded Fang! Leiyn sent her plea racing along her bond to the titan. *Come to me!*

The ash dragon already lay in wait. At her invitation, he raced through stone and lava toward her.

But their enemies rallied as well. Paladins formed into a line, shields raised as they advanced. The four bearing the titanbone greataxes and Iritu clothes hung behind with the odiosas and priestesses; their protectors, it appeared. Mahia rose from the Ilberian mahas, the enslaved humans rousing at their masters' commands, preparing to challenge Ekosa's defense. The priestesses sent their mahia elsewhere, seeking something beyond Leiyn's awareness.

She nocked an arrow, meaning to waylay their schemes, when a cackle cut through the foul fog. Osmet's unnatural shape scurried forward, bearing down on the small knot of Leiyn's friends.

Batu charged her, but the lyshan was too clever to meet a direct charge. With impossible speed, she evaded him and drove at Teya.

Leiyn withheld her scream until after she loosed the arrow. Still, it missed, flying beyond to ping into a paladin's shield.

Leiyn raced toward her beloved. She could only watch as Teya rolled beneath Osmet's attack, her spear raised. Spidery limbs trampled where the scout had stood.

Then the lyshan hissed and reeled back, beads of amber ichor peppering the air.

Teya rolled away, suffering no worse than a few scrapes. She flashed Leiyn a look before barreling toward the lyshan.

Trust us, Redlock.

Leiyn ignored her beloved's remembered words. For the moment she had believed Teya dead, all thoughts of the future had fled.

She would not watch her die.

The paladins had closed the gap and were nearly upon Ekosa and Ketti, still standing where they had first appeared. Half the odiosas battered against Ekosa's invisible wall, their mahia like sparks bursting from burning logs. Somehow, he held against them.

But swords could break them as easily as magic.

The paladins pivoted at Batu's roar. The wildsoul bowled over a handful in his initial charge, metal folding beneath the brutish strength lent by Sarryl. Terror rippled through their enemies.

Still, they rallied against his charge. Pushing, they drove their shields against her enraged friend. Swords dipped through the gaps, cutting through fur and hide to draw out red.

Leiyn vented her fear and fury in a blast of lifeforce. It stumbled and battered them, as powerful and overwhelming as a tidal wave.

The counterstrike found her a moment after.

It caught her like an unseen punch to the chin. Leiyn reeled as pain ravaged her being. She heard the tittering of the odiosas' mockery, their wordless voices whispering in her mind as they drove the knives in.

"*Get out!*"

She drove up her walls, shutting out the enslaved mahas. But they would not win the battle if she huddled behind her barriers. She had to go on the offensive. Keep their enemies on the back foot.

Don't let them die, Firebrand!

The sky lit up as lightning spilled down, drawing up Leiyn's gaze. For a moment, Monte Ardiente was illuminated. She stared at it, baffled, before rousing and nocking another arrow.

She had seen what it was in that moment. Not chasms spilling lava, but eyes weeping red tears. Not smoke from a caldera but issuing from nostrils and a yawning mouth. Not a mountain peak, but a head. The head of a titan.

The world titan was not buried beneath Refugio. It itself was the island.

Mehu'Ra screeched and dove toward the melee. Here in the grotto, his sapphire feathers were vibrant with hues of amethyst and emerald, undiminished by the dismal surroundings. Lightning shimmered across his coat, then blasted down among the huddled paladins. Screams rose. Electricity buzzed through Leiyn's feet and stiffened her muscles. The stench of burned flesh and cooked meat filled the air.

A moment after, Clouded Fang came roaring up behind

Leiyn. Fresh smoke billowed around her, fragrant with hot stone and reptilian musk. The black-scaled leviathan shadowed her as he circled overhead.

Leiyn set her sights on the lyshan, who still batted at Teya, toying with her like a cat would its meal.

Protect! she pleaded with her bonded titan. *Kill!*

The ash dragon opened its jaws. A glow exuded from it, portending what was coming. Leiyn raised her arrow, one of her last Iritu ones, and took careful aim. Osmet's eyes flickered toward her the moment before she loosed.

The lyshan disappeared.

Leiyn cursed even as the arrow flew toward nothing. Her titan scorched the ground where Osmet had been with blinding flames. Teya stumbled backward, arms raised against the blistering heat.

Stop! Leiyn commanded Clouded Fang as she raced toward her beloved.

The ground trembled, bringing her up short. Leiyn whipped her head around, searching for its source. Did the world titan still writhe in its death throes? Could the volcano of its corpse still erupt?

But she knew the strange pressure against her lifesense. That incessant pull only one creature possessed. Her mahia veered toward the blinding creatures taking form.

More titans approached.

Attack! Leiyn ordered Clouded Fang, focusing him on the priestesses and odiosas. *Quickly!*

The ash dragon wheeled around. Fresh fire built in his mouth. Before he could breathe it, two titans dove from the peak of the volcano through the low-hanging clouds. These monsters had his same shape. His same power.

The priestesses had called forth ash dragons.

As they came into view, she saw they looked different from her bonded titan. The larger one boasted dark gray scales and red horns; the smaller was ashy white all over. Neither was as big as Clouded Fang, but with fire building in their mouths, she knew numbers might still overwhelm him.

Survive! she bade him.

Draconic bellows boomed through the air. She watched Clouded Fang wheel away from their dives, seeking to outfly his pursuers rather than meet them straight on. All three soared into the gloom above, only remaining visible by lifesense.

She left the titan to fend for himself; others needed her more. Though Mehu'Ra had devastated the ranks of paladins, Osmet had reappeared, battering at both Teya and Batu as they sought to keep her away from Ketti and Ekosa. The wild-soul took the brunt of it, moving in to protect the *situal* from immortal blows she could not hope to survive.

Leiyn reached for her quiver of Iritu arrows and felt only two shafts under her hand.

Best make them count.

"Batu!" she shouted as she nocked the first arrow. "Pin her!"

Even without the din of titans and injured humans, her friend seemed beyond hearing. Snarling with bestial rage, Batu feinted a lunge, then committed to the second, grasping at her limbs. Osmet moved almost lazily as she dodged back and lashed him on the head with a spidery limb. A fresh cut sprouted across his brow.

"*Fesht!*"

Try as she might, Leiyn had no shot. The lyshan was too quick and clever. She had only landed an arrow on Khamo with the help of Ata and Clouded Fang. And one naming themselves She Who Remains had no death wish like Man'nah.

Fresh esse rolled through her senses.

With trepidation, Leiyn looked over as something emerged

from a river of lava along the volcano's slope. Even from a distance, she saw it was as long and wide as a creek—a hundred paces or more in length. Molten rock flowed off of it to reveal a gleaming carapace the deep red of dried blood. A thousand legs clicked together and against the stone as it turned its bulk toward them.

A giant centipede, born of lava. Come at the call of the odiosas.

Despair crept through her before she squashed it. A glance toward Clouded Fang showed he would be of little assistance. The three dragons tangled in the air, and from the feel of his esse, her bonded titan suffered the worst of it.

"Shit, shit, *shit!*" Cursing, Leiyn stopped long enough to shout, "Ketti, the new titan!"

The Eteman glanced back at her. "There are two!"

Only then did Leiyn recognize the fourth titan's awakening. Fire wreathed it, dying away as it flew toward them to reveal a hide streaked with bright orange and yellow. Its beak looked overly large for its head, for it was as long as the rest of its body. Wings more like a bat's than a bird's extended from its arms down to its back legs. For all its ungainly appearance, it was large, larger than Mehu'Ra, and burned with as much power.

The new titan angled for the tempest hawk, beak pointed toward it like a spear. Mehu'Ra screeched and banked out of the way. The opposing titan followed, far more agile in the air than it looked. Sparks billowed in its wake, flames simmering from its leathery hide.

Leiyn tore her gaze away. She could pay the fight no more heed. There was only one way she could help Mehu'Ra and Clouded Fang. Help her friends.

She had to kill the mahas.

Setting her eyes on them, she dashed forward. The only paladins remaining were those bearing Iritu artifacts, but all four stood in her way. Their eyes shifted, uncertain, as she stormed toward them.

"Leiyn, I am with you!"

Her lifesense revealed Teya sprinted beside her. Despite her resolution to protect her, Leiyn was glad to have her by her side. Without her falchions, with Clouded Fang requiring every bit of his own esse, Leiyn would have been hard-pressed to take on all four men on her own.

"Walls up!" she cautioned as she put her own protections in place.

The odiosas blasted against them a moment later. She had felt Ekosa's strength waning, the amber beads gifted him by Xepi all exhausted. But Leiyn's walls could withstand more than the enslaved mahas could deal even with the rampaging titans eroding them.

Leiyn replaced her Iritu arrow and nocked a broadhead. It would not penetrate Iritu armor, but a well-placed arrow could still kill a man in a single blow. Odiosas and priestesses, too.

"Cover me!" Leiyn called over her shoulder, and Teya moved forward to oblige.

The strangely clad paladins met the scout's charge. Animalistic helms lent them a fierce aspect. With axes heavy in their hands, they could not move them as adroitly as Teya wielded her spear. Even outnumbered, she harried and held them back. None were able to get in close enough to bring their axes to bear without being gouged by the titanbone spearhead.

Leiyn focused on her task. The odiosas looked at her as she aimed her arrow, their expressions blank. Their assault continued futilely against her walls, but they did not flinch away as she sent the arrow sailing forth.

One robed form fell tumbling to the ground. Even without sensing his esse, she knew he was dead or dying by where she struck.

She let a second arrow fly, then a third. Only with the fourth did Leiyn relent from targeting the odiosas and turn on the artifact-clad paladins.

Teya's defense had broken, and she retreated before their assault. Fresh wounds dripped blood down her arms from where the greataxes had cut.

Fury blossoming, Leiyn loosed an arrow. Distracted as they were, close as they had come, she could hardly miss.

A man tumbled to the ground. Red tears wept from his pierced eye. He twitched, then ceased to move.

One paladin broke off from Teya to attack Leiyn. She dropped her bow and drew her Eteman knife, then waited for him to reach her and swing. All too predictable—he expected the weight of the weapon to do the work for him.

Against another foe, it might have worked.

Leiyn channeled esse into strength and caught the shaft of the greataxe. The impact shuddered down her arm, but she had withstood blows from Iritu. A mortal man could not break her.

Leiyn drove her knife into one of the man's wide eyes, then tore the greataxe free of his nerveless grip. Returning her bloodied blade to its sheath, she took the weapon in both hands and glanced toward Teya. The Gast scout had taken the battle back in hand; it seemed Ketti had stunned one axeman with mahia, for they were rising from the ground, dazed by an unseen blow.

Trust us.

She turned from her beloved and dashed toward the remaining odiosas and priestesses. Instinct finally awoke in the enslaved men and women as they scampered back.

Not quickly enough.

The half-moon blade parted flesh like water. Blood sprayed the shadowed air. Leiyn tried not to see the bodies falling. She felt like a lyshan, like Ata among the Suncoats. A farmer threshing wheat. Her crop of corpses.

The odiosas fell before her. Soon, only strewn and bloodied limbs remained.

Panting, trying not to feel the carnage of her kills, Leiyn looked to the priestesses beyond. They fled across the desolate landscape, heading uphill, though the volcano could offer no escape.

Leiyn made to pursue them when Osmet flashed into existence before her.

The lyshan's horrid mouth was twisted into a grin. "I asked you once, Oldsoul. What remains after a scream?"

Fear for Batu froze Leiyn, but only for a moment. Channeling esse into speed and strength, Leiyn lashed at the forest of black limbs with the greataxe. Sever enough of them and the lyshan might slow enough to kill.

But Osmet was too swift. Shifting in and out of the grotto, she evaded Leiyn entirely.

"How?" Leiyn could not help the question ripping free of her as she stalked forward. "How can you reach within me?"

The dozen eyes widened in mockery. "Do you not remember my gift?"

"What do you—?"

She never finished the question. Agony seared through the back of her neck. Leiyn's head jerked backward—too fast, too sharp.

A crack, a snap—

Then nothing.

VIII
PART

BEYOND DEATH

54

THE NIGHT BEFORE

The breeze off the sea whispered against Leiyn's cheeks. Dried her eyes. Tears threatened to spill forth.

She blinked, swallowed. Forced them back down.

"Speak," Ata murmured beside her. "I will listen."

Leiyn opened her mouth, but the words did not come. She knew what she must say. Needed to say it. So why did she hesitate?

You're a damn fool, Firebrand.

Frustration rose with its usual swiftness, forcing out words both inelegant and bludgeoning. "If it comes to saving them or me, save them." She waved a hand toward their companions resting in the camp behind.

The Iritu smiled, amusement light on her features. "Are you planning something rash, little fox?"

"No. But you know the danger we face. The chances of all of us coming out alive."

Her expression smoothed. "I do."

"If someone has to die, let it be me." Leiyn lowered her gaze, fresh heat pricking her eyes. "It has to be me."

"I'm certain all of us would prefer to survive," Ata murmured. "You included."

Leiyn reached for Ata. She did not touch the dryvan lightly. Part of her still feared her strangeness. But she grasped her hands now. Her long talons were hard and knotted against her skin, but her esse was warm and strong as a snow-swollen river. Always, it raged just beneath the surface, threatening to break free.

"Please, Ata." She stared into the Iritu's eyes. "Swear to me."

Ata chuckled, half a smile curving up her face. The other half—the half with the milky eye—remained stoic and still.

"Very well, Leiyn. I swear it."

Leiyn clutched her hands a moment longer, then released her. "Thank you."

The dryvan laughed again, now devoid of humor. "If that time comes, we'll see if you still thank me."

Leiyn turned away to stare over the moonlit ocean. If that moment came, she doubted she would have time to thank her.

But knowing she would not watch another friend die was reassurance enough. Even if she had to die herself.

55

NOTHING

What remains after a scream?

The words peeled back the darkness, but numbness claimed her body.

Leiyn blinked her eyes open. She felt as if she drifted beyond life. Beyond death. Yet somehow, she remained alive.

Is this life?

The blackened body of the world titan spread before her. She lay on the ground, cheek pressed to the stone. She had fallen; the ache in her cheek told that much.

The fight. My friends! Back on your feet, Firebrand!

Leiyn tried to rise, but she could not move. Could not feel her arms. Her legs. Her torso.

Panic swaddled her, suffocating. Drowning.

Black legs scuttled into view and only heightened her terror. A roaring drone filled her ears. She heard nothing beyond that sound.

But Osmet did not need words to speak to her.

Little fly, little fly, caught in a web!

The lyshan sang in her head. Leiyn tried screaming if only to drown her out, but she had not the breath.

What's wrong with me?

Osmet cackled, the echoes of her laughter swelling to fill Leiyn's being.

Did you not enjoy my little gift?

Memories jangled in her mind. Her neck—it had snapped. She had heard of people becoming paralyzed but never witnessed it. Never felt the horror of your body becoming your tomb.

The prick to my neck!

How had she ignored it? She had wondered why the lyshan stung her in Qasaar rather than killed her but had thought it only a taunt. From the mad lyshan, it had seemed probable.

Now she knew the truth.

Leiyn's lifesense remained, allowing her to feel the inky blackness that metastasized throughout her body. It had lain invisible throughout the weeks of travel, but like a seed awaiting its moment, it had sprouted at Osmet's command.

The cursed toxin spread, claiming more of Leiyn with each moment.

Heal, damn you!

Mahia was connected to the body as well as the mind. Though some had been lost with her paralysis, enough remained that she should have been able to mend what was broken. But the toxin hampered her, blocking her efforts. All the while, Osmet rifled her soul, all barriers collapsing before her intrusion.

Nothing, nothing, NOTHING!

The mockery cut off as someone moved into Leiyn's hazy vision. She recognized her as much by her esse as her protective stance over Leiyn. Fear and hope surged in equal measure.

"Teya..." Her voice was rasping and weak. She barely had the breath to wheeze out her plea. "Go... Leave..."

If her beloved heard, she refused to comply. She heard a

distant cry as Teya charged the lyshan. Osmet did not dodge, but folded around her, aiming to crush her.

Fresh agony spasmed through Leiyn, its source the toxin. An echo of what its mistress felt.

Leiyn watched, uncomprehending, as Osmet crumpled before the *situal*. Teya stood above her, a hand extended, the circle of titanbone and sinew held in it and glowing with imbued power.

Xepi's artifact!

Darkness enwrapped Osmet's soul. Like the many threads of a web, she was trapped in it and further entangled with her struggles. Lifeforce flooded into Teya, making her as bright as the sun to Leiyn's hidden sense. Too much for one of her capacity to hold.

Leiyn willed herself to reach out to her, to say something that would warn her of the danger. All she could eke out was a single, breathy word.

"Stop..."

But she did not stop. Teya held the talisman there as every drop of life drained from the lyshan and trembled into her. Her wounds had healed, and now what seemed bubbles of esse made her soul look as sickly as any lyshan's. Leiyn had glimpsed similar growths on old animals. It always meant they were close to death.

Teya, stop!

Osmet tipped onto her back, black limbs twitching in the air. Then they stopped. Her body lay dark.

The mad lyshan was dead.

Teya dropped the artifact, now absent of power, and fell to her knees. She was shaking, her muscles trembling.

Dying.

Heal, Firebrand! You have to heal!

Even with its master's death, the toxin lingered. Leiyn set her mahia against it, trying to purify it as she once had Isla's infection. So little strength remained to her. Even the amber beads at her hip were beyond her reach. Her grasp on her body faded more with each moment. She slipped free of the world.

Heal, damn you!

A spasm rolled through Leiyn. For a moment, she thought it was a sliver of feeling coming back to her body. Even pain would have been welcome if it meant her control was returning.

Then she felt the truth.

Her bond to Clouded Fang had frayed to its last thread, but she felt him still. Felt as he crashed to the ground, pinned beneath the talons of the rival ash dragons. Their teeth and claws rent through scale and hide and magical barriers and into the flesh and esse beyond. His agonized roars rattled through her being.

"Help..." she gasped, flailing her mahia after the titan. "Help him..."

Then Teya was there beside her. She was on her hands and knees and shaking. The feverish brightness of her esse was awful to bear. It grew more painful still when she collapsed atop Leiyn, the treacherous arm splayed across her cheek.

"Take it," the scout gasped. "Please!"

Memories of when she had taken too much flashed through her mind. Licky lying still, eyes staring. The forest animals arrayed around her, their bodies shriveled and dry. The desiccated corpses of Suncoats.

But if she did not take lifeforce from Teya, both of them would die.

Leiyn rallied the little control remaining to her and grasped at her beloved's lifeforce. Her greedy mahia sucked it down to inundate her body. The rush was both euphoric and agonizing. Healing was never painless, and the more when it was her spine and soul she repaired.

The toxin held out a moment longer, then relented under

the bright torrent. Snapped discs of bone repaired and realigned. Ligaments and muscles knit back together.

Needles pricked her fingers and toes. Leiyn might have wept for gratitude. Any feeling was more than she had expected to have again.

But she did not stop. She stole still more life from Teya. The *situal's* seizures ceased, but she still lay prone and unmoving. Leiyn feared she suffered from more than an excess of life-force. That the artifact had done harm that could not be reversed.

Fresh torment along her titanbond jerked her back to other concerns. Clouded Fang still fought, but his efforts weakening. The opposing ash dragons were getting the better of him. Though his font of esse had seemed endless, before their relentless attacks, it quickly dimmed.

Without help, he would not last.

Leiyn tore free of her beloved and rocked to her feet. Teya tumbled to the ground. Leiyn's balance pitched, her legs feeling as firm as bundles of straw.

What she saw of the battle nearly drove her to her knees.

Clouded Fang was pinned. The larger gray dragon had her titan's wing folded under his claws. Only Clouded Fang's vigilance kept the gray from tearing into his neck. Their heads weaved atop their long necks, the gray trying to push its advantage, her bonded titan not giving an inch.

But the smaller white dragon soared down to land next to the pair. As Leiyn's titan lashed once more at the gray's attempted bite, the white darted in, latching its teeth onto her dragon's neck. Mahia blasted from it. Heat radiated as fire built in its belly.

For the first time, Leiyn felt her titan grow afraid.

Helplessness threatened to overwhelm her. She could not fight titans. None but another titan could.

But she could kill their masters.

Torn between loyalties, Leiyn looked back at Teya. The scout's eyelids fluttered, her movements sluggish. Yet though Teya's lifefire burned low, Leiyn saw no darkness that would signal lasting harm. She could do nothing for her—nothing but protecting them all.

"Watch over her!" she shouted at their friends.

Ketti glanced at her, expression pinched with concentration. Even as her tempest hawk held off both of the flying titan and the fiery centipede, she managed to noticed Leiyn's plight and gave her a sharp nod.

Knowing it would have to be enough, Leiyn left her beloved and weaved across the pitted ground. Between the smoke and confusion, it took her a moment to locate the mahas. Four priestesses remained, fled up the side of the volcano. Out of reach of her knives and arrows.

But an invisible arrow was more difficult to avoid.

Drawing on her mahia, now brimming to excess, Leiyn shot it forth. The first priestess buckled at the blow, stunned but alive. Their hold on the titan they commanded slipped.

Leiyn concentrated on the next one, but had to withdraw to defend before she could lash out. One priestess had enough talent to both leash a titan and attack. But without the advantage of surprise, it was only enough to make Leiyn's head ache. And they remained vulnerable to her counterstrike.

She hit the offending priestess harder, arrowing into her esse. The woman collapsed, unconscious.

But neither of them commanded the dragons. The giant centipede turned its body just shy of the battlefield and turned back toward its river of lava. The flying monster also peeled away to fly back toward the volcano. It made for fewer enemies, but she knew it would be better still if they could become allies.

Then it came to her.

"Ekosa!" she called. "Help me!"

Even a dozen paces away and her voice still tremulous and weak, he heard and looked around. His face was streaked with sweat and his shoulders were bowed, yet his lifeforce showed no greater affliction than weariness.

She pointed at the flying titan. "Leash it! Help Clouded Fang!"

Even as she finished speaking, the world shook. Leiyn threw up her walls, understanding it for the attack it was. As she regained her balance, she took in what had happened.

The two remaining priestesses had attacked her together. If it had worked, it might have been a sound stratagem.

Now, they had made themselves more vulnerable.

Leiyn snarled and sent out a retaliatory blow. The first priestess folded at once, exhausted from the attack and holding onto her titan. The second threw up barriers to Leiyn's intrusion, but they collapsed as Leiyn pressed in.

Their leashes severed as they collapsed. All the titans were untethered.

Leiyn looked back to Clouded Fang. All the while, she had felt his agony deepening, but no cessation of their bond. She saw now that was only just accurate. His esse had dimmed to levels she once thought unimaginable for titans. He struggled against the dragons pinning him, but his movements were weak and growing weaker.

She thought freeing them would be enough, that they would cease to attack, but the ash dragons acted otherwise. Neither the gray nor white even seemed to notice the absence of their masters. Now that the fight had begun, they were determined to finish it.

They would fight until they claimed the kill.

Desperately, she reached into the white, who had the deadlier position of the two. *Yield as I yield!* she pleaded with it. *Leave! Cease your attack!*

The white dragon ignored her attempts to command it.

Caught in the throes of battle lust, it had no intention of letting off.

Swallowing hard against her tightening throat, Leiyn left Teya lying where she was and ran toward Clouded Fang. She sent the same supplication into the gray dragon and tried leashing it to her will.

The gray paused. Its slitted eye slid up to regard her running toward it.

Then it looked back down and bit harder.

She put on a fresh burst of speed, drawing off of her bloated lifeforce. Glistening golden blood streamed down her dragon. Death approached on swift wings.

She fumbled for the knives at her hip. Feeble and short next to a dragon's teeth and claws, they were all she had. But they would still cut where she aimed.

She was still too far away, though. As she raced toward the tangled dragons, the white spasmed. Its throat undulated. Smoke puffed from between its lips. The air danced with heat.

Blue flames poured out over black scales.

Clouded Fang roared and writhed. His esse further darkened. He tried dislodging the white, but its grip was fast. There was nothing he could do.

She flew across the cracked ground. Twenty paces away; a dozen; only a handful remained. The titans loomed above her, even the smaller white four times her height at the shoulder.

Leiyn channeled energy into her legs and prepared to leap when the winged beast fell out of the sky.

She stumbled back as the titan's long beak dove into the base of the white's skull. Stunned and injured, the white dragon loosed its hold on Clouded Fang, then scrambled back. Golden blood shimmered from the wound as it raised its head, searching for its attacker. Spotting the yellow-and-orange beast, it roared and spread its wings, its intentions clear.

Leiyn did not need to glance back to know what had

happened. Ekosa had come through. He commanded the titan on their behalf. If only Clouded Fang could rise, it would almost be an even fight.

She knew of no way to free her dragon. But she had to try.

Screaming wordlessly, she bunched her legs and leaped into the air.

The hellish world blurred as she soared toward the gray's head, knives held aloft in both hands. The enormous blazing eye slid toward her, pupil dilating. It did not release its grip on Clouded Fang, but its lifeforce blew against her in a searing torrent. It spread its wings to buffet her back.

None of it was enough. Half-blinded and crazed, momentum carried Leiyn toward her destination: that same giant eye that watched her hurtle toward it. Half as big as she was, with all the force of a titan behind it, she almost drowned in its gaze.

Her bond to her titan saved her. Anchoring herself in it and Clouded Fang's pain, she directed all her remaining focus at her knives.

Eteman belt knife and ranger anelace stabbed into the gray's eye.

It was as soft as any other eye. Steel drove in past the hilts. Her hands sunk into the jelly. Golden blood gushed over her arms.

The dragon bellowed and bucked. Loosing its teeth at last, the titan raised its head and reared. Leiyn had no grip on it. Sluicing with lifeblood and vitreous, she slipped at the first shake.

And went soaring.

With what little presence of mind remained to her, Leiyn layered esse over herself, preparing for the impact. She could barely see. Her nearness to the dragon had sapped all moisture from her eyes and blurred her vision. All she could see was a vast darkness racing toward her.

The volcanic rock greeted her with a bone-breaking embrace.

Her left shoulder hit first. The rest of her body followed. For all she knew how to take a fall, she had never been thrown from so far up. Leiyn rolled with the impact, but everywhere that hit the stone seemed to shatter.

When at last she came to a stop, Leiyn huddled together, quivering. Agony roiled through her. Only a wave of anger pressed it back.

Don't die now, Firebrand!

Osmet's lifeforce still seethed within her, and the twenty amber beads at her hip were full of life. She sent it all rushing to her injuries. Under her guidance, bones pieced back together. Muscles and ligaments wove themselves whole. Her skin closed, sealing in what blood had not spilled. Fresh blood manifested to surge through her veins.

As she healed, she opened her eyes and reached out with her lifesense. Beholding what had become of her dragon.

Clouded Fang was no longer pinned, her attack on the gray dragon having freed him. He stood once more and stared up defiantly into the sky. Her titan seemed capable of little more. The volcanic soul that had brimmed with lifeforce had reduced to a smolder.

But other titans had taken up the fight. Ekosa's beaked monster was leading the white dragon on a chase. It looked to have taken the worst of it since its initial strike and was unable to gain another advantage.

The gray met its match in Mehu'Ra. The tempest hawk chased the dragon, bolts of yellow lightning striking from the dark clouds. Scorches upon its flanks and tears through its wings told of a fight that would not last long.

They were surviving. Perhaps even winning. Osmet dead. The Suncoats devastated. The priestesses downed. The titans freed and harried. And her companions still alive.

She shuddered with a sudden realization. *Where's Ata? Her Saints-damned brother? The rest of his minions?*

Her healing was not yet done, but Leiyn pushed to her feet. Swaying, she lurched across the porous rock to the Eteman knife where she had dropped it a dozen paces away. Her anelace, she could not immediately find. One of her last possessions from the Wilds Lodge, she could only hope it had not disintegrated in a lava-filled crack.

She had no more time to search for it. Not all the Suncoats were felled. She sensed the remaining two in Iritu clothes and greataxes creeping forward behind Clouded Fang. Her dragon sensed them as well. The black dragon turned his baleful gaze on them, his jaw parting.

But he had no more fire. Even the light in his eyes had dimmed to a muted yellow. As he was, could he even hold off two mortals?

Leiyn picked up the Eteman knife. Her grip still felt weak, her balance tenuous. But she had no time to waste. Setting one foot in front of the other, she made for her bonded titan.

Her pace increased as her healing completed. Her life-force resolved at levels similar to her natural amount. She had no more sources to draw from. If she took another lethal injury, there was no guarantee that she would survive.

Then don't get hit!

The two Suncoats looked fresh for the fight. Perhaps they had been waiting for just this occasion, coming in after their quarry was too exhausted to resist. None of them were headed for her, however. Though they cast her glances she could only call nervous, both advanced on Clouded Fang.

Leiyn set into a stumbling run. "*Feshtado* bastards!" she hissed between clenched teeth.

They were closer to her dragon and flanking him. Clouded Fang, as soundless as ever, darted forth to bite at the one on his right. The paladin dodged out of the way and landed a glancing blow on the dragon's snout, but the black scales defied the titanbone edge.

Yet the dragon had left himself exposed. The warrior on his left swung his axe. Its half-moon edge found the flesh exposed by the earlier dragon attacks. Fresh blood spurted out as it gouged into the neck.

Leiyn stumbled as pain wracked her once more. Ordinarily, she could have shrugged off her dragon's echoed agony. But in her weakened state, it took her longer to recover.

The second paladin's axe fell, gouging a fresh injury.

"No!" Blindly, Leiyn ran at them. Her vision twisted with her lifesense. Her mahia spasmed like an overwrought muscle. Still, she pressed forward, desperate to reach her titan. Desperate to save him.

Her foot caught, sending her sprawling.

Leiyn gasped with the impact, but did not evaluate the fresh wounds. Scrapes and twists could wait for afterward. She had to keep going. Clouded Fang needed her.

Before she could regain her feet, someone ripped into being before her.

Leiyn held up her knife before recognizing them. Ata stood before her. Dripping with gold ichor, she swayed where she stood. Her armor was battered and broken. In one hand, she held her scythe in a wearied grip. The other carried the hourglass artifact Ayda had turned. Her lifeforce, so bright before as to be blinding, had dimmed to a firefly glow.

Their eyes met. But before Leiyn could call out and warn her of Clouded Fang's peril, the smoky air between them filled with more shining beings. And these were no allies.

The lyshans had come.

56

OATH

Leiyn staggered to her feet as she took in the fresh foes.

She recognized them from her glimpse in Vasara. The burly gray one with a long horn projecting from the tip of their snout. Enthil, the one with dragonhide armor and mothy wings and a crest of antlers. The Iritu like a deformed tree, weapons bristling from the ends of a multitude of limbs. The one on all fours that resembled a huge panther, eyes glimmering.

And standing in their midst was Sharo.

Only the lyshan lord was free of injury. The rest dripped with amber ichor, evidence of Ata's scythe in the tears through their armor and flesh. But their diseased souls still blazed, conflagrations against the night. Even Ata, as deadly as she was, could not fight five of her immortal Kin.

Sharo glanced at Ata, then turned to Leiyn. She flinched under the full force of his gaze. Those gray eyes burned like twin suns from all the heritage concentrated within them.

"Oldsoul. You have been as resilient as we hoped." The lyshan lord glanced toward Osmet's crumpled form. If her death touched him, neither his expression nor esse betrayed it. "She Who Remains was cunning and dangerous. To have overcome her is no mean feat."

She yearned to strike at that subtle sneer, to batter in his revitalized flesh. But for the moment, all she could strike with were words.

"We've killed lots of Iritu. I'll kill you, too."

His smile widened. His eyes flared. "Without your Vast One?"

She looked past him just as the next blow fell. Leiyn clutched a hand to her neck. She felt the deepening cuts of the greataxes as if in her own flesh. She choked the same as Clouded Fang choked on his blood. Felt his essence draining as if from her body.

She could not force out words past the sensations. All she could do was moan and remain upright.

Sharo took a step closer. "It was ever the weakness of your kind, your reliance on titans. But take them away, and what have you left? A frail mortal."

Leiyn lunged. Blind with Clouded Fang's pain, she acted on instinct. Prayed to the Saints that Sharo was too absorbed with his gloating to dodge.

The Eteman knife sank into his chest, down to the hilt.

Leiyn hesitated, baffled she had struck true. She looked up, though her lifesense told of her enemy's fate.

Sharo shone with life still. This was no Iritu blade to eat away at his layered souls. The wound she had dealt him dimmed him so little she could detect no difference.

"Now do you see, Oldsoul?" he breathed, his smile widening. "The futility of your resistance?"

Leiyn braced her free hand against his chest and jerked the knife free. Before she could strike again, red flashed across her vision. She spun to the ground, iron and salt flooding her mouth. Her jaw felt wrong as it throbbed.

"No, we thought not," Sharo spoke as he stood over her. "You shall require more convincing. But we are equal to the task."

The other lyshans moved to flank her. They left no gaps between them.

She knew it then. Knew how this would end. Ignoring the enemies ringing her, she caught Ata's eye from beyond them. The dryvan had not moved. Despair clawed through her, paired with another emotion just as potent. Regret.

Fear stronger than for herself wrung Leiyn out. Channeling esse she could not spare into her broken jaw, she mended it enough to push out garbled words.

"Remember, Ata!" She spat, the pain of it almost robbing her of speech. She forced through it. "You swore!"

The dryvan grimaced and looked aside. Leiyn could not tell her intentions from her esse alone. Dimmed and convoluted, it waged war with itself.

"Enough." Sharo shifted his gaze to Enthil. "Take the Eteman. Kill the others."

The winged Iritu pulsed his magic with acknowledgment. But before he could move, Ata spoke.

"Let them go, Sharo."

The lyshan lord twisted to face the dryvan. "You are in no position for demands, Sister."

"You know I am." Ata grazed a talon across her ichor-spattered chest. "If you wish to claim our Mother's seed, release them and meet me at Her ashes in peace. Even now, I will welcome you."

"Even now?" Laughter rang from his gray lips, all the more jarring in the infernal landscape. "That is good, Sister. For when we come, we will have forced the mortal realms into peace. Perhaps then you will see it was the only way."

Slowly, Leiyn levered herself upright and worked to get her feet under her. She was trapped, outnumbered, and outmatched. But only death could part a ranger from their duty.

Spitting blood at Sharo's feet, grimacing at the pain shooting through her head, Leiyn looked around the battlefield. She could only catch glimpses of her friends, but her lifesense told her what her eyes could not. Teya had arisen and limped toward her, her spear acting as a cane. Ketti and Ekosa walked next to her, their mahia strained as they commanded titans in their pitched battles. Batu and Sarryl lumbered behind the others, their white fur turned pink with blood, much of it their own.

They were battered and injured and weary. But they were alive.

She looked at Ata again. "Ata. Please."

Leiyn did not know if the dryvan heard her over the thundering sky and the screams of titans. But she knew Ata understood as her mismatched eyes alighted on hers.

The dryvan's expression twisted. Beyond, their friends rushed faster toward them. Preparing to fight, though they could not hope to win. Fight for her.

Teya screamed. Batu roared. Ketti and Ekosa reached for her with their mahia.

Ata's shriek drowned it all out.

Heritage rode on that keening sound. If the dryvan spoke words Leiyn understood, only one was recognizable.

"*SHARO!*"

Leiyn watched through her lifesense, fearing the dryvan would throw herself at her lost brother. Instead, Ata expanded her magic.

The lyshans tensed. The one shaped like a panther pivoted and pounced at her—but too late.

Ata had vanished.

She did not leave alone. Teya and the others were gone as

well. Leiyn felt Mehu'Ra, ablaze with lightning, break off of the gray dragon to disappear among the clouds.

Her friends were safe. But her relief was short-lived.

As the final blow fell, Leiyn collapsed to her knees. She felt the moment the axe severed Clouded Fang's spine. When his billowing lifeforce succumbed to darkness.

When her ash dragon died.

His death welled up in her, freezing her limbs and sapping her strength. She could not move, could not strike at her enemies. Even if resistance was futile, she meant to struggle on. Needed to.

But it took everything in her just to lift her head.

Sharo kneeled before her, bringing his face close to hers. Through the coppery taste of blood, she caught his repulsive scent. The perfume of flowers overlaying honeyed decay.

"Still, you struggle on. Such spirit." He reached out a taloned finger to stroke her cheek. "We shall cherish it."

Leiyn jerked away. Had her jaw not been beyond her command, she would have bitten his finger.

The lyshan lord laughed. "You will break before the end, Oldsoul. We shall break you."

She tried to lift her hands, tried to drive the knife into her enemy once more. But an invisible force slammed into her. The numbing shadow of Clouded Fang's death, barely held at bay, became an inevitable tide.

Leiyn flailed against it. But where could she go? Death ringed her, penned her in. There was no escape.

Doubt made her hesitate. It was the opening the darkness needed. The waves swept in, battering down her resistance. She clawed for consciousness, but drop by drop, it filtered away.

The umbra flooded over her, and she drowned in it.

EPILOGUE

Ayda tightened her hands around the bloody arrow resting in her lap. She had known to expect the beings flashing into existence across her audience chamber. Known it was the only outcome.

Still, she flinched as the Undying Ones made their return.

She squashed the mutinous part of her that had hoped they would not return. If any stood a chance against the Saints' Servants, it had been the Tideraiser and her fellow invaders. If the conquerors told true, they had defeated the Armada nearly on their own. Won the war against the greatest navy Unera had ever seen.

But she had witnessed the power her immortal masters possessed. Knew the futility of defiance. There had only ever been one end.

Ayda had not risen so high by choosing the losing side.

The immortals did not arrive alone. The living and dead both came in a gust of brimstone and blood and offal. Those few remaining of her paladins and priestesses staggered a step away from the immortals as soon as they reappeared.

Of the soldiers, only two had come through, both wearing

the strange, enchanted clothes given to them. Around them, the bodies of their compatriots littered the ground, dark with death. Their bone axes dripped with a golden liquid that shimmered to her lifesense. The same that had filled the artifact that had sent them away.

The blood of titans.

Four of the priestesses had survived as well, though only two remained conscious. Ayda had the distinct displeasure of seeing Sister Martina was among them. She even had the gall to look up at Ayda, triumph evident in her expression.

Conniving cockroach.

The odiosas had fared worse. None had survived, for someone looked to have brutalized them. Heads and limbs scattered about their bodies, leaking blood onto the gleaming tiles of her floor and dying the golden carpets dark. Ayda's stomach bucked. Only a lifetime of trained composure kept the bile from rising past her throat.

Of the invaders, only one remained. Ayda stared down at the Wilds Witch with dispassionate pity. When Leiyn of the Titan Wilds had stood before her, defiant and brimming with power, she had seemed untouchable.

Now, her lifefire had burned down to embers. Her jaw was swollen and disfigured. Burns layered up her arms and reddened her flesh. Her eyelids fluttered, but she seemed far beyond waking.

The she-devil of Baltesia, the slayer of the World King, the symbol of colonial rebellion—she lay only as a fragile, broken thing. Horrifyingly mortal.

Yet she lived. For now.

Ayda quieted her curiosity. Deadened herself to the suffering and slaughter before her. Stilled her expression to the placidity of cattle. The witch had spoken words that pierced the veil of Ayda's willful ignorance, arrows much like the one she shot through Ayda's shoulder, but they were no truths she had not known before.

She knew the master she served.

Sharo alone remained unscathed. He claimed to be a servant to the Sacred Saints, yet others always served in his stead.

A foolish thought. Ayda squashed the defiance within her once more. Now, such feelings could only grant her a similar fate as the broken woman below.

"Another awaits the Crypt," the Saints' Servant told her, gesturing at the prone witch. "See that she is confined."

"It shall be done, Undying One." Ayda hesitated, then dared a question. "What of the others who came with her? Have they survived?"

The immortal dismissed her questions with a lazy wave. "For now. If you fear for your life, you need not. We have ensured they shall not disturb our work here again."

Ayda glanced at their prisoner and doubted his words. They had followed this woman into the heart of the Basilica Sóveran. How much more would they risk to rescue her?

But she knew better than to speak against her master.

The immortal continued, heedless of her internal struggles. "We have the one that matters. The Caller to turn the tide. With her in our power, we shall usher in your Epoch of Belief."

Sharo turned a smile on her. False. Mocking.

How long had Ayda known she served a lie? Long before the woman dying at her feet had decried her loyalty to him.

But not all prisoners were bound by chains.

"Omn blesses our mission, Undying One." Ayda signed the sun over her chest.

Sharo laughed, then stepped out of existence. Vanishing as easily as he ever had, for purposes she could scarcely glimpse.

The other immortals stared at her for a long moment, each

more horrific in their appearance than the last. Then, one by one, they followed their master into thin air.

Ayda banished the unease from her mind and looked to the fresh paladins standing at the entrance to her audience chamber. They stared with undisguised horror at their compatriots, but it was a testament to their faith that none broke from formation.

"Take this woman to the Crypt of the Six. She is to be restrained and kept alive." This last she spoke to the Sister Martina and the remaining priestess. The two nodded and moved to the colonial woman, power rising within them. Paladins moved forward to join them.

Ayda watched as they lifted Leiyn's inert body in rough hands. With the priestesses sustaining the she-devil's feeble lifeforce, they marched her through the grand doors, bloody footprints left in their wake.

But bodies could be cleared away, blood mopped from the floor. Soon, her audience chamber would shine in Omn's light as it always had. Soon, there would be no sign left of Leiyn of the Titan Wilds. Ayda had witnessed what became of those left to Sharo's devices. What remained of them afterward.

If she saw the Wilds Witch again, it would be as a husk.

And what then? Ayda let herself wonder. *What form will his Epoch of Belief take?*

She prayed to the Saints it would never come. Prayed, though she herself ushered it closer.

Forgive me, San Inhoa. Forgive my sins.

But what forgiveness could there be for sins as black as these?

AUTHOR'S NOTE

Thank you very much for picking up *The Wilds Exile*! I hope you've enjoyed it.

...And my deepest apologies for where we ended.

But never fear—you won't have to wait long for the fifth and final book, as *The Titan Revenant* is well on its way. To be sure not to miss it, follow me on Amazon or sign up for my newsletter on my website, *jdlrosell.com*.

After that cliffhanger, you won't want to miss how it all ends!

While waiting for the release, why not be part of this series' story? One effective way you can join in is by leaving a review.

Reviews, as I'm sure you know, help other readers take a chance on a new author and book. A glowing recommendation is often what it takes to convince someone to pick a book up.

There are several places to leave reviews for *The Wilds Exile*. The primary ones are Amazon, Goodreads, and Audible.

And if you haven't left a review for *The Last Ranger*, you can also do so on those same sites.

If you're especially loving this series, consider sharing it with a friend or two! Word of mouth is my personal favorite way of finding new books, and I'm sure I'm not alone in that.

Thanks again for reading this book, and if you take any of the above actions, a double thank you.

Best of luck coping until *The Titan Revenant* arrives!

Josiah (J.D.L. Rosell)

APPENDIX A

THE CHARACTERS

Acalan Tikau - Chieftain of the Gast tribe the Tekuan, which translates to "Jaguars." Also now Toa'Yao, or "War Chieftain," of all the Many Tribes.

Adelina - A priestess of the Holy Catedrál. First encountered at the First Temple of Baltesia in Southport, where she tricked Leiyn into confinement below the temple.

Altun - A plainsrider of the Gazian Greathouse. Has a contentious history with Batu, Leiyn, and Isla.

Adama Ta'Rul - A distant ancestor of the Ta'Rul family. Sister to Eshun.

Arash Ta'Rul - An Eteman of Hold Ta'Rul. Father to Ketti, grandson-in-law to Oro.

Arias di Carille - A young Ilberian soldier first met while stationed at Fort Ribereño. Leiyn was responsible for cutting off one of his arms.

Arlo - The surgeon of the Wilds Lodge.

Armando Pótecil - A now-deceased conqueror, or general, of the Ilberian military.

Arwia - An Eteman ancestor briefly referenced as a possible source of a quotation.

Ata - Also known as "Hawkvine," "Rowanwalker," "Rowan," and "Foxfur." True name is "Atastimina." A dryvan who fights on the side of Leiyn and humanity.

Awera Talabi - Title: "Cloud." The chancellor of Ore-Ofe.

Awidan - Also known as "Mooneyes." An owlish dryvan of Glade. Deceased in a lyshan raid.

Ayda Santidad - Also known as "Ayda di Inhoa," "Mother of Mercy," "The Altacura," "The Bride of Heaven," and "Holy Mother." The spiritual leader of the Holy Catedrál.

Azarah - A lyshan who resembles a giant, black-coated jaguar.

Baltesar Veda IV - The current Caelrey, or ruler, of Ilberia. Also called "the World King"—a grandiose misnomer, him only being the ruler of the Ilberian Union.

Bane - Teya's draconion.

Batu Khatas - An older plainsrider pupil of the Gazian Greathouse.

Belen of Wharfhaven - A wall captain of Southport.

Biqqa - A spirit hummingbird of a brilliant emerald hue. Often seen around Ketti Ta'Rul.

Brine - A reef whale (an ocean titan) named by Teya. Primarily appears as a large formation of blue coral.

Bristle - The spirit boar bonded to Rhun. Also called a "hill hog."

Carles Collon - A middle-aged servant in the governor's villa. Also a mahita of the Order of Mahia.

Celia of Quay - A teenage daughter of fisherfolk, now a mahita of the Order of Mahia.

Chispa - The silver-furred spirit fox who has tailed Leiyn after different points in her life. Sometimes merges with the dryvan Ata.

Clouded Fang - The ash dragon (a variety of titan) bonded to Leiyn. First encountered at the erupting mountain in the Titan Wilds known as Nesilfo, the Clouded Fang.

Coyoti - An odd-mannered Gast scout who served with Teya among the *situali*.

Cual - A Jaguar warrior accompanying Acalan in Qasaar.

Demesu Gol'Tor - A distant ancestor of the Gol'Tor family.

Dinis Sorje - The mayordomo to the governor's villa in Southport.

Eghe Ilori - Title: "Talon." Captain of an Ofean outpost outside of Kunu.

Ekosa Siza - An *eesu*, or Ofean maha, of the *Kekére*.

Eld - A dryvan whose shape resembles a young elm tree. Deceased in the lyshan raid on Glade.

Eloxo - A Jaguar warrior accompanying Acalan in Qasaar.

Emilio - A smooth-talking rancher living in Carmenar, a Baltesian frontier town.

Enthil - A lithe lyshan with the wings of a moth and a crown of antlers.

Eshun Ta'Rul - A distant ancestor of the Ta'Rul family. Brother to Adama.

Estel of the Fifth Quarter - A reluctant mahita of the Order of Mahia. Also a successful merchant.

Feral - The unruly, brown mare that once belonged to Lodgemaster Tadeo, and is now Leiyn's loyal steed.

Francesc - A Baltesian youth from Carmenar hung for having sympathies for the Ilberian Union.

Gan - A ranger of the Wilds Lodge. Originally from Altan Gaz.

Genevieve of Orille - Also known as "Evie." A mahita of the Order of Mahia. Named after the author's niece.

Hector - Also known as "Halftooth Hector." A vagrant on the streets of Vasara.

Ilaoti of the Wind - Chieftainess of the Red Hawk tribe among the Gasts (tribe of Teya). Part of the Tetrad.

Ish'tar - A lyshan with twice as many limbs as a human and spindly in appearance.

Isirat Fai'Don - An Eteman friend of Ketti's.

Isla Ogbi - A ranger of the Wilds Lodge. Died by an arrow from Taban Khyan. In life, Leiyn's best friend.

Itzel of Folly - The mayor of Folly and premier over the Baltesian portion of the Titan Wilds. It is a widely known secret that she had a long-standing romantic relationship with Lodgemaster Tadeo.

Izan of the West Woods - A mahita in the Order of Mahia. Husband to Reyna.

Jegu Qayag - A wisdom of Altan Gaz. Leader of the wisdoms assisting in Southport.

Joaquin - A ranger of the Wilds Lodge.

Joromi - A male skystrider of the Ofean Stormhold.

Ketti Ta'Rul - An Eteman of Solace. The youngest member of Hold Ta'Rul and heir to Mehu'Ra.

Khamo - A lyshan often seen wearing red titanbone armor with seemingly malevolent intent.

Kyaka Ndaye - The current Odisi, or ruler, of Eyi.

Leiyn of Orille - A ranger of the Wilds Lodge. Protagonist of the Ranger of the Titan Wilds series.

Luca di Eño Vasara - The conqueror, or general, in charge of Baltesia's military. Named after the author's nephew.

Man'nah - Deceased leader of the lyshans. Once said to have been the strongest among them.

Marina - A ranger of the Wilds Lodge. A middle-aged, no-nonsense woman.

Martina - A priestess of the Holy Catedrál encountered on Refugio.

Mauricio di Siveña - The Elected Consul of Baltesia (formerly the governor).

Mehu'Ra - The tempest hawk bonded to Oro Ta'Rul. Guards the borders of Solace.

Mooneyes - A dryvan whose shape resembles a humanoid owl.

Mottle - The horse formerly belonging to Isla Ogbi, now shared by Ketti and Ekosa.

Moyo - A Red Hawk *situal* (from Teya's tribe) who guards the Whisperspire in Qasaar.

Nabo - A tentacled lyshan who has mastered the ocean.

Nahui - A loud-mouthed, small-statured Gast scout friendly with Leiyn and her companions. Served with Teya among the *situali*.

Naia of Southport - A mahita of the Order of Mahia. Formerly a serving lady in a merchant lord's manor.

Nathan - Sometimes called "Old Nathan." A curmudgeonly ranger of the Wilds Lodge.

Nava Eño Villanova - An Asraichean mask seller on the streets of Vasara.

Nestor of Saints' Crossing - A former Baltesian soldier, now a mahita of the Order of Mahia.

Nidinu Ta'Rul - An Eteman of Hold Ta'Rul. Mother to Ketti, granddaughter to Oro.

Noemi of the Docks - A mahita of the Order of Mahia. Also a young mother of three.

Odowa - A female skystrider of the Ofean Stormhold.

Oktai of the Spears - The current Hesh Jin, or ruler, of Kalga.

Onah Salako - Also "Wing of Moons." One of the two leaders of the Kekére.

Oro Ta'Rul - Also "Ab-Abi." Eteman patriarch of Hold Ta'Rul. Bonded with Mehu'Ra and primary guardian of Solace.

Osmet - Also known as "She Who Remains." A lyshan who has embraced the Iritu's reputation as shapeshifters. Has many features combined into a grotesque combination, including those of a bat, lizard, jaguar, spider, and raptor. Can also transform fully into a bat at will.

Qara Gegeen - A wisdom of Altan Gaz. Temporarily the head of the Order of Mahia in Leiyn's absence.

Ram'bal - A large lyshan with many features of a bull.

Reyna of the West Woods - A mahita in the Order of Mahia. Wife to Izan.

Rhun - A wildsoul living in Ilberia. Bonded to the boar Bristle. One of the remaining free wildsouls after the raid on his village.

Rúben of the Docks - A Union sympathist guard in the governor's villa and would-be assassin.

Saikan - The horse of Batu Khatas.

Samu Oyabola - Also "Wing of Stars." One of the two leaders of the Kekére.

Sarryl - An albino spirit bear known as a "moonbear." Sarryl means "moonlight" in Kalgan. Named by and bonded to Batu.

Sergi of Southport - A mahita of the Order of Mahia. Son of a cobbler.

Sharo - The new lyshan lord with malevolent intentions for Leiyn and her friends.

Shu'eil - A giant lyshan who has adopted the form and chitinous armor of a crab.

Simó of Lake's Edge - A youthful vagrant and mahita of the Order of Mahia.

Steadfast - Leiyn's black stallion. As loyal as his name implies, he barely makes any sound, not even a whicker.

Taban Khyan - New moorwarden of the Gazian Greathouse. Suspected association with Sharo. After killing Isla, Leiyn slew him in return.

Tadeo of Lake's Edge - The lodgemaster of the Wilds Lodge.

Tecla of Wharfhaven - A grandmother and widow, now a mahita of the Order of Mahia.

Teya of the Hunt - A Spear, or leader, of the *situali*, or Gast scouts. Also Leiyn's lover.

Tinoch - An Uman chieftain. One of the Tetrad.

Tozi - Their *tekip*, or caretaker.

Urta - A lyshan with the bulk and long horn of a rhinoceros.

Wynn of Saints' Crossing - An odiosa briefly freed from his brand before succumbing to a titan attack in Southport.

Xepi - A shaman of Qasaar who once taught Leiyn about magic.

Yavin - An Ilberian fruit seller in Bayo Sol.

Yolant - A ranger of the Wilds Lodge. Fond of singing for the Lodge and playing her stringed gourd.

Zaki Gol'Tor - An Eteman friend of Ketti's.

Zezé - A Baltesian soldier under Captain Belen's command.

Zuma Apisi - A Gast shaman of the Tekuan tribe.

Zyanya of the Wave - A Gast chieftainess and member of the Tetrad.

APPENDIX B

THE WORLD

An overview of the locations in the world of Unera.

THE VEILED LANDS

The three colonies of the Veiled Lands are also called "the Tricolonies."

Baltesia

Former colony of Ilberia.

Southport - Capital of Baltesia.
Orille - Leiyn's home village.
Folly - A Titan Wilds town.
Saints' Crossing - The bridge town that spans the Gorge de Omn.
Lake's Edge - Lodgemaster Tadeo's hometown.
Breakbay - An abandoned city ringed by titans. Ruined during the Titan War.
The Wilds Lodge - The Titan Wilds stronghold of the rangers.
Carmenar - A town in the Titan Wilds along Frontier Road.
Wharfhaven - Coastal town near Southport.
Quay - Coastal fishing village near Southport.

Altan Gaz

Colony of Kalga.

Orolt - Capital of Altan Gaz.
Helkist - Fur-trading town.
The Greathouse - Also called the *Baishin*. Stronghold of the plainsriders.

Ore-Ofe

Colony of Eyi.

Kunu - Capital of Ore-Ofe.
The Coterie - Also called the *Kekére*. Tower of the *eesuwé*, or the mahos of Ore-Ofe. Located in Kunu.
Lamayo - Fortified trading city; acts as a secondary capital of Ore-Ofe.
The Stormhold - Also called the *Izul*. Stronghold of the skystriders.
Solace - Hidden Eteman village in the Ofean jungle.

The Titan Wilds

Borderlands spanning the Tricolonies. In Baltesia, these lands extend beyond the Gorge de Omn.

The Barren - Arid wasteland beyond the Silvertusk Sierra.
Qasaar - Capital of the Gasts and other indigenous tribes.
Haven - An Iritu ruin that provides a refuge for Leiyn and her comrades.

THE ANCESTRAL LANDS

The continent is also called "Forye."

Ilberia

The Ilberian Union.

Vasara - Capital of Ilberia.
The Devilwoods - The forest north of Vasara, so known for its reputation for harboring wildsouls.
Refugio - "The Hallowed Isle." Stronghold island of the Holy Catedrál. Also considered to be a sacred place by Omnists.
Bayo Sol - "The Golden Harbor." The port town attached to the campus of the Holy Catedrál on Refugio.

Eyi

The Eyin Empire.

Mumsi - Capital of Eyi.
Kaiam - Important city of Eyi.

Kalga

The Kalgan Dominion.

Galkhir - Capital of Kalga.
Betgol - Important city of Kalga.

APPENDIX C

BESTIARY & BOTANICAL

BEASTS OF THE TITAN WILDS

Coral trout - An ocean fish that congregates near coral reefs and reef whales.

Draconion - *Axolto* to the Gasts. A large lizard that resembles the monitor lizard of the Ancestral Lands, they have been domesticated over eons to be riding animals to the native peoples of the Veiled Lands. Docile unless threatened, they have spines along their backs except where a rider is seated. Draconions typically appear in four colors: orange, yellow, red, and black. They sometimes combine variations of these and have striped or mottled patterns.

Rainbow birds - Birds common to the Ofean city of Kunu. So-called for their iridescent feathers. Much like pigeons or seagulls elsewhere, they make themselves a nuisance and thrive near the city congestion.

Snow ape - A large ape with a shaggy white coat, a red snout, and blue around its eyes. An apex predator of the Silvertusk Sierra. It can be incredibly aggressive when provoked or when hungry.

Spirit animals - Little is known of the creatures that appear as animals, yet also seem to be more. Travelers through the Titan Wilds have reported being assisted by creatures who are often of silver or golden coloring. These have taken the forms of wolves, large cats, foxes, deer, and all other manner of beasts. Many believe them to be spirits from Omn, sent by the Saints to keep their followers safe. Others have reported the native peoples have stories of them as little gods taking forms that humans can understand, and that often their favors granted will someday need to be repaid.

Thorned lion - One of the largest predators in the Titan Wilds, it typically poses little harm to humans unless starving. They have been known, however, to prey on livestock. The rangers of the Wilds Lodge have learned torches burning fennel are sufficient to drive it away from human populations. With a mane of spines, it is deadly to contend with. Engagement should be avoided whenever possible. Thorned lions typically travel alone, though females will care for their cubs until they are several years old.

Titans - Also called *"kainox"* by the native peoples of the Veiled Lands. Straddling the line between beasts and spirits, they appear as enormous animals or mythical creatures that ravage the land. Titans are not always present in the landscape; they "awaken" or materialize in cycles that can vary from months to years. Many appear to be tied to a certain feature in the terrain, but this does not appear to be accurate in all cases. Following is a list of the titans known thus far:

Ash dragon - Volcano titan.
Gorge spider - Rock titan.
Hill tortoise - Earth titan.
Mirror swans - Lake titan. Always appear as a pair of swans.
Rain mammoth - Rain titan in the shape of an elephant.
Reef whale - Ocean titan made of coral.
River serpent - River titan.
Sand stampede - Desert titan in the shape of stampeding wildebeest.
Sea kraken - Ocean titan. Also called "The Wight on the Tide."
Tempest hawk - Storm titan.
Vine jaguar - Jungle titan.
Fog swarm or "Winged Death" - Fog titan. Said to take the form of a swarm of flesh-devouring bats.

Tusked jackal - An aggressive canine species known for their destruction of other animal habitats. Tusked jackals travel in packs of thirty or more and bring down their prey through numbers and ferocity. As they pose significant threats to humans and livestock, they are best driven away

Wolfdeer - A species of fanged deer that appear to be particularly aggressive. Unknown if they are carnivorous or not. Like other deer species, they travel in herds. Stags compete for the rights to mate with a herd's does. Fights have been known to be to the death. Mateless young stags often travel in a herd of their own.

PLANTS OF THE TITAN WILDS

Drybrush - A fern-like plant that shrivels upon a touch, then slowly stretches back out its leaves and limbs, regaining color and moisture and seeming to come back to life.

Echinacea - A pink flower whose extract is often used as a natural antibiotic.

Everscent - A flower that changes its aroma throughout the seasons, and sometimes over the span of a few moments. Usually, these scents are quite pleasant. Its blossoms have long, sky-blue petals streaked with white around a fuzzy red pistil, from which long, pink tendrils emerged.

Firefruit - Aubergine berries that burn one's skin for hours. There are stories among the Gasts of using firefruit to incapacitate one's foes.

Hangman's vine - A carnivorous plant that strangles any creature unfortunate enough to be snared by it. Known by the red coloring of its vines and leaves, it is exclusively found wrapped around full-grown broad-leafed trees.Travelers are advised to be wary of which trees they rest against.

Nacatl - A mushroom found in the caves on the northern side of the Silver-tusks. Has hallucinogenic qualities when ingested as a tea.

Peyotl - A cactus whose flower is used for a hallucinogenic tea by the Gast tribes.

APPENDIX D

GLOSSARY

Many of the terms not defined in previous appendices can be found here.

Ab-Abi - "Great-grandfather" in the Eteman tongue.

Abu - "Father" in the Eteman tongue.

Akan'Oala - Translates to "Those Who Came Before." This is the name given by Gasts to their ancestors. Legend has it that they came long ago to the Veiled Lands and conquered them by benefit of their superior magic. In the eons since, time and war have robbed the Gasts and other indigenous peoples of many of these secrets, leaving their history shrouded in mystery.

The Altacura - The leader of the Catedrál. Addressed as "Gran" or "Her Sanctity." The Altacura has always been female. Many of those who reached Ascendance to become one of the five Saints have previously been the Altacura. Though officially a religious leader, by benefit of her station and the Catedrál's resources, the Altacura has traditionally wielded great power both in Ilberia and in the world at large.

Ama ek akkir - "I am yours" in Eteman. Used as the binding words for a titan.

Ara'buru - The Eteman "seeing pool" located in Solace. Used to observe and learn from afar about the peoples, languages, and events of the Veiled Lands.

Ascendance - The process by which a person is made into a saint. Often, saints have arisen from a previous Altacura, though not exclusively. Holy miracles must be attributed to the person in order to achieve Ascendance, as do revelations of morality as divinely inspired by Omn. Only five individuals have thus far Ascended in the Catedrál's history.

Asraicheans - An indigenous people of the Ancestral Lands, particularly in Ilberia. Identified in part by their red hair and light-colored eyes. Largely conquered and incorporated into Ilberian society in modern times, but with a denigrated status.

At-Iti - "Great-granddaughter" in the Eteman tongue.

Bantu - "Mother" in the Eteman tongue.

The Basilica Sóveran - The fortified home of the Altacura at the heart of the campus of the Holy Catedrál.

Bond(ed) - "*Kamit*" to Etemans. References to either the mutual attachment of a maha to a titan or to the attached titan itself.

The Caelrey - Also known as "the World King." The political leader of Ilberia. In practice, often has to share power with the Altacura and her Catedrál. Reigns from Vasara, the capital of Ilberia.

The Careta Desfil - Also called "the Procession of Masks." A spring celebration and parade in Ilberia in which participants wear animal-inspired masks. Spectacles include star dancers, bull riders, and fire breathers. Stolen from Asraichean tradition.

The Catedrál - Also called "the Holy Catedrál." A sprawling religious institution worshiping the prescience of Omn and the god's revelations. The Catedrál has largely acted as a matriarchy, with precedence given to women for positions of power. Though officially a religious institution, its significant resources and moral sway often translate to geopolitical power that its leaders are unafraid to wield.

The Cherished - The name Eyins and Ofeans have for themselves as worshippers and believers in Okulukulu, the Mother Goddess.

Ciudad Abultado - The section of Vasara outside the inner wall where lower classes live.

Ciudad Interna - The section of Vasara within the inner wall where the more affluent members of society live, including the Caelrey.

Cloaking - The induction of a ranger apprentice into a full ranger by giving the apprentice a ranger cloak, a resilient and warm article dyed a forest green. Inducted rangers are also referred to as "cloaked rangers" by benefit of this ritual.

The Cloudholder - Leader of the Stormhold, the home of the skystriders of Ore-Ofe.

The Colonial Order of Mahia - The arm of government relegated to the training and deployment of mahas within Baltesia.

Conqueror - A general of the Ilberian military. In the colony of Baltesia, conquerors wield authority only surpassed by the Caelrey and, contentiously, the Altacura.

Council Domo - The building where the Liberty Council confers.

The Crypt of the Six - Mysterious catacombs associated with the Holy Catedrál.

The Culling - "*Palaq*" to Etemans. The long period during which the Iritu winnowed magic from the Etemans' and Gasts' ancestors. These events led Etemans to hide within grottos and Gasts to lose their most powerful shamans and forget the deepest secrets of magic.

Deq ama - "Tell me" in the Eteman tongue.

Dryvan - Also called "skin-walker" and "forest witch." Known as "*sach'aan*" to the Gasts. Among themselves, dryvans refer to themselves as "the Kin." Dryvans are shapeshifters. Though often possessing shapes approximately human, they are changed with attributes of animals and plants. Rarely seen, it is unknown what their disposition is toward humanity, for stories have been told of both boons and harms.

Eesu(wé) - The magic wielders of Ore-Ofe and the Eyin Empire.

Egreshti - An invective of the Gasts. Also "*gresht.*"

Elected Consul - The leader of Baltesia. Elected by a host of representatives from across the former colony.

Epochs of Unera - According to the Catedrál, the first age of Unera was the Epoch of Sin, when all of humanity was mired in ignorance and transgressions. During that time, those with mahia were worshiped as gods, and all quailed at their power. Then, with the founding of the Catédral came the Epoch of Epiphany, the current age, which began with the miracles of the First Saint, Inhoa the Merciful. This is believed to be a time of civilization and virtue, when the truth of the Saints will be spread to the far corners of the world and all will be saved from their sins.

Esse - Also called "lifefire," "lifeforce," and "essence." Known as "*ilis*" to the Gasts. Esse is the vital life energy of a being. Invisible to most, those who possess mahia see it as bright life, often moving like flames throughout the body. Each individual possesses a unique esse, and those with an attuned enough lifesense may identify any being by it. Though mostly isolated to a being's body, mahia allows one to either draw it out of individuals or manipulate it to different effects.

Etaro - "Spirit" in Eteman.

Etemans - A people related to Gasts and their ancestors. Etemans now only exist in isolated pockets within grottos.

The Eyrie - A substantial island that forms part of the Eyin Empire. Believed by Eyins to be the birthplace of humanity.

Ferino - Translates literally to "feral" from Ilberian. A derogatory term used by Ilberians and Baltesians toward Gasts and other indigenous peoples.

Fesht - An expletive common in Baltesia referring to an aggressive sexual act. Thought to have originated from an indigenous tribe. Similar to the Gast expletive "*egresht.*"

Fiend's nectar - A strong Gast liquor. Has a slimy mouth feel, a hint of sweetness, and produces a burning sensation on the throat.

Gasts - Refer to themselves as "The Many Tribes" in inclusion of other indigenous nations. Though perceived by colonists as a homogenous race, Gasts entail various tribes bonded by cultural and spiritual beliefs held in common. During the colonization of the Veiled Lands, the Gasts resisted the Ancestral Lands, which led to the Titan War. Following their capitulation, the Gasts largely retreated to beyond the Silvertusk Sierra to the arid lands beyond the mountains called the Barren.

Gerinakku - The annals of Solace. Contains many artifacts of the Eteman people as well as their history.

Ghosts - Called "*timili*" by Gasts. These ghosts are typically found in ancestral ruins and manifest as whispers and a lingering sense of esse.

Great Teyao - The larger of Unera's two moons.

Gresht - An invective for the Gasts. Also "*egreshti*."

Grotto - The Iritu term for a space outside of the ordinary world, created and sustained by magic. Also called "*haru*" by Etemans.

Harmony - "Heaven" in Omnist faith.

Heavens' Reach - "*Aafinsowa*" in Eyin. The luxurious estate of the chancellor and the head priest of Ore-Ofe.

The Hells - Modified commonly as "Ten Hells," "black hells," and "Legion's hells." The afterlife for sinners in Omnist tradition.

The Hesh Jin - Also called "the Ocean Lord." Leader of Kalga.

Inheritance - The Iritu term for magic. Also "heritage," depending on the usage.

Kasadum il denu - "Adapt or die" in the Iritu tongue

The *Kekére*, or the Coterie Tower - The tower in Kunu where the eesuwé live and train. The center of magic within Ore-Ofe.

Kilakt - "Forsworn" in the Gast tongue.

Kuit - An expletive in the Gast tongue.

Lakan - "Ghosts" in the Gast tongue

Lakti - The western cliff of Qasaar.

Legion - The force of evil to the Catedrál, opposing the good force of Omn and the Saints. Seen as a fragmented being with many faces on account of the tormented souls it has captured screaming for release. Some believe Legion manifests demons in Unera to serve his purposes. For some, titans and dryvans are a few of these demons, while others see them as natural manifestations akin to animals and plants.

The Liberty Council - The ruling council of Baltesia.

The Lodgemaster - Leader of the Wilds Lodge, home to the rangers of Baltesia.

Lualli - The eastern cliff of Qasaar.

Mada - A familiar term meaning "mother" to Baltesians and Ilberians.

Macua - A club-like weapon lined with shards of obsidian wielded by Gast warriors.

Maha - A user of mahia; specifically, one located in Baltesia.

Mahia - Known as "*semah*" to the Gasts. Mahia is a magic of life and death, allowing its user to manipulate esse to various effects. These effects include healing, killing (by draining an individual of esse), and strengthening or energizing one's body. Mahia also seems to have something to do with titans, as the creatures appear to be at least partly magical in origin. While seen as having come from Omn by the Catedrál, it is also seen as a tool by which Legion could exploit human weakness and lead people into sin. The other Ancestral Lands have higher levels of tolerance, though most view it with distrust. Among the Tricolonies, these attitudes are often passed on, though more leniency has evolved.

Mahita - A pupil of the Baltesian Order of Mahia. I.e., a maha-in-training.

Makayo - Translates to "Unity." The Gast afterlife, in which an individual merges with the world. The losing of oneself to the great whole of being is anticipated with eagerness.

The Moorwarden - Leader of the Greathouse, home to the plainsriders of Altan Gaz.

The Mothertrees - "*Ialadta*" to the Iritu. Also called simply "the Mothers." The great magical trees that gave birth to the Iritu. Now extinct, burned by the ancestors of Etemans and Gasts.

The Murmuring Canyon - A ravine near Qasaar where the stone is alive with spirits.

Nappahi - Workshops, like smithies, armories, and forges, to the Iritu.

Odiosa - A witch hunter of the Catedrál. By virtue of possessing mahia, odiosas sense out those with magic and either recruit them to their cause or have them executed. It is unknown how people become indoctrinated as odiosas, though their odd temperaments allude to some sort of torturous process that addles the mind.

The Odisi - Also called "the Sky Queen." Leader of Eyi.

Odisi wangu - Literally means "My queen" in the Eyin tongue; used as an exclamation similar to "My God!"

Okulukulu - Also "Mother Goddess" and "Mistress of Stars." The central goddess of the Eyin and Ofean peoples.

Omn - Also called "the Unknown" and "Omn Almighty." The god honored by the Catedrál. Most often depicted as a faceless, genderless orb of astral origin, similar to the sun and the moons, though distinct from both. Omn is believed to be the creator of all, including magic and titans.

Pada - A familiar term meaning "father" to Baltesians and Ilberians.

Plainsrider - A protector of the Tricolonies dwelling at the Greathouse in Altan Gaz. Akin to rangers and skystriders.

Plaza dil Jadiel - A plaza along the Promenada Palacia featuring a fountain dedicated to San Jadiel, a Saint of the Holy Catedrál.

Premier - A provincial governor in Ilberia or Baltesia.

Prima Maha - The leader of the Baltesian Order of Mahia.

Promenada Palacia - The main street running through Vasara that leads directly to the Caelrey's castle.

Qelpu - "Disorienting" in the Eteman tongue.

Ranger - A protector of the Tricolonies dwelling at the Wilds Lodge in Baltesia. Akin to plainsriders and skystriders.

The Ranger's Lament - An invocation spoken by a ranger after taking a life. Often spoken to alleviate guilt at the killing. The phrase is as follows: "Your spirit touches mine."

The Ranger's Oath - An oath taken by rangers at their cloaking ceremony, which they vow to uphold during their service. The oath is as follows: "Perceive. Preserve. Protect."

The rising sun - The symbol of the Caelrey.

The Sacred Saints - The five individuals in Catedrál history who have Ascended from mortals into divine representatives of Omn. The Saints are seen as intermediaries between the faceless god and humanity, and interpret what is good and what is sinful. The Saints and their associated virtues are as follows:

San Hugo of Resolution and Equity
San Luciana of Sincerity and Candor
San Jadiel of Grace and Beauty
San Inhoa of Mercy and Quietus
San Carmen of Loyalty and Justice

Seedings - In reference to the Iritu, the birth cycles of their kind (through their Mothertrees, the *Ialadta*).

Shaman - A magic wielder and religious leader of the Gasts. As those possessing mahia, shamans serve many vital functions within Gast society, including healing the sick and wounded, communing with the ancestors and the spirits of the world, and warding against titans. They are often highly educated and serve as advisors to chieftains. By benefit of magic, shamans have also historically been reservoirs of indigenous history. Unfortunately, if a shaman dies before they can pass this knowledge on, it is forever lost, a problem that became particularly difficult during the Titan War and was one factor that led to the Gasts' retreat.

The Shroud - "*Kai'am*" to Etemans. The protective barrier erected around Solace.

Skystrider - A protector of the Tricolonies dwelling at the Stormhold in Ore-Ofe. Akin to plainsriders and rangers.

The sun and stars - The symbol of the Holy Catedrál.

Taht - Meaning "father" or "mother," it is a respectful address for shamans.

Takah - "My people" in the Gast tongue.

Talisman - Also called "*periaptu*" by the Iritu. Items imbued with magic that produce various effects.

Tekuan - A Gast tribe with a reputation for being continued aggressors since the Titan War. Their name translates to "Jaguar" and their people are tattooed with this symbol.

The Ten Virtues - The ideals upheld by the Catedrál as being good and worthy of pursuit. All are associated with one of the Sacred Saints. The virtues are resolution, equity, sincerity, candor, grace, beauty, mercy, quietus, loyalty, and justice.

The Tetrad - The council of four chieftains that leads the Many Tribes of Qasaar.

Titan's awakening - The event when a titan first emerges from a natural body, such as a hill or river, and forms its body. It is believed titans may lie dormant in places for years before rising. Upon their awakening, those with magic perceived it as radiating very strongly from them, often so much so that it is impossible to resist their pull.

The Titan War - The war over the colonization of the Veiled Lands, fought between the Gasts and other indigenous peoples against those coming from the Ancestral Lands. After years of failed negotiations, the Gasts finally pushed back against the people invading their lands. Using magic, their shamans sent titans against the colonial settlements, devastating them and killing thousands. Though those possessing mahia from the Ancestral Lands did not know how to control titans, they used their magic against the shamans themselves, leading to the deaths of most of them. Following the loss of their shamans, the Gasts and other natives retreated beyond the Silvertusk Sierra to the lands known as the Barren. Only a few remained behind, and these were discriminated against, often to the point of violence.

Toa - Translates to "chief," the title given to a Gast chieftain.

The Tumult of Titans - "*Nox'mekva*" to the Etemans. The event during which Eteman ancestors are claimed to have "broken" the world.

The Uman - Another of the indigenous people of the Veiled Lands, and included in the Many Tribes.

Unera - Called "*Tlalli*" by the Gasts. Unera is the planet, the world at large.

The *Uphathi* - Also "the Cloudholder." The master of the Stormhold.

The Veil - The misty boundary that separates the Veiled Lands from the Ancestral Lands. Once penetrated by a wisewoman from Kalga, it allowed for the conquest and colonization that followed.

The Whisperspire - *Tepe'laka* in the Gast tongue; the tower where the Tetrad meets in Qasaar.

Wildsoul - Also known as "beastfolk" in some parts of the world or as having "tainted blood" to the Etemans. Humans with Iritu blood that have the ability to merge with spirit animals.

Wisdom - Also "wiseman" and "wisewoman." A wielder of magic in Kalga and Altan Gaz.

Young Chiuni - The smaller of Unera's two moons.

Za'qu - "Ghosts" in the Eteman tongue.

READ THE FREE PREQUEL

If you would like more of Leiyn's adventures, you can find a free short story about her contending with a company of titan trappers on my website at: *jdlrosell.com/ranger*

BOOKS BY J.D.L. ROSELL

Sign up for future releases at jdlrosell.com.

Ranger of the Titan Wilds

1. The Last Ranger
2. The First Ancestor
3. The Hidden Guardian
4. The Wilds Exile
5. The Titan Revenant

Legend of Tal

1. A King's Bargain
2. A Queen's Command
3. An Emperor's Gamble
4. A God's Plea

A Battle Between Blood (Novella)

The Runewar Saga

1. The Throne of Ice & Ash
2. The Crown of Fire & Fury
3. The Stone of Iron & Omen

The Famine Cycle

1. Whispers of Ruin

2. Echoes of Chaos

3. Requiem of Silence

Secret Seller (Prequel)

The Phantom Heist (Novella)

Godslayer Rising

1. Catalyst

2. Champion

3. Heretic

ACKNOWLEDGMENTS

Many thanks to each of the following people:

Kaitlyn, my wife, first reader, and, increasingly, business partner! I'm so grateful for your support and collaboration.

Sarah Chorn, our fabulous editor.

Joemel Requeza, the new amazing cover artist for this book.

Shawn T. King, our same immaculate cover designer as before.

Sutthiwat Dechakamphu and 21, the two new awesome interior artists for this book.

Shawn Sharrah, our usual keen-eyed proofreader.

My patrons on Patreon, who continuously provide their generous support: Debbie, GhostCat, Tarris & Ruth, Riley, Don, Tony, Ben, Nick, and K.C.

Julia, the first proponent of Ranger of the Titan Wilds. I hope you've enjoyed how I brought archery back more in this book!

And a massive round of applause for all the *Kickstarter backers*:

Chloe A. | Kurt Adam | Brett Adams | Emma Adams
Joseph W. Aguiar | Julien Alessio | Peter Allen
Walter E. Alvarez Jr | Hank Alward | Gregory Amato
Angelika | Amelia Armstrong | Boyd Atkinson | Jon Auerbach
William Cody Austin | MH Ayotte | Cortney Babcock
Patrick Bächli | Jack Baer | Beth Ball | Robert Barbour
Connor Barrett | Peter "Tonour" Basak | Steve Batezel
Cassandra Baubie | Dave Baughman | Polina Bazlova

Howard Blakeslee | Brett Blakley | David Bobbitt
Christopher Boisvert | Bradley Bolt | Lorraine Bondi
Kurt Boulianne | Jason Bowden | Joe Bower | Virgil Bower
Elli Breakspear | Kaleah Brewster | Justise Briones
Jonathan Brown | Robert Brown | Derrick Bucey
Paul Bulmaga | Ashley Byrd | Steven Cairnduff
Dan Calderman | Nick Calderon | Joshua Callahan
Franchesca Caram | Meredith Carstens | Peter Casale
Scott Casey | Garret Castle | Giuseppe Centineo
John Chattaway | Tyler Cheek | Cliff Chen | Clarissa Ching
Scott Chisholm | Duncan Chisholm | Dennis Choi
Gianna Christopher | Vivian Cicero | Elena Clark | Lee Clark
H.M. Clarke | Christopher Clayton | Cynthia Coffman
Paden Cogswell | Matthew Corbin | Alexandra Corrsin
Eric Cotti | Bridget Cowne | Tim Cregar | Janet Crespo
Cole Cross | Katie Cross | Sarolta Csik | James Cunningham
Travis D. | Natalie Daman | Susanne Daniels
David Daughhetee | David | Dyfan Davies | Starr Z. Davies
Elizabeth Davis | Joanna Davis | David DeHaan
Andreas Deller | Destinee, Mother of Seven Sons | H. Deur
John Devlin | Aaron DeWaard | Chelsea Dietz
Jamie Dockendorff | Justin Dorian | Martin Dovina
Heather Dow | Katie Dresel | Gabrielle Duncan
Nirkatze Durner-Feiler | Richard Earl | Kristopher Ecklof
Mark Erickson | Doug Erling | Hugo Essink | Andy F.
Emily F. | Lukas Feinweber | Miguel A. Fidalgo
Richard Fierce | Stephanie Fischer | Marie Fisher
Russell Fisk | Emma Flaws | Danny Flood | Mychal Ford
Scott Frederick | Kallen Frieling | Christopher Froebe
Darren Fry | Morgan G. | Mike Galligan | J. Gabriel Gates
Zeke Gates | Geek & Dad | Mark Geier | GhostCat
Quinn Giguiere | Ronnie Gill | John Gilligan | Patrick Ginter
Richard Giovane | Jeff Glasgow | Drew Gohmann
Mike "Gonzo" Gonzales | Vannessa Goodwin | Gordon

Derek Gorny | Falk Graepel | Sean Gray | Miranda Green
Justin Greer | Vickie Grider | Mark Griffith
Marie Grimaldi-Clermont | Michael Grovenburg
Kris Guthrie | Michael H. | Ryan H. | Taylor Haddock
Kristian Handberg | Michael Haney | Matias Hansen
Dylan Harney | Debbie Harris | Jase Hartly | Michael Hayes
Laura Haymond | Shane Heaton | Jackalope Heelein
K. Hendrick | Billye Herndon | Alicia Hintzen | T. Hise
Austin Hoffey | Grace Hoffman | Sasha Hoffman
Kelly Hogue | Jack Holder | Christian Holt | Karin Holt
David Holzborn | Neil Houston | Terry Mitchell Hulett
Peter Hutchinson | John Idlor | Neil J. | Ernie Jennings
Zachary Jennings | Jennifer Johnson | Michael Johnson
Celia Jones | Jacob Joseph | Solene Joubert | Alex Joyner
Jessica Juby | PJ K. | Axel Kallesøe | Kevin Kastelic
Kenneth Kauffman | Laura Kaylor | Christian Kegley
Katie Keith | Boe Kelley | Tanvir Khan | Matt King
Nick Kirkland | Christopher Kirke | Thomas Kjelsen
S.A. Klopfenstein | Sarah Kocich | Heiko Koenig
Christian Könemann | James Kralik | Benjamin Kristofice
Reinier Krouwer | John W. Ladley | Annik Lamoen
Samantha Landström | Steven Ray Lane | André Laude
Christiana Laudie | Joe Lee | Mathieu Lefebvre | Kevin Leintz
Donald Lenhart | Kyle Leubka | Rocco Levitas
Richard Libera | Nicolas Lobotsky | Sarah Long | Jason Lovell
Ronald Luck | Alex Luco | Lorenzo M. | Karen M.
Megyn MacDougall | Johnny MacIsaac | Erick Madrid
Tommy Maguire | Gianluca Marcheselli | Kris Marchesi
John Markley | Jason Martin | Krista Marx | Charli Maxwell
Connor Mayo | Rory McCabe | Gerald McDaniel
James McGinnis | Karl McGurty | Michael McLendon
Cathy McLoughlin | Andrew Medeiros | Sancho Melis
Pedro Mendes | Bas Meulendijks | Christian Meyer
Zephyr Mini | Michael Mitchell

Alberto Mohammed-Dawson | Benjamin Molina | Matt Mollo
Tyler Montgomery | Rochelle Moore | Alan Morgan
Brandon Neal | Korbyn Nelson | Samantha Newberry
Hank Nordic | Charles Norton | Petar Novakovic | John O.
Angel Ocampo | In loving memory of Basil Martin
Mark Olson | Mike Olson | Josh Oplinger | John Orefice
Chip Orlikowski | Darren Pallant | Nicholas Paynter
Kait Peace | N. Scott Pearson | Jeff Pena | Sarah Phillips
Palmer Pickering | Ellen Pilcher | B. Plaga | Duane Powell
Victoria Price | Wayne Priddle | Rob Priest | Jason Pulham
Qavee | Scott R. | Jens D. Racherbäumer | Ian Rankine
James Rao | Colin Rayburn | Tana Reeve | Ryan Reeves
Austin Regan | Xiomara Reyes | Matt Ritter | Joe Rixman
Todd Roark | SaraBeth Roberson | Will Rodd | Suz Rodgers
Trevor Roelfs | Chris Roeszler | Sarah Rogers
Tarris & Ruth Rosell | Matthea W. Ross | Rasheed Ross
Dale Russell | Wilma S. Murphy | Josh Samples
Sarah Schroeder | René Schultze | Nathan Seaward
Shawn Sharrah | Katherine Shipman | Sunny Side Up
Kindreth Silverwing | Henry Simme | Chris Skowronek
Paul Smith | Dakota Smith | Brad Snyder | Stijn Soethout
Justin Speck | Melissa St-Pierre | Herman Steuernagel
Justin Swift | Melissa T. | CM T. | Jason T. | C. Taormina
Tassilo | Rosa Thill | Lloyd Thistle | Vancil Thomas
Andy Thompson | Andrea Tolu | Kiefer Tonkin-Caudery
Josh Torrenga | Arild Tvedt | Rodney van Valburg
Mike Vance | Eric Vilbert | Jezza Vlasic | C.V. Vobh
Vulpecula | Andrew Wainwright | David Walters
Aubrie Walters | Madge Watson | Ben Wehner
Floyd Weitzel | Michael Welch | Kenyon Wensing
Duncan Wilcox | Kyle Wilkinson | Annarose Willhite
Charles Williams | Blaine Williams | Margaret Willinsky
C. Wilson | Debra ann Wilson | Carly Winchell
Lia Winnard | Lori Wolbrueck | David Wolfson

Alex Wrigglesworth | Keelyn Wright | Spencer Wright
Jasmine Young

Finally, thank you, dear reader. I appreciate you taking the time to read this book.

Josiah (J.D.L. Rosell)

ABOUT THE AUTHOR

J.D.L. Rosell was swept away on a journey when he stepped foot outside his door and into *The Hobbit*. He hasn't stopped wandering since.

In his writing, he tries to recapture the wonder, adventure, and poignancy that captivated him as a child. His explorations have taken him to worlds set in over a dozen novels and five series, which include Ranger of the Titan Wilds, Legend of Tal, The Runewar Saga, and The Famine Cycle.

When he's not off on a quest, Rosell enjoys his newfound hobby of archery and older pastimes of hiking and landscape photography. But every hobbit returns home, and if you step softly and mind the potatoes, you may glimpse him curled up with his wife and two cats, Zelda and Abenthy, reading a good book, or replaying his favorite video games.

You can learn more about him and his books at *jdlrosell.com* or contact him at *josiah@jdlrosell.com*.

www.ingramcontent.com/pod-product-compliance
Ingram Content Group UK Ltd.
Pitfield, Milton Keynes, MK11 3LW, UK
UKHW040031040425
5313UKWH00002B/263

9 781952 868542